MW01178942

The Last Trumpet

A. JOHN ELLIOT, MD

ARCHWAY
PUBLISHING

Archway Publishing books may be ordered
through booksellers or by contacting:

Archway Publishing
1663 Liberty Drive
Bloomington, IN 47403
www.archwaypublishing.com
1 (888) 242-5904

ISBN: 978-1-4808-5025-5 (sc)
ISBN: 978-1-4808-5342-3 (e)

Library of Congress Control Number: 2017916290

Printed in the United States of America.

Archway Publishing rev. date: 11/16/2017

Author's Note

This novel contains anti-Semitic ideology necessary for historical accuracy. It is not a reflection of my personal beliefs, nor do I endorse this ideology

JUDITIH ELLIOT; FOR HER
SUPPORT, ART WORK, AND PUTTING
UP WITH SLEEPLESS NIGHTS

DIANA LEVY; FOR PUTTING UP
WITH A COMPUTER IDIOT

ROBERT WHITCOMB: THE RED PEN EVER AT
THE READY, A GREAT EDITOR AND FRIEND

The Last Trumpet

The wolf shall dwell with the lamb, and the leopard shall lie down with the kid; and the calf and the cub lion and the fatling together; and a little child shall lead them. And when He opened the seventh seal, there was silence in Heaven.

—Revelation 8:1 NKJV

Contents

Chapter 1
Spree Canal, Berlin, August 1933

IS WELL PAST MIDNIGHT. Andreas Eckhart waits and listens. A crowd has gathered on the corner in the alley off Lutzo Strasse.

"I never thought he'd do it—not this way. He didn't do this by himself. He needed help. I mean, you can't nail yourself. Shouldn't we get someone—a priest?"

The stranger next to him points to the leering faces, smiles. "He's a Jew."

The stranger's hands are empty of nails. His bald, smooth head bears a curious smile. "He picked a good day, quite an audience," says the stranger.

Slowly, the gathering slips away and is replaced by the clopping of a milk barrow and a cry "Fresh milk."

Andreas, overwrought and fidgeting, squints into the rain at something hovering in the sky- as if expecting to see a ghost—something he does frequently since returning from France and the war.

"Do you know him?" the man asks

"Never saw him before," Andreas answers, inhaling sharply.

The nails holding him are rusted and driven crooked. They tear at him.

Andreas stands back. He is quite sure he doesn't know him, though he does resemble the jeweler down the street.

I'm late for my meeting with the hospital board. What am I doing here? I was brought in by the yelling and the vendors. God, it's filthy hot. He has on only his underwear. No one should die wearing only his underwear.

He drives past the Spree Canal. The waves, whipped by the oncoming storm, make the placid stream seem like a river. He knows the man at the canal's edge. Stops, opens the car window, and leans out. Despite his graying hair, he appears young and virile.

"Hey there, Andreas!" Gunther bawls at the top of his voice. "Don't just sit there ogling—give me a hand! He's a Jew." Gunther adds in explanation.

Struggling, he drags the limp form toward the edge of the canal. Andreas hesitates. He and Gunther are not good friends. They had shared a trench in France. Andreas feels obligated. Gunther had saved his ass in a night raid during the war. Glancing at his watch, he jumps out of the car, leaving the door open.

"He looks like the same guy they just took down from the wall back on Lutzo Street."

"They all look alike," said Gunther.

"I haven't much time. Have an important meeting at the hospital," Andreas says, hiding the guilt rising in his face.

"Do you have permission?" he asks as they drag the limp form to the edge of the canal. "Heydrich won't like it."

"Won't like it? Christ, he paid to have it done—not much. I mean, he's a Jew, but it still costs. Even a Jew. I mean, even a Jew costs."

"Why? I mean. Why did he die? Did you have to kill him?" asked Andreas.

"First of all, he killed himself," said Gunther. "By being a Jew."

"Heydrich wants him dead. That's reason enough. Jesus Christ, Andreas, you don't get permission to kill a Jew—you just do it. No one is going to care."

"You've never killed one before?" he asks, clearly surprised.

The sun disappears behind a cloud, and it starts to drizzle. Wind rustles the beech trees, and a melancholy mist hovers over the canal. Andreas, shivering, buttons his raincoat and looks out over the canal at the large, gray clouds scuttling over the city. It seems it is always raining. He had been born and would die in the rain.

They stand together in the rain at the edge of the canal. Not far off, cars whiz by.

Kicking at the water collecting in the gutter, Andreas repeats, "There was no reason for killing him."

"First of all, I just told you he killed himself," says Gunther.

"By nailing himself to a wall?" asked Andreas, incredulous.

"With a little help," added Gunther, laughing. "There's no reason for letting him live. A Jew!"

The canal writhes its way into the morning, into a new day. Past smokestacks, warehouses, and a car parked on the side of the road. A young woman and a child approach the car. The child carefully wipes her shoes before getting in.

"I don't like it," Andreas says, turning to leave. "I've never killed anybody. At least, not like this. Why are you pulling the nails out?"

"Christ, I don't know, didn't even realize I was.

"It looks better, more orderly. Habits take a long time to die." How about during the war? You're almost forty. You mean you never killed anybody before?"

"That was different."

"He killed Christ," said Gunther. "There," he said, pulling the last nail from his hands.

"That's no reason," said Andreas, sinking into his Mackintosh. "Besides, you don't believe in Christ. When was the last time you went to church?"

"So? You were looking for a reason. You have a reason," said Gunther. "We have to make sure he's dead. Can't take any chances. I didn't know you were a Jew lover." Gunther laughs. "Did you take the names of the soldiers while you were in Flanders? For Christ's sake, nobody would have been killed." He fumbles through the man's pockets. "Here. His name is Mischa Lowenstein. Write to his parents." He tosses the wallet to Andreas. "C'mon, help me. Let's get it over."

Andreas picked up the wallet and started to open it.

Gunther, annoyed, says "Give me a hand. I've wasted enough time."

Gunther pulls his pistol and fires point blank into the Jew's skull. His head explodes. "Just in case. Now we're sure. He's dead. Pick up the pieces. Throw them into the canal."

Andreas stuffs the wallet into his pocket. "Why me? I had nothing to do with it. I never touched him."

The body floats upstream, arms spread. With a limb from a fallen tree, Gunther turns the body and pushes it underwater. "It won't sink and keeps popping up. I forgot to put those rocks in his pockets," Gunther said, "to get him to sink."

"What do you do if he won't sink?"

"Put a few more holes in him. He will. Give him time. Bullets cost money. This way, it looks better. More orderly," he answers, smiling.

"Did you decide to kill him before or after you found out he was a Jew?" Andreas asked.

"What's the difference?" asked Gunther.

"I don't know. It seems important."

"He was stealing me blind," Gunther said, turning toward Andreas. "Besides, I don't need a reason. Why the hell are you so nervous?"

It is raining harder, and sheets of water begin flowing down the street and into the drain. The trees across the road bend in the wind.

"I've got to get going," says Andreas, concentrating on the puddles at his feet. He avoids one only to splash into another. "I'm Catholic. It's a mortal sin."

"Money in the collection box goes a long way toward penance," said Gunther with a laugh.

"I wonder what it takes to be a good Jew," said Andreas as he walks d back to the car. The door is open, and the seat is soaked. "Christ, I left the door open."

"Serves you right." said Gunther, stuffing several bills

into Andreas's coat pocket. "Better spend them quick; tomorrow they won't be worth crap."

"Look, Andreas," said Gunther, leaning into the car, "there are two kinds of people in this world—those who kill and those who are going to be killed. The war should have taught you that."

Andreas shakes his head. "Wait a second. You killed him. I just watched."

"I see. So that makes you innocent? What about that thought, word, and deed stuff? Or were you asleep?"

Leaning forward to wash his hands, Gunther picks up a piece of skull he had missed in the cleanup. "Don't want to leave any litter," he says, skipping the fragment of skull into the canal.

The car, parked by the side of the road, pulls up. A young woman jumps out, takes her camera, snaps a picture of the body floating in the canal, gets back into the car and drives off. Next to her, a child fondles her doll, uninterested in what is happening outside. *How do you explain murder to a child?* Andreas wonders

"He'll never come back," Andreas mutters staring blankly into the fog. Only the lapping of the waves to certify the canal's existence.

"Of course not. Would you if someone nailed you to a two-by-four?" Gunther laughs.

"He'll never come back," repeated Andreas.

The body, barely visible but for blood flowing out of the wound, makes a lazy path in the river.

"He sure has a lot of pimples," Andreas says.

Lightning flashes. Thunder rumbles in the distance the wind rising. whips around his mackintosh.

"Relax. What are you worried about?" Gunther asks.

"My sister. She's alone," Andreas replies.

"She's dead, and so is your father," said Gunther. "They're both dead. For Christ's sake. How much have you had to drink?"

Gunther doesn't understand.

"Well, you don't look as if you're starving. You have money in your pocket, a place to sleep. What the hell else do you want? I know how it is. Don't feel bad. You argue and fight, but in the end, you are family. You're together."

"With us it was different," said Andreas. "In the end, we were angry, bleeding. If my mother hadn't died… If she was alive, it would have been different."

"Why?" asked Gunther. "You're a big boy. What are you looking for? Someone to hold your hand?"

"I don't know. I'm all used up, over my head. I've no place to go." Andreas shrugs.

"You worry about everything. You're becoming an old lady. No place to go. What do you call that castle your father left you? Sans something or other. Jesus, no place to go."

"I almost wish we were at war. I had a place to go then."

"I feel sorry for you—all alone in thirty-some rooms."

Lightning flashes. Andreas winces.

"If you're worried about the lightning, why not put a wire in your hand? You can talk to God directly," Gunther says.

"I already have. He won't kill me until I'm ready. I might kill him first."

"Who?"

"God"

A shadow glides across the windshield. Andreas climbs into the car. He pretends not to see it. *It will go away, the way it has in the past. I died in Flanders. I'm living among the corpses on the battlefield. There are a lot of us.* Andreas turns, waves goodbye.

"You're nuts," said Gunther, leaning into the car. "You've got it knocked. Stop looking for trouble. One of those shells must have gone off a little too close."

Gunther hesitates, turns, and pulls a roll of bills from his pocket. "For your help."

"Forget it," Andreas says. "You already paid me. I didn't do a thing."

Gunther shrugs "Have it your way."

Chapter 2
Sans Souci, Potsdam, 1933

ANDREAS SLAMS THE DOOR and drives East toward Sans Souci, the family residence since the Crusades. The road is empty but for the debris: —fallen trees, limbs, leaves, and garbage tossed up by the storm. The rain slaps against the car as it rattles over the earth and climbs slowly into the hills, past the statue of Fredrick the Great, past the planned site of the Erbgesundheitsgericht, the health court. He smiles. Only in Germany—a court for sick people, not a hospital. Of course, the cure would be to kill the plaintiff, the Jew.

Is being Jewish—a hooknose or a sloping brow—hereditary? He looks at the stain on his hand. Not a disease, a… hereditary marker. He doesn't like the sound of it. Hooknoses and receding foreheads have become diseases. Jewish, Gypsy, Polish have become diseases like typhoid and cholera—fatal. He must submit the names of his new patients and justify why they'd been admitted. Several had disappeared from the wards before he'd had a chance to see them, reasons not given.

He drives west to the park, into a different world, a different time. Past the rose garden overlooking the Havel River. his face, harder than when he'd last visited, his hair, whiter, the set of his jaw firmer, the lines in his face deeper. He stops above the long, central staircase flanked on either side by vineyards, a prefabricated palace atop a prefabricated mountain.

Sans Souci. Each plant, rosebush, peony, and tulip carefully chosen and planted, a scherzo of color suspended above the river. Bombed during the Great War, broken pavement, slippery, leads below. The sun is beginning to come out. The glare of a cold, hard morning illuminates the stairwell. He walks back to the car carefully so as not to stumble on the broken concrete. Uncomfortable among memories, he grows silent.

His father had used the castle as a convent. He was never allowed entry. It was reserved for beautiful women and, strangely, priests. Sundays, they would trail into the inner sanctum with arms crossed, bearing a chalice and mumbling liturgy. Strange echoes and wailing would issue from beneath the closed chambers; women, their clothes in disarray, would emerge staggering, often naked.

His father was anything but religious, and the women parading through the castle were anything but bruised, unfortunate Christians. Many were wives of prominent generals and gauleiters. Every Sunday, they solemnly presented themselves for the holy ritual. Shivering despite the roaring fires.

The castle was never home. He'd never had a home unless you could call the Kaiser Wilhelm Military School home.

Branches whip out of the blackness and claw at the car. Wind threatens to carry it into the river. He is tired. He has rehearsed the coming struggle many times: his father would try to settle the argument as he had many others with fists and threats.

Shifting closer to the windshield, he flinches as he dodges the leaves and branches rushing by, his father sitting in his frockcoat.

"It was an ugly death. There were so many better ways for you to kill me."

"Yes, perhaps," Andreas answers. "I have no apologies, Father. You are dead, and finally, it is over." Andreas can't help but feel something more has died. *Why the sadness? Why the despair? The longing? I hated him. I'm glad he's dead. He always left me just enough to make me come back thinking I might win next time. Well, it's over now.*

He drives subconsciously, half asleep, thinking, remembering.

"I was a soldier. My business was killing. I had duties," his father would reply.

His father's last days in the nursing home would flare suddenly like a pilot light about to go out, he would sit up and remember something. His father's death had awakened in Andreas a new respect—not love, but an urgency to know him. For some reason, he felt his future depended on it. Sentimentality for the past? Perhaps. Painful and melancholic, it would not go away. When asked if he was sorry, his father smiled. "For what? My life demanded making decisions. I am a German. My soul required that I make them, and I had to respond. It's the Jews who have committed the crime. I have never asked for apologies. So, this is how the voyage ends," he adds, a wry smile crossing his lips.

"You never understood, Father. A hug and a warm handshake would have been enough. Just to show you cared. Not that 'You're a man, not a boy' bullshit. You never touched me without leaving me bloodied."

In the distance, he sees the outlines of the castle atop a small mountain overlooking the Havel River. Like all dreams, abandoned, it shares the fate of those who'd inhabited it. As if only yesterday, he and Ernst swim in the small lake below, the water always cool beneath the oaks, deep and cool. The castle is crumbling. At night, he hears the stones shift and the voices of dead knights. Squinting between the windshield wipers, he forces a dark laugh indistinguishable from pain.

His family, all of them, are an open wound. His mother's incessant whining—unsure, abandoned, searching for someone to love, dying slowly. His father's murderous bellowing and addiction to violence, his sister's open seductiveness—half clothed, swishing her perfect body as she crosses the room, enjoying her father's suffering. Driving him. Relentless.

"He's my father," she says when he points out his father's slack-jawed interest.

"He's human," he replies.

The slap of waves against the seawall hurls foam like snow into the courtyard, a gust of wind, a searchlight sweeps over the crenelated towers, the wail of a fog horn seeps into the stones, the bluish-white light turns his SS uniform- black. Andreas stares at his uniform. The one he had worn in Belgium had been gray. *Only nine, or was it ten, or fifteen years ago?* He wasn't sure. Wars, like uniforms, seem to blend, distinguished only by their color.

The light flashes, pours off his forehead and into his eyes. He remembers scrambling through the rain and up the cement stairs, the mountain stark above him. A small window has blown open, drenching the stairwell. The castle is dark like a tomb, lit only by the searchlight sweeping over it. A single candle wavers in the wind. A tingling note floats from the piano in the living room.

"Father?"

"No," his sister answers. "Father's here, upstairs."

"Well then, who's playing the piano?"

"Nobody. Must be the wind.

"He's here I tell you! Father's here. He's after me!" A mixture of fear and disdain fill her eyes.

Her legs are tanned, her breasts young and firm, her bottom curved and small. Her hands are held in prayer; her instincts vibrate with desire.

"I know his footsteps, how they sound, sticky like something sucking on the marble and soft on the stairs. He's close."

Andreas wraps her in his arms. The scent of wet dust and mold mix with cracked and splintered plaster make it difficult to breathe. He is aware of her body pressed to his, her nightgown torn and hanging. The bulge in his groin grows, the open window bangs, the pane shatters. Splintered glass litters the stairs. The searchlight continues across the walls, peering into abandoned rooms. Rats scurry, their claws scratching on the wooden floor.

"He will never harm us. You're here," his sister murmurs. Her eyes glassy, her speech garbled, she clings to him, her hair falling over her forehead and into her eyes. His fingers fumble on the buttons; her nightgown falls to her feet.

"Kill him!" someone yells. Her mouth wide, her lips, red, are on him. The gnawing in his groin becomes her command; his blood rushes. He is aware of a shadow, strong arms, large and heavy fists, and his father's voice. His hands, dripping blood.

His father hurls her across the room. "Is that the best you can do?" He sneers. "A boy? Find a man."

"It's all a mistake. I never touched her!" Andreas pleads.

"In thought, word, and deed," his father says with a laugh. "What do you call that bulge in your pants? I'd respect you if you did. But no, you're going to pretend and go to your room and jack off. Just as well. You never would have satisfied her. You don't have what it takes. She's too much woman for you."

Andreas grips the steering wheel. His knuckles are white. The thud is real. Close. His father's face looms. Tara holds the smoking pistol.

"Who did I kill? Whose blood is on my hands?"

"Father's?" he asked.

"No, mine," she said. "It is my blood he's shed."

"Shadows and ash," she sings, dancing around the room. "Shadows and ash."

He left and run into the night, into the rain, into the thunder, past the flames licking at the walls, past the shadow and the light—to war and the sanity of battle.

The years have not softened the memory. Andreas sits in the car, listening to the metal as it settles, pulls the Luger out of the holster, feels the cold steel against his temple. The light plays over his hands and then moves on. In the gloom of the flooded street, Andreas trembles. The rain splatters onto the pavement.

Wiping the perspiration from his face, he opens the glove compartment and takes a cigarette from a pack of Camels. He would run that night, leaving behind the promise of butterflies and picnics on the lawn. He'd run down the long hill—to certain death, to salvation.

Fifteen years. Hitler sentenced to jail, like Christ to rise again, the hope of the Weimar Republic a façade, triumph over communism, assassinations, and blood, the Great Depression, mass poverty, and the obscene wealth of a few. Blame and blood and the face of anti-Semitism.

Heine had predicted, "The demoniacal forces of the old German pantheism would rise from the shadows and again spew ash." Volk blood, German blood, would again shake the earth—not for gain, not for love, but because it was German blood and it thirsted.

Too bad he had burned his old copies of the *Simplicissimus* magazine lampooning Communists and National Socialists alike. It hurt to look at the faces. *Who knew what was coming? They did. We did. Heine did.* Beatings and torture, caricatured and waiting. It took courage to publish the photographs: breads lines, people picking coal from slag heaps and heating their hands over trash barrels.

The French have already evacuated the Rhineland. They'd be back. Repaying the war debt with proceeds from rail bonds maturing in 1988! Even '38 was ridiculous. The past and present were uncertain.

Who knew that Ernst would die? Who knew I would kill

him? Who knew I would become a doctor and become head of
German undercover in London? Who knew my father would be
right and I would be a fag and fall in love with Ernst?

He pictures Ernst climbing from the lake, watches
him sway toward him, his mouth screwed into a knowing
smile. *Who knew?*

Andreas sank down, perishing in the white light of
the searchlight. The castle is dark. The wall has crumbled
and lies in rubble. The wind whistles, tunneling through
broken and decaying stones, vanishing in empty memories,
only to awaken again in moonlight. A bitter howl, it creeps
over graves and coffins.

Listening to the wind, he thinks again of his father and
of his sister, Tara, a casualty of his father's war. If only he
could find her, he would heal her; he was sure he could. She
had disappeared like the light from the wavering star shells.

"So you became a priest?" he asks himself, staring into
his reflection on the windshield.

"No, a doctor. We have a lot in common. Like a priest,
I use God, an excuse, a shield—it was God's will. Who's
to say otherwise? Having soulful, gray eyes, a handsome
face, and a disregard for life and death helps. If you have
nothing to lose, you rush toward shells, saw off legs, and
patch up wounds under the swaying light. Sometimes, they
live. You get good at it—perhaps even enough to earn the
Iron Cross. Perhaps your title had something to do with it.
You even lose the desire to off yourself, though at times it
comes back when you least expect it."

Light from a passing car glances off the windshield
and blinds him. When the glare cleared, Emil, the butcher,
is smiling, the postman is smiling, his sister, holding the

revolver and standing over his father's body, is smiling. Ernst, standing over him, bends toward him, and his lips part. The trees bend, rubbing their bare bark together, and then with evil hunger clash and separate.

His cigarette, burned to a nub, Andreas opens the window and flicks it out. The wind and rain are cold on his cheek.

Chapter 3
Sans Souci Castle, Potsdam

FIELD MARSHAL ELOISE ECKHARDT. His father's will lay crumpled in the fireplace. Turning to smoke, it twists and hovers over the fire, then slipping into the study, it settles onto the desk, the chairs, and soaks into the drapes.

"I have chosen my old firm Codding and Carter to manage the disposition of the estate." The stationery is stamped with the seal of the Gestapo; the letter written on Field Marshal Himmler's private stationery. His father and the field marshal were close friends.

He had never been consulted or received notice of his father's burial, and after the inquest, his sister had mysteriously disappeared. Just as well. She'd escaped and wanted nothing further to do with it.

His father was and would forever remain a stranger behind a locked door. *It could have been you, Father, who said as Hitler did, "My will is your belief." Who were you? I never knew you. Was it you who told me what and how and never to talk back? Always ready to show with your fists who was right? You who said, "Love hurts. Everything worthwhile hurts"? Your*

war would go on for forty years, and all that time, I would be
powerless to refute you.

The castle was empty of soldiers, empty of cars
and guns. Empty of salutes and clicking heels but not
of memories. They, like a drunkard, reel from room to
room.

Andreas leans forward, his hands on the smooth,
lacquered wood. The casket is warm as if something inside
were alive. "Finally, you are quiet. No voice, not even a sigh.
Your rage silenced. All your friends came: Hitler, Göring,
and Himmler. Heydrich placed flowers, shook my hand,
and said they were sorry. There was not one tear among
them. Their presence and the flowers were the measure of
their sorrow.

"Tara? She's fine until she tries to sleep. Then she
is pursued by the beast, the same one who's been after
her since she was a child. You remember. She'd wake
up screaming, 'It's going to get me!' No. She doesn't feel
sorry. No, she doesn't feel guilty. She thinks you deserved
it. "There are things left undone" His voice answers from
the casket. "Not for me, Father. I expect to be left alone—to
live and die."

"Your sister, Tara, will receive the property in India."

He hadn't seen her since that night, until the reading
of the will.

"I looked for her afterward, father but she'd disappeared
again. Tara's deep, malicious eyes, pouty smile, and—pain.
Madness. A disease, an illness, concocted by you, Father,
nurtured and spread by an entire nation. She distributes
pain like flowers, her lithe figure floating into a room with
her lilac scent. Death and pain and lilacs, always lilacs

And I inherit the remainder? Sans Souci in Germany, the flat in Mayfair, and Landscheide? I knew it. You knew I hated Landscheide."

"I would advise you, Andreas, to learn more about Landscheide before you indulge the impulse to sell it. You were born, raised, and spent most of your years there. It is an ancient property, and many of Germany's heroes are buried there. You will find many heirlooms—particularly in the desk in my study."

"I am not going near that place ever!"

His stepmother, a princess in India, had arrived before her marriage as bright and colorful as her dress, her dark eyes flashing with laughter, only to be greeted by dark-paneled rooms without sunlight and the boot of German legend.

"I was her hope, and she turned to me for help. I tried to protect her, but your war, Father, was without end. Violence and suspicion, your sole means of expression against a rival—your son. When the end came, her laughter still rolling with life, you, her husband, were still too self-absorbed to realize her despair."

"I also bequeath you the vermilion stain you have so often tried to wish away," his father whispers.

Andreas studied the red-purple birthmark running down his arm and onto his hand.

"As long as it is with you, your inheritance will be safe. If I have been relentless and unforgiving, it has been to prepare you for the ordeal to come. Now, I am tired and wish to sleep."

He hesitated, reread the letter. There was something unsaid, a warning, or perhaps a plea, the same plea he'd seen in his father's eyes before he let loose one of his swings. Lately, he'd noticed there was no power in his swing; it didn't hurt, more like a pat. Releasing the letter, he watched it flutter into the fire. It occurred to him that perhaps it was as close as his father would come to an affectionate touch.

"Goodbye, Father," he said. Surprised, he snatched at the letter. It escaped, turned black, and coiled into ashes.

He next opened the letter from Himmler: "Congratulations on your promotion to chief of staff at the German Charity Hospital, London. I am sure you will serve with distinction."

Charity Hospital? A fantasy. A cover for the Gestapo in London; a way to find Jews who'd eluded them in Berlin.

"Regarding your recent assignment, your contact, I believe, is already known to you. She will give you an envelope and further directions. She will contact you."

To his surprise, the contact *was* known to him though he wouldn't recognize her for months to come. Tara had the unique ability, like a chameleon, to alter her appearance and with it her personality—all but her eyes. They would always give her away, intense and malicious.

No, Tara wasn't dead. She'd been spirited out of the castle the night of the shooting and sent to a cloister. She had reappeared at the funeral, a changed woman.

He'd come close to recognizing her. The scent of lilacs and her eyes, tiger's eyes, had again given her away. She'd grown into the legs of a woman, tall and beautiful, smooth and dangerous. She walked in long, slashing strides—not touching the ground—the moment when she was beside him, her blouse open, her skirt above her waist, when she'd given him the envelope and slipped into the darkness.

"Whoever presents this ring is entitled to the wish that goes with it."

Tara had given him the envelope and swayed away that night. Disappeared stealthily like a jungle cat. A woman still infatuated with fairy tales, rings, and ring givers. He'd shouted to her, but she had her own course and paid no attention to his game.

Chapter 4
Cheapside, London

He held the envelope against the window, the seal of the Gestapo embossed like a vaccination mark. He would meet this Lebenfels and then collect his prize.

Cheapside, the hunger and poverty no different from what he'd encountered in the war. His headlights cut through the mist and outlined a black ribbon of track. A whistle screamed. A train sped by. Sheets of smoke and cinder fall over the brick walls. He followed the tracks past crooked buildings, past the church, past his charity clinic, Mr. Andreas Eckhart barely visible in the fog.

The explosion from a leaking gas main had destroyed city blocks, and the smell of gas lingered. Streets, mostly deserted, sections of row houses missing, gaps like empty sockets in a row of decaying teeth. shattered bits of children's crayons had turning the pavement red, yellow, and green.

The church was empty, the charity offices shuttered. The Mayfair ladies had come, stared at the starving figures, opened their pocketbooks, lifted their skirts above the garbage and urine, and rushed back to care for their cats and parrots. Himmler had put the charity hospital in the Cheapside section of London for a reason. It was excellent cover.

The windshield wipers kept time, *swish thump, swish thump.* "Where the hell is number twenty-two?" Andreas leaned forward, searching, shivering, and regretting he'd accepted the assignment. A vague uneasiness. *Must be getting colder.* He felt for the Luger, placed it by his side, studied himself in the rearview mirror—a thick shock of black hair, a lean face, prominent cheekbones, deeply set gray eyes, long, black eyelashes, and jutting, defiant chin. A ray of light from his car darted past a shop window. A man attracted by the sound of the car leaned out the doorway and spat.

"April in Paris" played on the car radio. He stopped the car but left the beams on. Pulling his collar closer, he hunched his shoulders against the rain and pulled his hat tightly over his head. He ran up steps. Steeper than the others, they set the house apart from the other row houses. The water poured off the lintel, off the brim of his hat, and down his neck. He peered closely at the numbers. "Twenty-four. Damn!" He hurried to the next house. His shoes squeaked, and his trousers stuck to his legs.

He rang the doorbell. A lace curtain fluttered inside. He pushed the bell again, bent forward, and lit another cigarette. He pushed against the door. To his surprise, it swung open. "Mr. Lebenfels?" he whispered. He turned on the lamp and looked behind him. There were two sets of footprints on the carpet, a half-empty bottle of wine on the table. Dirty dishes filled the sink. The room had the stale stench of air that hadn't been breathed. No window had been opened.

He heard a hum. He put his hand to the sharp pain. Blood flowed onto his collar. A razor stabbed into the desk. It vibrated like a saw. Something moved in the half-light from the street. A passing car threw light on the wall highlighting the cheap floral print as it swept downward and was extinguished.

The front door flew open. The wind rushed in. Someone was running down the steps. He chased the sound into the empty street. He went back in and pulled the blade from the desk. He had never seen one like it, a disk no more than five inches wide shaped like a star with five points. Blood dripped onto his collar. Sweat gathered on his forehead. He had never felt so cold.

He left the house. Stepping over puddles, he slid into his car. About to turn on the ignition, he heard a sound, someone walking on broken glass. He appeared in front of him in the windshield, withered, old, and stooped. Tapping a walking stick, his fingers, like dead twigs, stuck out of cutoff mittens. His face was worn. He held a large cup. He shook it like the one before communion, when the priest blessed the wafer and the bells tinkled. He liked that part the most.

He tapped on the car window. "Help."

Andreas opened the window and tossed a coin into the cup.

"Are you lost?" Andreas asked.

"Kyrie elusion," the old man said.

"Must be a fuckin' priest," Andreas whispered. There wasn't a church in sight. The stranger turned and riveted him with a stare. "The man you seek is not coming." He melted into the fog.

Perhaps he'd imagined it. He reached into his pocket. The coin was missing. He pulled into the street. "Stupid," he said aloud. "Just an old drunk."

The rain spattered against the window. Growing stronger, it blew in sheets. *How the hell have I gotten myself into this? "Just do this one little thing for me," she'd said. To get laid. Why else? God, she was beautiful. Careful. You've seen what happened to General Blomberg, and he was head of the army. You're a successful surgeon and head of the German Charity Hospital in London. It's turned into a community center for deadbeats and young whores, but still, it serves its purpose. Charity? All you need to make the irony complete is to add, "Jews not accepted." What the hell do you care? You have it made. Don't fuck it up. Stop the bleeding. Sew it together or cut it off.*

The wound in his ear was small, superficial, and would require little attention. His reputation as one of the best was courtesy of his female patients. Many he had seduced were wives of highly placed government officials. The Gestapo was pleased: "Bed them, get their husband's secrets. If things get too tough, photographs are available to convince them." He wondered where they hid to get the close-ups. It might not make him a hero, but fucking his way through the next war wasn't too bad either. Playing hide-and-seek on a lonely street in the worst section of London was stupid.

Chapter 5
Admiral Nelson's Square, London

IAN MCDONALD SLOUCHED IN the rear of the square, his hat cocked on his balding scalp. A newspaper reporter, he wore his sallow complexion, yellowed teeth, and rheumy eyes as badges of his job. It was stinking hot, and he was hung over.

He knew and admired Andreas, the young man sitting across from him. It took someone with courage to stand up to his father, one of the toughest bastards he had ever known. Andreas had returned from the war distrustful, a hero, and a loner. He had agreed to meet Ian in Trafalgar Square before a speech he was to give to the Anglo-German Friendship Society.

"Nothing's changed," Mac said as he pulled a chair and wiped the sweat from his face. "Yesterday, we were killing the French. Tomorrow, we'll be killing them again. It's a comedy."

The square was strangely quiet; the heat was oppressive. *The damn heat*, thought Andreas. *It's running over the tables, the chairs, the faces, the walls, the children. Even the trucks are covered in sweat.*

He knew Mac would want to discuss the Eiger episode. Up to then, Andreas had refused to discuss it or give any interviews. Mac was an old friend and in danger of losing his job. He needed an exclusive.

London: Grim faces, crowds, placards, chants of "Juden! Juden!" Andreas thought that at least there, he'd be free from the madness in Berlin—blood and God around every corner, men and women standing against walls, waiting. Assassinated—not by bullets but by taunts, insults, and spit. Jews—flesh to be used. *Mine to use. The madness!* Thoughts that pursued him into churches, onto roadways and sidewalks, and even into brothels.

Andreas had never wanted to be a hero, had never believed in heroes. Yet just to survive was heroic. He had been surprised when he'd been offered the chance to lead a German team up the north face of the Eiger Mountain in the Swiss Bernese-Oberland, one of the most dangerous. He'd accepted.

He knew the climb would be good publicity for Hitler and the Fatherland. Climbing appealed to him—balancing on the edge of the thinnest margin between life and death. The danger, the immensity of the mountain appealed to him; it made more sense than death by random shooting and murder. *What are the alternatives? Die in a car crash? Get shot by a jealous husband or by Heydrich or Himmler? Why worry? Anything can happen.*

Still, he hadn't expected his name to be coupled with the word, *hero,* in the daily newspapers, over the radio—and on Hitler's lips.

Andreas had risen in the Nazi Party aided by fortune, his father's fame, and civil war. The Freikorps—veterans returning from the front—thought they could have won the war but had been stabbed in the back by the big business interests, "the fucking Jews."

He was fortunate some might say—destined. His father was a decorated general. Andreas, in the right place at the right time, had rescued Heinrich Himmler from a gang of Communist Spartacists. Together with the publicity from the Eiger climb, it had made him a hero.

He took chances and survived, sometimes miraculously. His contempt for death and God became legend. "Why not?" he was quick to ask. His blood was German blood, Siegfried's blood. Many times, his men did not survive. Always, he returned.

If death had already marked him, it would be of no matter. His death would be for Germany.

McDonald, working for the *Manchester Guardian*, had met Andreas purely by accident. They had both sought refuge under the same roof during the Putsch engineered by Hitler in 1923, a year when it all fell apart: the French occupied the Ruhr, the currency disintegrated, the Bolsheviks roamed the streets.

"I remember the day you said you'd accepted the climb," recalled McDonald, sipping his wine. "It was a day just like this, white and hot. I remember because despite the heat I was cold."

"I remember I asked you if you were afraid. 'Afraid?' you asked as if it were out of the question. You said, 'Don't you see? I'm guilty.' Those words have haunted me," said McDonald.

Andreas stared into the red-hot ball hanging in the sky like a balloon, scorching the square, the glare from the metal tables reflecting and multiplying the heat.

"Guilty?" asked McDonald. "Of what?"

"We are all guilty," said Andreas, laughing.

He pulled out a chair. "Christ," he said, shaking his hand. "Hotter than a whore on payday." Gingerly, he leaned forward, his hands on his knees, "All right, Mac, what's so important? What's bothering you?"

"Three dead men. Deserves a story, don't you think?" McDonald shot back. He seemed to swim in a vortex of shimmering heat. "Can't say I didn't warn you not to go."

"Why don't you take off that damned hat," said Andreas.

"I don't need a sunburned scalp," replied McDonald. "It doesn't look good, and it hurts."

Andreas asked, "Was I to say no to Himmler—to God?"

"God? Where the hell did he come from?" asked Mac, studying the table.

"He runs the lottery," said Andreas. "We have no choice but to play."

"Have you forgotten it is an honor to die for Hitler and the Fatherland? Siegfried and Wotan say so. They're gods." McDonald smirked, a good Scottish smirk. "Come on, I mean *God*," he said, pointing up.

"So do I," said Andreas, pointing the other way. "He's played with me for thirty-eight years. In the end, what does it matter? Death is the end, win or lose, here, in Flanders, wherever."

It was Andreas who wore a smirk.

"Everyone died except you, Andreas. You were supposed to die on the mountain with those men."

"Nice of you to say so. I think so too. I'm alive. He'll get even. He has something special planned for me." Andreas looked around as if someone were listening. "Mac, can I trust you?"

"Of course you can."

"I met him on the mountain. I'm not kidding. I met him."

"Climbers are always talking about meeting God on the mountain. It's almost a cliché. He lives there." Mac paused, a reporter's pause calculated to elicit an intimate response. "What the hell happened? I got this garbled view from the trial. What *really* happened?"

"What really happened was that I saw and spoke to him, and he and I had it out."

"Is that all?" asked McDonald.

"I'm standing there, and out of the blue, I hear a voice. It tells me he's God and not to be frightened. He has things for me to do. He would make me a hero. I said, 'No way.' I wasn't interested. I'd looked, and there were no heroics on my chart. All I wanted was to be left alone." Andreas stopped. His face changed. He took a long drink of wine and then looked into the distance.

"I was frightened, scared shitless. Not because of who it was. God, I mean. Not even because I was afraid to die. I'd committed a crime, but against whom? Certainly not humanity. I'd done them a favor. Cowardice? Perhaps. But I'd faced war without shrinking. What was it that had me so frightened? He just stood there and laughed at me. What could he do to me, kill me? I realized death wouldn't be enough for him."

"Obey!" He said. "You will obey!" Then I got angry." I'm thirty-eight. I've spent four years patching up your wounded." I said." I really lost it. I swear, Mac, I don't know where I got the courage. Why the hell can't you take care of your own problems? Why should I obey? Kill me. I don't much like this world you created anyway. I've spent thirty-eight years building a life without help from you, and with a fucked- up father to boot, and you want me to work for you?"

"Then this roar. When I turned, an angry sky was tumbling toward me, a white wall of snow and rock. I yelled to the others. They were still yoked together. I was buried. A huge boulder whizzed past me. Most of the snow was deflected by a mound of rock in front of me. It was a miracle. It saved my life. I know. You think I'm imagining it—that the old shell shock had returned, but no, Mac, it was real. I know it was real. The next thing I knew, the sun was shining and I was hanging on the edge of a ravine—silence and snow—and his voice, 'You could have saved them if you'd obeyed; now it is too late.' They wanted facts at the trial. I didn't have facts. I will never forget the silence, like a church. And his laughter. I was fed up. He promised one day he would return. I looked for him. He never came."

Mac said, "Jesus, Andreas. Why are you still here? I mean, if I were God, you'd be a spot on the pavement."

"He took it quite well. Didn't move a muscle, didn't bat an eye. Though I thought for a moment I saw a flicker of sadness and even perhaps a tear. When I next looked, he was gone. "Who knows? I know he isn't finished with me. When you think about it, what can he do to me? Whatever it is, it's going to be grisly. You can bet on that."

"He speaks quite fondly of you." Mac smiled.

"I'm not afraid of him if that's what you mean. I think he's a phony He never meant to keep his promise. Besides,

I like being a martyr," Andreas said, his head dropping onto his chest.

"I fled Him, down the nights and down the days;

I fled Him, down the arches of the years;

I fled Him, down the labyrinthine ways

Of my own mind; and in the midst of tears."

"I'm impressed," said McDonald. "Didn't think you read poetry."

"Those words have become my bible," said Andreas. "I repeated them over and over during the war. At Verdun, listening to the bullets slap into the bodies piled in front of the trenches. Whenever God asks for something, it is for his reasons, not ours. Run, you can only suffer. I found that out during the war."

He paused, considering whether to continue. "I wonder what he wants. Why does he keep trying? Says he's chosen me. I'll never forget those dreadful eyes. I think he's nuts. Perhaps I'm nuts. In either case, I want nothing to do with him. I told the prosecutor that at my trial. It took some time to quiet the courtroom.

In the end, he always wins. I died with Ernst that day on the mountain. Oh, he's clever. The mountain lures you. The breeze whispers, 'Come on, come on.' Nothing is important—nothing except the next step, the next gulp of oxygen. He'd been looking for a reason to take Ernst."

"Why should God care about Ernst?"

"It wasn't Ernst. It was me. Because I loved him," Andreas said with a strange sadness.

"How much of this can I print?" McDonald asked, worried.

"The whole fucking thing as far as I'm concerned. One

other thing. What do you think he did when those men plummeted into the ravine?"

"He laughed so hard he peed his pants."

"So, there I was, Mac, three dead men and me staring into the white heat while he laughed his ass off. Why, Mac? Because he wanted it. He was the boss. It was his choice. Because I wouldn't throw myself into a ravine."

"Well, as you just said, he's the boss," said Mac tongue in cheek.

"It wasn't my affair. It wasn't my problem."

McDonald motioned for the waiter, a short popinjay, his hair parted in the middle, a dripping attempt at a mustache. "A pitcher of red, the cheapest," he ordered, trying to contain his laughter.

Not a shot had been fired in London. Yet the war had, like a drunkard, wandered into garbage thrown from thousands of lorries, into stores with secondhand clothes.

"The war," said the waiter apologetically, returning with the wine.

Since his divorce McDonald was chronically short tempered as well as short of money. He needed a shave. He also needed this interview to save his job with the *Guardian*.

"Thanks for the interview," he said. "It will save my ass." He poured the thin red wine into a stemless glass. "Why the jacket by the way? It's hotter than hell. Are you going after some of that jailbait over in Piccadilly?"

"Sex is my obsession," said Andreas without a hint of irony. "This business with the Jews, where is it going? From what I can tell, the Nazis don't want them to leave the country with or without their money. They've got something in mind for them."

"They can use their Wiedergutmachtung for money," said McDonald with a smirk. "Jews get that in exchange for Marks when they leave the country. Supposedly good for exchange into foreign currency. Trouble is no government recognizes it. It's worthless."

"For enough, you can still get out," said Andreas. "Ten kills over France. Shot up a farm yesterday," he added.

"Who?"

"A friend of mine. Well, not a friend, an acquaintance. He's an asshole, a coward."

"What made you think of him?"

"You were talking about getting laid. Made me think of his wife. One of the best pieces in England. A real bitch."

"Well then, I won't bother getting to know her," said Mac.

"They do look a lot like sheep from up there."

"Who?"

"Children," said Andreas.

McDonald took a long swallow of wine, grimacing slightly. "God, this is swill. Come hell or high water, I'm going to get laid tonight. Trouble is, I'm close to broke."

"Here's fifty pounds. Pay me back when you can," said Andreas, placing the bills on the table. "Find a Jew. You can get her for a few of those Wiedergutmachtungs or whatever they're called. She will be so horny that she'll do whatever you want and not even charge you. The language of love. It must have been invented by Germans. Get. Have. Do."

"Every man is an island." McDonald shrugged and passed his hand over his swollen jaw.

"What happened to your jaw?" Andreas asked.

"Bad tooth."

Andreas eyed him suspiciously.

"All right. I ran into a door. Make you feel better?"

"You've been running into a lot of doors lately," said Andreas, a worried scowl crossing his face.

McDonald moved his chair into the shade of the umbrella, carefully removing his hat to not disrupt the few remaining strands of hair. He resettled it on his head and motioned to the waiter. "'Nother pitcher." His voice, slurred, was coming from a shadow.

"You know you got it wrong," Andreas added. "It's not every man. It's no man."

The sky began to darken over the statue of Nelson.

"Looks as if we might get some rain," McDonald said.

"It does that a lot. The sky darkens, but there's no wind, no rain. The poison without the antidote. Just the way it did on the massif," Andreas said, staring at the pavement. "You know, I've never done a nobler thing than refuse him."

"Those dead men might not agree with you."

"I've climbed the Eiger since the accident. I've met those men at the top. They just stare at me and disappear into the mountain. They're not angry."

"Good thing I wasn't one of them. I'd have killed you," said McDonald.

"My friends complain that God's turned his back on them. They are the lucky ones. It's those he hasn't turned his back on, the ones he's got in the crosshairs that have to worry," said Andreas. "It started with that show-stopper Crucifixion. You have to admit, great theater—and that promise to return. It was all for show. Suckered a lot of us, but not me. I mean, who gives a shit?"

"You're better off if you don't listen, pay no attention to

the bellowing and noise," said McDonald, fanning himself. "It's tough, though. I mean, what does that leave? Hitler? The Nazis?" "Unless!" Andreas said with a broad smile. "Unless you're insured."

"How the fuck can you be insured?"

"Become a Jew. If you're a Jew, you can have it both ways. If he's coming back, you're covered, and if he's not, it doesn't matter. He wasn't the Messiah, and you didn't expect him to anyway. This promise to return is brilliant. It keeps you in the game." Andreas shrugged. "Tara, my sister, refused to put up with the bullshit."

"Where the hell you been hiding her. In a convent?" Mac said.

"Yes, as a matter of fact. I haven't been hiding her. She's been hiding herself. She blames me. I didn't shoot father. She did."

"Man, one fucked-up family," said McDonald.

Andreas slid a photo onto the table. McDonald reached to move the chair closer. "Son of a bitch, it's hot," he said. He carefully picked up the photo—a long, sensitive face, a questioning face, mocking, unnerving, and strangely alone. Andreas remained fixed on the pavement with a look of anguish in his eyes as if any show of affection and she would disappear.

"She's half German, half Hindu. My stepmother was Hindu. She's not really my sister. Her mother was my stepmother. The important thing is she's a Buddhist."

"Why is that so important?"

"Kept her from buying into all that Nazi crap my father was dishing out."

"Don't they practice the caste system in India? That's

a form of Nazism. If you're on the lowest rung, you don't stand a chance. It all flows downhill," said McDonald.

"You just have to buy into a higher rung in the next life," said Andreas. "The price is what you have done in this one."

"Who judges?"

"For Christ's sake, how do I know?"

"That's the rub. There's always someone who judges," said McDonald. "As for me, I'm fifty percent German," he boasted with exaggerated emphasis.

Andreas's speech became very droll and with exaggerated malice. His face puckered. "You're quite sure. You looked it up. I mean, wouldn't want anyone to think you're a Jew."

Mac, his face red, said, "Don't be funny. That's not what I meant."

"What did you mean?" Andreas asked.

"It's just that there's no sense in looking for trouble."

"Of course," said Andreas with an impish smile.

"This new law, the Erbgesundheitsgesetz, pretty much says if you aren't German, you own nothing. In fact, as far as the Reich is concerned, you are nothing, don't exist. It's going to be very important to have those papers. Tara. Beautiful name," said McDonald, changing the subject.

"You wouldn't like her middle name, though, Lilith. Try that one after a few schnapps."

"And? For Christ's sake tell me more. She's beautiful. I'd travel around the world for her."

"You'd be disappointed," Andreas said. "She likes women."

"Haven't you made any effort to find her? Maybe you can change her mind. I bet I could," said McDonald, pouring another glass of wine.

"She doesn't want to be found. Every time I get close, she disappears."

Children began to filter into the square carrying balloons and ice cream in honor of Peace Day. "I'll get you!" a girl taunted, hiding behind Admiral Nelson's column. "You didn't count to a hundred! Do it over."

Eight... nine. They were running toward the chestnut tree that overlooked the lake. Tara's legs flash in the sunlight. Each flash cut into Andreas's heart. Tara is fifteen. School is over, and they will have the summer together. She stops, lightning traces across the sky. Perhaps it will rain. Leaves toss and sizzled over them.

"A hundred!" Andreas shouts. "Here I come, ready or not!" Carefully, she opens the lunch box and anxiously searches among the dead husks and butterfly wings, fragments of time, demons hidden and yet to come.

Between two worn pieces of paper is a ring, a ring you might find in a Cracker Jack box, a ring that is plain and worn and fake.

"The ring-giver's ring," she says. "Promise again. Promise again!"

"I promise that whoever brings me this ring will be granted the wish that comes with it. Without fail. Without fail," he adds solemnly.

She places the ring back into the box, orders Andreas to close his eyes, and carefully returns it to the tree. Climbing onto the rock and onto the swing, she glides higher and higher. The wind and leaves whirl overhead.

McDonald laughed. "Put a penny in the box and it will buy? What? Sin?" he answers, laughing.

"You'd have to promise to bring the ring, the ring-giver's ring," said Andreas.

"For a piece of that I'd promise anything," said McDonald leaning forward and almost falling out of the chair. Jesus Christ, Andreas."

"Him too?" asked Andreas with a smile, attempting to disentangle himself from his chair and spilling his wine.

"Bullets, firing squads, death are the order of the day. Ring givers?", McDonald bellowed throwing a chair across the square, "While civilization is sinking into hell."

There was no one else in the restaurant. The proprietor was not amused. He approached with a smug grin, his mustache quivering with contempt. Andreas turns away from the little girl running delightedly around the one-armed admiral.

"My friend is not well. I will gladly pay for the damages," he said, hustling Mac into a chair.

Mac shook him off. "We were good Germans. We prayed a lot and obeyed our father," said McDonald to the waiter "My father had a way of expressing himself with these, he said, holding his hands in front of the waiter. "He had a way of praying with them too. I knew the Bible better than the priest did. I went to church. The wafer stuck to the roof of my mouth. It tasted bitter." Mac continued, staring at the pavement while he spoke, the pen hanging limply from his fingers. "Not the whole story." He said slurring his words.

The waiter smiled.

The anger and indignation that had carried McDonald through endless horrors was dying. He was tired and could no longer sustain the despair, the broken bodies, the broken lives. He looked at his glass and softly putting it down said, "Shouldn't be drinking." He was as drunk as Andreas had ever seen him. There was a long silence and the sound of the heat. "Don't give up on me, Andreas. Not yet. It doesn't mean anything."

Looking away, Andreas said, "I know," his eyes still on the glass. He did know. Mac was torn up inside. The depression and starvation, the violence, yelling, shooting, barricades, Kashmir's death, and now his mistress's departure. But it was Kashmir he mourned. McDonald picked up his glass and in defiance drained it in one swallow.

Looking into Andreas's eyes, he said, "It was murder. I never struck her, but I killed her. It's all a blur ... riots, fists, order, duty, vengeance, and obedience—all the things that are dear to a German's soul, but it isn't the story, the whole story."

"What is?" Andreas asked.

Splintering the pencil, McDonald looked past Andreas into the heat-laden air. "Don't you see it? We're locked in a cave. Waiting his return. Waiting. Down in this cave, praying, waiting for the wind. But there is no wind—not even a chaplain. Only death."

Throwing the fragments of the pencil at the wall, he sank onto the floor. "Kashmir left me because I couldn't love. I couldn't. Me! The stud of the press corps. She was warm and alive, there for me to love, but I couldn't." Looking like a wounded animal and staring into the hot September Day, he said, "I couldn't. I see her staring at me behind barbed wire, anointing me for a piece of chocolate, a gumachtungs, just another hour."

"She wasn't Jewish?" asked Andreas.

"Oh God, if there is a God, forgive me. I've never stopped loving her. I'm just treading water, waiting."

"Less booze might help," said Andreas.

"Less? I can barely make it now. You know that island, the one you say is a myth? I'm on it—alone." McDonald looked up. "It's simple. After the war, someone, I don't know whether he was a civilian or a deserter—didn't make much difference in those days—sitting in the window of Sackler's department store. You knew he'd been shot. You could have driven a truck through his bullet wound. He just sat there with this look on his face, as if he were asking, 'What happened? One minute I was sitting here, and the next I was dead. Why here? Why me? I just came in to get a drink—and now I'm dead. I've been dead for days. Christ, I'm turning green. I smell awful. Doesn't anyone care?' He raised his head and repeated, 'Doesn't anyone care?'

"Well," McDonald said, staggering to his feet, "I don't know what came over me, but I'm all right now. We've survived. In fact, that Eiger climb has made you Hitler's darling, a hero."

"Almost made me a dead one," said Andreas.

"Don't you feel at all guilty?" asked Mac.

"I didn't kill them. Look, Mac, I told you it isn't my problem. Blame him, God. Resurrection is for priests and pallbearers. The Olympics are coming, the chestnut trees are blooming, people are happy. The Tiergarten is full of happy, well-dressed, and polite Germans."

Restless and impatient, McDonald continued feverishly. "Perhaps it's better to kill them than to let them suffer. Freedom doesn't include Jews. We should have known better than to think Germans would put up with democracy. The republic. Bertolt Brecht and the Bauhaus school were dreams. Seems impossible. Germany has become the world's center for art and music. We have displaced Paris and New York. Some very important people have come over to Hitler's side."

"We are living in a cultural paradise, or so the *Berliner Zeitung* says."

Andreas took McDonald's arm and still gesticulating, gently steered him across the street.

McDonald stared at the billboard. "I saw Hitler at the performance of *Tannhäuser*. He was escorting his niece, Geli Raubal. She killed herself." He laughed, tears streaming down his face.

Andreas shrugged.

"Should get hold of that fellow who writes for the *Berliner Zeitung*. He'll know the true story. Haven't seen anything from him lately."

"Is he Jewish?" asked Andreas.

"Yes, I think so," answered McDonald. "Otto Reinhart, probably dead. Murder? Suicide?"

"They're both options," answered Andreas. "A lot of suicides."

"Hitler's mistress? Christ's mistress? Who knows? Who cares?"

"Some with latchkeys on the ramp. Living in a sort of peace. In a concentration camp," McDonald muttered as he performed a sort of jig, almost falling flat on his face.

"What was that?" asked Andreas, steadying him.

"Oh nothing. Cute tune, don't you think? How old are you, Andreas?"

"Thirty-nine."

"What do you think the odds are of another war in ten years?"

Andreas laughed. "I don't know. Pretty good. Why do you ask?"

"Your lucky day was when you came across Himmler when he was attacked by those Commies."

"Luck? Never believed in it," said Andreas. The sun hurt his eyes. He covers his eyes. He started to say something, hesitated, and then turning and looking McDonald straight in the eyes, broke into a long, nervous laugh. Annoyed at himself, he added, "Of course it's all nonsense, and I probably dreamed the whole thing. But you know, Mac, I did see him. I did talk to him."

They slowly made their way across the street toward the square. A crowd had gathered awaiting Andreas's speech. Men in brown and men in black patrolled the square, their boots flawlessly polished, the Eisenkreuz vaccinating their arms. The square was spotless.

"And it will sell papers," Mac said as he turned to find a seat.

The president of the Explorers Club, Sir David Bees, took the podium. Photographs of Hitler and King George lined the platform. Pointing to the man to his right, Sir Bees introduced the hero of the Eiger Massif, Dr. Andreas von Eckhart—caring physician, philanthropist, and head of the German Charity Hospital.

Andreas approached the podium, his speech in his hand. His SS boots shone in the proscenium lights. His stride was commanding, his knuckles were white. Smiling, he looked out at the audience and across the square toward

Whitehall. *Could God have deceived so many for so long—and who gives a damn? He's dead. A beer, a piece of ass, a place to curl up, and we're happy. So what's the answer? Have no illusions. Eat, sleep, get laid, and wait. But will he come? The man you seek is not coming. And does it matter? Nothing will change. Nothing ever will change.*

"... and Germany and Great Britain will always be friends and will always be partners in the fight against tyranny."

The applause continued as Andreas returned to his seat. Andreas looked at McDonald.

"You can feel it, Mac. You can see it in their eyes."

"What?" he asked.

"The despair, the fear, even worse, the desire, like a narcotic—another war. Only twenty years, Mac! The Germans have succumbed to it already. The British will be next. They'll have no choice. Either that or rename London. He's won. Hitler's won," said Andreas.

Chapter 6
Regent's Park, London

A GRAY MIST AND the smell of burning coal settle over London. Two men in dark-leather coats grunt and sweat, they take turns, leveling punch after punch on their victim. Spittle drools from their lips; Their faces glow. Their veins swell under their collars.

They are British, but they might be any number of believers in a cause. They obviously enjoy their work. They beat their victim as if they are beating dust from a rug.

Finally, like a sack of straw, the victim sinks to the ground.

"We have to find that code," says the larger of the men. "Run your fingers under his tongue and the back of his throat. Do it!

Now inside his bum."

"I hate this job," the smaller man says.

"The boss ain't gonna like it. All this work for nothing. Get his clothes back on."

"How the hell am I supposed to do that? The bones keep catching."

"Make sure he's done for," says the larger man. "I said get out and check him!"

The smaller man examines the body. Bony ends stick out from torn clothing in every direction. He gets back into the car and wipes his shoes.

"Get out and get the briefcase. Pick up those papers. For Christ's sake, do I have to tell you everything? Can't you think for yourself?"

"They're all covered with blood," says the smaller man getting back into the car.

"I can see that."

"Who the hell can make sense of all these diagrams and numbers?"

"That's not our problem. The boss said to bring back anything we found, and that means blood and all."

The same mist that covered London congealed into the fog that surrounds David and Mary Lean as they drive home.

"David, drive slowly," Mary says, her patrician voice cutting through the silence.

"Yes, my dear. We are barely moving now."

David had never explored anything more than the inside of a bottle, but he took pride in being a large contributor to the Explorers Club.

"That young officer is an excellent addition," said Mary.

"Yes, rather," said David.

"He's good-looking, an excellent surgeon, and from what Eleanor says, not too bad in bed."

Jesus. He had to be pretty hard up to fuck Eleanor. "Yes." David nodded, his mind fixed on the hatcheck girl at the club. Suddenly, he swerved to the side of the road and stopped.

"Why are you stopping?" Mary cried.

"He needs help!"

"Who?"

"That man—didn't you see his face, all bloody?"

"I saw no such thing," said Mary, "and even if I had, I wouldn't stop! Probably some Jew." She reached over and jerked the shift back. Pushing his foot aside, she slammed her foot on the gas. The driver of a car coming up behind saw the red taillights and swerved, barely missing them before careening off into the fog.

"It was probably just one of those striker thugs beating up another kike Bolshevik. No need for us to get involved," Mary said.

David's thoughts returned to the hatcheck girl as they pulled back onto the road. "At least for a moment it looked like a man," he muttered.

In a hurry to leave after his talk to the Explorers Club, Andreas barely missed a car backing into the highway and struck his head on his rearview mirror. He was on emergency room duty that evening. He would have the hospital registrar look at the wound on his forehead. The nick in his ear had stopped bleeding.

He hurried to the hospital dressing room where he changed into his scrubs. He was thankful the room was empty. He wouldn't have to take the ribbing and Hitler salutes.

Except for the sporadic cries of despair, the hospital was silent. A single light in the nurses' station lit the hall.

The nurse on duty, Deborah, a pretty blonde, stood as he entered.

"Good evening, doctor."

"Jack and Jill went up the hill to fetch a pail of water," he sang softly to himself. "Why, Deborah? Why did they climb the hill? Of course, because someone told them to. A sergeant, a corporal, a father. Rachel didn't, nor did Joseph. He was dead, and there was no angel to warn them. There was a machine gun at the top."

"What the hell are you talking about?"

"Nothing. Just no soap and two more dead children. No soap. Never enough soap."

"Where were they killed?"

"Cheapside, near the clinic, God's waiting room. Throats slit."

"What has the nursery rhyme to do with it?" she asked.

"Remember, cleanliness is next to godliness, and God demands that the little ones be clean before they enter heaven. Were the innocents cleansed before they were slaughtered? Rachel didn't get a chance to wash her children. Perhaps that's why she was weeping."

"You *are* crazy," she said.

"And you have a nice ass" he replied

"Later. Have these charts to finish."

Gingerly, he felt the bruise over his forehead. At most, he would have a small scar. His ribs hurt, and the darkening discoloration was spreading to his jaw. *Where the hell had that Bentley come from?* He poured a cup of coffee and took a deep breath. He noticed his operating shoes were covered with blood. *Have to have them cleaned before the next performance.*

Glancing at his watch, he wondered why he wore it. His time was kept by food trays and the medicine cart.

The loudspeaker crackled. "Dr. von Eckhart, report to emergency." The monotone announcement was followed by a giggle. "No, not here, silly." A click as the monitor was turned off.

Andreas lifted his leg from the desk and brushed the crumbs from his white coat. He put the cup of coffee on the table and both hands on his knees, heaved himself up, and sauntered past the flashing red light from the ambulance. *Time to play the part.*

The registrar, stethoscope in hand, burst through the curtain. *The play will begin.* A second actor entered, twisting her hips and thrusting her large breasts. She minced toward center stage and handed Andreas the magic potion. He plunged the needle into the heart ... the beat quickened, *thump, thump.*

A life had been saved.

"Is he dead?" the policeman asked.

"No. We saved him."

"He's a murderer," the policeman said.

"Who isn't?" Andreas replied. "It's not over yet. The show has just begun." He fondled the nurse to the beat of the heart: *whoosh, thump-thump.* The heart went silent.

"Death. You see, you never know."

"Dr. Eckhart, room 215," said the same bored voice.

"Let the next one on duty take it ... Jesus, I'm tired." He pushed back a shock of hair. His eyes were red rimmed. *Like throwing the dice. The man's number was up, and there wasn't a damned thing anyone was going to do to change that.*

He lumbered toward the dressing room. Cries for help.

Despair mingled with curses from faces turned toward the wall.

"You might want to look at this one," the blond nurse said.

Andreas leaned over the body.

"Jewish?" he whispered.

"Lowenstein. What else?" she answered.

"How the hell did he wind up here?"

"The ambulance driver was new and took him to the first hospital he could find. I explained the deal to him, but it was too late. It won't happen again."

"Great, but in the meantime, we're stuck with him."

"Not for long. Only until he dies. He's terribly beat up, lost a lot of blood, needs a transfusion, won't last the night."

"What else?" Andreas asked, throwing his hands skyward. "You know what this means if Himmler finds out?"

"He won't. We just have to find a way to keep it secret until he dies. Then throw him out with the rest of the trash."

"Why not before he dies?" asked the intern. "What the hell's the difference?"

"Murder," said Andreas.

"He's a Jew," the intern replied. "How about the incinerator? It's where he was headed for anyway. Himmler will never know."

The Jew stirred and turned his face. "Am I going to die?" he asked in a whisper.

"You are still very much alive," said the nurse.

His scrawny fingers, like a spider, fought to find hers and crawled onto her palm.

She shrugged and in disgust untangled his grasp. She held up a vial of morphine. "He's going to die anyway," she said.

"We could shoot him," the orderly said.

"The noise," she said.

"The mess," added the orderly. "I'm the one who's going to have to clean it up."

"We can't let him suffer," said the nurse. "It's the Christian thing to do."

"He's Jewish," said the orderly.

"Go ahead, shoot him," said Andreas.

No one moved.

"Our job is to care for him. He's a human being," said Andreas.

"A Jewish human being," said the nurse. "It's obvious he needs blood. It will leave a trail—who gave it and who got it."

"That's it," said Andreas. "I took an oath. Give him the transfusion."

"So long as your name is on the order. I want nothing to do with it," said the nurse.

Andreas leaned close to the Jew. "My name is Dr. Eckhart. I want to help you. I'm going to give you a transfusion. We have to."

"You have to kill me. It won't matter." He gestured and pulled Andreas toward him. He whispered, "Find my son. Give him the message: On land and in the sky. In the sky. It's in … Oh, my God," he pleaded, as if in prayer, "just a few seconds more." And then he fell back.

"I guess we won't need the transfusion," the nurse said, looking at Andreas.

"This wasn't the time to be a hero."

She rose. "What you do with him is up to you. I never saw him," she said, looking grimly at the intern.

"He never saw you, either. He's blind," said Andreas. "Look at his eyes. They're solid scar."

"He's seeing as much as the rest of us now," said the nurse.

"Not the sun and the moon," said the orderly.

"When did you last see them? What color are my eyes, my shoes? No, don't look. Tell me."

"I don't remember."

"Are the stars out?"

"I don't know."

"You can see, can't you?"

"I have—"

"It has nothing to do with seeing."

"We'll have to hide him in the bottom of the garbage," said Andreas.

"It can't be that bad. What can they do to us?" asked the orderly. "This is England."

"Did you see those people demonstrating?"

"Yes."

"They aren't from the local B'nai B'rith," said Andreas.

"I don't want my ass in a sling for some Jew," said the orderly.

Andreas smiled. "Now you're beginning to see. Stuff him in the laundry bag in the broom closet. We will toss him out with the infected linen in the morning."

Chapter 7
Kensington Court, London

THERE ARE SO MANY corpses. What's one more? What am I supposed to do? Andreas walked through the twilight and feeling chill, he pulled his collar around his neck. His concern for the Jew was little enough, but it was all he had. What the hell, his devotion to the poor had opened the pocketbook and legs of more than one debutante. Himmler ran the clinic with an iron hand, mostly for show. Medicine, even soap, was scarce.

"Verdammte English weather!" he cursed, tugging his scarf closer around his neck. He hailed a cab and glanced at the *Daily Telegraph* someone had left on the seat. "Hitler to Become Supreme Commander of the Wehrmacht." In a Reichstag speech, he had declared, "the protection of German blood and honor: the law of genetic inheritance." Carefully, so as not to alarm the British, French, and American press, he was laying the groundwork for war and for Jewish annihilation. War was inevitable. *At least it's honest.* Andreas laughed.

He was about to put the paper back when he saw the headline: "Two Children Killed," this time in Bayswater, another ghetto. Again, the dead children had been washed and an amulet found beside their bodies.

They drove past the bars, the darkened alleys, and the prostitutes who haunted hospital emergency rooms. "You got it wrong," one of the black ambulance drivers said. "They don't come here to be cured, just patched up so they can go on a little longer until they disappear down some street where murder is an everyday event. There are no jobs. The banks have no money. The soup kitchens no food. The rent is due."

"Awful fog," the driver said as he searched for Andreas's flat.

"What do you think of these marchers?" Andreas asked, reaching for his wallet.

"Well, sir, they all wants something. And in the end, I'm the one who winds up giving it. If you really want my opinion? I say fuck them."

Andreas paid the driver and walked up the white cement stairs to his flat, felt for the lock under the large brass plate that read, Mr. Andreas Eckhart, General Surgeon.

"Fuck them," he said. "Well, Yorick, what do you think of that?" He entered the apartment, laughing. He smelled the immaculate odor of furniture polish, the coffee brewing in the kitchen, and the aroma of roast in the oven, each indicating the person responsible, Anna.

"Ist das Sie, Herr Eckhart?"

He was still laughing when he walked to his desk to check his mail.

Again, his housekeeper called out, "Ist das Sie, Herr Eckhart?" Anna walked into the living room. Tall, regal, petulant, overbearing, Göring's former mistress, he'd insisted that Andreas hire her.

"Yes, Anna," he answered. A character out of an Ibsen play, a ramrod back, petulant, smug, and efficient. Tight lipped, she kept to herself and rarely went out even when invited.

"Is something funny?"

"No, Anna. Any messages?"

"Yes," she said close to tears and sitting bolt upright in her chair. "Minister Ribbentrop has called several times. His secretary said it was important. You are to call him as soon as you arrive."

When the phone rang, Anna reached for it. Annoyed, he took it from her, noticing the worry lines around her eyes.

"Who?" he stammered. "Why are you calling me? I'm off duty."

"I had no choice," said the registrar at the other end. "Someone called from the German embassy. I think it was Ribbentrop. He said to call you and no one else. The man is terribly beat up, looks as if a bus ran over him. There is really no reason for you to come in. There's nothing you can do for him. Don't think he'll last an hour."

Anna stood clutching her apron. Tears ran down her cheeks. She knew this man. She was no more a servant than he was Jewish. Andreas hung up. Seconds later, the phone rang again. That time, Andreas answered, unsurprised to hear it was Ribbentrop himself.

"We would be most appreciative if you could look into a situation. It is very delicate and must be handled with the utmost caution." Andreas visualized Ribbentrop's monocle slipping. "A close friend has been involved in an accident. I believe you know him, Herr Lebenfels. I believe you paid him a visit just recently."

The flat in Cheapside. That's why he didn't show up.

"Would you be kind enough to look in on him at the hospital? There's someone on the way who can fill in the details. He should be at your door in a few minutes."

"Herr Lebenfels," he murmured as he hung up.

Anna started to say something but stopped and looked away.

"Do you know this Lebenfels?" Andreas asked.

She shook her head, on guard, waiting.

"It seems someone tried to kill him. Are you certain you don't know him?" He felt it important to be right about this. It was evident that the accident had affected her immensely. She had never lied to him in the past. Her perfume was overwhelming. He didn't recall her ever using perfume. "He's been badly hurt," he added.

Anna's eyes widened. "No, Herr Doctor, I've never heard of him," she said flatly, bending to pick up a nonexistent object. She brushed some lint from his jacket and straightened his tie.

A few minutes later, Andreas stepped into the backseat of the embassy car and sat next to Herr Weber, a short, wizened man. He wore a large bowler that seemed to have been poured over his head, a trench coat, and an Eton tie knotted under a silk scarf. He smiled from beneath his clipped mustache and extended a soft, wet hand.

"Good of you to help," he said. His voice was smooth and sibilant. Andreas thought of a confession booth.

"I believe you knew Herr Lebenfels."

"Yes, I knew of him. I never met him."

"He's dead," said Weber.

Andreas started to correct him, but Weber ignored him and continued. "Herr Lebenfels was carrying important documents, in code. They must *not* fall into the wrong hands." Looking directly at him, he said, "I assume you will be successful. Meet me tomorrow at the Connaught Hotel. Have the documents with you."

He opened the door. Andreas was barely clear of the running board when he ordered the car to drive on.

Andreas nodded to the ambulance driver busily wiping down a stretcher. He shook his head as Andreas walked by. "Not much you can do for him, Doc."

Andreas shoved his hands into his coat pockets, squared his shoulders, and nodded to the admitting clerk. He walked into emergency. The new secretary was young and pretty. Those days, they all seemed young and pretty. He gave her six months watching the flotsam pass through the doors before her warm, bright eyes became as cold as agates—pimps, hustlers pushing for a story, the clap, a prescription, a pill, something to dull the pain, children with worms, the palsied, the repentant. He was in the middle of a shithouse, and it overflowed. He was tired. There was nothing he could do about it.

Medicine, like the church, had promised more than it could deliver. And he was left to collect the tab. He noticed the tattoo on Lebenfels's arm, the double-armed lightning bolt of the SS. The nurse repositioned his arms. Again, they fell away.

"No veins," the anesthetist said, placing his arms back on the stretcher.

"He must be bleeding into his belly," Andreas said. "Get him to surgery—fast."

The familiar rush, bottles, and instruments flying. Lebenfels's clothes, unnoticed, dropped to the floor. The janitor threw them into a hamper.

"Back again?" the scrub nurse asked.

Andreas looked at her over his mask and murmured, "Tonight?"

"You always say that," she said with a laugh.

"Damn it!" The nurse reached around and wiped Andreas's mask. Like a wet hose, the artery had slipped from his fingers.

"We're losing him," the anesthetist said, leaning over the ether screen. Andreas laughed. "You've got it backward. He found us."

"We're losing him," the anesthetist repeated, looking up from his novel. "We're pouring blood down a rat hole."

Andreas had seen the plot before. It was farce. It was too late. Lebenfels was a dead man, but the actors had already gathered. The scrub nurse, rubbing her ass against the chief registrar, looked up and smiled under her mask.

"We gather together to ask the Lord's ..." Andreas murmured, leaning over the screen that separated him from the anesthetist. "Perhaps he was better lost. Keep the blood coming," he said in a calm voice, taunting the anesthetist, who had returned to his novel. "His will be done. Don't want the play to end too soon—before he gets his final scene."

He paid no attention to the shower stall next to him, assuming it was one of the doctors.

"I decided to take you up on your offer," said the nurse as she stepped from the steam. Her large breasts jostled as she reached for a towel. Her nipples were hard. Her flat belly tapered to the cylinders of her thighs. She ran her hands, then her lips, over his erection.

"You promised," she said. He lifted her onto the counter. Her buttocks squeaked. She threw her head back. He lunged into her. She met him with a deep moan and pushed back. He drove deeply, more forcefully. She clawed. He released himself into her with a cry. She too cried out as she felt him collapse.

Spent, he felt her push him away. She slid off the counter, dressed, and without a word, left the room. Andreas leaned against the sink.

"Has anyone been here to see him?" he asked. The Gestapo had positioned a Brynnhilda as Lebenfels's private-duty nurse. "Remember, no one except me gets near him."

"Don't worry," she said, pointing to the outline of a revolver under her skirt.

"Where are his clothes?"

"They didn't come back with him. Probably got sent to the basement to be incinerated."

Panicked, Andreas started for the elevator, changed his mind, and took the stairs.

"Where are Lebenfels's clothes?" he asked.

"Who?"

"The patient I just operated on. He came in a few hours ago."

"Probably in the basement with the rest of the stuff."

The admitting secretary was new, pert, with the tight

body and wide-eyed innocence of a teenager. "Why is everybody looking for those bloody rags?"

"Someone else is looking for them?"

"Yeah. A few minutes ago. A big fella, said he was a relative."

"What relative?"

"I didn't ask, and he didn't say."

Andreas rushed to the basement. The room was rank with mold. A single bulb hung from the ceiling. He yanked on the string, sending it into orbit, throwing light on discarded clothes, dolls, toys, pocketbooks … the refuse of the dead. He heard shoes scraping along the wall; he smelled aftershave, sweat, breath.

"Don't make me kill you," Andreas whispered with feigned bravado. Perhaps he hadn't heard. Shadow and light fell over the unknown face making it seem there were two. His arms dangled at his sides, and there was the odor of tobacco. "I don't want to kill you. Christ. I don't even know you. Whatever you're getting paid, I'll double it."

The shadow slid along the wall, immense. Perhaps he hadn't heard—understood.

"Gehen see sofort Ich will sie night schiesen!"

Perhaps, even worse, he had.

Silence. An eternity. Then in another heartbeat, eternity came to an end and the unknown figure was before him. Like cats, they circled each other, and with each circle, the stranger drew closer.

The stranger was on him, his soft belly pressed against his back. His sleeve rubbed against Andreas's throat; steel flashed in the dim light. Andreas kicked a foot back into his attacker's knee, felt him buckle, and turned to face him.

He has just come from the barber, a smudge of shaving cream still on his ear. Fat but agile, his large head sitting between broad shoulders, in a crowd he would be one of the many—faceless, expressionless, invisible.

The stranger spread his legs for better balance, jabbing and circling, passing the knife from hand to hand, making it difficult for Andreas to guard against the stroke.

Andreas searched for a weapon, something, anything. The stranger grunted. Cunning and deceptively quick, his small eyes darted, his arms moved in wide circles; looking for an opening to plunge the knife.

"Dr. von Eckhart. Are you down there?"

It was the admitting clerk, Claire.

The stranger cocked his head, looking away, briefly off guard. Andreas reached for the dagger, turned it, and plunged it into the attacker's chest. It ripped through his shirt, glanced off a rib, and then like going through butter slid in to the hilt.

Eyes wide, spittle dripping from the corners of his mouth, the dying man looked at Andreas in disbelief. Andreas pulled the dagger out. It was followed by a puff of air but little blood. He gave an involuntary kick, the last nervous agitation of his life. Searching his pockets, Andreas found fragments of uneaten coffee cake wrapped in greasy waxed paper and smelling of fish, nothing that looked like a message. He quickly dragged the body to one of the iceboxes that served as the clinic's makeshift morgue and stuffed it in.

"Are you all right?" Claire asked. "I heard a racket down here but didn't pay it much attention. I thought maybe one of the ambulance drivers had come down looking for spare parts." She smiled a sweet, sexy smile.

"I found someone rummaging around in the clothes, but I scared him off. Ran out the side door," he said, pointing to the basement exit.

"Geez, I don't know how anyone can wear that stuff. Most of it is covered with blood and stinks to high heaven. It's the kid's stuff that tears me apart."

Maybe she's being truthful, maybe not, but once the corpse is discovered, she's bound to put it together.

"You know, I've been waiting to ask you to dinner," he said, looking soulfully into her eyes. He slipped his arm around her waist.

She left him with her phone number and a promise.

"Has there been anyone to see him?" Andreas asked, returning to look in on Lebenfels.

"Two men had walked by down the corridor."

He checked Lebenfels's blood pressure. He was dead but for an occasional agonal beat. He looked at him, at the thin mustache curling over his lip. *Had he in his wildest imagined that this was his end? Why here?*

He left the hospital and headed for the nearest pub. He was too tense and full of adrenaline to go home. *What the hell has Tara gotten me into?* It was dark. He turned frequently, looking behind him. The knife that had nicked his ear at the apartment was called a *sheruken*, used mostly in Asia. It took a professional to throw it. If it hadn't been for that dipsy clerk, he'd be sharing shelf space with the other corpses. Well, he'd take care of her later; a little concern and some money should do it. Whoever was after Lebenfels knew his business.

It was nearly midnight when he entered his flat. Anna was out, and the flat was silent. Jumped when the phone rang.

"Willoughby here, Scotland Yard. Is this von Eckhart? Sorry to intrude at this late hour."

Scotland Yard? Could they possibly have found the body already? Andreas felt his heart beating faster, and he consciously worked to avoid expressing concern in his voice. "Yes, it is Dr. von Eckhart. How can I help you?" The words came out slowly and steadily. He reached for the decanter and shook off the chill. Anna had at least built a fire before leaving. It must have been some time ago judging from the dying embers. He poured himself a large whiskey and went about rebuilding the fire. An ember exploded. Andreas felt for his gun. He had left it in his coat pocket. He drew back, sensing there was someone in the room.

Willoughby trundled on. Would it be possible for him stop by the Yard in the morning? But Andreas could not answer. Instead, he fell to his knees as the blow struck him across the back of his skull.

"Who are you?" Andreas asked, rubbing his head.

"Willoughby," he answered, "Inspector Willoughby, Scotland Yard."

The voice was hollow and came from a long way off. He wore a long mackintosh, too long for his slight form and dripping onto the Aubusson rug. Anna would be upset. "When you didn't answer, I thought something had happened, and I rushed over. That's a nasty knock on the head. Perhaps we ought to go to the hospital and have it looked at."

"I'm a doctor. I'm all right."

Willoughby seemed disappointed. "Well, if you insist, but I'd get it looked at."

"It's just a knock on the head. By the way, how the hell did you get in?"

"Ah, well, we have a few tricks you know."

Stretched out on the sofa, Andreas described his attack. Saw nothing. No enemies. Couldn't explain. Simple burglary probably. Lies of course. *Does the inspector believe me?* As he spoke, Willoughby toured the flat, opening doors that led to the living room and bedroom.

"Why are you here, Inspector?"

"Yes, sorry. Forgot to explain. There's been a sort of a murder at the hospital, someone stabbed in the laundry room."

"What could they have been after in the laundry room?"

"That's the question, isn't it?" said the inspector archly.

"Certainly not the moldy rags. We talked to the clerk, ah, secretary. She didn't know a thing. Hard to imagine she didn't hear a ruckus, insists she didn't hear a thing," he said.

"Well, inspector, I don't know anything about it, but of course I'll help any way I can."

"Right, of course. We'll straighten it out. Anyone live here with you?" he asked, opening the door to Anna's room.

"Just my housekeeper who lives here. She appears to be out this evening."

"Well, obviously you are in no shape to answer questions now. Suppose I call and arrange to meet you tomorrow."

"That would be very generous of you." Andreas eyed the decanter. "Can I offer you a drink?" he said, pouring one for himself.

"No. I never drink on duty. I'd be careful. I mean, so soon after that nasty blow."

Andreas fought the urge to laugh. Willoughby fit the caricature too perfectly. *I never drink on duty?* "I apologize, but Christ, just once I'd like to meet an inspector who *did* drink on duty."

Andreas threw himself into a chair and watched Willoughby drive off. Holding his gun, a standard-issue nine-millimeter Luger, he waited, expecting the door to creak open at any moment. As though his worst fears had been realized, he was certain he heard someone on the landing. He jumped to his feet and flung open the door, the Luger held stiffly at arm's length.

"Jesus!" shouted McDonald, staring at the Luger pointed directly at his chest. "What the hell is wrong with you? You could have killed me," he said, staggering into the flat.

"Sorry, Mac." Andreas closed and locked the door. "I've had rather a bad night."

"It certainly looks that way. What's wrong?"

"Murder," Andreas said.

"What are you talking about?"

Andreas's voice was almost a whisper. "What I am talking about, old sport, is that my life has been threatened twice in the last two weeks. You already know about my trip to Cheapside and my meeting with this Lebenfels."

McDonald spied the decanter and poured himself a drink.

"Mac, it's only seven a.m."

"So?"

"Suit yourself. Mac, someone tried to kill me last night."

McDonald tasted his whiskey. A highland single malt. "That's what you get for screwing all those women, probably a jealous husband. Besides, if someone meant to kill you, you'd be dead."

"Funny, that's what I told the inspector. You just missed him. Amusing fellow. You wouldn't like him. Doesn't drink on duty."

"You are assuming that both attempts were by the same person."

"Christ, Mac, how many people do you think are after me? It has to be this Lebenfels."

"I thought he was dead," said McDonald. "I've just come from the hospital, and they told me what'd happened."

"He is, but whatever they are after isn't."

"You're probably right," said McDonald, but he looked dubious. "After all, killing an SS officer would mean a body and an investigation, the last thing they'd want."

"I'm going to have to go back and get rid of the body."

"What body?"

"The guy I killed, whoever threw the knife. Hell, how do I know?"

"What knife?"

"The one someone threw at me at Cheapside."

McDonald was silent, his face suggesting a man trying to piece together a difficult puzzle. "Don't play the fool, Andreas. This is serious." He suddenly exhibited genuine alarm.

"Now it's serious, but only a few minutes ago, it was a joke."

"Things have changed," said McDonald.

"Like what?"

"A body. That's what. What did you do with the body?"

"I didn't have many options. I stuffed it into one of the iceboxes. No one saw me. No, that's not true. There was one person, Claire."

"Who's Claire?"

"A secretary."

"So there was a witness."

"Not exactly."

Andreas explained the events as they had happened.

As a reporter, McDonald had seen his share of murders, and he'd seen his share of killings as well. He finished his drink at a gulp and poured another. Nothing shocked him anymore. Nothing hurt him anymore. "The first thing you need to do is get rid of that body. Then make Claire an offer. Buy her off. Or get her out of town."

"Shame she had to get involved."

"The way you tell it, if she hadn't, you'd be dead," McDonald said with a reporter's attention to detail. "Of course," he added sarcastically, "you could kill her yourself. That's what a good Nazi would do."

"It's what my father would do. Where the hell did that come from? I haven't thought of him since the funeral. Should have known he wasn't through with me."

"And when do you start taking responsibility?" McDonald asked.

"I'll take responsibility for my own actions bur not for someone else's. I've been through that."

"When does it become your problem?"

"Never. Why should it be? I didn't create this mess. I don't hate Jews. I don't hate anybody. I just want to be left alone to live and die. I didn't create this damned world!"

"What did you say the name of the man was? Not the guy you killed, the one you were supposed to meet? The guy with the code?"

"Hans Dieter Lebenfels. Whoever killed him had it in for him. Every bone in his body was broken." He dug into his pocket and produced a thin, black booklet. "I found his passport," he said, wiping the blood still on the edges. "He'd just returned from Cairo."

McDonald exhaled audibly. "This is no game, Andreas. Keep your head down."

Andreas detached himself from his thoughts of Claire. He shifted his focus and said in a loud burst, "It has to be her. She's the one."

"Who? You mean the secretary?" McDonald asked.

"No, my housekeeper. She's frightened me from the day I met her."

"Christ, man, the woman is in love with you," said McDonald. "I could see that the first time I met her."

"This is her sanctuary," Andreas said, leading McDonald into her bedroom. The room was dank, cold, and musty. What light there was filtered through heavy shades and drawn drapes. McDonald reached for the shade.

"No! Don't."

"How's she going to know?"

"She will," said Andreas.

"I had no idea you were this frightened of her. Why the hell don't you fire her?"

"Because, my dear fellow, she was Göring's mistress." It was almost a whisper. "And I was afraid. When my father returned from India, he brought with him a new wife and a new terror—Anna. You just don't fire Göring's mistress.

My father had just married and needed a servant for his new bride. One he could trust, which to him meant someone who believed in his Aryan ideas.

"The Aryans were big in India in the Sanskrit days. Even then, they thought it their duty to link all parts of the world together—one Reich you might say. The Persians called themselves Ariana—hence Iran. At any rate, Göring provided him, my father, with—his lover, Anna. The crazy woman became a passionate follower of Helena Blavatsky. The one who preached secret doctrines and fantasies that Aryans had proceeded from the Atlantians and were descended from the Brahmin ruling class. The same ones the Indian nationalists embraced.

"The only difference, these were in Sanskrit. A royal priesthood. Brahmans, and caste were the defining ingredients. Sound familiar? You know, all the mythic tradition and Volk knowledge that's so popular these days. Anyway, to make a long story short, Göring was gravely wounded in the putsch in Munich in November '23. Everything was in turmoil when Anna somehow appeared out of nowhere and carried him off to Schorfheide, his hunting lodge, and nursed him back to health. That's where he became addicted to morphine, by the way. We Germans are great at substituting fidelity for caring. What Anna cared about was the Reich, the Black Forest, Hansel and Gretel. My mother needed a servant, and my father gave her the Antichrist."

"Look." Andreas pointed to a carving on the mantle. "Kali Tara, the Hindu goddess of death."

"Jesus, I wouldn't want to meet her in a dark alley."

"It's grotesque, but it's only a carving. Would you feel

better if it were a cross with a man hanging on it with nails in his hands and feet?" Andreas asked. "I am Kali Tara. I am Time, the devourer. I swallow all that exists. I stand on the corpse of existence," said Andreas, his voice trembling.

"Tara. Isn't that your sister's—"

"Yes. My mother liked the sound," Andreas said, swiftly looking away. "You may laugh, but if my mother were here, she would be in despair. You know how women are. My mother would tell me stories at her knee. Kali Tara often appears as a goddess with four arms, a lolling tongue, and holding a garland of heads."

"That's an awful moniker to put on such a pretty woman," said McDonald. "You need to get some sleep. You look like hell."

"I keep waking up, can't sleep for more than an hour. Could you with that around?" Andreas said with a desperate chuckle.

"You need a good lay," said McDonald.

"That's the last thing I need for Christ's sake. All you have to do is wander outside and you'll be faced with a dozen young whores."

"Well then, get a dog." Mac laughed.

Andreas's voice became very low. He spoke slowly. A sadness had fallen over him, and he looked on with bitterness. "It's not the same. It will never be the same."

"What?" asked Mac.

"I don't know if I can put it into words. I just know that life will never be the same," he said with sadness that infected them both.

"This is probably the work of a cheap thief. It has nothing to do with your life."

"What is my life?" said Andreas, weary, grinding out his cigarette.

"Look, Andreas. You're one lucky son of a bitch. You are Heydrich's trusted spy, you have Himmler's ear, and in this world, that's all you need."

"Yes, that's all you need," he said with overwhelming sadness. He looked searchingly at McDonald. "Mac, I don't like the Jews any more than the Nazis. I just want to be left alone. I want nothing to do with the whole damned business. Somehow, I got dragged into it, just the way Anna did, the way we all did."

"We were born," said McDonald, a smirk crossing his face.

Andreas went rigid as if struck. "Why didn't I think of it sooner? Lebenfels! He's famous for his work on runes, and I think he designed Wiligut, where they keep the cyclotron."

"What the hell are runes?"

"Symbols, like the alphabet. The Schutzstaffel, the SS lightning bolt, pagan. The cross, Christian, both symbols."

"Interesting," said Mac, "but what the hell does it have to do with the knock on your head?"

"I don't know, but put Anna, Göring, Lebenfels, and Himmler in one pot, add murder, and you have a stew."

McDonald rose to take a closer look at the statue. Andreas was ashen and sweating. He'd won the Iron Cross but was afraid of a fifty-year-old woman.

"Doesn't prove a thing. So she's a little mad. Half of Germany is locked up in their rooms worshiping a man with a funny mustache and the other half a man nailed to a cross."

"This is London, not Berlin."

"London, Berlin, Calcutta, it's not the place. It's not my father. It's not Anna. It's me! I can't seem to get it together."

"So?" said McDonald smiling, trying to keep Andreas from wandering into one of his dark moods.

"Getting back to Anna. If she wanted to kill you, there are easier ways, like poisoning your knockwursts."

Chapter 8
Connaught Hotel, Carlos Place, London

Andreas slept fitfully, aware of the slightest noise. The next morning, he showered and dressed. Satisfied there were no bruises, he reached for his umbrella. He called Scotland Yard and postponed his meeting with Willoughby, claiming a headache. It seemed that Willoughby had cleared most of his questions already and the others were not pressing. Strangely, Willoughby ended the conversation with "I would still be careful, Dr. Eckhart."

The sun was pale yellow. A damp chill wrapped around his neck and seeped under his clothes. He was being followed. He turned around several times, stood in front of windows, but saw only a middle-aged couple, the man dressed in a tweed coat with a pink carnation in the lapel, the woman in a flower-print dress and severe headmistress shoes.

He entered the Connaught Hotel, headed for the grillroom, and ran straight into Henry Sloat, married to Diana Bellows, the air attaché's daughter.

"Hello, Andreas. Fancy meeting you here. I say, you haven't forgotten our shoot this Thursday. Marbury and

Dwight will be there. And don't forget our party next weekend. Bring your friend Ernst."

Andreas's face made a slight, involuntary twitch.

"Oh, I am sorry, old boy," said Sloat sincerely.

"Should be loads of fun," Andreas said quickly and headed for the bar attempting to escape. Sloat was a throwback, a familiar but depressing story, a man who found solace in war, a man with no place to go and hanging onto his past. His promise lacerated by the end of the war, he hung on hoping for another. He followed close on Andreas's heels. *Shoot?* thought Andreas. *Might as well toss a bunch of dolls into the air. The birds stand as much a chance.*

It was hotter than hell in the grillroom. Sloat joined him. Despite the heat, he was still wearing his Oxford scarf with club colors over his Royal Air Force uniform. Despite his uniform, Sloat looked sallow and sunken. His gray, streaked hair hanging over his collar, he refought his battles without the courage to take on a new one.

"It is different up there," he said noticeably animated, "the noise of the engine and the bullets and the ..." His voice disappearing into his scarf. "It's all confused: horses and cows and sheep and men and the smell of death. You'd be surprised how much a man looks like a sheep from up there. Couldn't be sure. I just grabbed the trigger and let God decide. It's his flock."

"Nothing official," said Andreas, "but the rumor is the Germans are going to send Ernst Teuer and the Condor Legion to Spain."

"Once you have heard the scream from one of those dive-bombers..." Sloat could barely contain his glee, his hand swooping over the bar in pantomime. The patrons knew the drill; they'd heard it many times before and had grown bored. They turned away, shrugged.

Agitated, Sloat leaned forward on the edge of his stool. "He spoke to you, didn't he?"

"Who?" Andreas asked.

"God," Sloat said, his hair spilling over and the perspiration dripping onto his collar. "He dared you too, didn't he?" said Sloat, grabbing Andreas's lapels. "He dares me every time, plays with me, and makes a fool of me."

Andreas looked into the blank faces. Smiling. *What the hell am I doing here? Why here? Is there someplace I should be?*

"Can you believe she once loved me?" Sloat asked, fidgeting with his scarf, one elbow resting on the bar. He pointed with his chin toward a woman just entering and glancing longingly at his wife from a distance—a dog allowed to drink from the edges of his dish. Andreas pitied him.

Aware of her good looks, she posed. Removing her white gloves, finger over finger, and surveying the battlefield with all the skill of a field marshal, Lady Diana Bellows strode toward the bar. Patrons moved to make room; elbows gave way. Slat pushed himself away from the bar, the tumbler of whiskey still in his hand. Diana Bellows barely noticed.

"Do you ever take off that scarf?" Andreas asked. "It's hot in here."

"I'd be naked. They might not recognize me," he said, downing the whiskey in one gulp.

Diana Bellows had already met her newest conquest, Major Ernst Teuer, a German ace. They were often seen together at Gstaad. A marvelous skier, his family had a house in Grindelwald, in the mountains, where the snow was white and clean and fell silently.

Diana—haughty, impudent, and beautiful. A woman who passed you on the street with the self-assurance of her class and looks. Pale blue eyes and Nordic cheekbones, full, red lips, and greedy breasts straining at her blouse. Andreas had met her before, had felt the point of her rapier tongue. Not anxious to be the target again, he started to leave—too late.

"This lovely fellow is really a full German colonel, a hero," she announced to no one as she slipped onto a stool. "He climbed the…" She faltered. "What was the name of that mountain?"

"The Eiger," said Andreas, remaining standing. Bored, the assembled looked at him with increased curiosity, frowned as if awaiting a clap of thunder, wondering about a man who'd met God. Perhaps God would show up here at the bar and have a drink. Minutes passed, a half hour and he hadn't come. They'd been waiting a long time. They had important things to do. Why should they wait? Why here? Why now?

They knew nothing and cared nothing: Sloat, his love, his sorrow, his defiance. They knew only that they'd put money in the basket and deserved better.

Diana Bellows flicked an ash from her cigarette, turned, and introduced Sybil Long, an attractive, flat-chested actress who resembled one of the characters out of a Noël Coward play. Stately and waving a long cigarette holder, Sybil ran her tongue over her lips and offered her hand in the same indolent way she did on stage. She drifted away toward a young woman at the end of the bar leaving Andreas with Diana.

"We have met," Andreas said. "You are much lovelier than even your photograph." The words fell off his lips automatically. She was lovely, haughty, beautiful, and frightening. Her eyes were killer's eyes. He knew them, had looked through them. Despite her arrogance, she was alone.

Her legs crossed, her elegant thighs moist, her skirt above her knees, Diana Bellows, a huntress looking for game, searched her purse for a cigarette, desperately trying to hide the pangs and hunger for adoration, for fawning attention. She lit a cigarette, placed it in a diamond-studded holder, and disappeared in a cloud of white smoke. Waving the weapon in front of her, she said, "You are the hero of the Eiger climb, aren't you? The one where the entire team died. Except you," she added, staring down her aquiline nose. "You killed your best friend, and you told God to fuck off. Marvelous. I read the newspapers."

Her cold, defiant blue eyes swept over him, undressing him, leaving him bare. She was the real thing. A bitch.

"It's far-fetched. I mean that you should meet and talk to God—even tell him to go to hell. You didn't, really?" She smiled. "But with Hitler and Wagner, all this stuff about the German gods, who knows? I have to hand it to you. It's a good story."

Fingering her necklace and swinging her foot, she looked around at the others sitting at the bar. She knew them. They were the same ones, always there. But something had changed. A ghost hovered over the bar. Uninvited. Smiling. Dampening the laughter. Reminding them of the hopelessness, the weariness. There was no escape. They were tired of being alone, of waiting.

On the streets, in alleys, in bedrooms. Life was changing. Things that mattered no longer seemed to: love, courtship, seduction. Men assumed you would go to bed. They planned the evening around it. They would never realize it and wouldn't care if they did. A woman had to be at ease, her feet warm, words of love in her ears, hands traveling like soft cotton over her body, caressing, exploring ... then, at the right time, yielding. Now, it's important to be an actress, to fake it. She couldn't remember the last time she'd had an orgasm.

The luster in her cheeks, her coiled hair framing a porcelain face, seduction became her objective—not because she desired to, but simply because she could; it reaffirmed she was still in control.

Diana's gaze settled on the white collar of a priest entering the room. Glass in hand and eyes wandering, fighting off the boredom of his collar, he became the unfortunate object of her remorse. She had a score to settle.

"Isn't that so, Father?" she asked as he walked past. "You don't remember me?" She ground her cigarette into an ashtray. Her face twisting into a smile, she said, "I'm Diana Bellows, Steven's mother. You remember, we buried him—you and I, after the miscarriage. That's what they called it, a miscarriage, one with a crushed skull. Have you seen many of those, Father?"

"Miscarriages?" He was clearly startled. "I'm afraid I don't remember."

"It had to be a miscarriage. After all, you don't preside over abortions, do you, Father?"

The man stared, working to place the face. His collar had suddenly become tight, and he pulled at it. "I believe I know your family, but … ah … forgive me, I can't just at this moment recall …"

"Of course, it's difficult to remember one whore from another, Father. Perhaps this will jog your memory. We are generous supporters of the church. Your church."

His face changed, and he looked suddenly tired and weary, like a beaten dog. He had made a mistake, burying the child with church rites, but it had resulted in a large donation. He'd taken only a little for himself, just enough to get away for a few days. The chance meeting brought back the guilt and shame. He knew he would pay. Well, here it was. He looked at his reflection in the long mirror that ran along the bar wall. He had undergone many reinventions. With each compromise, each one so small that it hardly mattered, his face changed and his visage hardened until, like Dorian Gray, he hardly recognized himself. He took out a large handkerchief and blew his nose. The ceremonies—births, deaths, marriages—all ran together and carried no significance past the donation that went with them. He searched for the appropriate stored phrases and condolences.

"Goodness, now where is your mistress?" Diana scanned the taproom, saw her tucked away in a dark alcove. "Pardon me, Father," she said with a voice too cordial. "We are being rude. Mary," she called out. "Don't sit there all alone. Come and join us."

Mary, a woman wearing a plain dress and a shabby, old-fashioned hat and carrying a parasol, was overwhelmed with shyness. Her first thought was to retreat.

"Oh, it's you, Lady Bellows," she said with an attempt at a curtsy.

"Don't go," Diana said, sensing complete victory.

Undecided, Mary reached for her bonnet and fled. Father Nicholas, genuinely frightened, stammered from foot to foot.

"There is something you can do for me, Father, but it doesn't have to be this minute. I'll call you," said Diana, feeling the first pangs of guilt.

He started to move away, hoping he'd escaped the worst of it. "At your convenience," he said, turning to scrape out of the room.

Waiters moved like shadows in the noise and leaned in to ask diffidently whether Lady Bellows "would like another drink" and whether "Miss Sybil Long would like to have hers refreshed."

"I hate it. Being a bitch."

"Well then, stop it," said Sybil.

"I can't help it."

"Ernst," Diana said suddenly, looking directly at Andreas. "Of course, Ernst Langer. Hitler dedicated the climb to you. Was it for Hitler that you killed him?"

"Climbers die. It's part of the game. The jury found me innocent. It was an accident."

"You knew they were going to die. That's murder."

He laughed. "It's easy to demand heroism from someone when you yourself may not have it. Why would I kill him? I loved him."

"It's as good a reason as any," she shot back.

The admission, torn out of him, startled him, and he stared into the mirror.

"Smoky in here, isn't it?" she said, dismissing the tears forming in his eyes. She hadn't meant to wound him.

"It's been hell," he said. "I mean … I did love him, you know."

His confession, honest and unashamed, shook her. "I never loved anyone until Ernst. And I killed him." There was no hate, no attempt to cover his crime. It was fact, there for all to see.

Searching her store of set phrases marked for use in awkward situations, Diana said, "You *are* coming to my party. I won't take no for an answer." She had turned the pages and found a phrase that both deflected the need to go further and yet made Andreas feel he was acceptable. He was a lost soul, and she would change him with a woman's love.

"Ribbentrop will be there. You have no excuse," she teased with an impudent laugh.

"Of course," he said, relieved.

Andreas knew he'd been a witness to murder: she had killed the minister with a flick of the tongue just as she could espouse causes with her mouth full of caviar. But how her breasts strained at her sweater. And there was that moment of truth when she'd faced him and didn't cower.

Was that necessary? she asked herself. *He's a fool to go around bruiting his love for another man, but who in this room isn't a fool?*

She tried to force the hours ahead into a meaningful pattern but really had no place to go, nowhere she had to be at any time. Nobody was waiting for her. They had all played the game with her and grown bored. This was a new game with new partners. She was through, she told herself with something like conviction, finished playing games.

She stared at the whiskey left in the glass. She could hear it, the soft violence, the ice melting, settling, each cube jostling as it shrank into the brown liquid. She dropped her face into her arms. Her hand shook, and she felt herself tremble. Behind her, sunset reflected in the bar mirror.

Andreas, conscious of his birthmark, tugged at his sleeve and thrust his hands into his pockets. The clatter of the silverware, the hushed glances, and the whispered slights made him cringe. He excused himself and drifted to the other end of the room, ordered a whiskey, and settling into a chair, reread the note from McDonald. He smiled: "P.S.: Marry Claire? Lock the door."

Chapter 9
Connaught Hotel, London

HIS HAIR WAS WHITE and brushed back at the temples; his forehead was high and overhung two deep eye sockets with narrow-lidded, blue eyes. His uniform impeccably cut, Hans Weber Berlin, Gestapo, entered the cafe, sauntered up to Andreas, and stood beside him. The boisterous room quieted to a muted hush as Weber took Andreas's arm and led him to a table at the far end of the room.

"You must forgive me for being late. All turned out satisfactorily, I trust." He removed his gray suede gloves and carefully placed them on the table in front of him. "Did you find the code?"

"No, just this." Andreas handed him Lebenfels's passport. "The last entry is Cairo."

"Useless rubbish," said Weber, putting it in his pocket and pacing back and forth. "Colonel, we know he had the code." He leaned forward. "We are certain it was on him," he said slowly, enunciating each word.

"Yes, sir," said Andreas. "Unless someone has already taken it. You know of course that I killed one of them."

84

"So our friends in Scotland Yard have informed us. We knew there would be others looking for it. Were there any witnesses?"

Andreas hesitated. If he mentioned Claire, she would be dead by morning. "No," he said. "I don't think so." Though a familiar figure at the bar, there was something about Colonel Weber that commanded attention, extra consideration. You knew with absolute certainty that nothing got past him. You dared not toy with him.

"We will take care of it. The information we are after will determine the future course of the Reich." He lit a cigarette and leaned across the table.

"I've searched every piece of his clothing," Andreas said.

"Up to now, Colonel Eckhart, we have let you pretend that you were aloof from our cause. We have let you continue the fantasy because it served our purposes. Now you are in it, Colonel, up to your neck. The code cannot fall into the wrong hands. The consequences would be catastrophic for all concerned. Is that clear?" He took a draw on his cigarette. "Colonel, I repeat, search again!"

He ground his cigarette into the ashtray, squeezed his water glass so tightly that Andreas thought it might crack, picked up his gloves, and left.

Chapter 10
Marble Arch, London

ANDREAS TOOK THE ENVELOPE and stood to one side in the foyer, holding it to the light. It bore the seal of the British air attaché, Sir Harold Bellows.

"Dear Herr von Eckhart,

Lady Bellows and I wish the pleasure of your company at a reception in honor of Herr Ribbentrop next weekend."

He took a deep breath and dialed Guy's Hospital. It took a moment, but when Claire finally arrived at the phone, her voice was exactly as he had remembered. He launched into a well-rehearsed speech. "I've been thinking about you … all this time, and I really haven't gotten to know you … Why don't we take a weekend together?"

God, he had gotten good at this. He had never thought of her except to get her into bed. When he looked at her, he looked through her at the wallpaper.

As for her part … the great doctor asking her to go away with him? Was there any question? She allowed herself a small grin. She had always considered herself good looking but had resigned herself to the one-night stands with the registrars and interns.

Andreas finished with one of his sweet lines and then, as though an afterthought, inquired about the hospital. As he suspected, the body had been found. *Scotland Yard is practically living here. Of course. Willoughby.* "Any inquiries?"

"They asked whether I'd seen you recently. I told them you'd come in to do some surgery, but other than that I didn't know a thing. I lied."

Andreas felt his gut tighten. "Strange business," he said. Then abruptly changing tone, "Can I drop by your flat this evening? Perhaps we could go to the cinema."

The cinema with the great doctor … and then … who knows? It was a girl's dream.

"Eight it is then." Again, it seemed the conversation was at an end, but there was one thing more. "Would you please put me through to Pathology?" He listened; the first line did not click off.

"Yes, this is Perkins."

"This is Dr. von Eckhart. I wonder if you could do me a favor."

"I'll try."

"I have a banged-up corpse there. The guy who was killed in the basement. Have to make out a death certificate for Scotland Yard. Could you delay his cremation? It would mean a lot to me."

"He's been here for nearly a month now, Doctor. We've been waiting for someone to claim the body. We're getting short of shelf space."

"Certainly, another day or two won't matter. I'll put a hold on it."

He barely had time to dress. The note had arrived by special messenger: "We are to meet, courtesy of Herr Himmler: 17 Chancery Lane." He knew the street, not far from the British Museum.

Entering a large ornate room, he encountered a sea of floppy hats, rouged skin, and white arms and gloves. With swaying hips, lovely legs, and wearing a light blue chemise, she drifted past. He knew her at once, the way he would have known a beach from the sound of the waves, the surf, and the feel of the sand.

"Andreas Eckhart, I believe," she said.

A strange feeling. He hadn't seen her since the business with Lebenfels, but it was as though he had unfinished business with her—a score to settle. But where or what? "Herr Himmler suggested we meet."

He bent over and brushed her hand with his lips. Their eyes met. That she was beautiful was unmistakable. That he felt something deeper than lust was confusing. "I believe you have a message for me." Such banal words, but it was not a time for poetry. An inner voice told him, *beware—she is seeking your death*. There could be no doubt that—she was dangerous.

"A message and a challenge," she continued, looking into his eyes and her own reflection in them. Reaching behind her and with a smile, she said, "The lawn, the chestnut tree, the hiding place, the swing, the ring giver, it's been a long time."

Memories flooded back. A door opened, and he was inside. The room was bare, empty. At one time, it contained something fantastic. The smell of lilac, long, flashing legs, soft skin, leaves sizzling in blinding sunlight. An awakened moment. A dream?

"You don't remember," she said with a laugh, seeming to read his thoughts. The sky darkened, and the distant rumble of thunder hugged the sky. "We will be seeing a lot of each other. You have already taken care of the Lebenfels assignment?"

"Yes and no," he said. "He's dead. I haven't been paid yet."

"You will be—in full," she said, her green eyes flashing.

Dazzled, he watched her sway back toward the terrace and into the crowded room; her lithe stride was like that of a jungle cat, her buttocks whipping side to side.

The taxi sped past the Marble Arch and turned into Hyde Park. Marchers twisted down the street carrying banners and chanting in the name of world peace. Andreas saw Claire, fist extended, her woolen cap pulled over her blond curls, her scarf crossed over her shoulders. Caught up in the excitement, her face flushed; she was really quite pretty. Sex with her would be good until he grew bored. Christ, he grew bored almost as soon as he rolled over.

Claire introduced him to a knot of people forming at the rear of the cinema. They were grouped around a man wearing thick spectacles, his jacket worn and patched like someone who had tried to pass as a professor but had done a bad job of it. Still, someone addressed him as Professor Lindner.

"Why don't we go to my flat and continue the discussion?" the professor asked Claire. In hushed tones, he quoted Marx and Engel, his eyes fixed on Claire's breasts, his hand thrown loosely around her waist. That was a cliché that even she could recognize, and laughing, she disentangled herself and went to meet Andreas, who was standing on the opposite side of the street. Was Andreas really going to take her away and spend money without asking her for anything? Oh, she'd have to pay; she always did. But so what?

"This isn't the best place to talk," said Andreas. "How about tomorrow night, Waterloo Bridge, about nine?" The bridge would be deserted. He squeezed her hand. *God, she is easy.*

As Andreas drove away, a woman stepped out from the crowd and stopped beside Claire. She lit a cigarette and put an affectionate arm around the younger woman's shoulders. Claire could smell her heavy perfume, lilac. "Men," she scoffed. "We're just a piece of ass to them." The woman was lovely, her voice soothing and gentle, almost angelic. It was easy to like this woman, to trust her. It was obvious that the woman was attracted to her. Maybe she did want to sleep with her, but so what? Claire had slept with so many men; maybe a woman would be a welcome change.

"I have an appointment tomorrow," she said in response to the woman's invitation, "but if it doesn't work out, I might meet you for a drink."

"Ten then, on the Embankment."

"If I'm free," Claire said.

"That would be lovely," said Tara, gently kissing Claire goodnight.

Chapter 11
Waterloo Bridge, London, 1934

WHAT WAS I THINKING *when I suggested Waterloo Bridge? It's so damned damp and dreary.*

Because you can count on the fog rolling in at this time of night, an inner voice said. *You should get it done tonight.*

I still have no clear idea what I'm going to do with her.

Don't you? You're running out of time, said the voice, laughing.

To let her disappear seemed the only solution. They would never know – just a *pipe dream. The Gestapo knows everything. You are followed everywhere.*

Fog enveloped London Bridge. There was only the sound of the lapping waves and distant traffic. He could barely make out the approaching figure. Claire's heels beat a tattoo on the steel plates as she walked toward the center of the bridge.

Andreas stopped. A splash. Panicked? Relieved? He started to hurry. *No,* he pleaded. *If only. Give me more time! I would have found a way.* He rushed toward the sound. There was no one else on the bridge. Maybe Claire hadn't come. Maybe he had only imagined seeing her.

Stillness. But he could hear soft breathing; there was someone not far away. The fog parted. In the water below, a shadow swayed on the surface. The fog congealed. The river slapped against the pier. Tripping on the steel plates, he went sprawling. Footsteps hurrying away. Moisture off the cables splashing on the railing.

Footsteps walking away, toward the Tower of London.

Tossing the knife into the dark water, Tara said, "Paid in full."

Trembling, Andreas hurried down Southwark Street to Guy's Hospital. Slipping into the side door, he stumbled into the morgue. Dissecting instruments lay on the autopsy table. The floor was wet but spotless. Formaldehyde and disinfectant stung his senses. Fluorescent lights buzzed. He pulled the corpse from the icebox, but it wasn't the man he'd killed. It was Wagner! His monocle covering a gaping wound. *Christ! I'll be next.* He found Lebenfels in the next icebox, and as he lifted the body onto the dissecting table, one of Lebenfels's fingers hooked the seam of his apron. He pulled at the finger, but it remained hooked. *I should give the whole damn body to Ribbentrop and say, "I couldn't find the code, so I brought you Lebenfels." Wouldn't that go over well?*

He bent down and unhooked the rigid finger. As he did, Lebenfels's arm and the tattoo were just inches from his face. *Of course—the tattoo! Lebenfels himself is the message.* Taking a scalpel, he gingerly cut the code from the dead body and dropped the layer of tissue into a specimen jar.

A grotesque laugh escaped as he realized he was bringing Lebenfels to Ribbentrop after all. He pushed the body back into the icebox and made his way out of the hospital, walking toward Chinatown along the embankment. Stopping frequently to be sure he wasn't being followed, he turned onto Jermyn Street, detoured onto Sloane Street, and walked briskly up Sloane past Knightsbridge and then followed Park Lane to Berkeley, where he paused to light a cigarette. He then turned onto Mount Street and lingered a few moments before going to his flat. He considered hiding the specimen but decided to keep it with him. He returned his gun to his desk drawer and poured himself a drink.

Why feel guilty? Claire was just another piece of flotsam. A millstone. Someone took care of it for you. Be grateful.

The sound of glass hitting the floor woke him. He threw himself on the sofa and fell into fretful sleep. He awoke the next morning to the sweet odor of dying roses and the broken vase. There was blood on the sheet and a large abrasion on his knee. The roses, black with a sickly brown, were strewn over the floor around his bed. In the next room, Anna's bed hadn't been slept in.

Chapter 12
High Whitcomb, England

ALREADY OVERDUE FOR MRS. Loudon's tea, Andreas studied himself in the mirror. His Savile Row jacket with pleated vents fit him well. With his walking stick, he cut the fashionable figure of an English gentleman. It was a bleak October day as he set off past St. James Park.

He struck his walking stick in time with the loneliness that often accompanied him. "Can this be a dream? It has to be," he said aloud, looking at the stranger approaching him. "Nonsense," he said, startling him. The stranger continued to stare at him long afterward. House parties, teas, gatherings in the country—the cold, gray sunlight drifting, dancing on the pavement, and walking with him. A war, dead Jews, crucified, seemed ridiculous, distant, and far away.

Mrs. Louden prided herself on her good works. Her benefit functions and weekly literary gatherings took up most of her efforts. There was much tut-tutting about responsibility to the poor. *Pity*—a word heard often and a tear at the ready if needed.

Mrs. Devi Bose, a leading proponent of the Aryan myth, was the day's guest speaker. He remembered her when his father had been stationed in India. Her husband, a leader of the Indian nationalist movement, was a close friend of Sir Harold Bellows.

Andreas nodded and smiled as he circulated among the guests, several he had already taken to bed, and their hands lingered. He tried to imagine England after Hitler. The guests at this gathering would prosper. A fool's paradise, they would barely notice if the Nazis took over. It wouldn't interfere with their luncheons and dinner parties.

"I would like to introduce you to our guest speaker," said Mrs. Loudon, taking Andreas's arm and towing him across the room. He looked into dark eyes set in a perfect, heart-shaped face.

"Hello," she said, looking up from an autographed copy of her book. Her voice was a husky whisper, like a note played from a cello, her skin like polished sandalwood. A green sari held over her shoulder by an emerald clasp fell to her feet interrupted only by the swell of her breasts. "I understand you are now a colonel in the German army."

"Mere formality," said Andreas, dismissing the rank with a wave of his hand. And thinking what the curve of her abdomen and ample hips would feel like. "I live in London. I am, you might say, a German Englishman."

"I knew your father and mother." She smiled, stretching out a gloved hand, her face a picture of intimacy, barely masking her resentment. "I was only a child when your parents left for England, but I remember them." The mask she wore, woven from years of dissembling, smiled brightly. Behind the mask, Andreas could detect a deep and penetrating hurt and a desire for vengeance. Remembering his appointment at Bellows Castle, he put away the tightness in his groin and the promise of her hips and breasts; shutting out his desire, he left.

The driver at the wheel, the emblem of the General Staff on the fender, Andreas's car followed the long, curving driveway to Bellows Manor.

Sir Harold Bellows glided down the carpeted stairs and greeted them, tall and slender with reddish brown hair, fashionably gray at the temples and a rosy complexion, his eyes a placid gray. A daydreamer, he'd never accomplished much in Parliament and less as air attaché. He was from an old family, and his main function seemed to be to preside over parties and banquets.

Still, there was something about Sir Harold that set Andreas on edge, something cunning, a caged animal waiting for his prey to come to him. Hidden behind his placid exterior, he was prideful and arrogant. The German high command had changed their minds about him several times. He was well known to the priestly class in India and Tibet and necessary to their plans. He greeted Andreas in the large hall under the grim portraits of ancestors long dead.

"The servants will take you to your rooms," he said, a line long practiced. "Dinner is not till eight." As he turned to leave, he added, "Mrs. Bellows isn't feeling well and won't be down."

"Please offer her my sympathy," Andreas said.

"You know of course that Herr Ribbentrop is coming. He has asked to see you in particular."

Andreas followed the servant up the staircase and turned down a hall covered with a threadbare carpet, once quite fine, to a double door leading into a large oval room carpeted in pale-blue Islamic prayer rugs. French doors opened onto a balcony overlooking the terrace and gardens leading off to a park and stables.

He placed his suitcase on the bed and passed his fingers over the books lining the room. Thackeray, Dickens, Dante, Homer. One section was devoted to politics and philosophy: Spinoza, Kant, and Nietzsche, Hitler's *Mein Kompf,* and Lebenfels's *The Ahnenerbe: The Prehistory of the Aryans from the Brahmins to the Present.* Next to it, *The History of the Lost Tribes of Israel,* Orson Pratt, 1876.

He removed Lebenfels's book from the shelf. The cover was black and engraved with gold letters and the Tibetan symbol of life—the swastika. He turned to the table of contents. "Origin of the Aryan People from the Brahmin," "Thule Society," "The Jews in British Society." Andreas returned the book to the shelf, poured a drink from a decanter of sherry, and sat back in a worn but exceedingly comfortable leather chair. Fading light slanted through the long curtains.

He turned on a lamp. A statue on a side table flashed an image into the mirror of a female figure, her breasts hanging over a swollen abdomen, in one hand a sword and in the other a head. A belt of small heads hung from her waist. Repulsed, he turned her toward the wall.

"Come on, you old fogy, are you going to spend the whole weekend in your room?" Diana Bellows called from the hall. "We have just enough time for a ride."

He had hoped yet had feared she would be there. He hesitated, unsure. *What the hell. In for a farthing, in for a pound.* "I'd love it! Let me change."

"Be quick!" she said.

She gripped the horse between strong thighs; her back was straight and strong, her head up, her hands high and in control. It was the first time Andreas had been on a horse since France and the war. The horse shied, reared, whinnying as a snake slithered across the road. The high-pitched cry brought back screams, flailing hooves, the earth churning, a rider, flying shards … and blood—the stumbling, deafening agony of the Argonne. He had loved the horse more than any living creature, and holding his head, the light fading from him, he tried to make sense of his death, his devotion—senseless. The bell tolling slowly, the smell of rain and turf and gunpowder. Lost in a hell he had no part in creating.

Another war? He didn't have the courage for another war.

Diana grabbed the reins. "I don't understand. She's usually so docile. Andreas?" His gaze was stark, blank. "Andreas! Are you all right?"

Returning to himself, he smiled a little too broadly and took off at a gallop, Diana close behind. She had inherited her horsemanship just as she had her good looks and money. Andreas rose in the stirrups, felt the mare's mane in his face, and whispered into her ear. She broke into a canter. They entered a freshly mown pasture, and without hesitation Diana urged her horse over a high fence.

"Come on," she said, patting her horse, shining with sweat. Andreas followed, clearing the fence with ease.

"I'm impressed," said Diana.

A hedge blocked their way. "I dare you," she said as she urged her horse into a gallop and cleared the hedge. He felt the thrill, the animal responding to his commands. "Up," he whispered. They sailed over.

"That's enough," he said.

"All right," said Diana reluctantly.

They rode over the rolling hills where for centuries knights had ridden. Diana's auburn hair falling over her shoulders, her thighs gripping the back of her horse, seemed in one instant haughty and in the next enticingly warm. He wanted her, to touch her, lie against her, her legs gripping him.

I have spent all my life chasing women yet don't know them. I know horses. I know when they are sad, and I grieve for them, but women? All I know about women is how to get between their legs. Once I have caught her, the magic disappears and I am mute. Knew. Taken. Had. The words of love are those of war, of combat. When it's over, I have nothing. He stared at his hands, holding the reins as if they and the voice belonged to another person, a stranger.

What did you expect?

Peace, he answered. *What the hell is wrong with you? Most men would die to be as successful. You are getting soft.*

The horse broke into a canter. Tara's face appeared out of the sullen sky, her arms slid around his neck, her hair fell over her face. Her lips were red and begging, her perfume reeking of violence. His father's fists were on him. The shot rang out. "No! He's dead? Father's dead. No, he's alive—a ghost. As long as he lives, you will never find peace."

The horse bucked. Andreas reined her in.

Take her. His face was against the curve of her belly, her navel, a secret grotto. *She's asking for it. Each man is an island. Satisfy yourself. There is no reason past your own desire.* He'd walked past the statue of Christ for years without stopping. He suddenly needed meaning. *There is no meaning. There is no reason past wanting. You must decide. Meaning is what you make it.*

Confused, Andreas tore away from the voices in a gallop, his indecision and impotence turning into anger and recklessness. He directed his anger at Diana. She reached for his hand. He pulled it away, his love inexplicably turning to hate, his tenderness to cruelty. The feeling deepening until all the warmth and pleasure vanished. *I am a fool, a buffoon. These hands are good for nothing but to deliver pain. They are my father's hands. I am nothing more than I inherited—a repetition of what has been handed to me. I am no different from my father.*

They rode along the edge of the meadow swathed in silence but for the rustle of dead leaves and the hypnotic clop of the horses. He felt the familiar ache and loneliness at the end of the day when the light was fading.

Diana, all her life, even as a child, has been aware of the mystery of approaching dusk, the monkey's hour when familiar shapes took on strange outlines and new meaning. Suddenly, impulsively, she pulled Andreas down to her, and their lips meet. His horse reared, ears erect. Gently, Andreas brought her under control. Diana took his hands and led him to the stable. From beneath a cloud, the orange light burned and then died.

Ian McDonald, short of breath, trudged up the stairs. *Bellows Manor,* he said to himself as he studied the chipped plaster and flaking paint. *Moldy wreck. It's going to fall down before the Germans get a chance to bomb it.*

The newspaper reporter unpacked his aged dinner jacket and placed it neatly on his bed. Sir Harold had kindly given him the room down the hall from Andreas's. He heard a woman scream, a door slam, and china crash. *Lady Bellows venting her temper on the maid?*

"You careless fool!"

McDonald heard sobbing.

"If you'd pay attention to your family instead of that ridiculous Jewish business."

"This Jewish business will bring us a fortune."

It was Lord Bellows' voice. Unmistakably. The heating vents had been opened, and like a long earpiece, they carried the voices audibly into the next room. McDonald pulled up a chair ready to enjoy the intimate details of society life.

"The library is full of Jewish encyclopedias and language dictionaries. Are you going to turn Jewish on top of everything else? Our friends make fun of you behind your back. Call you hikey."

"Now, never mind. You know I'm no Jew lover. But you have to admit they know how to make money."

"That's inherited along with the nose. Ever since you and that fool Balfour promised them a homeland in Palestine, this house has been full of them. Next thing, you'll be asking them to dinner. Is this the latest and most dreadful of your hare- brained ideas? Jews! Who gives a damn? Find a cause that makes money. We are close to destitute, Howard."

"Well, in fact, I have done just that. I've invited Chaim Lowenstein this weekend."

She drew herself up, and he cringed, expecting the onslaught. "I can't bear another minute of it. Bellows is crumbling. I haven't enough money for proper clothes. I owe everyone. And you're having Jews for dinner! And while we're at it, what's this all about?" She brandished a check made out to Chaim Lowenstein. Sir Harold stumbled against the bed in his hurry to calm her. Money was safe ground. Money meant position, dignity; nothing else was important to her.

"It's a payoff to the people in the Sanhedrin," he said hesitantly, polishing his glasses. "The Jewish supreme court. It will never be cashed," he hurried to explain. "The Jews did away with it in the fifth century." His voice was taking the form of caution, careful not to raise her ire. He needed her opinion, her razor-like insight into people and schemes. She had suffered through several schemes with him.

"What Jews? Where?" she screamed.

"In Tibet," he said, cringing. "We're not sure, but Chaim doesn't want to take any chances."

"Another of your inspirations," she said bitterly. "So you're giving him money for Jewish judges who may or nor be there? Is that why my diamond broach is missing?"

"I was going to wait to explain, but I can see that's not in the cards. I need your word that you won't repeat any of this."

"It had better be good."

Harold took a deep breath. "Chaim Lowenstein is a member of the Hagana, a Jewish resistance group," he said with a frightened note in his voice.

"You mean assassins."

"No, these are reasonable people, not like the Lekhi or the Irgun."

"So you say. How do you know? Are you in the inner circle? You saw fit to pawn my finest piece of jewelry without my knowledge or permission to support Jewish terrorists? You can kiss your political career goodbye."

"Give me a chance, please, before you fly off the handle."

"I'm waiting."

"Chaim and I have worked before. He handled an espionage case, you remember, the explosion in Hyde Park last year. It was solved quietly without any publicity."

She arched her brow; the entire affair had offended her delicacy. As far as she was concerned, Hitler had the right idea. Having Chaim and his kind in her dining room was repulsive.

Harold went on. "… and I wanted someone who could handle the job in the same quiet manner."

"Job?" she asked. "You sound like a mobster. Soon, you'll be calling me doll!"

"Fabricating a fake Jewish state in Tibet—"

"Where? Have you gone mad, Harold?"

"Hear me out. There are rumors that there are Jews living in Tibet, escapees from the tribes that settled Palestine over two thousand years ago. Ten of these tribes went missing."

"Two thousand years ago, Harold?" Lady Bellows directed the words like daggers at her husband.

"Well, my dear, we are going to bring them back to life."

"Good going, Harold, just what the world needs, more Jews."

He sighed. "I'll lay it out as simply as I can." Harold felt himself getting stronger in front of the onslaught.

Her daggers were soft and didn't penetrate. "You don't

have to insult me. I'm as capable of understanding as the next one," she said, sensing his growing confidence.

I didn't mean to insult you. The rumor is they may have solved the riddle of the atom and have harnessed the power. You know how good they are at math. We are years from even beginning to do that. Hitler can't possibly allow that to happen."

"But they are not real. He must know that."

"He doesn't care."

"We win either way."

"Hitler's been looking for a reason to go into Tibet to get control of the passes into Afghanistan, India, and Suez. What is the one excuse he can't ignore? There are Jews there, and they have the means to destroy the Third Reich. Wait, you haven't heard the best part," he added, stifling his wife's unspoken objection. "I'm certain war is inevitable. To win, we'll need India, control of the Suez, and those mountain passes in Afghanistan and India. I can deliver them. That here may be Jews in the mix makes it doubly attractive. You know how paranoid Hitler is about Jews."

Nellie sat quietly, deep in thought. "I still don't see why we need this Chaim person. I don't like it."

"We need him to set up the fake Jews—letters, photographs of prisoners, radio intercepts, and unexplained bombings—everything that would indicate a Jewish population ready to go to war."

Indeed, he was alive, and he would be important after all. There was still life, purpose. He might yet outlive the old lady.

McDonald pushed back from his seat under the heating register and went to the window in time to see Andreas and

Diana saddled and galloping across the meadows. An abyss separated him from his days as a young reporter. His wife, their flat in Buckinghamshire, bleak and cold—he thought of her often and at times even heard her voice. He'd tried to make the best of their lives in England. But Kashmir yearned for the call of the tree lizards and the warmth of the tropical sun. Alone in the English countryside, she withered, and her laughter died.

On edge and drinking, he fell into loneliness. Kashmir and he rarely spoke. They ate dinner silently. Then she was gone, and he was alone. Kashmir's brother confided to him that the Indian nationalists planned an action against the British. The British raided the headquarters. Kashmir's brother was killed. The rebels exacted revenge for his apparent treason and killed Kashmir. Since then, he had knocked about the world living largely on alcohol and opium.

"Sir, just a reminder," said the servant. "Dinner will be at eight."

McDonald turned away from the typewriter, finished his whiskey, dressed, and walked to Andreas's room.

"Those are beautiful studs," McDonald remarked.

"Awarded by Hitler personally after the Eiger climb," said Andreas. "Cold as ice," he added absently.

"What was?"

"Hitler's blue eyes. Shall we jump into the fray?" Andreas gestured toward the door.

Lifting their Schiaparelli gowns, the gathering, the world's social elite, stepped from their limousines ignorant of the strangeness of destiny, confident that the rest of the world would first consult them before doing anything as rash as going to war. The ladies stepped from the porte cochere into the grand entryway sure of themselves and their position.

"Fools," said Andreas. "Can't they see they are irrelevant? They are crawling like bees into a hive that's barren."

The guests seemed distracted. A sudden storm coming after a sunny day had caused the lights to flicker. The servants lit candles. The great room was like an eerie church. People whispered and wandered from group to group. Cardboard women prefabricated with built-in motives, women who neither loved nor hated, who were not mean or consumed by lust—that took too much energy—sleepwalking through life, their habits a necessity to justify their existence. If he were to paint them, he'd color them brown, soft and brown. *Now Diana*, he thought as she entered the ballroom, *she would be hard and blue and dangerous.*

Adrift, Andreas leaned in on the edges of the conversations. "It's difficult to assess the real intentions of the German government."

He took another glass of champagne.

"Goebbels will have to go. Hitler has to rid himself of the mad-dog strain in the party."

"Laws have been passed. People are being brought to justice."

For Christ's sake, thought Andreas. *Why the hell are they whispering?*

"Remember, Hitler promised war—even worse, another crusade."

"It will take blood. Luxemburg and Liebknecht are dead."

"But Heydrich and Roehm aren't."

"Versailles."

"All those dead men."

"We made promises, hoping we could keep them on the cheap."

"Mark my words, we will regret our decision about a Jewish homeland."

"All those dead men."

"There is something in the German psyche that thirsts for war. There are parts of Germany where they still worship Siegfried and Wotan, where they still practice witchcraft," said Lord Somersby, tall and athletic, rosy-lipped, his blue eyes like cold agates. His long fingers clutched an ebony walking stick he moved hand to hand between his patent-leather shoes.

"But that was always true," said Sir Neville. "There will always be those who make capital out of the natural longing of people to be free and united in a national identity."

Sir Neville, looking into Somersby's eyes, saw the future; it was the past. "The Germans have retaken the Saar and reinstituted compulsory military service. This law protecting German blood and honor that Hitler mentioned at Nuremburg. Hell, you might as well bequeath your inheritance to Hitler."

"They'll get it anyway. That was some rally." Sir Neville shook his head. "You'd think Christ himself was at the podium. Did you see it? Too bad. It was a revelation, at the very least a wake-up call."

"Destiny, omens, and promises," began Somersby. "God and politicians. God loves making promises. He

promised Satan—I've always wondered about this one—
that he'd be released from hell after a thousand years.
Rather peculiar notion, don't you think? A thousand years
by what clock? The time is up. I mean, with all this time
and space relativity."

The rain spattered against the windows.

"They haven't the men willing to fight. They're Jewish.
They have syphilis."

"It's all about the banks, the money."

"If we manage to split the atom, there is no end to what
we can accomplish. No more of these five-year wars. It will
be over in hours. We will be able to destroy each other by
simply pushing a button."

"And now that Hindenburg's dead, there will be no
stopping him—the plebiscite was ninety percent for Hitler."

"If I were Jewish, I'd be making plans to leave,"
said Lady Neville, her voice shrill, her laugher ugly and
hysterical.

"Speaking of which, the newspapers claim there is a
lost race of Jews living in the Himalayas of all places," said
Sir Neville.

"Must be that rabble rouser who writes for the *Guardian*.
He's always stirring the pot."

"Careful. I understand he's one of the guests."

"Here?"

"What's the world coming to?" asked Lady Neville.

"Who is he?" Andreas asked, leaning over the balustrade.
"I mean the one with the walking stick."

"Lord Somersby. I know him," answered McDonald.

Andreas looked away, following Ernst Teuer and Diana,

unaware of the loathing in McDonald's eyes. "Family has been around since the Magna Carta. Chairman of the East India Company for a while. One of those who believe the world was theirs from the beginning."

The musicians struck up a waltz. Andreas was surprised to find Diana beside him. Her moon-colored gown set off her ash-blond hair and green eyes. Because she was no longer on a horse, she seemed taller than he remembered. Teuer sidled up. Bowing, he asked Diana if he could have the pleasure of the next dance. Off they went, leaving Andreas in Sybil Long's hands.

"Rumor has it that we and the Germans are racing to find them," said Sybil, nodding toward Chaim.

"Find whom?" said Andreas, distracted by Diana.

"The missing Jews. I can't imagine why. We have enough of them."

"Don't worry. Himmler has the address of every Jew in Germany."

"No, silly. The missing Jews, the ones in India or Tibet or whatever."

"There aren't any missing Jews. They are either murdered or in camps."

"Or in the Cabinet. My father was a minister. He was fascinated by the story and drilled it into me. The Jews were a wicked people given to bacchanals and orgies. God had to keep after them to be good. They went missing, lost. You'd have to go back to the Bible to find them. This is after the exodus—Moses, Joshua, and that crowd."

"After spending about two hundred years in Egypt, they wound up in Canaan—all but Moses, who was not allowed to enter the Promised Land. About six hundred thousand of them divided into twelve tribes. They were in Assyria longer than they were in Egypt. After Sargon captured the Jewish capital, Samaria, in about seven hundred BC, about twenty thousand were carried off to Halal, near the River Gozan, a tributary of the Euphrates.

"At about the year six hundred, I may be off by a hundred years, they escaped north to a country where 'man never dwelt, where mountains and precipices and mist loomed over green lush valleys.' That part I remember distinctly. They were about one hundred thousand when they left.

"That man, the one over there." She gestured toward Chaim Lowenstein, a tall, thin man standing next to a beautiful brunette. "He told me all about it." She smiled. "Or at least what the Jewish texts remember. His wife is writing a book about it. They're Jewish. Kirstin Lowenstein's her name."

"You mean the brunette?"

"The one you're undressing?" she countered.

"You can't blame me," he said.

"Her father was a close friend of the PM. She's Scandinavian or something. Göring's first wife was Swedish, you know, von Katznow, the love of his life. She died in 1927 while Göring was on duty. He married Emmy Sonnemann, an actress. Two people that much in love can't be all bad, can they?"

"The Reich's marshal? In love?" He smiled at the thought.

"Where the hell have you been? Everyone in Berlin knows."

"I didn't."

"Why are you surprised? She's beautiful, an actress. Of course, most of her friends are Jewish. There's nothing wrong with that. It just means they're intelligent."

"Careful," whispered Andreas, moving closer. "Not too loud, not here."

"Why not? Your esteemed Reich marshal's stepfather was Jewish, Ritter von Epenstein or something. Of course you know the scandal."

"Anyway, to get back to Göring, a great tragedy. He falls madly in love with Carin von Katznow. She gets sick, doesn't let him know how sick. He leaves for duty. She dies. He built Carinhall in her memory. Designed every inch himself down to the doorknobs. Fresh flowers every day."

It was clear that Andreas's focus was elsewhere, on Diana.

Ignoring him and looking away when their eyes met, Diana's face turned crimson. She was not a novice. Certainly, not a naïve, helpless virgin. The idea that this, with Teuer, was a seduction angered him. He was behaving like one of the romantics he was fond of ridiculing.

Following Andreas's eyes, Sybil said, "I don't know what's stopping Teuer from proposing. He's obviously in love with her."

"How can you tell?"

"You can see it in his eyes," she said with unexpected sadness.

"She's not ready," Andreas said.

"What do you mean? Ready for what?" asked Sybil. "You certainly don't think she's a...?" She broke into raucous laughter.

"Just what I said, she's not ready. I mean ready to be a—Forget it."

"You mean a frau," she said.

"No, I meant, she's happy being herself."

"Of course she's going to divorce Sloat. She's tired of dragging him around, but I hardly think that's an issue. I haven't seen him this evening, but he's probably here passed out under a potted plant somewhere. I think the fellow would kill himself if she jettisoned him. He'd have no place to go. The only other place he knows is in an airplane, and there's not much call for that these days."

"Hmm, I wouldn't be too sure of that," said Andreas. "Sounds as if she needs a doctor."

Studying Andreas, she asked, "Do you have anyone in mind?"

Avoiding her innuendo, Andreas said, "He may be back in a plane sooner than you think."

Andreas watched Diana and Teuer disappear under the portico, and a moment later, she was once again standing beside him.

"You can put away your binoculars," she said.

Andreas, alive to the scents and colors and the seductive antagonism between them and turning toward her, asked, "May I have the next dance?"

"Of course."

Dinner was announced, and Andreas discovered he had been placed next to Kirstin Lowenstein. He offered his arm, and together, they joined the other guests as they took their seats. Diana entered the dining on the arm of Major Teuer, her smile too wide, her laughter too loud, and a tear welling in her eyes. The dining room glittered with silver.

The Irish linen, Limoges serving pieces, and Queen Rose china crowded one another for a place at the table.

His eyes never left Diana. He fought the jealousy welling in them. "I love you. I hate you. God damn you, Diana."

Sir Harold stood and offered the inevitable toast. "To peace and to our brothers in India," he said, bending toward Lady Bose.

The rosy-cheeked assembly gave a hearty "Hear! Hear!"

Andreas pulled the chair for Mrs. Lowenstein and again was aware of her beauty, taking notice of her Scandinavian complexion and the lovely curve of her buttocks. He went out of his way to be polite and found himself enjoying the evening. A brandy on the veranda coming on top of the wines at dinner made both slightly heady.

"It's all changed for me," Kirstin said. "I feel rushed as if I don't have time, all the things I want to do. Unfortunately, Chaim is not interested in those things."

"What things?" Andreas asked.

Her face turned slightly pink. "Some of the new ideas, you know, Freud, love, sex. I'm still not sure. I mean, what I'm looking for, what I want."

"I hope I'm around when you are. Judging from what you are now, it should be something to see," he said, smiling. "It's the threat of war. It makes things we have postponed seem urgent."

"Yes, perhaps. There will be no putting it back together. The pieces will be too small, atoms," she said bitterly. "Do you have children?"

"I'm not married."

"I'm sorry, I don't mean …" she said, blushing again.

"I know," he chuckled. "Please go on."

Andreas ordered another brandy, and together, they sat under the stars among trees like drawings. Kirstin was silent. Chaim hadn't approved of her working, she explained, so when they married, she'd become a Jewish housewife. "And you know what that means—luncheons, meetings, fundraisers. Thank God Chaim's not religious. But we still see the family for Seders and the holidays. The Jews have lots of holidays!" A pause. "I'm bored to death."

Herr Lowenstein sat across from them, deep in conversation with Lady Marlborough. Andreas didn't envy him and could imagine the conversation: *Oh yes, we must support them. After all, they didn't ask to be Jews.*

"I'm tired of pretending and of dealing with pretense," said Kirstin. "A few days, a few nights, and it's over. Covered in nettles and briar decayed and over. If that's our end, why are we wasting time? I'm tired of Jews who are trying to be something they aren't, flying about from one do-gooder function to another. Where does it lead? Nowhere! Chaim is intelligent but confused. It leads nowhere. Do you know we're members of the New York Yacht Club on Manhattan's 44th Street? I've never been inside it, not once. The only reason I know we are members is from the donations requests."

"That's a long way to go for a sail. You're beautiful. Come, let's not waste, the evening."

He overheard Major Teuer talking to Diana. "Let's get out of here."

"Chaim is in New York often on business," said Kirstin. "Says the contacts will help his business. We don't even own a boat. Chaim thinks a jenny is a distant relative."

"You know," began Andreas, straining to hear the conversation across the table, "if you are ever free, I'd love to show you around Wiligut Castle, perhaps even the cyclotron. I'm going to take over the research at Wiligut."

Wiligut meant nothing to her, but realizing the not-so-hidden meaning behind the invitation, she said, "Yes, I would like that."

Her figure bent over the table, her face crimson, Diana rose unsteadily. Teuer attempting to drag her back, and pulling on her gown, he exposed her breasts. In a frenzied burst, she tore free and with a hoarse cry slapped him hard across the face. She ran from the room in tears. Teuer, realizing his compromised position, stood and stiffly turned to his host. He bowed and apologized; he said she had unfortunately imbibed too much of the fine wine, a lover's quarrel. He clicked his heels, turned, and left, his iron cross swaying from his neck. How quaint but understandable said the guests exiting for coffee and fine brandy awaiting them on the veranda.

The next day, wind rattled the windows and rain poured off the roof. The servants slid silently around the dining room, asking in confessional tones, "Would madam like something else for breakfast?" Lady Bellows remained in her room as she had the night before.

With the skills of a seasoned adventurer, a skilled surgeon, and a trained agent, Andreas had ended his evening in conversation with Lady Carlton, wife of the minister of the exchequer—slightly overweight, middle aged … and alone for the weekend. Another drink, a hearty laugh, a few kind words. Not wasted on a woman whose husband had not slept with her in years, preferring his club and his mistress for company. When he emerged from her bedroom before dawn, he had learned that the new appropriation bill did not include funds for increasing the British antisubmarine force. A large appropriation for Tibet was curious and without further details. *Do we? Do they? Have the strength for another war?*

Chapter 13
Bellows Castle

EVERYONE SEEMED ON EDGE at breakfast. *What an awful day this is shaping up to be*, Andreas thought.

"Did someone die?" asked Diana as she burst into the room. They had reconciled, and she had spent the night with Teuer. Feeling a bit guilty, she shrugged. *Love? Sin? How do you spell it? Another word for ... alone. You are never more alone than when you are making love.* Shaking her head and rubbing her upper arms, she declared, "Christ, it's cold in here. Can't we afford some heat?"

"A glorious day for tennis?" She laughed, her lithe legs flashing beneath her short skirt. The rain beat a merciless tattoo on the roof.

"How about a tarot reading?" asked Mrs. Devi Bose, sweeping her arms toward the game room.

Diana and several others crowded around the table. "I don't know the first thing about it," said Diana.

"You, Colonel von Eckhart, will be our victim," said Mrs. Bose. Andreas obligingly sat as instructed, not wishing to deny the formidable woman her fun. She selected a deck of cards and proceeded to count out separate piles—wands, pentacles, sword, cups.

"Now," declared Mrs. Bose, "there are two orders of cards: a major group and a minor group. The cards in the groups are called arcana."

Andreas's mind wandered to the small blond hairs on Diana's arm and her tiny wrist. *She is a saint*, he thought, *lonely and tormented*.

"The cards in the major group represent the intellect; the minor arcana represents the elements—fire, water, earth, and air. I prefer to choose from the major arcana first." She turned up a card; it was the devil: a horned creature holding a naked man and a woman in chains.

"The man is waiting to unshackle the passion in the woman," she explained. She next drew the knight of pentacles mounted on a black horse. "You are awaiting the culmination of your task." Next the seven of wands, "The card of victory. All three cards depict battle," she declared. Next, she drew the three of swords. "Oh! The sword pierces a heart." She looked at Andreas with sorrow. "You will have a great disappointment that will break your heart."

She chose next a card from the deck of wands. She slowly turned over the king. "It is the king of wands. When the battle is over, you will have achieved victory. You will go to a place of knowledge and understanding."

"Well, that's something at any rate." Andreas managed a polite smile; he was surprised this silly woman had actually affected him. "But I wonder what good is understanding if you are dead?"

"There are many ways to interpret the cards," assured Mrs. Bose, placing a comforting hand on Andreas's knee.

They rose to leave; Diana had waited for her chance. She needed someone to talk to. His eyes resting on her, Andreas was aware that not only was she beautiful, she was also frightened. "Are you all right?" he asked.

"Well, that reading was kind of nasty," she said.

"Nothing like being told you're going to die with a broken heart," he said with a chuckle. They walked on together, and she took his arm and placed it around her shoulders. "There, that's better," she said, nestling into the embrace. "Don't be frightened. I just wanted to feel warm, loved, secure."

If ever there was a woman who didn't need support, it's Diana, thought Andreas.

Relieved, Diana smiled. *Let it be*, she thought. "It means as little to Teuer as it does to me," she said with faint amusement. "It's as though last night never happened." Then, as though reading Andreas's mind, she said, "Everyone thinks as you do—that they don't need anyone. I have news for you, Andreas. Everyone, even you, will find you need someone."

Diana, her face flushed and her eyes bright, cast a backward glance at Mrs. Bose.

She and Andreas walked into the chill, late-afternoon shadows following the path that led past the fountain to a small, secluded cemetery. "Sometimes, Andreas, I feel you are the only person I can talk to. The only person who understands." She spoke softly, almost in a whisper. "Bellows Manor is dying, Andreas. Brick by brick, it's dying. Soon, it will fall down around our heads."

They sat next to the fountain. Andreas softly touched Diana's hand. "Everything dies. Lancelot died, Arthur died,

Beowulf died." Water trickled into the fountain, and there was the smell of dampness in the air.

"I feel that when Bellows dies, a lot of other things will die with it."

"Like what?"

There was a longing in her voice, one that had nothing to do with him. She was up and striding around the fountain, her footsteps making small indentations in the soft, pebbly earth.

"God. Grace. Me. A way of life. Do you believe, Andreas?"

"Believe? You mean in God?"

"In miracles. Like a shadow. Eric, my son, always turning the corner one step in front of me."

"Who?"

"Eric, my son, the one I killed. I want to believe, I try to believe he's still with me," said Diana.

"The way I try to make sense of that climb and pretend I didn't kill Ernst, to make sense of … those—dying. No! I don't believe," Andreas said, suddenly angry, hurling a stone at the wall. "King Arthur and the Holy Grail. Death with dignity," he continued, a wry smile scarring his face. "I've seen a lot of death. None of it was with dignity. It's ridiculous. We are alone flying on the wings of a dead moment in history. But it's the only thing that stands between us and murder."

She studied him for what seemed a long time.

"I haven't forgotten him, Andreas. I never will."

"I killed him, but I won't forget him. He's with me every day."

"I know you believe in such things, Andreas," she pleaded.

"Believed," he said, turning to her, his gray eyes almost black. "Perhaps if he'd bring those men back to life the way he did Lazarus, I'd believe."

"They are dead. He's dead."

She turned to him. Her face was grim, a mask; her body was tense with hope. "Do dead things leave anything behind?"

"If you mean anything tangible, no, I don't think so."

"So you don't believe that buildings are alive, have a soul, or lovers leave a trail of passion? Evidently not," she said, looking out over the fountain and the crumbling walls.

He thought of the previous night. He'd felt something when he watched her across the table, something he desperately wanted to feel again. He was suddenly tired and fed up with talk. He wanted to plunge his head into her, between her legs, feel her warm belly against his face, but she was so immersed in her dream. Gasping, he said, "Make love. Let's make love."

She stepped back and jumped to her feet. "No! I can't, not just like that, on order. I can't just deliver love as if it were a sandwich. Even if I did, what good would it be? It would be sex, only sex. You can get that from any whore, Andreas. It wouldn't be me. You saw me, the real me, the bitch, last night. This would be only a reflection in a mirror." Tears were running down her cheeks.

Perhaps a bitch, he thought, *but right or wrong, it is honest, and I love you even more for it.*

Andreas sank to his knees. Lifting a handful of stones from the fountain, he asked, "What harm is there in that? We have only so many days, so many chances."

"Perhaps, but women see it differently," she said, cupping a handful of water and letting it drip slowly into the fountain.

"Diana, they're dead. Romeo and Juliet are dead! Your son is dead. For him, it was essential he be dead. Then Ernst too could die. I still see the edge of that cliff. I will see it forever jutting out, daring me. I'd still cut the rope."

"I believe they lived on," she said.

For a woman, they had to.

"If you walk into a room where there has been a murder or a tragedy—like a child dying—the spirit of that child continues to exist, to be felt by the living long afterward. There must be something left. There has to be."

"You mean do I believe in ghosts? I hope not," he said, rippling the water with his fingers.

"No, not ghosts, a presence."

"I don't see the difference."

"You wouldn't. You're a man."

The occasional raindrop wrinkled the fountain, threw sparkles into the night, died away in silence. They were two small vessels becalmed.

"He is buried over there," she said, pointing to a small plot ringed by a stone wall. A large oak hovered over a stone tablet. The gardener had dutifully removed the weeds, and the grave was well tended. There were no flowers. "Funny, I remember everything about him, every movement until his last."

The rain left small spatters like grapes on the stones.

"My father wouldn't allow him to be buried inside the castle walls."

"Do you always do what your father asks?"

"Demands," she said. "I did then." She turned toward him, and he shuddered.

"I killed him. I loved him." Her face was a living portrait of hopelessness. "To hell with them," she yelled. "He isn't dead. I killed him, but he's not dead. Not in here," she said, pointing to her heart. "Not in here. Have you ever felt as if you'd rather die? No, not die, start over?"

"Often," said Andreas, "but the mistakes are built in. Like ghosts. You repeat them, you cherish them, you can't get away from them. No matter where you go, they follow you—like salmon returning to the ocean."

"I want to get away, far away, to some place where they need me—some small island."

"Where there are lepers," he said, mimicking her. "Escape to the savages. To the bush where there are pygmies, even a few cannibals. Of course, drinking would be out of the question. As for sex?" He jested, throwing his arms in the air. "It's always easier in the jungle." His face became serious and his voice became low. "But beware the dark, beware the void, Diana. Beware. You may get to know yourself then. I did in Flanders and discovered I didn't like myself. You don't need lepers or cannibals, only yourself—alone. The man missing his nose, the woman with a stump for a leg is easy to identify. And you'd care for them. Of course, pure of heart and pure of limb, you'd care for them. But there are others as deeply wounded. Just turn around. You see them every day, wounded, with their beards, limping along, heads down, afraid to look you in the eye. And you'd care for them. Of course. Until you couldn't stand it any longer.

"The blood, the moans, the missing arms, legs, faces are easily recognized. What of the men, women, and children with green pieces of wool stitched to their breasts waiting their turn in the slaughterhouse? Would you care for them?"

Andreas lit a cigarette and inhaled deeply, his thoughts wandering to the trenches of France. "War is a great dare. It brings you close to yourself. If you are a coward, you know it in a thousand ways. Oh, you can get around it, but deep down, it gnaws at you. When you're alone, it eats away at you. External wounds are easy to recognize and care for. The wound that put me in the hospital could not be seen or touched, not even by me. It was deep and well masked. You don't have to travel to a battlefield to see them—even now. Just as far as Berlin. Just step outside or go to the Jewish market. Sit for a moment and watch them try to pass the day without thinking of the final moment, animals in a pen."

"Didn't you win the Iron Cross?"

"Yes, but heroism isn't bravery."

"Then what is?"

"To be able to sit and wait, look at the sun, feel the warmth on your face, and be alone. You are alone when you die, and you wait and ask, 'Why? Why?' You search then for the reason for living, and you see yourself, perhaps for the first time—no trumpets, no flashes of light, just your watch ticking away. You panic. You have to find a reason for living. Search! Was it only a dream? There's no time. A glimpse. A shadow. A dream. Shut the gates. Turn on the gas. The last trumpet's near—about to sound."

The music of the fountain, like rain gently falling in the silent night, held them in its grasp. It seemed like a lifetime before he heard Diana ask, "The Eiger? You saw him—God—then. Didn't you?"

"Him? Was it him or myself I saw—dressed as a fool?" He wrinkled the water with his fingers. "You must know each man, his reasons for living and God's reasons for letting him die. Love and hate are always at the bottom of tragedy, and they were on that day. If only he hadn't forgiven me, given me his blessing."

"Forgiven?"

"I expected, hoped, to die, but that wasn't meant for me. You see, instead, he let me live. I was a coward. Would you believe he went to all that trouble to show me what I already knew? It would have been easier if he'd killed me, but that would have taken away all the fun. We do his bidding. Break his nose, he's a Jew; his leg, he's a Gypsy; crucify him, he's a fag. A bayonet or a grenade? He's speaking a foreign language. Latin, you say? Hell, they are all speaking a foreign language. Dominus vobiscum—I baptize you in the language of death. It takes time to learn, the language of death. I learned it from the men I patched up and sewed together. Every general should have to learn it—the language, the smell, the last puff of air. He judged me then. I'm judging him now. I have nothing to lose."

His face dazed with weariness, he tossed a pebble at the wall. The fountain came to life and shot into the air. The water gurgled into the basin.

"There you are, Andreas. I've been looking all over for you." Sir Harold approached the fountain shaking his head. "The German ambassador is practically a prisoner in his own embassy. Even I, the air attaché, can't get in. Ribbentrop is very anxious for you to see him. He won't be able to land in this weather. God knows how you are going to deliver your package. We've got to get to the embassy."

Diana watched as Andreas and her father drove off. The light rain subsided only to be replaced by thick fog. She stole past the cemetery, running her hands along the moss-covered bricks, past the dead paintings, up the staircase to her mother's room.

"Teuer is what I deserve. I hate you. I love you. God damn you, Andreas. I thought I was through with you." Her voice became sad. "Love. I'll be damned if I'm going to huddle under some bush waiting for you. The nights—it's the nights, alone, my dreams. If only," her voice close to tears, "I hadn't borne the child and not torn it to pieces."

The door was open just enough to see inside. The lights were out. The radio was on, and the program played across her face. Her mother lay on the bed talking to the shadows. Mumbling. *A nursery rhyme? A secret passed on through the ages of women whispering the secrets of sorrow known only to women?* Diana crept to her room and closed the door.

Andreas and Sir Harold drove past Mayfair, Hyde Park Corner, and the Marble Arch. Andreas was unsure how much Sir Harold could be trusted. He had no choice. "The package Ribbentrop is expecting is a piece of skin with a code tattooed on it," he shouted over the roar of the Morgan. Sir Harold turned his eyes off the road, almost striking a mail post.

Andreas continued. "I was able to remove it and put it into a specimen jar thinking I could slip it to Ribbentrop at your party. A crazy pattern of sticks called runes. Someone was coming, and I had to leave. But I'm sure I have it all."

Sir Harold knew that Göring and the Nazi High Command were on tenterhooks regarding Lebenfels and the missing code. Göring was biting his nails: the invasion of the Middle East, Tibet, India, and Suez depended on finding the code.

"You know of course that once you are on embassy grounds, you are in Germany and MI5 can't touch you," said Sir Harold.

Chapter 14
Bellows Cottage, Buckinghamshire, England

SIR HAROLD SAT IN the living room staring at Diana, dressed in a chic gray suit with accompanying bonnet. She had driven up the gravel driveway and jumped out of the driver's seat, not bothering to open the door.

"Beastly weather," she said, throwing her bonnet on the sofa. "How are you feeling? Have you been using the crutches?" She knew damned well he hadn't. Quickly abandoning the false sympathy, her interest flagging, she decided she really didn't care.

"You know, Father, we ought to come here more often. It's so much more comfortable than that huge mausoleum."

Two months and he's still limping around on those crutches. "It's only a sprain, Father," she said, amused.

Apologetic, he said, "I'm almost as good as new." Dropping the crutches, he hobbled to the couch and threw himself on it. "It's all falling together, Diana. There will be no stopping us. Have you heard the latest? Hitler just won ninety-two percent of the vote. He's been appointed chancellor. We've left the League of Nations and the disarmament conference."

"We?"

"The last time I looked, we, the British, were still members, and Ramsey McDonald was still our prime minister, and the swastika wasn't flying over parliament. Not yet. It won't be long," said Sir Bellows.

"Whose side are you on, Father?" Diana asked.

"Ours. Bellows'. We stand to gain most with a Nazi victory—wealth, our former position. We. Those who believe."

"In what? What do you believe in, Father?"

"The same things you do, Diana—tailored clothes, lobster, quail, the races, weekend parties. Need I go on?"

"No, you've made your point," said Diana perusing a copy of *Vogue* magazine.

"We are one of the first families of England. We along with the Germans were meant to rule. We utter the same catchwords, smoke the same cigars, use the same perfumes, go to the opera, the symphony, and the ballet."

"It's expected," said Diana, inhaling sharply, suddenly angry.

"Because it's our responsibility," countered Sir Bellows.

"And Father, how do you feel about gassing women and children? Is that our responsibility?"

"That's propaganda. We are doing no such thing. We would never." He waved his hands. "Well, it's preposterous."

"Let's drop it," she said, thumbing the pages.

"Would you mind taking my crutches? Where did that damned Aston Martin come from?" he asked, throwing the *Times* across the room.

"We can sit under the umbrella. It's a shame to waste this sunshine," said Diana, ignoring his tirade.

Feeling the warmth from the champagne at lunch, Diana was pleased that she and her father were getting along so well, but she was still uncertain it would last. She found the conversation depressing. "The Yard," he continued, "insists there was someone else in the car."

"Of course there was," she said, turning the pages. "Andreas. Unless you dropped him off before the accident."

"Does he chew betel nuts?"

"There are a lot of things Andreas does that I'm not aware of, but chewing betel nuts isn't one of them, and who gives a damn?"

"Scotland Yard. Seems they found betel nuts at the accident. Whoever wanted me dead chews betel nuts."

"They are an Indian delicacy, aren't they?"

"The Yard be damned. I don't care if they think it was Gandhi. I don't want them to know about Andreas."

"Why?"

"If you have a minute to stay in one place and not dither about, I'll tell you—and put that bloody magazine down."

Her hand gave an involuntary jerk as she tossed the magazine across the room.

"I'm sorry, Diana. I'm getting weary of hobbling around. I'll make it brief. This next war will be different. There will be millions of dead, but no bodies. There won't be anything to bury—a tidy, clean war."

He looked directly into the sunlight shielding his eyes. "What does that sound like? And while you're at it, pull those damned drapes."

"Hell. The Apocalypse," she said, drawing the curtains.

"There," he said, satisfied. "Would you mind handing me the ashtray? And one of those chocolates if it's not too much trouble. An *atomic* bomb." Enveloping himself in a cloud of white smoke from his pipe, he appeared extremely satisfied with himself.

No, she didn't see, and furthermore, she didn't give a damn. "So what?" She and her father were allies in one cause—continuing the Bellows title.

"Don't be foolish. You have much to lose—property, position. Think, Diana. There's a new source of energy—atomic energy. Uranium. The Germans want it, and it's sitting on top of one of those mountains. I'm the key to their getting it. I have the contacts that will get us through those mountain passes. Bellows Manor will be restored to its former glory, and our family will be wealthy once again."

"You are being a bit dramatic, aren't you?" she asked.

A gust of wind rattled the windows. She felt suddenly cold.

"And would you mind closing the windows? It's getting chilly," he said, shivering.

The wind rose as a small patch of clouds passed overhead and then as abruptly as it started, the calm returned; only the patter of rain against the windows remained. "There are so many ways to profit. Himmler is opening new camps at Ravensbrook and Sachsenhausen to make bricks." He laughed. "The German brick king. Stone works, iron foundries, textiles, leather. Not bad when you have no labor costs and no limit on the hours they can work and an accounting arm that's under the direction of your friend, navy paymaster Obergruppenfuhrer Oswald Pohl.

All controlled by Himmler's holding company, Deutscher Wirtschaftsbetrieb.

"That will seem like small potatoes compared to what we're after, and all we'll need is a bunch of short swarthies with big noses and receding foreheads. The answer to war is to start one. If worse comes to worst, we'll just invade. We need those passes. We need that uranium. It won't take many men to control the passes."

"Why would a Jew want to help you?" she asked.

"It's just a hoax. Of course, there are no Jews in Tibet. and if there are we couldn't care less It's the dead Buddhists we care about – the ones who've been killed by the Jews"

"Exactly! We are going to supply a few—dead ones. Hitler will go in. The Jews are a convenient excuse. If they're not there, we'll manufacture them. Hitler's going to do the same thing in Czechoslovakia and Austria—invade to protect. Neville Chamberlain will lead the charge."

"Who's going to go to war for Jews?"

"Not for Jews, for Buddhists. To save them from Jews. Christ died for our sins. The Jews killed him. The Germans are making sure we don't make his martyrdom meaningless. We are not going to invade to save the Jews, we're going in to save the Tibetans *from* the Jews. You haven't grasped the depth of the hatred Hitler has for the Jews. They are vampires waiting to suck the blood from every virile Aryan. It doesn't matter if it's true. You can hide behind it. It's a diplomatic reason. No one really cares. If you say it often enough and have a few photographs."

Diana was beginning to get the picture. "You are going to strike a deal to protect Buddhists from Jews? Is that it?" and the mountain passes just happen to be part of the bargain."

"Well, yes, exactly! We'll release photos of bodies of Buddhist children strewn about. We can get them from the camps—Auschwitz, Dachau. Goebbels will dub in some mountains. How is anyone going to know? They will have to take what we give them as gospel." He winced as he tried to get up. Falling back, he put out his hand. "I need you," he said.

She ignored his hand. "If we find what we are looking for, what do we do with it? And what do we do with the Jews?"

"I told you, there aren't any Jews."

"And if there are?"

"They will be dead Jews. It's been three thousand years since they were kicked out of Assyria and God gave Ephraim the covenant. The Germans have detected several instances of unexplained radiation. If they are there, they're dead."

She looked at him with renewed admiration. How stupid not to have seen it. "So while everyone is concentrating on uranium while they are searching for the Holy Grail, Germany is going to occupy India, Sikkim— the entire region. Is that it?"

"Precisely. And before the international community wakes up, we will own the Middle East and the oil under it."

"What of the people who are sitting in Tibet? What do we do with them?"

"Build concentration camps, use them for labor. The same thing we are doing with the Jews. No one will care. In fact, they'll rejoice. Cheap dresses, cheap oil, cheap housing. We'll turn the Buddhists into shopkeepers. No need to brave the mountains for a few dollars. Divine mystery will evaporate from religion. Buddha will become an amiable uncle. The Jews, if they are there, won't give us much trouble. In the meantime, we'll hold the world's energy—oil. We must be smarter. Be ready for the unexpected." Letting go of the crutches and falling back, he said, "Leave it to me." He sighed. "Oh, to be young again. I don't know how Göring does it. Keeps up with all the young, beautiful women. Have you met his latest? Tara Lilith?"

"It's an exotic name," said Diana.

"She's an exotic woman."

"Who is she?"

"A relative of Andreas's, I'm told."

"Really?" Diana's felt her pulse quicken. "Are you quite sure? You'd think he would have mentioned her."

"It's a crazy family," said Sir Henry.

Diana chose a cigarette from an ornamental box on the piano and held it like a pointer, her hand poised in midair. "What if the whole thing is a waste? If we go through this charade and it has no purpose? There are no Jews. There is no uranium. It's all just a gigantic game."

"But there are those mountain passes There's going to be a war, Diana. There will be an atomic bomb no matter what. The Nazis have Heidegger and Schroeder, both physicists, working on splitting the atom. What did you think Andreas was doing at Wiligut?" Sir Harold smiled, pleased to see that he had caught his daughter off guard. "I was lucky," he continued. "Those brakes had been tampered with. I won't be as lucky next time."

"You will live forever, Father. Your kind always does."

"Don't underestimate me, Diana. Your mother has.

Without those passes, no one gets into Tibet. Jews or not, they come with a price. I've traveled to the Tashilumpo Monastery to meet the Panchen Lama, Sendhin Tulpo. It sits at the confluence of the passes that control the entry into Tibet and to the mountains. I've made sure Göring realizes my importance.

Kongzhengchenga has never been climbed by a German." The sound of his voice giving him comfort, he said, "You could hold it with no more than a company of men. You" —he pointed at her— "you are going to be the first woman to reach those passes."

The old man made gave an old man's laugh. "Those bleeding hearts, the Astors and the Vanderbilts, are going to pay for the guns and ammunition to protect the Tibetans from Jewish wolves. The British will never know until it's too late. By that time, we will have invaded Mesopotamia, and we will have air support and heavy equipment."

He took a long pull on his pipe, exhaling leisurely, waiting for his words to sink in before he continued. "Your expedition will travel under the cover of the new craze, you know, to find herbs and plants, fruit and nuts—God's food as the fools call it. And of course, if there are natives, they must be abused natives! Never underestimate the stupidity of the public, my dear. In fact, Göring's worked it out so that the green worshipers will pay for the occupation. I'm sure you've read in one of your fashion magazines that it's possible for the Tibetans to live to a hundred and have delicate skin and raging desire."

"So you see, as far as the public and the government are concerned, we will be climbing to discover new flora, preserve our species, and protect one of the worlds most respected and loved peoples. We must link hands with these oppressed people, the Tibetan Buddhists. The open door," he said. "Brilliant, yes? The British will be overwhelmed with the publicity and will have to issue permits for us to forage around in their backyard. Once there, the guns and ammunition will follow. Only later will they discover that it is the master race doing the foraging."

"Have you heard the news?" Sir Harold asked at breakfast. "Hitler is head of the Wehrmacht. Now, all that's left is to get rid of Roehm, the head of the SA, and a homosexual."

She didn't know Roehm from Mickey Mouse, but still, there was no need to know him; her father's excitement told the story—a war wasn't far off.

Diana stared across the table as though she'd confronted the March hare.

"What do you think?" he asked, pleased with himself.

Diana could think only of something she'd learned in history class at Miss Horten's school. It was from Heine. "The German angst for battle and war for war's sake would once again arise. Beware, you French, beware you, British, for when it does …" She couldn't remember the rest.

Lord Harold leaned back in the couch obviously pleased with himself, a look of triumph on his face. as though he had just attained the highest peak in Tibet. And the flag that he placed at the top of the mountain bore the crest of Bellows Manor. "I'll see to it that Himmler picks Andreas to lead the expedition. Your job is to stay close to him."

"What do we do if the press doesn't buy it?"

He smirked. "What we have always done. We use force."

Chapter 15
Bellows Chapel, Buckinghamshire

DIANA CLIMBED INTO THE car, settled back, and turned on the radio "A kiss is just a kiss --- the fundamental things of life as time goes by" "The fundamental things of life as time goes by..." She repeats wistfully "And when two lovers woo, they still say I love you ..." But what do they mean? She laughed. "Life is short, and love is fleeting, I want you while you are still young and firm. I don't want to grow old and watch you wither. What else could they mean"

"Louis Armstrong, the black singer" she said, recognizing his voice He launched into a second melody. "the ring around my finger What a life. I'm in love". More like around your neck, if she's not black", she laughed. On second thought if life does go on.? I'll be damn if I'm going to be trapped, settle for someone I don't love."

"I'll apologize to Mary. Why not. It's on my way. That should do it."

The Chapel was part of the pastor's cottage tucked away in a dark wood, in a quiet corner of the Bellows' estate, it, had served the castle and surrounding parish, Buckinghamshire, for centuries

She fumbled at the door, and leaning, pushed it open. "Father?" she murmured, and then louder, "Father?" The odor of incense. permeated every nook and crevice, seeped into the walls and onto the ceiling. Petals from discarded flowers dotted the floor. A casket loomed in the dusk like a ship in a fog. It was steering right for her. Of course, that's where the petals had come from; There were no flowers on the casket or in the room. She'd been in the room once before, when she'd buried her son.

There were no mourners. The cottage was dark. She entered the room. Walking up to the casket, she ran her fingers over the polished wood. She turned when she heard footsteps.

"Father!" she breathed. He didn't answer but stood looking at her. His eyes, red, sparkled. The hatred in them, the poison, flowing onto his face with his tears.

"You!" he hissed. "How dare you show your face here? She meant nothing to you. You are a little late for cakes and coffee."

Taken aback, Diana stuttered, "Whose?"

"You know whose!" he hissed.

"No, truly, I have no idea."

"Mary!" The name was a sob. "She shot herself the day after you called her out at the Connaught. Why are you here? Did you love her or care? Would it have made any difference to you—to be a friend—if not a friend, a Christian? To have shown some kindness—not love, just kindness. But instead, you chose to ridicule and mock her, she, who was a Christian and wouldn't hurt a dog."

He fought for air as he continued to speak. "By the rules of the manor, you should have led the procession, at least should have provided refreshments for the mourners. There were many, and they won't forget. Oh, they'll forget Mary soon enough, but they won't forget that you didn't supply them with cake and coffee!"

The large man looked small now, hunched and shrunken into the depths of his sorrow. "I once believed there was nothing that could hurt you once you were a man of the Lord. He would comfort you under all circumstances. You have robbed me of the one thing I loved. I promise I will get even. I will take from you all that you prize."

He fell to his knees. "We weren't sinners. We were lovers!" His hands raised in supplication. He was suddenly alone with his faith, with his God, an unforgiving, frightening God, and he was afraid. Still crouching over the casket, he broke down and covered his face.

"You are looking for a scapegoat," Diana said, backing away toward the door. She heard herself speak but wondered where the voice had come from.

He was alone, surrounded by dead saints. Just as she was alone, surrounded by servants, hangers-on, but alone. He stepped forward to strike her but restrained himself at the last minute. Holding himself still, he said, "You are not worth it. You are not worth my anger. I pity you," and walked away.

The house was silent. Wiping tears from her eyes, she climbed back into the car. Throwing the copy of *Vogue* onto the backseat, she slid into the driver's seat. Her courage faded, and she was suddenly, terribly, infinitely unhappy and alone. Staring at the wheel, the keys jingling in the dash, she was overcome with sadness. "I can't go on like this, I can't," she said. "But I will—decaying like Bellows." She sunk onto the steering wheel. She turned the key, and the engine started. She drove off.

The explosion was heard for miles around. Little was left of the church other than a blackened silver chalice and the brass handles of a coffin.

Chapter 16

Anna's Apartment, Unter den Linden, Berlin, February 1935

A WOMAN'S FOOTSTEPS SOUNDED out of the fog. Anna flicked the light switch at the top of the steps. Balancing a large black bag against her knee, she bent over, looking for the key to her apartment. Major Heydrich slid from the car; Glancing up the street, he bounded up the steps. He caught her from behind. The chloroform took effect quickly.

When she awoke, Heydrich was standing over her. "Untie me, you bastard," she demanded. "What the hell do you want?"

Staring out the one window, Heydrich, tall and slim, every bit the Prussian officer, bore a cruelty more of a thug than a soldier.

Anna felt for the amulet she'd worn around her neck. Panicking, she realized it was missing.

"We used to have such good times." Heydrich sighed. He turned from the window and the faint sunlight filtering into the room. "I thought together we could summon the devil. One more mass for old times' sake."

"What do you want from me?"

"The amulet, Anna, the amulet."

"If you cooperate, it will be over quickly. If not …" He shrugged.

"I don't know what you're talking about."

He leaned forward. "Where is the amulet? It tells the way up the mountain. Anna, you've run with wolves—don't die with dogs. Where is the uranium?"

Incoherent images floated in her mind—dead children staring, their throats slit.

"Don't play games, Anna. This will make it easier." He held an ampoule of morphine up to the light. "Renew your vows in one final mass. Lust is the bounty of life. Be mine, part of me."

His hand closed around her throat. The last of her life still on his tongue, the devil so close.

Heydrich bent forward and released her bonds. She stroked his forehead—lovers.

"Remember," she said wistfully, "when Göring was wounded in the Putsch in '23? Hitler in jail? I never gave up hope. I relieved my pain with opium, and years after, I never lost faith. After all those years, did you think I would abandon Andreas, my son, my dream?"

"Well then, you have chosen," said Heydrich.

The spasms started. Convulsed in agony, she reached out for him. He held her head and smoothed her brow. Bending, he kissed her gently on the forehead. "Don't be a fool, Anna," he said, holding her in a lover's embrace. "Please, just say the word."

It was hopeless. She was a dead woman. But she could save Andreas.

"In ice and in fire. In the air and on the ground," she said, her face flushed and the words barely audible.

"The attack has been planned," replied Heydrich. "All we need is the right time. We will find the amulet, the uranium. Let there be no doubt. Man will put it to its fated purpose. We will make religion out of the fear and terrorism that follows. The Nazis will be almost a relief. I laugh to think how juvenile mankind still is, to think he can combat the evil in himself by knowing himself. It is the devil he must know. If it were himself he was fighting, he would have uprooted it long ago.

"We're suffering from the same evil two thousand years later. Christ is dead. Nonetheless, we will have to fight the same battle that was fought so long ago. There will be a reckoning, a judgment. And this time, you might not win."

Anna could barely see him in the fading light—his voice savage, possessed.

Chapter 17
Guy's Hospital, Southwark Street, London

ANDREAS WALKED TO THE hospital disappearing into the fog. Few people were on the street. He hadn't much time. He would need antiseptic. an anesthetic to reduce the pain and a scalpel.

He hurried down the stairs to the morgue; he found a needle and a small vial of Novocain in the dissecting room. Taking a deep breath, he injected the Novocain into his left arm. Making a small incision and parting the tissue over the muscle, he created a small pocket. He opened the vial and inserted the piece of Lebenfels's skin, closed the wound, put his jacket on, and walked up to the admitting desk.

"Who's on ambulance duty?"

"Tony," said Natalie, the new girl. She was cold and indifferent by nature, but her eyes were moist. A soft sob escaped.

"What's wrong?" asked Andreas. Natalie motioned to a gurney by the ambulance entrance. "Someone we know?" Andreas asked, already guessing the answer.

"Claire. They just fished her out of the river."

"Good God, what happened?" Andreas's face convincingly bore the expression of pained surprise. How many times had he used it when confronted by a spurned lover?

"Murdered, robbed. Some son of a bitch killed her for a few measly pounds."

Andreas shook his head. Disgust, anger, pity. A show for Natalie. Or was it?

"Where's Tony?" Andreas asked.

"Coffee."

Andreas ducked into the hallway and walked to the pharmacy. He pulled open a drawer marked Tuberculin Vaccine, BCG. He injected the vaccine into his right arm and slipped a nitroglycerine pill into his pocket. He could count on the BCG to stimulate an immune response and raise his temperature; the nitro would dilate his vessels, raise his pulse, and give him a good flush. In an hour, he would look sick as hell. The incision in his arm was already beginning to throb.

The coffee shop was empty except for the ambulance driver, who sat at the counter staring into his cup.

"Too bad about Claire," said Andreas. "How about giving me a ride?"

"Yeah, sure."

Such a dejected look. One of Claire's lovers?

"Just let me finish this coffee."

Andreas went to the lobby, picked up the phone, and dialed Scotland Yard, asking for Inspector Willoughby.

"He's off duty."

"It is very important. Tell him Dr. von Eckhart called to report a murder."

"Where? Who?"

"Claire Hutchins, at Waterloo Bridge. Her body's been fished out of the river."

"Who are you?"

"Her murderer. Don't bother sending a car—I'm coming in on my own."

Andreas climbed into the front of the ambulance. Tony turned on the flashing red light.

"I feel bad about Claire," Tony said as he exhaled cigarette smoke. "She was just in the wrong place at the wrong time."

"I guess so," said Andreas. "Let me out at the corner."

As soon as the ambulance had passed from sight, Andreas took the nitroglycerine from his wallet, emptied the packet into his mouth, and walked the rest of the way to Scotland Yard.

"I'm here for questioning," he said. "I'm the man who reported the murder a short time ago."

The medicines had begun to take effect. His temperature was rising, and his pulse was racing. Willoughby had just returned, and Andreas was led into his office. Two hoppers and an assortment of pens were scattered over the desk sharing space with half-eaten cake. Willoughby seemed to have shrunk since Andreas had last seen him, but his head seemed to have grown. His coat appeared two sizes too large, his hat too small.

Willoughby looked up. "Are you all right?"

"Of course. It's just that it's hot in here."

Willoughby heaved himself into a chair not bothering to remove his coat; he sat tapping the desk with a pencil.

"Can I get you a cup of coffee?"

"Black, very black," said Andreas.

Willoughby removed his coat and again collapsed into his chair. It rolled backward under his weight and collided with the metal cabinets behind him.

"Bloody office is too small." He pulled himself back to his desk and rested his chin on his folded fingers. The elbows of his jacket were threadbare. "This young lady is the recording secretary," he said, introducing the stenographer.

Andreas smiled. She wore a severe skirt, blouse buttoned to the neck, short, swept-back hair, and no lipstick. Unsmiling, she held her hands poised over the typewriter.

"Well, let's review the facts," said Willoughby, removing his tie. "Tell me what happened."

My arm got infected, and then I died, Andreas thought. *Or was it in France that I died?*

"You didn't go back to your flat after you returned from Bellows Manor," said the inspector. "So no one has been there since you left, and that was..." he flipped his calendar, ...

"two days ago. And you returned early this morning?"

"Sir Harold was kind enough to bring me back to London."

"Were you in the car when the accident occurred?"

"No."

"Poor sot. He must have gotten into the accident right after he dropped you off."

"Will he be all right?"

"He will live, if that's what you mean," his voice trailing off. "By the way, do you like betel nuts?"

"Hate them. Why?"

"No reason. Why didn't you go directly to your flat?"

Andreas's temperature was rising, his faced was flushed, and his head was swimming. "I had to kill him!" he blurted.

Willoughby's eyes dilated. "Who? Pardon me. You had to kill whom? Yes, that's better, whom?"

"The big guy, in the morgue. It was him or me."

Willoughby seemed confused. "I thought you wanted to report the murder of a young woman." He looked at the dossier. "A Miss Claire Hutchins. She had her throat cut. Waterloo Bridge. Our men just brought her in."

Andreas fixed his gaze on the overhead light. A spider was busy devouring a fly.

"Her too."

"Doctor, are you here to confess to this Claire Hutchins's murder or someone else's?"

"Both." Andreas was sweating.

"We have only one body," Willoughby said.

"Someone must have taken it—the one in the morgue, I mean."

"When did that killing take place?"

"Which one?"

"The second one. The young lady we already know about. Tonight, in the morgue?"

"Yes, tonight … or was it yesterday? Or last week?"

"Perhaps the body just walked off?"

"Maybe you just don't know where to look. I just told you," said Andreas.

What right do they have to keep him here? Murder. How many had the Yard killed? Wagner and the stranger deserved to die. Claire—that was murder. His arm throbbed. He squirmed in the chair. He was burning up. *Tap. Tap. Tap.* The typist continued typing.

"What?" he asked, shaking his head.

"Dr. von Eckhart," said Willoughby, "why did you kill her?"

"All I know is that I'm responsible for her death. I guess I just didn't care enough to save her."

"Could these deaths have had anything to do with the strange case you took care of a few nights ago, the one your embassy called about?" The inspector shuffled some papers on his desk. "Here, a Mr. Lebenfels? The author who wrote all that Aryan rubbish."

The room was silent. The *tap, tap, tap* went silent. The inspector rocked in his chair.

"Did you know a Herr Wagner?" he asked.

"He was never my patient," said Andreas.

"You are a colonel in the SS?"

Andreas felt his head full of cotton. The endless, pointless talk around in circles. "I came here of my own free will," he said.

"Indeed you did, Doctor, and I am most grateful. But there are obviously a number of loose ends that need to be tied up. I'm sure you can understand that. By the way, we have been trying to contact your housekeeper. We'd like to ask her some questions. Might you know her whereabouts?"

"I haven't been home. Have you tried her apartment? She rents a little place in the East End. Sometimes, she's out late at her society meetings."

The room was deathly hot, and he didn't feel like answering any more questions. *What the hell could they do to me?* He was dead inside—dead. He pictured himself lying on the gurney withered, stiff, and white.

"Are you ill, Doctor? We won't be much longer."

The typing stopped.

Andreas steadied his legs and pushed against his chair trying to get up. "If I'm not under arrest, you know where to find me," he said. "Could you ask one of your officers to give me a ride? I really don't feel well."

"Certainly, Doctor. We will pick this up again tomorrow, when you are feeling better. Meanwhile, please leave us your passport. And of course, do not try to leave the country."

The room was spinning. Andreas held onto the side of the desk.

Willoughby summoned a young officer. "Take the doctor home, please. He will give you the address."

It was a late-model Rover. Andreas caught the scent of leather upholstery mingled with stale cigarettes. "Where to?"

Andreas got into the front seat next to the driver. *Perhaps my plan has gone too well. I'm not sure I have the strength to complete it.*

The patrolman unbuckled his tunic. The nightstick together with his flashlight and notebook lay on the seat beside him. Pulling out of the driveway, he turned to look for oncoming traffic.

Andreas struck him across the back of the head with the flashlight, and his head slumped onto the steering wheel, a thin line of blood trickling down his neck. Andreas jumped out, shoved the patrolman over to the passenger side, and put his tunic and cap on. His head pounding, he got into the driver's seat and headed for Belgravia.

He pulled the car in front of the German embassy. The patrolman on duty gave him a quick nod and turned back to his coffee. Andreas slipped out of the car and onto the grass. He vomited. *If only I can get someone to answer the buzzer, I'll be on …* Slithering on his stomach in the shadow of the car and still retching, he staggered up the steps and collapsed against the buzzer. A large eye spoke to him, a hot wire inside his arm. He tried to sit up. Someone restrained him.

"I'm a doctor," said the eyes leaning over him. "Dr. Milner."

Andreas pointed to his arm. "It has to be opened."

"It will hurt," said the doctor.

"Wait! Find … piece of flesh … carefully … formaldehyde." He struggled. A warm blanket floated over him. Voices, far away.

"Warm saline soaks. Betel nuts every two hours by the clock. We will know by morning if it has to be amputated."

"You have been delirious for a week. Do you feel well enough to sit up?" she asked. A tall, slender man stood next to her. His skin was drawn tightly over his face, and a long scar stretched to the corner of his mouth—Foreign Minister Joachim von Ribbentrop. Professor Nielson, a short, almost midget-sized individual, stood next to him.

The foreign minister held up a brown slip of paper the size of a cigarette wrapper. "We have it. We have found the cipher. The numbers from the tattoo were to a safe-deposit box. Our agents scoured every bank in London to find it. Ancient Aryan symbols," he said, puffing out his chest and standing on a chair while pointing to a copy of the cipher in the blackboard. "Runes. They have an interesting history. If you wanted to be a hero, you'd carve the runes in your own flesh and bleed to death, a red-letter day." He laughed a high-pitched laugh like a woman or a hysterical child. "Sundays and holidays are still printed in red. Runes were used to predict the future. Like casting the dice or shuffling tarot cards," he said, fussing with his trousers that hung over his shoes.

"They look like a bunch of twigs tossed up after a storm," Andreas said, sitting up in bed.

"You already know some of them," said the professor. "The sun wheel and Hagenkreuz are runes. You wear a runic symbol, the Schutzstaffel, the rune of the SS."

Andreas dozed off, and Nielson returned to his blackboard.

"Will you be up to traveling tomorrow?" Ribbentrop asked.

"Yes," Andreas said. "But I doubt Scotland Yard will let me out of the country."

"Don't worry. We have taken care of that. You will leave from my private airstrip at Bellows Manor."

It was late in the afternoon when the phone rang in Sergeant Willoughby's office.

"Colonel Eckhart is flying to Berlin at eight o'clock tomorrow morning." The voice clicked off.

Chapter 18
10 Downing Street, London, October

AS ANDREAS'S PLANE APPROACHED the French border, Chaim Ephraim Lowenstein was entering number 10 Downing Street. He was still trying to get to the bottom of his father's accident. He had died brutally. There had been a great deal of blood. His clothes had been covered with it.

Curiously, his father had been struck crossing the Embankment, close to Whitehall. The street was wide there, and the speed limit just twenty-five kilometers per hour. The ambulance driver had taken him to a nearby German charity hospital. When they deposited him he was already dead.

His father's death was as if he'd been swallowed by the earth. There was nothing left of him; his wedding ring and wallet were missing, and there was little to remind Chaim of him. Someone had removed the wedding ring while he lay on the sidewalk. It was curious. The ring, though gold, wasn't worth that much. The wallet he could understand. It contained at least five hundred pounds.

Chaim's former position as director of Israeli intelligence in England had led him to chase down alleys, all nonproductive and leading to all sorts of strange conclusions, mostly paranoid and unfounded. Chasing after eyewitnesses didn't help either. The mystery slowly receded into the background as life returned to normal.

He knew why he'd been called to the prime minister's office, and he would know exactly what he would say. He'd repeated it over and over, savoring every word: "Go to hell."

He walked toward 10 Downing past important-looking people in well-tailored suits, heads held high, smug swaggers, dismissive glances. If you looked, however, really looked, you'd see their inner turmoil, their sadness and fatigue, and their endless questions, *Why? In any event, it doesn't involve me. They can't blame me, accuse me. It's the Jews. Their cunning and licentious cheating has caused this. Why should I get involved? For what purpose? What's for dinner? What's playing at the Strand?*

Legions of men and women sweep by in both directions, their attaché cases and umbrellas clutched to their chests like medieval armament. *We are English*, they seem to say. But a few walks slower than the rest, stare at the sidewalk, heads bowed, faces turned away. They are English too but from a different army; armed with tefillin attached to their arms and tzitzit to their shirts, strings around their fingers.

The yellow piece of cloth they wear attached to their coats in Berlin is missing. They didn't need it to remind them they are Jewish. The looks on strangers' faces are all the reminder they need.

The day is raw despite the bright sunshine. The tall buildings are covered in soot. His shoes scrape on broken glass. The cracked pavement with bits of grass breaking through, the smell of rotten food, the chorus of people slouching toward him with hard eyes, grim faces, belies that this is London, not Moscow or Prague. There is a sense of violence in the air.

Cowering under his black homburg and the upturned lapels of his Saville Row coat, Chaim Lowenstein turns into 10 Downing, avoids the man urinating on the wall, and enters the servants' entrance. The butler opens the door and quickly ushers him into a tastefully paneled room. A small coal fire burns in the grate in one corner; a large mahogany table takes up the corner across the room. Several chairs are scattered about.

Next to the fireplace is a red-upholstered wing chair, its back to the entrance. A teapot and a partially chewed biscuit suggest someone sitting in the depths of the chair. A cloud of white smoke hovers over it. Not much has changed since he had last been a guest. *How long ago?* It seems an eternity. He was young then—young in many ways. He believed then. A young man, a Jew, had to believe—to kill, to follow the blood trail. There were no contradictions. Everything certain, simple. He follows the cigarette smoke to the ceiling, remembering.

Judea, an illusion illuminated like a dark grave by dark smoke and amber whiskey. They drink and tell stories. Their successes with women—never their failures. The strong fellowship of youth, of men imbued with hate not by experience but by stories passed down by parents told at dinners and bar mitzvahs, the light shining on their faces and young beards, their voyages just beginning. *We are brave. We will never change. No matter the sacrifice, until we achieve the end—a homeland. But we did change. We grew older, wiser, and we realized death and sacrifice could not be washed*

away with milk and honey. It is what it is, what it was, and what
it will be forever with God, their God, our God, an unforgiving
God, a cruel God, the God of Heydrich, Himmler, Hitler, Mengele,
Herzle, and Moses.

"Everyone's gone. I gave them the day off," says the
voice from the chair, arrogance and sense of superiority
stamped on each syllable. "I thought it better if no one
saw you," he said, grooming his white hair with his hand.
Dressed in a black, double-breasted suit, a red rose in his
lapel. In the dark room, his voice coming from the bottom
of the chair seems disembodied.

Of course, thought Lowenstein. *Wouldn't want a Jew to
be seen in conversation with the PM.* "No worry. I'm used
to being heard but not seen, Mr. Prime Minister," Chaim
answered, removing his coat.

The PM smiled ruefully. "I'll get right to it," he said,
turning to face his visitor and struggling to contain his
anger. "What a mess. This was found amongst your father's
papers." Expecting Lowenstein's response, he added, "I
have corroboration from my sources."

Lowenstein could not hide his amusement. Nor did
he try. "There are no Jews in Tibet, Mr. Prime Minister.
At least, if there are, we don't know about it. We don't
have anyone there to verify whether they are there. This
postmark is easy enough to fake."

"Suppose your father found out he was wrong, that
there were Jews living in the mountains."

"My father was extraordinary, but I don't think even he
could find Jews in Tibet. By the way, how did you get hold
of the papers? I searched everywhere after the accident. Or
should I say murder."

It was the PM who then looked amused. "Someone was crossing behind your father," he added with disdain. "He picked up the papers and brought them to us."

"How fortunate for you," declared Lowenstein, intent on completing the interview without giving the PM the satisfaction of witnessing his outrage. "We are still missing a few things, his ring and his wallet," added the PM in a nonchalant tone as though they were discussing the day's cricket results.

With special effort and withholding his temper, Chaim said, "Your assassin doesn't need them. I would like to have them back if you don't mind too terribly. I don't care about the wallet. Your man can keep the money, but the ring has sentimental value."

"I regret the death of your father, truly. It should not have happened."

"Thank you, Mr. Prime Minister, but I'd say the odds were even—an eighty-year-old blind Jew against a Bentley."

"Preposterous!" The PM heaved himself out of the chair and confronted Chaim, his waistcoat stretched tightly over his paunch. His face sallow-gray and bloodless "If you are implying that we intended to injure your father … Why, we are not thieves or murderers, man. Whether the letter is fake or not, we won't be insulted by a bunch of…" He caught the words, spilling out of his mouth, just in time. "… by a bunch of foreigners!" A flush creeping into his face. receded, leaving it more bloodless than before.

"Pardon me, Mr. Prime Minister, but murder, rape, and torture do not seem to upset you nearly as much as the messenger."

"Humph! Well, perhaps I owe you an apology."

Lowenstein had grown tired of the exchange. It was time to get down to business. "Why have you called me?"

"It's this Jewish affair. These Jews in Tibet. It has me extremely upset."

"So I gather. I can solve your problem—you can stop worrying. There are no Jews in Tibet."

"Easy enough for you to say. If there's the slightest chance, it's worth the extra effort to find them. We need to know. We need someone we can trust."

"If they are there, make them British citizens the way Hitler has made the Germans in Czechoslovakia and Austria. You are obligated to protect your sheep. The ones that strayed," Chaim said condescendingly. "Once they're protected, there's nothing to worry about. If wars are to be finished successfully, they must be started for the proper reasons."

"Don't you think that torturing Jews is a proper reason?" asked the PM.

"Rubbish! You torture them every day. You want to find Jews for one reason and one reason only—so you can blame them for killing Buddhists. No one cares about someone who dresses in black with black whiskers and curls. But blond innocence is always a winner. Who could be more innocent than Buddhists?" Chaim asked.

"There aren't any blond Buddhists," said the PM. "But there are legions of young blond English, and we can photograph them—boys holding prayer books marching on their way to save a bunch of Buddhist monks," said the PM smiling, his face bright, his lips red. "We want those boys to be British—not German. I don't think you understand. We *want* Jews to be there!"

The PM sank back into his chair and lit another cigarette. Lowenstein waited for him to continue. "Control of the Hindu Kush, India, Burma, Nepal—the whole damned area," the PM said."

"Ah, yes. Protect," whispered Chaim. "Well, take heart—there are no Jews in Tibet. And if there are? Make them an offer for the uranium. That's what you're really concerned about."

The PM took a deep breath. "Christ. Who doesn't know about uranium? That's just part of it. Control of the entire region is the real prize. The passes, Tibet Nepal Sikkim, Bhutan, northern India—the high ground."

"Uranium!" whispered the PM. "The word is bandied about as if it were fish and chips. We have no clear idea what it is"

. "This letter might just as well have come from a ghost."

Lowenstein accepted the letter from the PM's hands. A smile etched across his face. The letter had come from a ghost, one that had been strangled and left for dead many times. The lost tribes of Israel had gone missing around 600 BC but returned every time the Jews were persecuted and needed to escape. A story told at the knee, a figment of imagination and hope.

"Better off dead. It wouldn't do to have them come to life, would it, Mr. Prime Minister? This rumor has been circulated every time the Jews are in trouble. There are no Jews in Tibet."

Watching the PM carefully, he added, "But there may well be uranium."

The PM adjusted himself in his armchair, his legs

crossed, a slipper dangling from one foot. Only the alteration in the studied blankness of his face indicating he was alive and not a statue. He remained seated, a slice of white skin peering out from the hole in the side of his sock. Bending forward, he poured tea. The hum of the clock and the chimes sounding assured everything was as it should have been.

"You are wrong. We want the Jews to be alive," said the PM.

"So that you can kill them?" said Chaim.

"Not exactly. To protect the Buddhists from them."

"And you expect me to prevent it? "To promote it." he said.

Stunned, Chaim wasn't sure he'd heard correctly "Do you mind, Mr. Prime Minister?" Chaim said as he pulled the curtains to let in some sound, some color, some life. He stared into the window, the rain distorting his face, the words filtering through the windowpane darkly as through a looking glass. The concept was madness, a joke. yet the PM was deadly serious;

What has changed? A great deal. I am no longer a Jew. I no longer rejoice at dead bodies and heart-lifting songs. I am not one of the bearded with ringlets and soft hands. In fact, I despise them. But neither am I one of the strong faced, with fists clenched aloft, marching. My hands and my shoulders are stiff, too stiff to raise over the dead, too stiff to raise in celebration. I'm tired.

"Did I hear you correctly?" he asked. You want me to promote a war?"

The prime minister was silent. "You're a dreamer, Chaim," he said, pointing a finger at his visitor's chest. "And I thought I was an innocent."

He faced the PM, two combatants who'd forgotten why they were fighting. The PM broke the silence.

"Your father ..." He paused for a moment. "Do you mind if I refer to Saul as your father? You can't imagine how distressing it is to refer to Heydrich as your father. I still can't get used to it. Saul, how much better that sounds— more Jewish, I mean," he went on, the sarcasm never leaving his face. "You and he used to read a book or a scroll at Yom Kippur?"

"Yes, Yom Kippur, the Day of Atonement. Of course, the scroll about Jews who had defied God and were forced to leave for a place where 'man never dwelt.' The tribe was named after their leader, Samuel Ephraim Lowenstein. That's why I'm here."

I am who I am because my mother mounted him and I sprang from that union. Heydrich's son! I will go to meet that fate. No matter how hard I try to deny it, to turn my back on it.

"The lost tribes," said the PM.

"But they're not real. It's pure make-believe, a tribe of dead Jews! Ghosts." said Chaim.

"Don't you see, Chaim? We want them to be real. We want them to be alive."

"So you can kill them! It's the uranium you're after."

"It's not the Jews we are going to protect. We need their ghosts so we can protect the Buddhists from the Jews," answered the PM. "You can't turn away from it, Chaim. The people couldn't care less about Jews. They wouldn't know one if they fell over him. What they prefer to see is a man outlined against the sky climbing up a mountain, or kneeling in prayer. The sky and the unsullied mountain,

Never a money-grubbing Jew. The Buddhists must be protected—from them. We have two choices: to protect the Buddhists from the Jews or the Jews from the Buddhists. The decision is easy."

"You want a war so that you can go in to protect—the Buddhists! And of course, do a little looking around while you're there."

"Yes, in a nutshell."

"Uranium doesn't weigh much, and if you just happen to stumble across it?"

The PM fixed his eyes on Chaim. His hands falling by his side, Chaim hears the words. His thoughts are miles away; at his mother's knee in rapt attention listening! The room is small, pictures hang from the walls stretching over generations. A small ornate clock ticks

"I don't understand; why did you marry him?" The question no more out than he wished it could be taken back. He knows and fears the answer.

"I loved him. I wanted his child."

In an instant, his hope is swept away. "I don't expect you to understand," she says closing her eyes.

The PM watched and waited for the right moment. He reached into his vest pocket and withdrew a ring. "This is yours. I debated whether I should give it to you."

"By what right did you keep it?"

"Decency," answered the PM. "Look inside."

Chaim carefully turns the engraving toward the light: R.E.U.T.—Reinhardt Eugen Tristan Heydrich. The episode has the smell of fate. It is fate that determined his mother's return to the land she loved, ignoring it was then under alien skies. She is next to the open window, rocking. is seized by a hacking cough that will presage her death from tuberculosis.

Chaim speaks in a weary voice. "It takes time to know a man. Until you do, you hold your breath and hope." He knows Heydrich. He is a killer.

"One million dollars. The Stradivarius, a piece of wood, worth more than my family would see in their entire lives, enough to gain passage for the entire family, enough to escape, enough for her to risk her life."

"Love?"

He laughs, a sound not far different from pain. "They, she and Heydrich, fall in love."

They fall in love secretly. Heydrich, a naval cadet, tall, impressive, sinister, and ambitious, an ice-cold intellect untouched by conscience. They fall in love before Auschwitz and Buchenwald but not before torture and death behind locked gates in Papenburg and Pomerania, not before torture and death behind locked gates in bunkers and empty buildings run by the SA gauleiters, not before—death secretly in ones and twos, ordered on the distinctive brown paper of the Forshungsamtress. They fall in love.

"Heydrich is worth millions, you know," muses Chaim. "Amusing, isn't it? One minute you're a despised murderer—couldn't buy your way into hell even, and the next a hero accepted in heaven. Money! Money in the collection basket, money on the offering plate, money for the poor, money in your pocket. You can buy Christ for thirty pieces of silver. The Stradivarius, a million, is worth the risk."

"We don't get to pick our future," said the PM, clearing his throat.

"Or our religion," said Lowenstein.

"Of course, there is one bright spot," said the PM. "It's all yours. The money I mean."

Chaim's face darkened. He squeezed the stem of his glass and stared into the room as if planning an escape.

"I'm coming," Chaim muttered.

The PM turned to see if anyone had entered the study. "I'm coming." Chaim's eyes growing more piercing every moment, he repeats, "I'm coming," his eyes burning and penetrating.

The prime minister, despite himself, again turned to look. Chaim's expression had changed, and his voice was normal.

"I'm tired of the whole damned business. So my father is Heydrich, a Nazi, and I'm a Jew." The words fee like ashes on his tongue. "If it were up to me, I'd say forget the whole damned thing," he said with disgust. "It's over, done with. I'm not a hero. I don't attend synagogue or Schule. My kids are Timothy and Betsy. They go to school with children named Brad and Jennie." His face pressed to the window, he feels the chill that darkens an already dark October day.

"Do we have a deal, Mr. Prime Minister?" He turned to the PM. "I don't give a damn about your problems in Tibet. It's probably crap. I'm interested in one person, Heydrich, and for one reason—to kill him. He has to pay."

"For his crimes? Or for sleeping with your mother?"

Stung, Lowenstein turned toward the PM, his muscles tense, barely breathing.

"I thought you were already a member of the Lekhi," the PM continued, ignoring Chaim's gaze.

"Irgun, Lekhi, who cares?" said Lowenstein, his anger subsiding. "I'll join any damned organization that gives me the chance to kill my father. Do we have a deal then?"

The PM's soft mouth twitched beneath his large moustache.

"The price for my cooperation is that I get to kill him. It's that simple. I would think the British would want him dead."

"Then you think wrong. We need Heydrich. With him, we can bring in von Braun, the rocket scientist, and Heidegger—Germany's top atomic scientist. They can name their price. Why not leave well enough alone? If he is alive and if you kill him, keep it quiet? No one will be the wiser. This way. The press. The story. You are sacrificing your mother."

"I'm using the only weapon I have. If I need help, I have a friend who works for the *Manchester Guardian*. He'd love to get his hands on a story like this. I'll deliver it personally."

"Think, Chaim!" said the PM, turning away. "Heydrich is working for us now. It's hard to swallow, but for Israel, for your mother, for yourself. Few know of the camps, and they couldn't care less. One Jew will be quickly forgotten. Tragedies always are. Think of the pogroms in Russia. In 1918 alone, two hundred thousand were killed. Forget it. If you want to be helpful, track down Werner von Braun and Heidegger. Convince them to defect."

"It's a nightmare," said Chaim.

"One that's all too real," answered the PM. "Help us create those Jews. We'll need them."

"For the next war," said Chaim.

"We can't get involved in personal vendettas," said the

PM, opening a filing cabinet and removing two folders. "We have one on Heydrich and your mother and one on von Braun and Heidegger. Our parents. We speak as if they were cause and we are the effect. When they are only images. Because Heydrich is a murderer doesn't mean you are. Do you have any memory of him? A man is more than his myth, and your feelings are surely more complicated than that he is a murderer. He's brilliant, a brave soldier, a good musician, and obviously, a good lover. Does your conscience allow for that? Do you have any memories? Do you remember any loving moments?"

"I remember his playing the violin, the intermezzo from *Thais*. He loved to play it. His face, everything about him, would change," said Chaim.

"*Thais*. The opera?"

"Yes. It's about a beautiful woman full of life and song. Until a man of God convinces her that life and love are blasphemous, that she must dress in black and still her instinct for love. Love is meant only for the supreme being, a leader like Hitler. In this case, Christ, but it could have been Hitler." Chaim thought for a moment and then turning toward the PM said, "He's a sadist."

Who? Hitler? asked the PM

"God," answered Chaim

The PM shrugged. "If you agree to help with the Jews," he said, offering Chaim the folders. "You decide."

Lowenstein, his muscles tense, hesitates, takes the folder marked Heydrich, studies the photographs without any show of emotion. Heydrich is close to sixty, though he appears younger. Cruel and ruthless, there is no tenderness in his face. Chaim turns, sees the small Derringer pointed at him. "What are you going to do with that?" he asks. "Shoot me?" Spreading his arms, "here, be my guest. You'd be doing me a favor."

The PM, realizing his mistake. said, "I knew it would be useless. Whatever you hope to gain from killing Heydrich won't compensate for the damage it will do to your mother, your family, our cause. Let it go."

Chaim stared out the window. The snow falling gently gave the pane a looking glass, other-world appearance. There was a time when he was aware of nothing but being a soldier and a Jew. Citizenship in a fabulous world of sacred murderers, a world bestowed with ubiquitous approval and heightened by the applause of revenge. He remembers fighting, not afraid of the storm. Finding shelter in each other, in shared belief. Everything hanging in the balance, the past and the future—a shared homeland. The words fall like the snow gently, silently.

Staring at the ceiling, he mumbles, "Some with latchkeys on the ramp living in a concentration camp ... knights and bishops, pawns and all. In a game of make-believe, darkly through a looking glass." Turning to the PM, he starts to laugh uncontrollably. "It's the only way it can have meaning."

"Of course, if you by accident discover he fell under a train ..." The PM shrugged. "Now let's get to what we expect from you if you do take on this Jewish thing. You will invent an entire history—names and fake documents as well as scientific data to show that a population of Jews does in fact live in Tibet and they are persecuting the Buddhists, you know, dead bodies strewn about."

"Have you ever been to that part of the world?" asked Lowenstein, tearing himself from the window. "The mountains and passes are not easily crossed. Those troops had better be well conditioned."

"Toy soldiers can do amazing things," said the PM.

Chapter 19
Berlin Airport, 1936

THE TOWER AT THE Berlin airport had assessed the damage and given Andreas's plane permission to land. Colonel Stoss, the pilot, was dead, and the plane, riddled with bullets, was flying on a prayer.

Andreas had boarded the plane at Ribbentrop's private landing strip outside of London. He'd assumed from his uniform that his fellow passenger was Luftwaffe. Other than a few pleasantries, he and the stranger had little to say to each other.

Where had that Focke-Wulf 190 come from? It had no markings. Whoever was at the controls wanted him or the stranger dead. He owed his life to the stranger. He'd flown the plane after the pilot was killed, and it was only his skill that had allowed them to land.

As the plane jolted onto the grass, he unbuckled, and shouting at Andreas over the sound of the engines, said, "By the way, if I were you, I'd stay away from the cyclotron for a few days." He leaped from the still-rolling plane into a ditch at the end of the field and disappeared into the woods.

Himmler's staff car raced toward the plane; an orderly jumped out as the car slammed to a halt. Himmler followed, his mouth pressed into a thin line. "Not many pilots could have handled it," he said, looking Andreas up and down as though expecting to find something missing.

Andreas was about to explain that he had not piloted the stricken craft, but he suddenly thought better of it. "Skill had nothing to do with it," he replied. "I just got lucky."

Himmler continued to examine him. "You were alone?"

Andreas picked up a handful of dirt ignoring the question. "Back on German soil. The tower gave me the instructions. I just followed them. A child could have done it."

"Get in," Himmler ordered. "The fighter must have taken off from a private airfield."

"Who has the power to get that done?"

The answer was obvious. One of four men: Göring, Goebbels, Hitler, or Ribbentrop—each with his own reasons for wanting Himmler dead.

"Someone must think you have important information, Colonel Eckhart. Important enough to see you dead," said Himmler, putting on his glasses and studying Andreas's face.

"Not that I know of," said Andreas, "unless it's that damned code, but I have already delivered it."

Ribbentrop would have his reasons. In their power struggle Göring, Ribbentrop, Himmler, and Heydrich had become a law unto themselves. Since the SA had been eliminated and Roehm assassinated, the path was there for a takeover—assassinate Hitler and the road was open. A super weapon would make the new Führer invincible.

Soon, two SS men were going through his clothes. He had no baggage. After they'd finished, they directed him to the bathroom, where he was searched more thoroughly.

Andreas waddled out of the hangar. He winced, sat gingerly as Himmler leaned into the backseat. "You will report to Professor Schroeder at Berlin University first thing in the morning. I recall you had almost finished your thesis on high-energy radiation and the effects on human tissue when we selected you for this position."

Berlin cafes, cabarets, the gayest capital in Europe, was gray and dark. The advertisements, the humor, the easy sex and vibrancy soured, sordid and chafing with Teutonic reality. The Jews, formerly ubiquitous in the pleasure haunts, slinking along the avenues heads down, listening, looking, herded together in ghettos—watching. Andreas opened the window and looked for the car that was to take him to the university.

At nine, the car slid to the curb in front of his flat. He was driven to Berlin University. As if in a church, people moved in an eerie hush silently from room to room.

"Andreas! Welcome!" Professor Schroeder greeted him. Short and squat, he moved with the agility of a prizefighter rather than a world-renowned physicist. His blue eyes darting from under short-cropped gray hair missed nothing. He rushed Andreas though a door marked Particle Research. The room was dark and smelled of chalk. Equations were scribbled on blackboards.

"I remember you were one of my best students. Why

did you leave?" Schroeder asked, pulling his glasses from his face.

"To survive. I was ordered."

Shaking his head and with a grim smile, Schroeder walked over to the blackboard into a world of equations, his face wreathed in the odor of chalk.

"No," he said, erasing one symbol and replacing it with another. "Better. Now, where were we?"

Andreas repeated Himmler's orders. "To study the effects of high-energy radiation on human tissue."

Schroeder shrugged. "Why? For what purpose, Andreas?" His face colorless, like a lover who saw his paramour in bed with a stranger but refused to accept what his eyes were showing him—that he had been cheated. The jewel he'd chased all those years and came so close to mastering would bring death, and he would be the patron saint.

"When the cyclotron is on and running, it is like a symphony. It buzzes and throws out numbers, but still, the secret is hidden. The answer was so close. Then they replaced him. Einstein. We should have expected it," he sighed. "He was Jewish."

The physicist put his glasses back on with both hands and blinked rapidly. "Did Himmler give you any further details? I mean about why Herr Meyer is being replaced?"

Of course, he already knew the answer. There was something desperate in his face.

Andreas put his hands in the air. "I didn't ask."

"You will have to catch up," said Schroeder, busying himself with the equations. "There's been a great deal of progress since you left. How long has it been? The war …

medical school ... the ... twelve years? Hard to believe you must be thirty-nine, close to forty now. Andreas, there are certain inescapable facts. One is Hitler. The others are Himmler and Göring. If Hitler or Himmler withdraws support?"

"There won't be any need for us."

That was understood; the answer hung in the air.

"If we split the atom, a grain of sand will have enough power to light Berlin. Think of it, Andreas, what it would mean to mankind."

Andreas laughed a hard, staccato laugh like the sound of rifle fire. Schroeder was a well-meaning idiot. *We will find a way to use it—to kill.* Both understood that. Both were silent.

"So you will be taking over as head of research at Wiligut? Interesting place. Grim. Could use a woman's touch, flowers, something." He paused as Andreas lit a cigarette. He took one when offered and accepted a lit match. "Ulrich Meyer is head of the research division, one of our brightest. We have the best cyclotron in Germany. His results with heavy water are extremely promising. We have to be careful and disguise them. The British are watching. We don't want reprisals—not yet."

"I know him, if he's the same one," said Andreas. "I went to school with him, before the Jews were relocated."

"It was unfortunate," said Schroeder.

Andreas wondered at the adjective; it usually preceded the words *but it couldn't be helped.* "Why is he being replaced?" he asked.

Schroeder shrugged as if to say, *Isn't it obvious?* "He's Jewish." Anxious to get Andreas's opinion, he hurried to the blackboard. "God is playing games with us," he said, shaking his head. "If we fire an atom at a paper with two slits, the atom will pass through both slits at the same time and leave two patterns." He drew out the next words. "And if we close one of the slits and fire an atom, the atom will automatically choose the other slit. Would you say that I was crazy or making it up?"

"Neither, but I would ask how a single atom could pass through two holes at the same time and leave two patterns. And how does it know to pick the open slit?"

"Exactly," said Schroeder. "Perhaps light has intelligence? Remember, all was darkness, and God separated himself from the darkness. Perhaps light has intelligence just as God has intelligence." He shook his head. "Albert Einstein, Ulrich Meyer, both Jews. It's unfortunate. I mean unfortunate for Germany. We will regret it. Have you heard? Executions—beatings, Jews suddenly gone missing. Rumor? Impossible. The chestnut trees are blooming, the streets are spotless, crowded with German youth, blond and lean and smiling..." He didn't finish his sentence.

"So you are to study the results of radiation on human tissues?" he asked, marching about the room. "Why?" he asked, turning to Andreas. But he knew why. He knew. He'd looked into the accelerator, he'd looked into her mouth, had seen the twisted and coiled entrails. She was beautiful but hideous. Schroeder shrugged again, and there were tears in his eyes perhaps from the dust coming off the blackboard. Perhaps from lorries packed with soldiers traveling just outside the window. "Of course, it can't be helped," he said. "Ach, you know what I mean."

He changed the subject, returning to his research. His voice once again excited, a magician in a hurry to pull a rabbit out of a hat. "We are smashing atoms with more and more energy but with no result. We get out no more energy than we put in." He waved his hands over the scribbled equations. "We need more heavy water, heavier marbles, more uranium, more everything, and still the answer may not come."

The next morning had the pale color of an impending snowstorm. Andreas, on his way to Wiligut Castle, glanced at his watch, leaned into the soft seat, and smelled the fine leather. It had been good to see Schroeder again. He couldn't believe things had taken such a turn for the better.

"The castle is not a very pleasant place," the driver volunteered, studying Andreas in the rearview mirror. "It's dark and smells bad. The officers' quarters are bare, very bare."

They followed the rutted road through a pine forest. A tank rumbled toward them. It stopped. An officer pulled himself out, peered into the car window, and demanded, "Papers!" Andreas produced his papers. The officer waved them on.

They continued climbing. The castle came into view like a crouching animal. Two yellow eyes shone from the turrets, and between them, the portcullis formed a gaping mouth.

An immense fireplace dominated the entryway; hanging over it was a huge red-and-white swastika. Tapestries of Teutonic knights covered the wall.

Andreas's footsteps echoed in the vast space. A young officer greeted him. "On behalf of Field Marshal Manfred

Heinrich Himmler, we welcome you to Wiligut Castle, the headquarters of the renowned Totenkopf."

Andreas was shown to his quarters, bare and cold just as the driver had said. The Totenkopf remained aloof except for General Allard Richter von Kaltenbrun, whose function seemed to be as liaison between the aristocratic old guard and the new recruits. Wounded, a hero of the Great War, he wore an artificial hand. Andreas had yet to meet with the director of research, Herr Ulrich Meyer. The man he was scheduled to replace was mysteriously absent. Andreas chose not to approach the cyclotron. He was a doctor, not a physicist, and this was the most advanced cyclotron in Germany if not the world.

Chapter 20
Gstaad, Switzerland

BORED, ANDREAS INVITED McDONALD to tour the castle. McDonald had already been scheduled to attend the peace conference in Switzerland. There were skirmishes, and there was little doubt Italy would soon invade Abyssinia. The powers were to meet to sanctify the invasion with some tut-tutting and please-don't-do-it rhetoric.

As long as he was going to be in Switzerland, he decided to interview an aged witness to the Eiger massif climb. It held an unrelenting fascination for him. The tale had been clearly told at the trial without embellishment or personal inflection, but he had seen many men lie under stress. It had to be one or the other—Andreas was a liar, or God was a murderer.

The road to Davos was a curving one. Looking out over the precipice, McDonald could see nothing but blue. He was speeding but felt compelled to press his foot harder on the accelerator. He was driving a rented car. The maximum speed had been set at sixty kilometers per hour, possibly saving his life.

McDonald wiped the perspiration from his face, but his sneer and sense of disgust remained. Why did he bother? He wanted to leave. Should have left years earlier. He'd begun to loathe the people he was trying to alert—their excuses even when presented with facts. Nonetheless, McDonald wrote the story and sent it to London. Though nothing would change, he needed his job. The Swiss would live forever. They rarely found anything to die for, and he needed to eat. The conference had established a German-Italian alliance for peace. He shook with laughter. You couldn't make it up. The French and English knew the Italians would invade just as they knew there would be a war. Not yet. Why ruin it? Things had never been better. It wasn't time yet. A few more years of drink, women, jazz, and Josephine Baker.

The mountains dominated everything. Conversation revolved around famous climbs. He had managed to contact the member of the Swiss climbing team who had investigated the Eiger incident. The old man was still alive but very ill.

The sanitarium was one of those bright Swiss hospitals, whiter than white—white linen, white beds, white uniforms, and white lights. The nurse said that it would be all right to approach the old climber but that McDonald must be careful not to upset him and that he was not always lucid.

The reporter found himself sitting next to a short, wizened man with staring blue eyes. McDonald soon decided he was on a fool's errand. The world was about to go to hell. Why was he looking into an affair that had occurred years ago, had already been investigated, and was of no importance? Why waste his time? These were good men, not rapists or murderers. They'd volunteered for the climb. Why go grubbing into the details? It was fate, an unfortunate accident.

McDonald, in the ward among white bandages and empty beds, had started to leave when the old climber reached out his hand. Leaning forward on one elbow, he whispered, "He's sent you, hasn't he? How do I know I can trust you? You had to have been there. I was watching the climb through a telescope from the village, Kleine Scheidegg, in the Bernese-Oberland, a vertical wall of ice, snow, and rock. I saw it, the ice and rock plummeting toward them. My God, I shall never forget it." Even at that time, he had difficulty comprehending it.

"The look on Herr Eckhart's face. It wasn't fear, it was—I can't put it into words—it was satisfaction. He was smiling. He welcomed it. Mind you, I was far away, but I could see he was smiling. They were swept down the mountain to the edge and over into the ravine, all but him. He slammed his pick into the ice and hung on."

The old man paused. He was exhausted as though just recalling the moment had returned him to the bitter altitude of the mountain. "When the snow cleared, three hung over the precipice. He alone was clear. If he cut the rope, he would save himself but kill the others. I grant you, there was no way he could drag the others up—but he smiled when he cut the rope. He smiled as he watched them hurtle into the canyon."

"You didn't testify to that at the hearing," said McDonald.

"How could I? I was looking at him from across the ravine. But I saw him. That satisfied smile, the kind you get when your plan has worked. The lawyers would have torn me to shreds. And for what? They were dead."

"Andreas didn't deny cutting the rope," Mac said. "The watchers, you know, the buzzards who watch climbs hoping for an accident, said they'd seen something flashing like a steel blade or a reflection in a mirror. He took responsibility for their deaths."

"It had to be his or God's, didn't it?" the old man said, falling back onto his pillow. He pointed to the mountain. "There, nothing can touch you, judge you—least of all another man. You are alone."

McDonald left the old man staring blankly out the window at the wall of stone and snow reaching into the sky. He had a long drive to Geneva. Defiantly, he gunned the car, almost spilling off the road.

Chapter 21
Wiligut Castle

ANDREAS FOLLOWED THE MESSENGER across the courtyard, through a foyer, and up a metal staircase. On the wall lining the stairs were shelves of jars filled with a yellow liquid and suspended human heads—black, yellow, white. Some smiled and seemed to push forward to get a look at the visitor. "Specimens and trophies taken from all over the world by German soldiers," the messenger said. "We measure them to find which ones are Aryan."

Andreas had not seen Meyer since they had gone separate ways—Andreas chosen for the Hitler schools for promising Nazis, Ulrich for detention camp. It was only the professor's intervention that had saved Ulrich from the gas chamber. Ulrich had gone on to become one of the most famous physicists in Germany.

If it hadn't been for the Jewish madness, Andreas could never have replaced him. The invitation to inspect the cyclotron, delivered by a messenger, had been written in a scrawled hand and stuffed inside an envelope embossed with the death head, Ulrich's way of reminding him who was responsible for his new appointment.

They entered a cold, marble-floored room, off which was a door marked Director of Particle Research.

"Come in," an irritated voice said. The room was chaotic: coffee cups, books, and clothes were strewn everywhere. Papers lined the floor like discarded wallpaper. On the desk lay a Luger pistol; two bullets lay in an ashtray. In the middle of the mess sat a gnome. Peering at Andreas but not getting up, he said, "So, Andreas, it's been a long time. Thought they'd have burned me to a cinder by now, wouldn't you?"

"Yes and no," Andreas replied. "You are too valuable to kill."

"I am now, but it won't be long. Doesn't matter—I need just a little more time. Have a drink." He pointed to the decanter standing next to the revolver.

"What are the bullets for?" said Andreas.

"When my self-contempt exceeds my despair," said Meyer. "Don't worry, they are not for you. You'd like to inspect our campus? The cyclotron's in the basement."

They walked through a large wooden door and stood on a concrete landing. A red light cast an eerie glow into the stairwell. Meyer handed Andreas a pair of red goggles. "Helps adjust your eyes to the darkness," he said.

At the bottom of the stairs, high-tension wires hung like spider webs, a whine like a child crying. Pale men in white coats hurried. The whine grew louder, the pitch higher, and the floor shook. Andreas found himself shouting.

Meyer led the way into a white-walled monastery. Two large pipes circled the room; a dial monitored each pipe, and a high-pitched whine issued from them. Mesmerized, Ulrich stared at the dials. Andreas reached in and turned the power switch back. A man recovering from a nightmare, Ulrich's heavy breathing slowed and his eyes refocused. It took a moment before he roused himself, looked at Andreas as if seeing him for the first time.

"Why were you sent here?"

"To study the effects of radiation on animals," said Andreas.

"By animals you mean, of course, you and me. How do you intend to do it?"

"I don't know yet. I didn't ask."

Meyer laughed. "You won't have to worry about guinea pigs; the Reich has already picked them for you. Just go over to dormitory three. You will get to know them," he said with a strange, quiet hopelessness.

"What's dormitory three?" Andreas asked.

"You'll find out. Now, about the cyclotron, it's going to be your problem, so you'd better know where we are. If you can explain it to Himmler, it might save your ass. It's simple, really. What are we trying to do? Kick out more energy than we put in."

"What were those rods sticking out of the chamber that looked like a bunch of spears?"

"They control the neutrons. If we pull them all the way out, the whole damned thing explodes. You'll get the hang of it. You will need more yellow cake to make uranium. Thorium will disintegrate only so much. If only we had a compound that would disintegrate to half its size, liberate millions of neutrons," mused Meyer. "It's all about the number of bullets. If we get to the point where the uranium fires enough of its own, the pile will sustain itself. Then the problem is how to control it. That's what the spears, as you call them, are for."

Meyer led the way back to his office, away from the deafening whine of the machine. "Suppose," he began, "just suppose that there was a material that decayed enough to produce the neutrons on its own. That would change the whole picture, wouldn't it?"

"There is no such material," said Andreas.

"Isn't there? There is a material that will disintegrate to half its size, or there was. But it was lost—a very long time ago, when Satan and God fought it out. Where it landed, no one knows, except for Anton Losen, and he is dead. And so there is nothing in this world that will save my ass, as you so perfectly put it. But perhaps there is in the next," quipped Meyer.

"Anton Losen? He's been dead for years—murdered. That climbing accident in Tibet was no accident. I understand you know all about such things," said Ulrich with a twisted smile.

"We get the newspapers."

"Do you know where Losen was climbing when he …" He hesitated. "… fell?"

"Only know what I read. It was somewhere in Sikkim."

"Sikkim? I knew some of the climbers, and the story I got was somewhat different. They were all experienced climbers. Everyone who knew Losen knew he wouldn't climb unless he had proper equipment, and he never exposed himself or his Sherpas to unnecessary risk. That's why it was so strange," said Andreas.

"What?"

"He didn't pack ice pitons or crampons or carabiners with screw locks or nylon rope. You see, he never intended to come back. Instead, he packed a chronometer and a sundial. Losen knew he was going to die. He was committing suicide. He told his Sherpas he'd been entrusted with the responsibility—by God. The Sherpas thought he'd gone off his rocker."

"What was the mountain?" asked Meyer.

"Kongzhengchenga. Eight thousand meters and never climbed by a German. The Sherpas knew before they left. They said goodbye on the mountain, burned incense, and left. Losen disappeared into the mist. His body was never found. Nor was the amber."

"The what?"

"The amber. He carried a piece of amber around his neck. It was etched with the path."

"The path to what?"

"To the forbidden fruit, to nirvana. Who the hell knows? Somewhere up there on the mountain."

"Where is it now? The amber, I mean."

Andreas looked at Meyer. "You and half the world would like to know. The survivors built a series of signposts, stupas, tracing his path as far as they could. They celebrated his death by smoking incense over his last known stop, a ledge with an impassable overhang. Losen's Ledge, they call it now. Twenty-two thousand feet. It's as high as anyone has gone. The path ends there. The amber has never been found nor has the path up the mountain."

They had arrived back at the office. There was the acrid smell of old coffee. Meyers dropped into his chair. "If you get a chance, drop by the women's dormitory. Rebecca is there," Meyer said and looked away.

What the hell is she doing in this forsaken place? Andreas wondered. Drums and bugles, boots and breasts, brisket in the oven, Christmas trees in the living room and menorahs in the kitchen … red wine and black hair framing a soft face, eyes, white thighs straddling the Brandenburg Gate, the white pillars move, enwrap him. He's motionless. Dust in the wind. The wind. Rebecca stares at him with blood-dark eyes.

He was awake. *I thought I'd never hear her name or see her again.* He had wept, and her scent had died. Replaced by a recurring dream, he was carried toward a shore. He recognized it. He was not swimming toward the shore.

Apprehensive, he waited for the surge to decide. *Am I a lover? A relative? A friend? Why haven't I warned her—protected her?* He knew they would call. They were rounding up all Jews to be taken to the camp.

They arrived, three of them, on a cold October evening, well dressed, polite, and considerate. They climbed the stairs to the flat, knocked on the door, and announced themselves.

How many had climbed those stairs, turned the handle, entering the cluttered room, looked at the yellow flame of the gas fire, the pink lamps, the crochet table cloth, the menorah on the table? How many had been welcomed at that door? There should have been legions asking for Rebecca's hand. There had been only these few, and these would be the last. Passing through the door and squeezing into the room, they carried their intentions concealed under heavy woolen coats and pushed in.

"May we come in?" No words carried the weight of death as serenely. Their black visors reflected light from the pink lamps. A black sofa hid in the corner against the wall, and a candelabra with seven candles sat on the linoleum-covered table; an ebbing fire exhausting itself in the corner. The room was cold. The occupants wore sweaters and shawls.

Politely removing a card from his wallet, one said, "Courtesy of Commander Heydrich. Just a formality. We need your work papers."

"I am a physicist. I've been able to find only part-time work at the university," said Meyer. "I don't have any work papers."

"You are Jewish?"

"Yes," he answered hesitantly. There was no denying it.

"You will have to come with us."

"And my family?"

"Them too."

"Why?"

"It's the law."

"Miriam and Rebecca?"

"Yes, I'm afraid so," said the officer, shaking his head. "It's the law. Put on warm clothes. It's Christmas. Where is your Christmas tree? You don't celebrate his birth?"

"I'm Jewish. I don't need a Christmas tree. I searched for years in vain to find one, only to find it grows in the mind."

"A cross? Do you celebrate his death?"

"Many use it as an excuse for hanging," he replied.

"You don't celebrate his death?"

"No, neither do we scourge sin. We forgive it. It's cold outside."

Andreas's eyes were fixed on the ceiling. His thoughts were miles and years away. He barely hears Meyer.

The wind whips around their coats. They gather their clothes and start downstairs. One of the men stares with open-mouthed interest at Miriam. She is tall, blond, and her legs smooth and shapely, her breasts, just budding, are round and jut against her sweater.

The trip is to hell. The girls are in the back of the van. "Slow, Fritz," he says. "We have two to examine."

A rug is thrown on the floor. Pulling the curtain, he shuts out the waning day. He leans forward. "Who wants to go first?"

"Andreas! Did you hear what I said?"

Andreas turned to the voice. His face is blank.

"I said Rebecca is staying at one of the guest houses. Now I must get back to work. I have a lot of calculations to do." He held up one hand. "A Jew—think about it, Andreas. I, a Jew, have done it," Meyer said. "I'm having a few guests for dinner the day after tomorrow. A sort of farewell party," he explained, his voice distilled, satisfied, coming from a place far away.

Andreas looked at him questioningly.

"I'm their Jewish necessity," continued Meyer. "Don't worry. It's not your fault. It's time. If it weren't you, it would be somebody else. The contract was short and one sided but good while it lasted. Join us if you can. I'll have the figures and calculations for you then. About seven o'clock. My bungalow is at the edge of the compound, number two."

Though he was tired, Andreas chose not to spend the night at Wiligut. He had business in Berlin, a meeting with Inspector Oberman, chief of Gestapo, Berlin.

Chapter 22
Inspector Oberman's Office, Berlin

"WHO ARE YOU?" THE secretary asked.

Who am I? My step-mother was Hindu, a beautiful woman. Her name was Lakshmi. My father was German. His name was Eckhart, Adolph Eckhart. My mother was light from the stars. Her colors were many, and her voice was music. My father was heavy, as heavy as German honor. His colors were black and brown.

Geheime Stats Gestapo, the most feared name in Germany, was housed in a benign-appearing house on Niederkirchenstrasse behind the Bundesrat and next to Himmler's office on Prinz Albert Strasse. The flag snapping smartly in a freshening breeze sounding like gunfire, startled him.

"Why are you here?" she asked, misinterpreting his failure to respond.

Andreas showed the woman his identification and returned it to his vest pocket. "I am here to find out what happened to Anna, my ..." He faltered. *My what? What was Anna? Warm? No one could ever describe her as warm.*

Affectionate? Definitely Loyal? Yes, that's it, she was loyal. And devoted? She was certainly devoted to Göring.

"I am looking for my housekeeper. She seems to have disappeared," Andreas said quickly.

The woman behind the desk, her uniform tightly pulled over small breasts, just as quickly let it be known by her blank expression that she could not care less.

"She was always kind to me, and that's what counts," Andreas heard himself say as though it were coming from someone else. The secretary reluctantly consulted the inspector's appointment calendar. There it was—Andreas Eckhart, 2:00 p.m.

Andreas took a seat and waited. The door opened, and a short, balding man motioned for him to enter. Following a pointing finger, Andreas sat in a hard wood chair in front of a large mahogany desk. Where was he to begin? *Lovely place, headquarters. One would never know it was the most feared building in Germany. It hums with efficiency. Your office, Inspector Oberman, is small for one as important as you, but it befits your character—nothing showy or alarming. Your secretary is a trifle overweight. Her hair is black but gray around the roots. Her blouse is brown, and her breasts are small. You look worried, Inspector. Is that why you busy yourself stuffing tobacco in your pipe and why you stare out the window? It can't be the scenery—the concrete housing development.*

"So, Colonel, I understand you are here on the matter of a missing person."

Yes, let us get down to business. I understand. You must make the interview quick. You have much more pressing business than to chase after a maid's disappearance. You've agreed to see me as a courtesy to my rank as well as to your colleague in

Scotland Yard, Inspector Willoughby. I, too, am Gestapo and understand that Himmler will soon have control of this bureau and that you are in a hurry to leave before that happens.

"Our friends in Scotland Yard tell us that something happened to your housekeeper before you left London. But murder? Why do you fear murder? Is there a body? And if so, what has become of it?"

Andreas lit a cigarette with deliberate slowness, taking a moment to gather his thoughts. The smoke from the cigarette and from the inspector's pipe meets and mingle above them.

"Inspector, I assure you, I've no idea what has become of the woman. And I have never said she'd been murdered. Inspector Willoughby thought that was a possibility, but he had no proof. That is precisely why I am here."

What the hell am I supposed to say? It was foolish to have made the appointment. Should I admit I'm glad to be rid of her?

"Could your housekeeper have been unbalanced? Might she have committed suicide?"

"Unbalanced?" Andreas smiled. "I have her discharge papers from an asylum if you would like to see them."

"Colonel von Eckhart, everyone who walks through that door says he wants justice. What he is really looking for is a pass either because he's done something or forgotten to—and feels guilty. What justice would be enough for you? Or would you be happy to leave well enough alone until we are certain there's been a crime?" He shuffled through a sheaf of papers, chose one, and placed it on top. "Your mother was, is, a very interesting woman, ahead of her time."

"She dances in bracelets of gold, and her bracelets make heavenly music". Remembering, Andreas said, "My mother

was a beautiful woman. She was magic. Her name was Lakshmi, the goddess of beauty and fortune."

"Only music, I believe. The other two I don't know about," Oberman said, startling Andreas. "She appears from the waves atop a lotus flower as did another goddess, Botticelli's *Venus*." The little man in the black uniform smiled. *Yes, I too am infatuated with Indian mythology*, his smile said.

"Your sister's name is Tara Lilith, I believe." Stroking his chin and waiting for the other shoe to drop, he added, "Unusual names—Tara Lilith, Lakshmi."

Andreas realized that coming had been a mistake. He didn't give a damn about Anna. He'd hoped that her handbag or some other article had been recovered like the amulet she'd carried around her neck. At that point, he had alerted the Gestapo. There was no going back.

"Come, Herr Eckhart, don't play games." The little man stood up and with both hands spread flat on his desk leaned close to Andreas's face. "You were a breech delivery. The operation took place in the sanitarium. We have proof. Your housekeeper, Anna, is your mother."

Anna, a ghost growing out of the shadowy air, laughed a mirthless laugh, and her eyes filled with tears. Andreas's temples pounded, and blood rushed from his face.

"That's ridiculous. How can you be so damned sure? And what of Tara, my sister? Is Anna *her* mother?"

The inspector relit his pipe. It was his moment, and he was taking his time. "No. Nor is she related. In fact ..." He drew on his pipe and removed it from his mouth, a conductor leading his small orchestra. "In fact, we cannot find a species that we can match with her blood. As far

as we can determine, your sister is not related to you or
Anna. Or to anyone else on this planet. Our scientists are
mystified. Blood doesn't lie.

"We are sure about your so-called housekeeper. She
is, or perhaps was, your mother. And," he added with a
significant pause, "she carries the gene that produces that
red-wine stain," he said, pointing to the stain stretching
down Andrea's arm and onto the back of his hand. "It is
carried by the mother but shows up only in the male."

"You're wrong," Andreas said vehemently.

The inspector smiled, removed his pipe, and knocked
the dead ashes against the ashtray. He stared out the window
into the blank, sunlit day, turned, and said, "Colonel, as I
said, 'everyone who comes through that door is looking for
an excuse either for something he's done or hasn't done." In
this case, we don't even have proof that a crime has been
committed."

Chapter 23
Metropole Café, Berlin

ANDREAS STUMBLED OUT OF Oberman's office and onto the Kurfurstendamm. In need of a drink, he searched his jacket for his wallet. His fingers closed on an envelope that had come in the morning mail. The envelope was stamped with the Heugenkreuz; the return address was Captain Kurt Wenger, 1905 Niederkirchenstrasse. *Probably confirming my appointment with the Gestapo*. He crumpled it and threw it into the gutter, where it swirled on the way to the drain. About to disappear, it lay motionless as the brown water swirled around it. *Wait! Kurt Wenger. The driver of the van.* He ran after the envelope and snatched it just as it was to be sucked into the drain. He dried it against his coat. His fingers thick, he opened it.

"Dear Herr Eckhart, please accept my apologies. We found we've overcharged you for the trip to Gestapo headquarters and are remitting this 10-mark note. I believe this is the correct amount and represents payment in full."

Andreas staggered against the stanchion remembering a face, fair hair, loose and cascading over soft shoulders, large, blue-green eyes, and a mouth full and red. Most of all, he remembered the dignity in the young face.

A group of Hitler youth outlined against the yellow light from the stanchion was parading. The *rat-a-tat* from snare drums banging against smooth, hairless thighs echoed. "Tomorrow belongs to me" came from their hairless faces, secure in their mission, secure in their belief. "Tomorrow belongs to me."

"We had a delightful talk with the young ladies, they are well and under our care. Please accept our apologies. —Captain Kurt Wegner"

A face, a clown perched on a spring, leered at him from a neon sign advertising the Metropole Café. It blinked, turned bright red, and then bilious green. Women gestured, promising breasts and open mouths, lolling tongues and pouting lips, sex and booze, wine and the wafer, memory and forgetfulness.

The Metropole had just reopened, the owner having recovered from a nasty collision with among other things a truncheon and several pairs of boots. Andreas started to turn into the café. The man in front of him bent to retrieve his ticket. His tailored suit speaks of money. His accent was Polish heavily tinted with Yiddish. It was apparent from the familiar exchange with the ticker taker; He was a regular visitor. The ticket taker smiled and gestured to the usher, who obliged, supplying the patron with his usual seat next to the stage. The chorus line entered close by. One young lady, in particular, passed right by him. He could have reached out if he had wished. He was known to be an excellent tipper—even if the money was Jewish. He sat in the same seat, at the same table. He never touched, grabbed, or even spoke to any of the dancers, especially one. With her, he was in love.

The gentleman ordered a gin martini "with an onion, not an olive." Andreas ordered a dry sherry. The orchestra struck up a can-can, and the line of scantily clad chorus girls strutted onto the stage. The audience yelled appreciatively; the girls started to kick their legs and shake their asses.

On the edge of his seat and flushed with anticipation, the stranger allowed himself only a small smile. *When they come for the Rembrandt, they will find it in shreds.* He had thought about it long and hard. He had never felt surer of himself. It hurt to destroy what he loved, to leave it wasted in front of him. He bathed in the pain it would cause Göring.

The line had reached his table. His eyes searched for her. She would never look twice at a Jew. Blond, with the face of a doll, blue eyes, and dark lashes sweeping over her cheeks. It was as if he knew her though he had never spoken a word to her. He was sure he would be snubbed, or worse. Even the simplest human contact was impossible.

Had she looked for him in his accustomed seat? Would she miss him if he hadn't been there? He liked to think so. He searched for her. She was last in the line of girls. Her body stiffened, detached itself from the line. In an instant, she slumped to the floor, unresponsive, stretched over his legs.

His first impulse was to disentangle her carefully; there should be no physical contact, no show of emotion. She grasped his leg trying to get up, and as he looked down on her, his resolve crumbled under her helplessness. *"Du bist die schönste von allen,"* he managed.

Andreas had a swift foretaste of their destiny and could not disengage himself from them.

"Please," the stranger offered, pulling out a chair. Gently, he sat her in it. A prince bowing to his lady.

The orchestra started to play. The young girl rises to dance. "No," he said.

"I must," she answered, "if I'm to eat."

"You must do only what fits your position. You are a lady," he said, suddenly sure of himself. No longer the Jew, still in the grips of his fantasy.

She blinked and for a moment didn't know what to say. But there was something about the expression in his eyes and the look on his face—the strangest kind of loneliness.

He motioned for the waiter. "Please," he said, ordering the most expensive meal on the menu, one she could hardly digest. "How long since you have eaten?"

"I don't remember. A while."

He signaled the waiter. "Please wrap this for the lady and bring her a bowl of soup and ..." He scoured the menu. "... a plate of scrambled eggs." He reached for her hand, desperately curling it in his. "Pardon me if I appear forward, but I feel I've known you for a long time. At least I know everything I need to make a decision."

"Which is?"

"Will you come home with me?"

"I'm not in the habit of going home with strangers—least of all with Jews. You want me to go home with you?" Her hands flew to her face, and the tears flowed again. "I'm not at all pretty, and as you can see, I'm clumsy too."

"I want you to marry me but only if it suits you."

She had become expert at reading meaning into the tone of a voice.

They'd become the center of attention—the beautiful girl and the Jew, beauty and the beast. The audience applauded. "Here's to the Jew and the princess! But what if she's German?" Smiles grew hesitant and turned to leers. The Jew had found something. They could see it in his eyes, his face, something they'd been searching for. The Jew had no right to it.

The waiter signaled the orchestra. They struck up a well-known parody. The tuba gave a large blast, and the clarinet seconded the echo. One of the chorus girls bent forward, and the waiter did a series of thrusts into her rear to the accompaniment of the tuba. The stranger grabbed for the young girl and started for the door. She, uncertain, hung back. "I love you," he said. Their eyes met. She picked up her coat and followed him.

Andreas drank his sherry and followed the stranger onto the street. As he walked through the hard light from the stanchion, he thought of the young girl lying on the floor. When he'd entered, the Jew was alone, separate from everyone and everything. --except for his dream. When he left, he was ready to share everything. Perhaps she had saved the Jew's life, and hers. Perhaps.

Andreas stood outside, uncertain. A sharp cold permeated his topcoat, and he shivered. The Jew's decision, his bravery, nibbled at him and flashed a light into a dark corner. He walked aimlessly and without realizing entered the Hackescher market, a Jewish ghetto. There was a curious quality to the light, a grayish-pink, bloodless light, the last anemic drops from a dying sky. Lone figures, stenciled into the night, hurried by, outlined in the light from the stanchions. Odds and ends of discarded lives were scattered on the sidewalk.

"Is permitted for a price," she said, pulling on his zipper. She was young and pretty and used. Her youth still glimmering. A life that walked at odd angles and peered into light, cautiously, afraid of what it might see- but still hoping—a fairy tale? Youth and beauty had survived. What had they lived on? The Nazis have stolen everything; what was left was broken. And yet they were back the next day for a try at survival.

She led him up a nearby staircase to a shabby, dark room, the bed and a small side table the only furnishings. The last of the sun cast a pale shadow on the bare wood floor. She lay on the bed, inert, her eyes turned away. Andreas began unbuttoning her blouse. She put her hand up.

"No. Please, unless… Can you? I mean, I'm pregnant. I have no money. I heard you are a doctor. Please!" Tears were running down her face and smudging her cheap makeup. The ridiculousness, the absurdity. He wanted to run. On her knees, she said, "It will be my first, but I watched other girls and know how to do it. Couldn't you? I mean. You are a doctor." She turned her face away. She was sinking into quicksand. The hopelessness; he could see it in her eyes, the yearning for death, for a way out.

"Look," he said, "the world has changed. So you made a mistake and got pregnant. Just be more careful the next time." He had to get out, to get away. It was none of his business.

She crouched; her bare buttocks on the bare floor. He felt hopeless. He was incapable of even this sordid sexual encounter.

"Men are all the same. No matter how careful, it's us who must pay."

"Well then, become a nun."

"It's the answer, but a girl has to eat."

He had no answer, only to tell her she had to get out of Germany.

"Where should I go?" she said, her eyes pleading.

"Here," he said, counting out fifty marks.

"What's that for? I haven't kept my end of the bargain." She slipped off the bed and tugged on his zipper.

He said, "Promise you will buy a ticket to America. Start over."

She nodded. "I promise."

"Yes." Andreas nodded. "That's the answer." He left the room.

Outside, Andreas stood under the stanchion, light reflecting from his face, feverish, impatient. *What the hell was I supposed to do? I am one man. This doesn't involve me.*

Again, voices out of the dark joined by the *rat-a-tat-tat* of snare drums. Again, frightening in their devotion. The group of Hitler youth returning. Their brown shirts and black belts reflecting in the light as they marched. A savior had come. "The future belongs to me." Jews scattered, hiding under porches, behind locked doors, their faith and their faces lifted to God.

A leper smiled from among the young faces. Marching time, the voices sang, mesmerized. Everyone, British and German, stood with hands over hearts.

"The morning will come when the world is mine. Tomorrow belongs to me. To me."

Chapter 24
Ulrich Meyer's Cottage, Wiligut

THE VOICE ANSWERING THE phone was deep and resonant. "Don't be surprised. There are still a few of us. Ulrich Meyer asked me to call and remind you about dinner tonight at his house. Nothing formal. There will be just the four of us."

Andreas got out of the car in front of a small bungalow set back from Wiligut Castle and fenced by barbed wire. A tall, square-faced man answered the door.

"Rabbi Jacobson? You look more German than I do!" Andreas said with a laugh as he removed his coat.

"Ulrich's in the kitchen playing cook. Please sit down. Would you like a drink?"

The parlor had just enough space for the two armchairs and a small coffee table. Lamps stood behind each chair, and books were piled along the walls.

"You can tell Ulrich lives here," said Jacobson, smiling.

"Neatness is for those who expect to live a long life," said Ulrich as he came in from the kitchen accompanied by Professor Schroeder. He laid a tray of small cakes on the coffee table.

"They are traditional Jewish cakes. We usually make them during Purim. It's not Purim, but I don't know how to make any others." Ulrich poured coffee.

Andreas, tasting a cake, said, "I almost forgot how delicious they were. Prunes, apricot, and what's the other ingredient? Poppy seed? Now I remember. Hamantaschen. That's what they're called. The story of Esther. Rebecca surely could have vied with Esther for beauty. Where is Rebecca?"

"I told you she is in the dormitory the Nazis keep for them."

Andreas knew the finish.

Ulrich, a tear flowing down his cheek, unable to finish, excused himself, to see about dinner. "We Jews know how to make the best of it. But sometimes, even we can't." Swallowing hard, he fought back tears and regained control.

"Andreas is practically a Jew. He ate more brisket and matzo-ball soup at our house than our rabbi did. After they dragged us off to the detention camps, there were no more matzo balls. There was no more brisket. It was called roast." An edge had crept into his voice.

"No more German Jews—just Jews. Am I right, Andreas?"

Ulrich was speaking over the graves of the dead. As he had many times before. *Another wreath?*

"There would be many more. Unless …" He cringed at his solution. "Unless we become the tormenters. Then they would stop, would have to stop. Belief, understanding, invite more beatings and torture. An eye for an eye."

"Most of us didn't know that was going on," said Andreas. "It just happened."

The rage evident in Ulrich's voice threatened to boil over his self-control. "Right under your eyes. What the hell did you think had happened to us? That we had all vaporized? The truth is you didn't want to know."

"What would you have suggested I do about it?" Andreas asked pointedly. The emphasis on the "I" was clear—*Don't judge me, Ulrich. Not until you have done something to help yourself.*

Professor Schroeder squirmed in his chair.

"I was just Ulrich," Meyer continued, "the funny-looking Jew who walked to school with you. In fact, there were times when I thought you almost wished they would come and get me. I was smarter." He got up and passed the tray of cakes. There were no takers.

"Smarter, perhaps, but not braver—not brave enough." *Before you judge me, judge yourself,* thought Andreas.

Ulrich had evidently decided he would clear the air. He had placed the needle on the record. Studying his guests with a mixture of compassion and scorn, he said, "Of course, Andreas, you ate at our house whenever you could. Your family couldn't afford brisket. Slowly, one by one, we Jews were no longer part of your life. Except for Rebecca. That was a different story. You had a thing for her, Andreas."

"Yes, I did have a *thing* for her. I was in love with her," said Andreas. "As for the brisket, no, we couldn't afford it— and a lot of other things your family got from the Nazis."

It was finally out in the open. The many perks the Meyer family had received for cooperation were well known and universally disdained by German and Jew alike. The slights that must have hammered at Ulrich were out in the open.

"Don't misunderstand," said Ulrich. "You were better than the rest," he said dismissively. "But you, Andreas, were the only one strong enough. It was your responsibility. Andreas, they gang-raped Rebecca." The words hung in the room like dirty air. "Heydrich and his bunch of thugs gang-raped her."

The room was silent. "Tell me, Andreas, why do you think you are here?" Ulrich asked. "Light matter, dark matter, do you think for a minute Himmler gives a shit? Your job is no different from that machine gunner guarding the camp. Your job is to kill not in ones or twos but in thousands. That's your job. Do you think the Nazis care about a single woman? Go outside just a stone's throw from the barracks. You will find a woman, a girl, a boy— anything you want. She will ask for very little—dinner and something for her family," said Ulrich. "This is Rebecca I'm talking about, a girl you loved, at least you said you loved."

"I was once foolish enough to believe in such things," said Andreas, staring at his empty glass of whiskey. "I thought I was in love, that's all. It's absurd to fall in love. The gauleiter was in love. He wanted your sister. That was the long and short of it. I tried to warn Rebecca—and you too, Ulrich. I'm sorry. I won't accept that responsibility. I sound like a priest," Andreas said, suddenly angry. "Sorry for what? It wasn't my responsibility to protect her. Where were you?"

"Don't you see I wasn't strong enough?" Ulrich repeated.

"It's safe to be weak," said Andreas. "You don't have to worry about responsibility."

"I couldn't have done anything about it."

"Did you even try? That's the trouble. You people expect others to do your fighting for you. Well, this time, it didn't happen. And it won't in the future. You are going to have to get your own hands bloody."

"I know, but I couldn't do anything about it."

Andreas rose and took Ulrich's hands. "Nice and clean, Ulrich. Have they ever been bloodied?"

"How many times, Andreas, do we have to bloody them? The destruction of the temple, Bar-Khobar, Masada, Warsaw. I could go on. How many massacres are enough?"

"Ask Christ. He's the one who sets the table," said Andreas. "And it's not *we* Ulrich, it's *I*."

"I sometimes think it would have been better if my mother had let me drip down her legs than let me be born Jewish," said Ulrich.

"If you keep holding yourselves out as different, it will happen again and again. People never accept anyone who claims absolute knowledge and a privileged position—not even Christ."

Professor Schroeder had not uttered a word. He looked muddled, sadder, as if he had tried to figure out the solution to an equation and was disappointed with the result. The fire and candles had burned down. His shoulders sagged, and his arms hung heavily by his side.

"Have another whiskey. It will be at least an hour till dinner," said Ulrich.

The setting sun threw a red shadow on the small table.

"Who pays for all this?" Andreas asked, gesturing around the room.

"The Nazis," said Ulrich. "They got nervous after Einstein left. Not bad, a maid twice a week and often a cook. Not kosher, but then I'm far from Orthodox. For as long as it lasts. The contract's sort of one sided."

Jacobson seemed to have awakened from a bad dream. Getting up to poke the fire, he was eager to change the conversation. Used to hiding behind scripture, he could find little to say. His eyes were red from lack of sleep, his shoes were worn, and his soul needed mending.

Ulrich continued his reminiscence. "Andreas was one of the few who stood up to him, to that bastard Eccles. He spat on me. Did you know that, Andreas? He spat on me. I can still feel the saliva. I didn't desert her, Andreas. There was no way I could have stopped them by myself."

"And that's the discount you expect," said Andreas.

Andreas stole a look at Jacobson. He stared at the wall. The closeness had grown oppressive. Andreas opened a window. Ulrich would not be dissuaded. He had decided to unburden himself no matter the cost. He'd stripped himself naked, exposing feelings that had lain dormant for years. Jacobson, uncomfortable with emotion and not finding a place to hide, stared into the fire. Ulrich left the room "to see about dinner.". Andreas busied himself poking the dying embers. For a long while, no one spoke.

Andreas poked his head into the kitchen. "You have said that the there's a natural source of radiation. Do you really believe that?"

"Yes," Ulrich answered, closing the door to the oven.

"You know that makes your research obsolete."

"No," said Ulrich. "It doesn't. Quite the opposite."

"But it will start a rush to find it, and whoever does will have control of the greatest power ever imagined."

"We won't need the cyclotron," said Ulrich.

"What do we tell Himmler?"

"To keep looking," said Ulrich. "We have managed to isolate a few grains."

"Of uranium?" asked Andreas. "Ulrich, did you say that you had isolated some uranium?"

"No, not uranium."

"Well then, what?"

"Uranium will seem like child's play," said Ulrich. "Dark matter."

"But Himmler's putting together a team to go to Tibet to find uranium. He thinks he's stumbled on the final solution."

"Perhaps," said Ulrich, "it will do."

Professor Schroeder appeared weary. His head sunken into his neck. His shoulders seemed to be carrying him to his grave. "Chaos is the natural state of existence. It takes energy to make order out of chaos. Order is death. Chaos is energy, the energy of life. It has to exist—if life exists."

"Are you telling me that you have isolated dark matter?" Andreas asked, standing in the center of the little room staring at Schroeder.

"Whatever it is, it's opposite to anything we have yet produced. If you combine it with uranium or even thorium, the Geiger counter shakes as if it's going to come apart. And that's just a tiny amount. I don't know what it is. We might yet change lead into gold. The priests change wine into blood every day."

The professor emerged from his stupor; his eyes shone as he leaned forward, listening.

"There's another world out there," said Meyer, "opposite to the one we know—an upside-down world."

The professor rose hesitantly as though he'd been struck.

"Are you all right?" Jacobson asked.

Ulrich, turning toward the professor, said, "I think we understand each other. I will leave it to you, Professor, to decide."

"You can trust me. You will excuse me if I don't stay for dinner, Ulrich. I'm not feeling well."

"Of course," Ulrich said. He grasped the professor's hands, and for a long time, they stood looking into each other's eyes.

"We will meet again," said Ulrich, "if not in heaven, in hell."

There was a moment of uncertainty. The professor turned, left the house, and stepped into the cold night. There was a full moon, icy white, and his breath crystallized on his coat.

The church tower chimed ten o'clock. Pigeons fluttered and retook their places. It was suddenly daylight. A parachute floated out of the darkness. The searchlights crossed and then held it in their beams. The figure vainly tried to maneuver, each movement followed and recaptured. A volley of shots, and the chute seemed to gather itself and plummet to earth. Soldiers slowly exited the woods.

Kirstin lay in the midst of the parachute, her blond hair sneaking from under her cap. "A shame. A crime," said the German captain.

"Such beauty," said the Oberlieutnant, making a lewd gesture and pointing to the Star of David hanging from her neck.

The last of the papers the professor had consigned to the fire curled and drifted. Patting the dog, he said, "Emma will take good care of you."

He left the house and drove deeper into the woods. Turning off the road, he parked. And opening the window, listened. Trees stenciling the night sky shivered in the cold wind. He looked at his watch and the gray stubble surrounding the crystal. The shot echoed off the tree. The dog lifted its head. Whimpering, it stared into the fire.

Ulrich, wiping his hands on his apron, returned to the kitchen. "Sounds as if you have plans to leave," said Andreas. "Are you being transferred? Certainly, the Nazis aren't going to let you go free."

"No, the Nazis aren't," said Ulrich.

"He is going to turn into a golem and fly away," said the rabbi.

"What the fuck is a golem?" Andreas asked.

"A ghost. Not just any ghost, a Jewish ghost," said Jacobson.

"Less complicated than you might think," said Ulrich. "Underneath this mask, I'm really a bunch of electrons and photons whirling about. You could walk right through me. In reality, there are two of me—one polarized with a positive sign, the other with a negative sign—twins turning in different directions. If you untangled the relationship between the two, one of them would be free, traveling at the speed of light. The other would be dead. I've achieved something better than the alchemists. I have turned matter into time. The Jewish texts describe a golem. I'm describing a quantum man."

"I don't know anything about the quantum business," said Rabbi Jacobson, "but I can tell you about the religious texts. A golem is a mythical man created by man."

"From what?" asked Andreas.

"From death and dirt," Ulrich said.

"Like Frankenstein," Andreas quipped.

"Abraham made such a man. By arranging the letters of the Jewish alphabet, he found the combination," said Jacobson.

"A Jewish incubus," said Andreas.

"A duplicate," said Ulrich. "Don't you see? It validates everything you have read in the Bible."

"It's hokum," said Jacobson. "That's not all. Tell him the rest. If you're going to make one of these golems, do it during the week. The golem has to be buried within twenty-four hours of his birth. And I don't want to hear you clanking around haunting me—you can't be buried on the Sabbath."

"You should be so lucky," said Ulrich, ignoring the tremor beneath his feet and the muffled sound of the explosion.

"What the hell was that?" asked Andreas.

"Maybe that plane," said Ulrich, looking up as though he could see through the ceiling of the room. "It sounded as if it was in trouble. If you are finished," he continued, picking up the conversation, "after the golem was made and life was breathed into him, ELOHIM EMETH was written across his skull."

"So?" Andreas said.

"EMETH in Hebrew means life. But if you remove the first E, it changes the meaning to death."

"Jesus, you people are complicated," said Andreas.

"That is exactly what he said," the rabbi replied.

"So God is dead. What do I tell Himmler?" Andreas asked.

"The Buddhists are right," said Ulrich. "Everyone has his own reality."

Chapter 25
Landwehr Canal, Kreutzberg, Berlin, 1936

LATER THAT NIGHT, ULRICH Meyer slipped out of the house carrying a small valise. He walked past the guard who'd been paid not to see him, got into a black cab that waited at the bottom of the hill, and ordered the driver to take him to the Landwehr Canal in the Kreutzberg area of Berlin. There, he left the cab. It was late. The streets were deserted. He walked two blocks down Axel Spinnger Strasse to Schlosplatz and then to Spanndauer Strasse. Crossing the Spree Canal, he slipped into a doorway on Karl Liebknecht Strasse and waited. No footsteps. He was alone. He walked through the next intersection and down an alley. A splash of light marked the entrance to a small tavern.

He stopped to look in the window. A mannequin sat playing a tinny rendition of "Auf Wiedersehen." Two women sat at the bar, their flabby faces coated with thick layers of makeup. Ulrich cleared his throat and looked at his watch. It was already five minutes past the time. He turned his collar up, walked into the tavern, chose a seat at one of the corner tables, and ordered a schnapps.

It must have been ten minutes later when he entered. He was dressed in workman's clothes—a peacoat buttoned over a grimy lambs' wool sweater with the collar wrapped about his neck and partially hiding his face. He approached Meyer and sat. "Do you have it? he asked."

The room was empty except for the two whores and the piano player. He smiled as Ulrich pulled a small box from a satchel and placed it on the table. The box, made of lead, was heavy. He needed both hands to lift it.

"This is all I've been able to produce," Meyer said. "You remember our agreement?"

"I'm ready," said the man. He handed him a slip of paper. "I assume you have it all with you. Take the taxi to this address. The road is narrow, and you will have to walk the last few blocks. The taxi is waiting for you outside."

"We have to hurry," said Meyer.

The man carefully lifted the box, tucked it inside his coat, and walked out.

Ulrich waited. After a few minutes, he rose and left. Still perched on his stool, the piano player continued to play. The whores at the bar slept.

As promised, a taxi waited at the curb. The driver sat stiffly as if made of wood. Meyer opened the door and gave the address. "Heartsease am Spandau." The driver looked at him questioningly. "Where the Spree joins the Havel River."

Irritated, the driver jerked the car into gear.

"Hurry!" Ulrich shouted, banging against the glass partition. "For God's sake hurry!"

The driver guffawed. Dim, sulfur-yellow light reflected from the cobblestones. The cab jostled wildly, bumping toward the sound, the channel buoy's mournful call.

He bit his lips. *Soon, I will know. Yes, but too late? Nothing lost. I was going to die soon anyway. But suicide? That's a sin. If I'm wrong, it won't matter. I've tried to be a good Jew.*

Whatever the hell that meant. He'd honored his parents, attended synagogue. No, he didn't speak Yiddish, and no, he didn't attend services or observe Passover, but he would leave the Jews with something much more important: freedom, a weapon that would allow them to get even for their years of suffering. The past hurt. The insults of the past were as fresh that day as they had ever been. He could bring each one to mind. "I promised you, Rebecca," he said.

"There's an extra ten marks in it if you hurry," he told the driver, counting the change in his pocket. He glanced at his watch: 11:35. He had only until the stroke of midnight. He cocked his ear to the sound of the channel gong and the water lapping against the canal. Fingering his revolver, he felt with his other hand for the bullets amid loose change.

The taxi came to an abrupt stop. Ulrich studied the abandoned stretch of road, reached for the small valise, and set it beside him. The light from the lamppost reached only a few yards. A rat scurried across the cobblestones. For a moment, he had second thoughts. But he paid the fare. The driver ground the car into gear and drove off.

A small steamer was tied to the wharf at the end of the narrow road. A reddish glow from its coal fire lit the cabin. Hawsers and lines hung from belaying pins. The boat creaked against the wharf. Ulrich walked to the edge of the wharf and looked into the hold.

The man, his face still partially hidden by his bulky wool sweater, was deep in conversation with a mate. The mate nodded and went below. A cold rain began to fall, and the man pulls his hat over his forehead to hide his face in the shadow.

"You have decided to keep your appointment," the man said. "I am ready to fulfill my half of the bargain as well." He climbed the ladder. Hanging onto the top rung with one hand, he asked, "Where would you like it done?"

"The foredeck will be as good a place as any," Meyer answered.

He searched in the small valise and removed a cup and four bags. He withdrew a piece of paper from his jacket pocket. Equations and Hebrew letters were scrawled over every corner of the paper. The man seated himself athwart the deck, braced against the stanchions, and said, "Tell me when." The stranger stole a glance at his watch, and a wry smile crept across his face.

"You know the words?" Ulrich asked.

"I should. They are mine," the man said. "Ate, Mallkus, Vet Deborah, Vet Gadelha, Le Loam. I believe that's it."

Ulrich carefully opened each of the four bags filled with dirt. He mixed the contents in a small brass cup. With his knife, he scratched a carefully chosen selection from the various combinations of the letters YHWH. He turned to the man and nodded. The man repeated the incantation.

The metallic click was followed by the acrid smell of spent powder. The stranger held the still-smoking gun. Ulrich's brains lay scattered over the deck. His watch read 12:05.

The mate came up from below and started swabbing the deck. The stranger shook his head. "Sad," he said. "Particularly since it was the right combination." He put the gun down. "All that for nothing. Past midnight—he can't be buried tomorrow. It's the Sabbath, and he has to be buried within twenty-four hours for the spell to work."

"Shall I dump him in the river?" asked the mate, holding Ulrich's remains over one shoulder.

"No. Anywhere near the castle will do. Wait," he said. "Put him down."

The stranger took out his knife and carved the letters ELOHIM EMETH into the remains of Ulrich's forehead. He then carefully removed the first *E*. Satisfied, he glanced up at the sky.

"Now you can take him." He smiled.

Chapter 26
Oranienburg, Germany

IT WAS STILL DARK the next morning when Andreas awoke. He was hung over. His batsman rushed into his room. Pulling on his shirt and hopping about on one partially tied shoe, he shouted, "Herr Meyer's dead!"

Andreas hurried to the car and sped to Wiligut Castle. Barely waiting for the car to come to a stop, he rushed inside. Himmler was poised over the library table, his scar like a piece of leather stitched onto his face from his temple to his mouth.

"What can be fortunate about this mess?" Himmler asked.

"Look at it this way," began Andreas. "One dead Jew, and now you don't have to worry. No one will know the research was a failure. He killed himself. No one has to know why.

The money was worth it. As far as Göring and the British are concerned, you have the secret to a new weapon."

"This isn't going any farther than this room. He died of a heart attack."

"I'll take care of it," said Andreas. "We will bury him with full military honors."

"Like hell you will," said Himmler. "Enough is enough. Take Meyer's body to Oranienburg and burn it with the rest of the Jews."

Smokestacks jutting into the sky belched a slimy chalk. There wasn't a soul on the road. Oranienburg, a detention center for political prisoners and Gypsies, had been turned into a concentration camp for Jews. The odor of rot permeated the air and sweated from the huts lining a maze of alleys.

Andreas was ushered into a wooden clapboard hut sparsely furnished with a rickety table and lit by a single light bulb. The only source of heat was a potbellied stove. The room was thick with smoke. The commanding officer stood over a small grate warming his hands, his face, grotesquely disfigured by a shell fragment that had glued his eyelids to his forehead. He inspected Ulrich's cremation papers and then motioned to his aide, who dutifully recorded their arrival and took down the name: Ulrich Meyer, Jew.

Rising, the major shot his arm into the air. "Sieg Heil!" Returning his hand to the table, he paused to record the names of the new candidates. The old table was littered with the scratched remains of prior inmates as if the inscriptions would guarantee their existence in this life as well as their entrance into the next.

His eyes riveted, he watched as a large beetle inched over his finger and onto his hand, the antennae, sweeping and exploring, seemed to mock him. The inhabitant of a world that fed on human debris, it slowly inched its way sure and careful. The major smiled. Slowly raising his hand,. he held it suspended over the beetle. He brought it down and flattened the beetle, the antennae still searching.

"So," he said, smiling, "A new candidate." He recorded the name Ulrich Meyer—Jew. That was it, all that would remain of Ulrich. The commandant walked to a large blackboard on which the duty roster was kept right down to the officer in charge of each barracks: "Block Führer." Underneath were listed the names of the Kapps—Jews who would pick the next shovelful to be burned or gassed: Levine, Solomon, and Jacobson. The commandant looked into Andreas's eyes and laughed. "You have brought us new recruits, a new skull. The beetles will be happy."

Andreas wandered to the edge of the compound toward a long, high wall pockmarked with bullet holes. The tips of pine trees waved in a freshening wind and dripped white dust. He pulled a cigarette case from his tunic and offered one to Jacobson, lonely like a schoolboy, his coat unbuttoned, gazing over the barbed wire.

"They picked me up this morning," the rabbi explained. "I was still in bed."

Andreas lit Jacobson's cigarette and then his own. "There will be an investigation," he began, "unless …"

"Unless?" Jacobson asked.

"The Nazis, Himmler, don't want an investigation. Remember, this isn't about a dead Jew. I think Himmler's been cooking the books, and the last thing he wants is a serious investigation."

"By the way, what time did Ulrich die?" asked Jacobson.

"After midnight," said Andreas. Tossing his cigarette to the ground, he added, "I can get you out."

Jacobson stared at the wall pockmarked with bullet holes. "Where would I go? It's a gamble, but I'm going to find out if he's really out there. What better way to find out if I really have an immortal soul? This time, I will be playing with my own money." He smiled.

"Don't worry. I've already arranged it with the Kapps," said Andreas, turning away. "They will make sure it's quick and painless."

Chapter 27
Café Rudi, Tauentzien Strasse, Berlin

"It's NOT THE CURE for everything," said Andreas.

"Since when?" asked McDonald.

Andreas pointed to a picture on the cover of the *Berliner Zeitung*: Göring and Major Teuer, and beside them, Diana dancing at a ball at Schorfheide, Göring's estate.

"Have you heard from her lately?" McDonald asked.

Andreas didn't want to discuss Diana. He'd burned her letters. As far as he was concerned, she was dead. The pickups and one-night stands would have to do. He was alone and miserable.

"You know, Mac, everything is different when you're alone. You walk differently, you see differently, time passes differently. You're more hesitant about what the next instant will bring—even entering a room alone and having to stand and confront whatever is waiting within."

"Buck up, old boy. There must be a nurse who wants to get ahead looking for a bright surgeon if you'll pardon the pun." McDonald held Andreas by an arm and shook him gently. "Hey, it's 1936. The Olympics are in Berlin. The place will be crawling with women. If that doesn't roast your chestnuts, you can celebrate the Condor Squadron's arrival in Spain. Hitler's promised them to Franco. They'll be able to bone up shooting the bulls. You're acting like a jilted lover. If you love her, go get her. Enough of this gentle and patient crap. This is Germany, the twentieth century, not England and the eighteenth. Come to think of it, it wasn't any different then. Get over it."

He went on to press Andreas for details of Ulrich Meyer's death. He was running short of money again.

"Shot himself," Andreas said, pouring another beer.

"Where?" McDonald asked.

"In the head," Andreas replied.

"Damn it," said McDonald. "Where was he shot? I mean, where did he shoot himself? You're the one who called *me*, remember?"

"What's the difference?" Andreas asked. "I mean, where he was shot?"

"A big difference. Where he was shot makes a difference. I mean, maybe someone was trying to send a message."

"Look," said Andreas, "this is a story for you. If Himmler found out I gave you this information, it would mean—" He ran his finger across his neck. "We don't know for sure where he died, but there were traces of river muck in his clothing and seagull shit on his shoes. Does that help?" Andreas asked. "Bottom line, he died of a heart attack."

"On the wharves?" McDonald asked.

"You're the damned detective reporter. Ulrich's body was dumped outside the fence at the castle. I hope he haunts the bastards."

McDonald looked at Andreas.

"Forget it. It's too long a story," said Andreas.

"Try me," said McDonald.

"Ulrich tried to turn himself into a fucking ghost," Andreas said.

McDonald put both his arms on the table as he leaned forward.

"This ghost comes whenever the Jews are in trouble."

"Christ, that's a full-time job," said McDonald.

"This is how we found him," said Andreas, writing the letters *Elohim Emeth* on the tablecloth. "The first letter, *E*, had been cut from his forehead."

"So?" McDonald asked.

"He's fucking dead," said Andreas. "God, I mean."

"Why is everything a damned mystery when it comes to the Jews?" McDonald asked. "And what the hell are you moping around for? It's New Year's Eve. So you and Diana have split You have a built-in stable at that whorehouse you're running."

"You mean the London hospital? That's getting dicey. We may have to pull out soon. Besides, I'm very careful what goes on there. I don't allow—"

"Come off it. Doctors, nurses, empty beds. What the hell do you think goes on, and so what?"

"Not as much as you think."

McDonald snorted. "It's me, remember? Your old buddy?"

"I knew one girl. She was Jewish too, but what a body. I would have paid her to get her out of London," Andreas said.

"Didn't think you were the savior type."

"Money in the bank. I've got her family's number."

"What makes you think they are still around? I'd call Auschwitz or Oranienburg if I were you."

"It didn't go the way I'd planned. I wound up taking care of her."

"Not again! Why don't you set up a rescue service?" McDonald asked.

"I can't help it. I can't get it up unless I feel I've unloaded, and you know my guilt."

Mac rolled over laughing. "That usually comes second."

"Sure you're not Jewish?"

"She kept scrubbing and crying. 'What's wrong?' I asked. 'We can't have those tears contaminating the wound, you know.'"

"Great line. I have to remember that one," McDonald said.

"I can get one of the aides to hold the retractors."

"'Tell me what's wrong,' I asked, assuming my best fatherly pose. 'They spit on me,' she said. Well, as you can imagine, it didn't go exactly as I had intended. I expected a sob story about a boy, love gone badly, you know, something I could make her feel good about by holding her and some kind words. I'm not kidding. Those were her exact words. Only ten minutes later, she came to the real cause for her tears. What do you think? Take a guess. She was in love. It was tragic. He was one of the guys who had spat on her. She was the prettiest thing since Lil Dagover, and I was madly in love with Lil. Saw her last movie three times."

"Well?"

"She's dead. We went skiing, and she died—hit by a truck."

"What?"

"The trail we were on at Davos, Bramabula, ended just short of an overpass. It had been sunny all day, and then, colder, it was beginning to ice over. She was a good skier. I warned her. She didn't hear me. We'd fought most of the day, and she'd torn off on her own. We'd made up. I thought we'd escaped. I'd carried it with me the whole day. I didn't know it would be her death. All that day before it happened, I was jumpy, looking over my shoulder. I thought it would be me. She just wanted a chance."

"And of course you were going to give it to her, the chance, I mean."

"Yes, Mac! Believe it or not. That's what I wanted to do, but then she kept begging me, and I thought that if I didn't, someone else would, and he wouldn't care. I wanted to help her. It was noon, sitting at the bar, the piano tinkling." Close to tears, he said, "I tried to put my hand up her dress, and she slapped me. Later, she moaned."

Chapter 28
Landscheide, 1937

THE NOTE MADE HIS heart pound: "This was under the rug—the one she was murdered on. —Inspector W."

Andreas stared at the package delivered only moments earlier. Tearing at it, he opened the small box and turned it upside down. A thin piece of metal fell onto the table—an amulet shaped like a Celtic cross. Embossed on it were two entwined triangles forming a pentagram. He recognized it as the one Anna had worn. She was dead as he'd thought from the beginning. The package had been delivered from the grave. He held it to the light, half expecting it to glow.

"We are going to Landscheide," he said to his driver.

"You have an emergency call from Herr Himmler."

"We are going," said Andreas. *This time I won't be put off.* He fingered the amulet. *Anna, what are you trying to tell me?*

The car hurtled over potholes and cut through slush. Though Christmas was long past, small crèches stood by the wayside. Bavaria was the heart and soul of the Reich.

"We are here, Landscheide," the driver said.

"Are you certain?" asked Andreas, his eyes red, his face

drawn. He hadn't slept, thinking of Landscheide, a dark
fairy tale. The grounds were a shamble. A ruined meadow.
A ruined house. No worms stirred, no crickets crawled.
The grass was brown and crunched underfoot. Nothing
was alive. Wind swirled around corners and under eaves.
A dog barked mournfully.

"My inheritance, witchcraft and hypocrisy," Andreas
whispered to himself. "Fences down, hay left to rot, the
property abandoned."

The main house had been partially burned. The odor
of charred wood still hung in the air. The lonely remnants
of the farmhouse still rose above the trees, vines reaching
up as if to bring it down. The bridge had disappeared—only
a few pieces of planking remained to mark where it had
once stood.

The past was present. The antique clock, the desk, the
inlay of mother of pearl over the desktop. He ran his fingers
over the tiles—a circle outlining a triangle with what
appeared to be a seed inside. Memories, alive, leaped from
the dust-encrusted furniture—angels, trumpets reached
above the flames and wreckage, above doomed loves and
dead heroes, the images more alive than physical presence.

He remembered it had always been warm by the fire—
sitting on the stool, warm and alive. The firelight caroming
off his father's boots tucked under the desk, his cufflinks
gleaming, and the Schutzstaffel red like blood. He, staring
at the wall, at a man hanging from a cross.

"We were betrayed, duped. We should have known—a
Jew. Compassion. The cross. Lies, all lies."

Andreas saw, imagined his father striding around the
room shaking his fist. Strength. Power. Terror. Eyeless

monsters. Slimy horrors. Sharp fangs. The worms of death feasting. The fiery cross of the Inquisition. The stench of burning flesh. His father's true memorial was there—in these catacombs.

Andreas saw—imagined? —the figure standing beside the desk, next to his father, a cape thrown over his shoulders, a goatee on an otherwise smoothly shaven chin, piercing black eyes.

"I know you. I have seen you before," Andreas whispered.

The phantom gestured to the desk. Slowly, deliberately, he ran his fingers over the tiles, outlining a triangle with what appeared to be a seed inside. Around the seed were eight lotus petals.

He whispers, "The lotus flower, the seed of enlightenment. Resting on it is an offering to Buddha. It is a way to understand where understanding fails. When you have grown, you will appreciate the meaning. You are welcome to enter," he says, taking his hand. "Come, explore. The lotus is a welcoming symbol, and it represents understanding and the presence of the Buddha, an invitation to meditation, thinking, dreaming as when you are falling asleep. Christ, hanging from the cross, is just an image of a man. The blood pouring out his side, not real. Like his tears. He is weeping. You have to make it come alive in your mind," He said, kneeling to him and drying his eyes.

The water is lapis lazuli surrounded by shining jewels, pure and soft. "Imagine the jewels lapping over diamond sands. The throne of the Buddha, the lotus, iridescent, like the colors you see in the electric signs, shining rays of light streaming out, transmitting his image—and the miracle."

Andreas didn't understand, yet he did. The words were soft and warm.

"You are reborn, Andreas—pure. If you have faith"

Andreas turned and shook off the hand on his shoulder.

"Faith, understanding, and peace, and the gold bell will tinkle. Words for blind people clinging to a lifeline". He said.

A lightning bolt struck. He smelled sulfur. The black cape overhanging the desk and half hidden in darkness moved. A stranger stood next to him.

"Who are you?" he asked.

"The caretaker."

"This place hasn't seen a caretaker in years."

"I am *your* caretaker," replied the stranger. "I have guarded the secret." He pointed to the desk.

"The woman who lived here—does she come anymore?" Andreas asked.

"No one comes. Neither man nor God. She's gone. Quickly, before she returns. The amulet."

"Who?" asked Andreas.

"Why, the owner of course." He nodded at the desk. "You are the only one left. You have one hour."

The hour was almost up. Andreas, seated beside the desk, was weary. He had tried Anna's amulet in each of the desk's drawers, but none of the locks had responded. The mandala was a fresco of Buddha beside the tree of enlightenment, the bodhi tree. Angry, he said, "No one comes. You are the only one. Bullshit." He was about to pass over the remainder of the inlay. Frustrated, he pressed the key-shaped end of the amulet into the space. With a loud grinding, the inlay rearranged itself, revealing a tunnel. The brilliant darkness of the tunnel sloped on. He could not feel an end.

"Maybe it's not bullshit." Andreas slid his hand into the tunnel, and his fingers encountered a cloth bag with a ribbon tied around it. Inching his fingers into the bag, he withdrew a reddish- brown object shaped like a pyramid, rubbed smooth as glass, and polished by many puffs of breath. A thin line etched into the amber. Light suffused the gem until it was ablaze. The engraving led past a small insect that had been caught by the gently flowing sap and forever imprisoned.

A bolt of lightning bathed the room. The clock whirred, and the hands stopped at seven o'clock. He was certain the clock had read eight o' clock when he'd entered the room. He opened the clock. The gears were rusted and covered with cobwebs. Still, it was ticking. The only way time could run backward was if he had been going faster than the speed of light, if a cosmic ray or lightning had hit and expended all its energy in one burst, perhaps a bolt from the approaching storm.

He put the amber in his pocket. Leaving the farmhouse, he hurried through the blackness through claps of thunder. A tree was struck by lightning, and thick smoke rose. The heavy foliage writhed in torment. Andreas approached the car. He saw the shadow of a woman in the window. Mother? Lakshmi?" he whispered, but he could not make out her features. When he turned, she was gone.

"Drive," he ordered, leaning forward and scanning the rearview mirror.

"Colonel, that car is following us."

"Lose him!" Andreas said.

The road was narrow and potholed. They picked up speed. The gauge crept to ninety kilometers an hour. The car behind gained on them.

They rounded a curve. A lorry loomed directly in their path. The driver hit the brakes and pulled at the wheel. The car careened wildly and fell off the road and down an embankment. Briefly hanging on two wheels, it then righted itself. Andreas turned just in time to see the car behind explode into a fireball.

Chapter 29
Himmler's Study, Wiligut, 1937

RAIN POURED DOWN AS they rode to Wiligut Castle. The car splashed up the gravel drive. Andreas, reviewing the ways he would die for defying a direct order from Himmler, jumped out as soon as the car stopped, briskly saluted, and brushed past the sentry.

Running after him, his driver, handkerchief in hand, pointed to Andreas's boots splashed with mud. He bent over and quickly cleaned them. Andreas checked his pockets. It hadn't been a dream. The jewel was still with him. A carving of the Aryan sun wheel hung over the door to Himmler's study. Andreas knocked and entered. Himmler, facing the fireplace with hands clasped at his back, turned and pointed to a chair.

"Sit down," he ordered. "Do you have any idea why you were chosen for this mission? There are other men just as well qualified."

Chosen? He couldn't help laughing. Chosen meant trouble. He'd vowed never again to be chosen. *Everyone who was chosen, wound up dead. I happened to be available.*

Himmler traced his dueling scar with his fingers recreating and enjoying the pain. His eyes, normally lidded, almost closed. He slapped his swagger stick against his thigh. "Do you recall a Herr Losen?" he asked.

"Anton Losen? Of course. The explorer and mountain climber."

"Do you recall what happened to him?"

"He was lost on a climb in Tibet several years ago."

"Fifteen years to be exact. His body's been discovered by two climbers—at the foot of Mount Kongzhengchenga. In Tibet."

The stick hovered in midair. Andreas, on the edge of his chair, waited for the slap. When none came, he presumed to respond. "Is the body well preserved?"

"It's serviceable." Himmler strode to the other side of the fireplace and ran his fingers along the library table. "You would expect it to be, wouldn't you? Preserved, I mean. After all, it's been packed in ice." His eyes drilled into Andreas. "We have found the sword!" he shouted, banging his fist on the table.

Moving to the bookcase, Himmler took a worn copy of a book from a shelf and handed it to Andreas—*The Legend of the Sword, Anton Losen* etched on the cover in gold. "Read it," he ordered. "I'll see you at breakfast."

It was late afternoon. Andreas, alone in Himmler's study, poured himself a whiskey and set his feet on the well-worn leather hassock. He'd begun to read when the door cracked open and Allard von Kaltenbrun, Himmler's chief of staff, crept in. Seeming even more tense than usual, he whispered that a strange delivery had been made to the castle that day. A truck escorted by motorcycle riders unloaded a casket. Himmler himself had overseen the unloading. It had disappeared into the castle.

"Who was in it?" asked Andreas.

"Damned if I know," said von Kaltenbrun.

"Sit down. Have a drink," Andreas said as he returned to his reading. "I'll tell him I asked you to stay." Andreas began reading aloud. "He will have to die, and quickly."

"Who?" asked von Kaltenbrun.

"Christ, of course." Andreas read on silently, then sat up and exclaimed, "Did you know this? The Jews claimed that the true Messiah would not—could not—be tortured. So, they reasoned, Christ had to be tortured to prove he was not the Messiah."

"My father could have written that. Makes sense in a negative sort of way."

A live cinder exploded from the fireplace.

"Stop fidgeting," said Andreas. "He won't be back for a while."

"You never know with that man," said von Kaltenbrun. "He just materializes out of nowhere."

Andreas continued to read aloud. "'Pontius Pilate would have paid well for a crucifixion—it was good entertainment. But he knew this one would mean trouble; crucifixions dragged on, and he wanted this execution over quickly. He didn't want his name connected to any part of the affair. The crowd, already restless, would get out of hand.' Hell, the good nuns didn't tell me any of this when I was in school. Did you know any of this? It gets better. 'Pilate concocted a plan that would allow him to wash his hands of the whole mess. He enlisted a Roman centurion, Gaius Longissimus, as insurance.'"

Andreas read on. "'Finish him if the crowd grows restless,' Pilate ordered. The Sanhedrin, the legal ruling body of the Jews, agreed. If the crowd got out of hand, he was to be killed quickly.'" Taking a deep breath, Andreas said, "Now that's something right out of Himmler's book."

"You are Catholic, aren't you?" Andreas asked. von Kaltenbrun stiffened. Andreas waved his hand to cut him off. "Don't worry. I know you are not a Jew."

"Yes, of course," he said.

"Well then, listen to this. 'Gaius Longissimus, mindful of his order, rode up to the limp body and drove his sword into Jesus' side. Blood, ruby red, welled from the wound. The woman who had walked stride for stride with the cross, who had wiped Christ's forehead and cleansed the blood from his brow, stepped forward and placed a cup beneath the wound. The thick, black juice dripped into the cup and turned to stone.' Wow! A ruby that size made of Christ's blood. Can you imagine what that's worth?" He went on slowly. "'He, Longissimus, delivered the sword and the stone to Mary Magdalene before he committed suicide.'"

"What happened to the stone?" asked von Kaltenbrun.

"Probably stolen," said Andreas. He closed the book, carefully marking the page. He hesitated, then looking into von Kaltenbrun's eyes, said, "At the end, he must have called out to God. Suppose he realized that he was human after all and there was no one to answer?"

Andreas closed his eyes and fell asleep. The windows were closed, yet the pages flipped as if by a gust of wind.

Von Kaltenbrun threw a blanket over Andreas and left the room.

The next morning, he returned to shake him awake.

"Have some coffee, quick," said von Kaltenbrun, pointing toward the library table. He had prepared eggs and strong coffee.

Himmler sauntered into the room pulling on his black gloves. Von Kaltenbrun stood at attention to one side.

"You slept well?" Himmler asked. "von Kaltenbrun, that will be all. Eat some breakfast, Andreas, but careful, not too much. Have at least a second cup of coffee."

Himmler walked to the library wall, put his hand on a cornice next to the window, gave it a twist, and waited. The wall slid back. "Careful," said Himmler, "the steps are stone and slippery."

Though much of Wiligut had been rebuilt, the foundation, walls, and turrets were centuries old. As the two men descended, small rooms became more frequent, some equipped with chains. Rats squealed and scampered over their feet. A purple patch of phosphorescent mold gleamed like neon. They spiraled down several flights in the dust-laden air, murky pink in the torchlight, and into a large circular opening at the bottom. Tunnels ran off in several directions. In one corner lay a brown sheet covering a mound. Magically, the mound changed shape in front of their eyes.

"There's something alive there," said Andreas.

"Death," Himmler said, covering his nose. "Pull the sheet off."

Worms, fat and surfeited, clung to the sheet; beetles and roaches scurried away. Himmler smiled. "Well," he said proudly, "this is Anton Losen. Have you seen anything like it? Take a closer look."

The body was covered with sores and deep ulcerations, the skin had peeled loose and hung in strips, the skull was a tureen for roaches. The remnants of one eye, half-devoured, stared.

Andreas whispered, "Nothing, not even leprosy comes close."

"What would you say if I told you we have produced changes similar to these?" Himmler asked. His pride at having created such horror showed in his face. "If you took some tissue samples and compared them, could you tell if the same thing had caused the changes?" he asked.

"Compare them to what?" said Andreas.

"To the ones we have produced in compound three," Himmler replied.

Compound three. Andreas remembered Ulrich's warning: "You won't have to worry about guinea pigs. The Nazis have done it for you."

"Yes, I think so," said Andreas.

"Take the tissue samples and report back to me."

"It will take forty-eight hours to fix them in formalin and analyze them," Andreas stammered.

"Take some from compound three and compare them," Himmler repeated, his eyes expressionless.

So this is why I was sent to Wiligut. Why Ulrich killed himself.

"I want those samples quickly," said Himmler.

Andreas telephoned the laboratory. "Can you stain and have tissue samples cut and ready for the microscope?" he asked. The director, a woman, was not allowed to enter the main room of the castle, but she promised to have the slides for him as quickly as possible.

Andreas went back into the crypt for the samples, took a wrong turn, and chose a wrong passageway. Finally, having fought through the cobwebs, he'd staggered back to the castle. Too late, he noticed he was missing two of the slides. He'd taken six specimens from various part of the body. Two were missing. Not that it mattered; one slide would have been enough. Losen was already a goner before he had attempted the climb. His cancer had been well advanced. He'd devoured himself, his cancerous tissue eating him to survive. He was already dead when a bullet behind his left ear had finished him.

Andreas made his way to the laboratory. The technician shrank away, and covering her nose, said, "Christ, Herr Colonel, you smell like death."

The next day dawned a glorious, sun-swept morning. Andreas and the lab technician, Fräulein Gabler, walked across the courtyard and down a tree-lined path to a low, whitewashed building. They might have been lovers looking for a quiet nook. Attractive, in her late thirties, Fräulein Heidi Gabler and the soft return of green and quiet had almost made him forget the nature of his work.

They climbed a white staircase, went through a heavy metal door, and up another three steps to a second door. At the head of the corridor was a yellow metal desk; a patient's rolling cart stood to one side. A nurse, officious but pert, had prepared two "volunteers."

"How did you pick them?" Andreas asked.

"They have all had at least twenty hours of exposure to gamma rays," she said as if it were a sun lamp.

Stunned, Andreas asked to see them. She reached up and slid back one of the curtains.

"This is Mr. Steinberg," she announced, standing by a white bed in her white, starched uniform.

Mr. Steinberg blinked with one eye out of half of his face, a massive cauliflower eating away the other half. The eye for a moment looked Andreas straight in the face, and then basking in the warmth denied its partner, sank back. Andreas touched a piece of the cauliflower, avoiding Mr. Steinberg's eye. The white uniform smiled.

The second "volunteer" was a mass of ulcerations. Andreas asked the nurse for morphine. She hesitated. "Morphine!" he yelled, rising to strike her. He took a syringe and injected him.

"Bury him," he ordered.

"We will burn him," she replied.

Andreas and Fräulein Gabler walked back to the castle. The sky was unconcerned. The birds hunted for worms, the beetles for ants. They returned to the laboratory.

Two days later, Heidi stood beside Andreas as he put a slide under a microscope. The tissue was disorganized. Telltale streaks of purple relayed the message—each cell was multiplying. He focused down to higher magnification and turned away.

"I have to hand it to him for his style," said Andreas.

"Who?" she asked.

"God. No gun or knife, just a tiny particle of energy and sit back. He wouldn't have to be anywhere around or even alive when it decided to kill." Each purple dot was a mass of genetic material dividing and subdividing, devouring the remaining cells so it could live. "The sword of destiny," he mused. Radiation had caused the cancerous growths, the wounds, both to the "volunteers" as well as to the climber, Losen.

Andreas refocused the microscope and then slid away in silence. The technician looked away and then at him. He motioned for her to see for herself. There was nothing to say.

No sooner had he finished than Himmler was on the phone.

"He wants us to bring the slides and a microscope and meet him in the library," Andreas said.

"Are you sure?" Himmler asked, barely able to contain himself.

"Yes, sir," Andreas answered. "Only the radioactive decay of a high energy source could have done this."

"Do we have such a source?" Himmler asked. "Meyer had said that there was such a source but that it had been lost a long time ago."

"It's probably uranium 238. It has been shown only recently that these elements are capable of spontaneous decay."

"If enough of this material could be found … would it be possible to produce a bomb?" Himmler asked.

"Yes," Andreas replied.

"And the explosive power?"

"Unimaginable."

Himmler smiled.

The castle was crawling with Gestapo. It was impossible to concentrate. Not hungry, Andreas pushed his plate away. He couldn't work anyway, couldn't get near the cyclotron. Security had been doubled. Himmler advised him to take a few days off.

Chapter 30
Von Kaltenbrun's Estate

HE WAS TAKEN BY surprise but accepted the invitation from von Kaltenbrun to attend his daughter's engagement party and spend the weekend at his family's estate. The streets were deserted; the drive to the estate on the Spree River took less than an hour. Berliners had become indifferent to the black uniforms and black sedans. The one following Andreas and his host discreetly kept its distance. As their car entered the gates of the estate, it drove past.

Andreas slipped into waders, and fishing rod in hand, made his way down to the stream and into the cool water. The stream passed in and out of meadows and through a copse of trees. The clear water swirled about his waders. Von Kaltenbrun positioned himself upstream. They had little luck, only a few desultory rises. Von Kaltenbrun splashed his way downstream and joined Andreas and they sat on the bank and shared a bottle of Chablis. Andreas studied a nymph as it probed its way past his waders. Von Kaltenbrun was eager to open the conversation though not quite sure where to begin.

"In a few days," said Andreas, "even today perhaps, that nymph will become a gossamer mayfly. Will it remember its life as an ugly creature stalking along the bottom of the stream and living under rocks?"

It was the opening von Kaltenbrun had wished for.

"No more than the people of our class will remember the Germany we knew," said von Kaltenbrun. "Sadly, our German instinct and will, our love of music and philosophy, have deceived us. Hitler is going to be assassinated."

Andreas tossed his lure into the eddying current. Von Kaltenbrun turned his eyes on Andreas. "Hitler is going to be assassinated. Did you hear what I said?"

"Yes," said Andreas. "I've heard it before. So what? Germans will revert to their old ways no matter who heads the government. The Weimar Republic was example enough. The will to be ruled is ingrained as far back as the rule of the father. I've told you I want no part of it," Andreas said. "No matter who wins the next war—Germany, England, or France—nothing will change."

"It will," said von Kaltenbrun. "Don't you see? Hitler is a madman. Göring is reasonable."

Andreas was astonished. von Kaltenbrun actually thought that this horror was about bringing back the era of the von, the nobility. The German people who had been fed on Nazi hate would then just crawl back into their holes and become good, law-abiding burghers. He stared into the water, at the patch of weeds waving in the current, wondering what he might look like to a fish—a god outlined against the sky. A hatch had started; winged insects began to fill the air.

"There are gentlemen of honor left in Germany," said von Kaltenbrun.

You fool. You poor, weak fool, Andreas thought. *Nothing has changed, nor will it ever.* "You have the money and contacts. Take your family and leave. Go to Switzerland."

"My family have been ministers and ambassadors. There is no place for us to go."

The trout were just beginning to rise, slurping hungrily. In a long, arcing sweep, Andreas dropped his lure in the middle of the stream. It started downstream. The line suddenly went taut. Minutes later, he netted the trout, its red gills opening and closing as it gasped for breath, the bright rainbow along its spine already turning a dull pink. He lifted the trout and gently rocked it in the stream until it regained its strength. With a thrust of its tail, it swam away. As he walked back to the manor to change for dinner, a thought occurred to him—*It will strike again at the same lure tomorrow.*

He changed into his uniform, a coat cut much like tails but with the tails missing, a waistcoat, black bow tie, the shoulder patches of a colonel, and the death-head insignia of the SS.

The dinner was to honor von Kaltenbrun's daughter, who had just become engaged to Manfred von Gonten, a lieutenant in the First Panzer division, a distinguished unit with a storied history. "Honor and Service" was its motto. It was reserved for the aristocracy, obviously off limits to Jews and Slavs.

Nothing had been spared; the meal had been prepared by Berlin's Bristol Kempinski Hotel, and an orchestra played American tunes. But there was only a smattering of young people on the dance floor. Two couples straggled out to "When they Begin the Beguine." "Mood Indigo" brought out a few more, and then "You Do Something to Me" filled the floor. It cleared again with "Night and Day," and the bandleader then settled on an Anglo-Saxon version of "Du, Du, Liegst Mir," and the evening went on from there.

Louisa, von Kaltenbrun's daughter, looked insecure but lovely in a light-blue Schiaparelli gown. Manfred, her husband-to-be, was short and stocky with thinning blond hair. Andreas was seated between Louisa and Ulrika, von Kaltenbrun's wife, who was dressed in a white, off-the-shoulder gown cut to show her charms to best advantage. His mood dark, Andreas hardly noticed.

Langouste from Paris, truffles from Languedoc, pastries from Maxim's, wild boar from the von Kaltenbrun estates, Bordeaux and Burgundy and French brandy. The guests were polite, and the conversation was hushed. Ulrika directed the servants just as she directed Louisa's life: "No, the summer house is unsuitable and a honeymoon in Antibes ill advised." Louisa's fiancé responded with a nod and Louisa with a giggle.

Andreas felt sorry for the girl. Her fiancé, fashionably urbane, ignored her, dancing the first dance with her mother and then going off to talk with her father. They were still not aware that their time has come and gone. Hitler, summary death by firing squad, concentration camps were the new order. Frau von Kaltenbrun bent forward, threatening to spill her breast into her soup.

"It's awful, damnable that such things can go on in Germany," she said, her cheeks flushed with champagne.

When she looked up, Andreas caught the suggestion of a wink, an invitation.

"Lobster, madam?" asked the servant. The waiters flitted like ghosts among the guests.

After dinner, the men retired to the library. The silence was made heavier by the pall of cigar smoke. "Are you in? We must assassinate him. We must for honor. But I must know where you stand. Failure means certain death."

Von Kaltenbrun rose to give a toast. "What can be worse about a war with France than missing its wines?" The nervous laughter died. He went on. "I know many of you are uncertain about your duty to Germany, but I remind you, the good lies so near. Learn only to seize it. Remember Thucydides: 'Greatness is won by men with courage, with knowledge of their duty, and with a sense of honor in action.'"

There was a collective sigh of relief. There had been no mention of Hitler. "After all," said Manfred von Gonten, "von Kaltenbrun had not said anything damning. Hitler might not be so bad after all, and I'd like to keep my options open."

"That will be all," Ulrika von Kaltenbrun said to the headwaiter. Andreas wondered where the car that had followed them had parked. He was sure it was close by. He was just as certain that the occupants would have recorded the names of everyone at the party. They would list their relatives down to the last cousin, their addresses and working places, what they had enjoyed for dinner, and their sexual appetites. No fact would be wasted.

The cigar smoke and brandy made Andreas dizzy but wary. *Whatever you say can be recorded and later used as evidence*, he thought.

Von Kaltenbrun broke the silence. "Have you decided?"

"You mean about which lure catches the biggest fish? Without a doubt the streamer," Andreas answered. "It's easiest to cast and hardest to resist. Should prove effective wherever you decide to fish. But if you are looking to land the big one, I would suggest a guide—probably English."

"You know damned well I can't," said von Kaltenbrun angrily.

"Surely you can. I'll tie one up for you," said Andreas. "I'll make sure it swims deep, below the surface. Still, the trout may want no part of it. There are some days when they just won't bite and there isn't a damned thing you can do about it. They just want no part of it," he repeated, leaning forward, inches from von Kaltenbrun. "I suggest if you really want to fish for rainbows, you take your family to England."

Andreas slipped out of his chair. Examining the lamps, passing his hands under the library table, he pulled out a small, round listening device. Putting his fingers to his lips, he replaced it. He left the estate the next morning, again shepherded by the black limousine. Desperate to keep up and still hung over, they were stopped by the local police for erratic driving.

Chapter 31
Darmston Village, Germany

ANDREAS SLEPT WELL THOUGH it had been difficult after the fine down comforters and silk sheets of the weekend to become accustomed once again to the rough linen and lumpy mattress at Wiligut. He awoke to hushed voices, the clanking of metal, the mournful sound of marching boots, and the soft hum of engines coming from the courtyard below. Dawn had turned the sky blue at the eastern edges when his driver burst into his room.

"Himmler wants you downstairs in uniform. Now!"

Andreas had forgotten to hide the morphine syringe. The driver glanced at the table then quickly looked away.

"Get some breakfast," Himmler ordered as Andreas entered the castle's great hall. "We will be starting out in fifteen minutes. It's a beautiful morning for some sport." An aristocrat in a society of men marked by dueling scars and trained for murder, he looked fresh and trim. The wedding, Louisa, seemed far away; the trout didn't.

"What are we hunting for?" asked Andreas.

"The man who stole the Losen slides," said Himmler.

"But they weren't stolen. I lost them, and as it turned out, we didn't need them," said Andreas.

"Any excuse will do," Kalb shrugged.

The troops loaded into the lorries. Their black rifles slung over their backs caught the first glint of the morning sun. A machine gun was hoisted into the back, and a tarp was pulled over it. Andreas's car was second in line, behind Himmler's.

"What the hell is going on?" asked Andreas. "Where are we going?"

"To the village, Darmston," his driver replied. "Only a few kilometers. Seems that whoever stole the slides lives in the village. Himmler wants to teach him a lesson."

The troops were boisterous as the motorcade crossed a small brook. They grew silent as they approached the village.

A clean, new morning fell onto the window casements. Anton Muller, one of the villagers, placed a few pieces of kindling on his fire. He added a few pieces of wood and warmed his large, calloused hands, put a piece of bread into a large iron skillet, and adding a piece of lard, he waited for the water for his coffee to boil.

"Won't be long, Oskar," he said. He and the dog had practiced this routine for a long time. The dog, wagging his tail, lay by the fire as he did every morning waiting for the handout. Anton picked up the worn copy of a book from the kitchen table. The book was never far from his grasp even when he was in the fields. He bent, and the dog raised its head to the familiar face.

Anton understood the words only vaguely, but the images needed no explanation. The white charger, the silver armor, the lance in the stirrup, the knight riding toward the castle where he would win his lady. Anton could manage only two or at most three pages a night, having to stop often to look up the meaning of the words.

The door burst open. The blow struck Anton under the chin. Blood spurted. The dog snarling, teeth bared, rose to defend him. The soldier struck it with the butt of his rifle, and the dog crumpled and lay still. The soldier motioned Anton out into the snow. He fell, his crippled foot twisting under him.

"Get your ass out," snarled the soldier. Anton was dragged to the stream, where the villagers stood huddled together.

"My book!" The soldier had thrown it into the snow. Anton picked it up, brushed it off, and clutched it. Anton squinted through the sunlight, imagining the black knight on his black steed. His novel had come to life.

"Find the thief who has stolen from the castle!" the black knight said.

Anton didn't understand. No one at the table round would steal from the castle; whoever did should be punished. He heard the order to stand. Clumsily, he got to his feet. Certainly, the criminal would be found.

"Every seventh will be shot."

He had to let them know that he too was a knight.

"Step forward at the count of—"

The shots echoed through the woods, scattering birds in a volley of flight. Ten bodies lay on the ground. The book lays in the snow. Anton's glasses lay beside it.

The brook babbled, unconcerned. The dog dragged

itself to Anton's body and lay licking his hand, unsure of what had happened. Himmler gave the order to put up the rifles, and men climbed back into the trucks. They were about to drive off when the young man lifted his head. The dog sitting beside him wagged its tail.

"Andreas, let's see whether you are a good enough shot to belong to the Korps. Kill them both. Here, take this." Himmler handed him a rifle. Anton had crawled to the edge of the brook.

"He's dead," Andreas said.

"Make sure," Himmler answered. "Turn and fire."

Kill Himmler, Andreas thought. He lifted the gun, aimed, and fired.

The back of Anton's head exploded. The blood flowed bright red into the brook down to the next pile of rocks, turning them pink.

"Good shot," Himmler said. "Now the dog."

The dog lifted its head and looked straight at Andreas. He fired. The bullet kicked the animal's head back. The soldiers cheered.

Anton's book, barely noticed, slid into the brook. It was carried downstream. The dog bled into the snow. Andreas climbed into the car.

The day had turned hard and metallic. No one spoke. Andreas got out of the car, and looking straight ahead, strode into the castle and stumbled up the stairs.

"He shot him," his driver said.

"Who?" von Kaltenbrun asked.

"The dog."

Soldiers climbed down and in groups of twos and threes walked to the barracks.

Chapter 32
Wiligut, 1937

As HE DRESSED FOR dinner, Andreas studied himself in the bathroom mirror, barely recognizing his face. He was about to turn away when he heard a knock on the door.

"I need a drink," said von Kaltenbrun.

He was dressed in formal uniform—stone-gray tunic and matching carnelian-striped trousers. The Iron Cross hung prominently below his collar. "Wouldn't happen to have some brandy, would you? By the way, thank you for your advice. I've considered what you said about fishing in England and have arranged for Luisa and Ulrika."

Andreas placed his fingers to his lips. Von Kaltenbrun ignored the warning. He was determined and went on, in fact seemed to enjoy the danger.

"I've never been considered for the Totenkopf unit— wouldn't have accepted it if I had. I'm a soldier. Heydrich uses the Korps as his personal judge, jury, and executioner."

Andreas again put his finger to his lips. The man was committing suicide. Von Kaltenbrun seemed determined to sacrifice himself.

"The initiation has sent good men to asylums. I've seen men with their insides torn open, their guts spilling onto the dirt, but never anything to match the terror in their eyes. You will carry the death head until the day you die. You are married to death and the ring. When you die, the ring will be returned to the ring giver and stored in the vault." He emptied his glass with one swallow and turned toward Andreas.

"Like Beowulf," said Andreas. "Heroes and gods, courage and justice."

Seated, Von Kaltenbrun's shoulders sagged, and his arms drooped by his side. He rose slowly from his chair as if he never wanted to get up again. Andreas followed him down the stairs, past hanging banners and tapestries.

"Andreas, we have been waiting for you," Himmler said. "You have proven yourself today. We have decided to move your initiation up so you will be able to get to Tibet by the end of April. The monsoon season starts in early June. As of next week, you will be one of us, a member."

Andreas stood to a smattering of applause. His eyes met von Kaltenbrun's and the accusation in them.

Andreas began to sweat and his hands to tremble. The dog, bleeding, followed him.

"Mrs. Devi Bose will be our guest lecturer. I believe you know her," said Himmler, introducing a beautiful woman in a silk sari.

"I knew we would meet again," she said cheerfully, extending her hand.

"Mrs. Bose, of course. I am delighted to see you again. I recall your reading at Bellows Castle," said Andreas, bowing. "The three of swords will pierce the heart, remember?"

"Really, Colonel, I insist you call me Devi."

She let her hand linger before she slipped past him on the way to the podium. The lights dimmed, and she stepped to the lectern. "I will speak tonight on the German Aryan and the Hindu Brahmin classes. I might also mention the Jews," she added with a laugh.

She began with a quotation from Heinrich Heine from a hundred years before.

"The German revolution will not prove any milder or gentler because it was preceded by Kant's *Critique of Pure Reason*. The philosopher of nature will be terrible in this, that he has allied himself with the primitive powers of nature. He can conjure up the demon forces of the old German pantheism. Having done so, there is aroused in him that ancient German eagerness for battle, which engages in combat, not for the sake of destroying, not even for the sake of victory, but merely for the sake of the combat itself.

"When the cross, that restraining talisman, falls to pieces, then will break forth again the ferocity of the old combatants, the frantic rage. The talisman has become rotten and the day will come when it will pitifully crumble into dust. The old stone gods will then arise from the forgotten ruins and wipe from their eyes the dust of centuries. Thor, with his hammer, will rise again and he will shatter the Gothic cathedrals. When ye hear the trampling of feet and the clashing of arms, ye neighbors' children, ye French. Be on your guard. German thunder is of true German character. When ye hear a crashing such as has never before heard in the world's history then know that at last the German thunderbolt has fallen."

The lecture concluded to thundering applause and stomping boots.

Andreas was about to approach Mrs. Bose when Himmler took him firmly by the arm. "Andreas, you know Herr Heydrich?" Himmler took a cigarette from his case and studied Andreas over his monocle, aware of Andreas's dislike for Heydrich, the "butcher."

"You, Andreas, and Herr Heydrich are going to spend a lot of time together. You are going to lead a team up Mount Kongzhengchenga. Herr Losen will show you the way. Which reminds me, Heydrich, be sure to get Goebbels and the film crew ready, and line up those fake Jewish refugees."

Losen will show us the way to Losen's Leap, but after that—what? Andreas wondered.

"It's not going to be easy," said Heydrich. "Most of them have never climbed anything higher than the kitchen steps. Carry the Jews up if you have to.. We won't have to worry about getting them down."

"Losen died from radiation poisoning. He must have found the sword," said Himmler, casting a glance at Heydrich. "Weren't you on that climb with Losen?"

Heydrich's presence affected Andreas; just seeing him, his eyes become misty with tears of shame, a darkness descended, and he cursed. Heydrich, Hitler, and his father had turned Germany, a country dedicated to honor, into an empty excuse for murder. In anguish, he addressed his father in his mind. *Thank God I've had nothing to do with it. I no longer feel anything—not hate, not forgiveness. I have no regret. The opportunity presented itself, and I killed you.*

I am your father.

In name only—you played no part in my life.

I was one of Germany's heroes. And you are as well. You are part of this plague.

Father, I didn't ask to be.

Heydrich was still talking; Andreas nodded as if listening and smiled.

"We found nothing even suggesting uranium," said Heydrich. "He just disappeared. Walked to a spot and the mountain as if it expected him. It opened up and swallowed him."

"You can requisition any equipment you need. It's better if I am out of the picture," said Himmler. "We don't want to alert the British that you are going to climb in their backyard. Göring either for that matter. And you, Andreas, be careful. There have already been attempts on your life." Himmler slapped his swagger stick against his trousers for emphasis. The sound ricocheted through the room like a rifle shot.

"Of course," Andreas assured him. *Heydrich's the one I have to be most careful of—at least on the way down. He won't need me anymore..*

"Mrs. Bose will get the necessary permits."

"The British would never be stupid enough to let us climb in their backyard," said Andreas.

"Wouldn't they? Hitler will annex Austria. Czechoslovakia will be next, and the British will do nothing. Chamberlain isn't going to upset the apple cart if he thinks there is a chance of avoiding war. That has been the secret to all of Hitler's success."

"They haven't read Heine," said Mrs. Bose.

"But how can we get to India without the British knowing it? We can't just walk into Calcutta. MI5 will never let us get away with it. The British have India and Tibet in their back pockets."

"History is on our side," she said. "The Aryans and the Brahmins go back a long way."

Himmler peered at Andreas over the top of his monocle and smiled. "Lord Bellows and Mrs. Bose have worked that out. Come, I will show you."

Himmler studied the map spread across his desk and pointed to the mouth of the Hoogli River. He ran his finger to the border between Sikkim and Nepal, to a mountain circled in red, Kongdzengchenga twenty-six thousand feet.

"This is where they found Losen, at the bottom of the Penlong Pass. The mouth of the Hoogli River is a mass of small inlets, impossible to patrol. We will have the necessary permits, but we probably won't need them. The open door lies through Sikkim. We will have insurance if we need it. The Tibetans are preoccupied now looking for the new Dalai Lama."

You will need every deception you have—the British will see to that, Andreas thought.

"We will choose a place to land, shift supplies to shallow-draft boats, and go by water as far as the Tista Gorge. From there, by mule and yak."

"Can we get that far upriver?"

"Yes. It's been done before. Officially, you will be on an anthropological expedition—to find herbs, magical cures for medical purposes. They are all the rage now. We will cross the border and walk in. The Tibetans and the British will know we are coming and welcome us with open arms.

"Oh, and one less headache—our informant at Scotland Yard has told us they have found the culprit behind Sir Bellows' accident—an Indian trading in stolen art goods. So we are simply looking for medical cures amongst the fauna. They won't be able to do a damned thing about it without upsetting all the bleeding hearts. Who could possibly be against allowing the German expedition to proceed for the good of mankind? Particularly if Sir Bellows is sitting in our base camp with his crutches."

Himmler's laugh was almost childlike in its delight. "Think of it, my dear Colonel. It will be very hard to refuse Lord and Nancy Astor and Sir Neville Henderson, the peace activist. They are close friends of Sir Bellows. At this very moment, Dr. Werner, Otto von Hentig, and Oskar von Niedermayer are promising the Tibetans large shipments of humanitarian aid—and perhaps just a few weapons to defend themselves against poachers. Of course, the Jews."

Himmler's smile and thick glasses served as camouflage as they had on many occasions. No longer smiling and looking directly at Andreas, he declared as though defying anyone to contradict him, "Blute und Boden. Blood and land. Minister Eisner was wrong when he proclaimed us a republic, and he paid for it with his life. We are Germans, and this is German land, and it is special. It belongs to the Germans—the Aryans by right. We have a divine mission to link all parts of the world together under German rule."

He envisioned horseman, chariots, Panzers hurtling across the plains spewing death and destruction, subjugating the Dasa of ancient India—the French, the British, and the Belgians, Hitler leading them.

Round and round until you forget why you started, thought

Andreas. *There is always someone ready to betray.* He had chosen espionage precisely for that reason: it required no commitment to belief—either religion or love. In fact, just the opposite. If he wasn't wrong, Sir Bellows was providing the British with reasons not to allow them to climb. Careful man that he was, he'd have both sides covered. Nothing ever changed.

"Soon, Austria will be abandoned to her fate," continued Himmler, pacing back and forth on a handsome oriental rug. "Hitler was born in Austria. Austria is German. Do you think for a moment that he will not move on Vienna? Austria is practically a thing of the past."

"You will have a chance to climb again," Mrs. Bose said, eyeing Andreas closely.

"You are not going with us?" asked Andreas with alarm. "Surely, you are not going to try to climb Kongzhengchenga."

"Perhaps. Who knows? Looks as if everyone is. It's going to be crowded. But only to the base camp." She laughed, apparently having taken Andreas's concern as a form of flirtation. "But now I must be off. I have many things to attend to. I have to be in Berlin early."

"Andreas, you and Major Heydrich will have full responsibility. If there is anyone you want, requisition him," Himmler added.

"What about Sherpas?" Andreas asked.

"I will leave that up to you and Major Heydrich."

"How soon do you want us to be ready?" Andreas asked. "We have to beat the monsoons, which usually start in June. That gives us about three months, not much time."

"The sooner the better," Himmler answered. "After your induction, you can leave as soon as you can manage."

Chapter 33
Paris

AT TIMES, ANDREA'S FELT as if he'd been drugged. An intense longing gnawed at him. The expression in his eyes—the strangest loneliness. Diana and he had gone separate ways. His attempts to quiet his longing for her had been fruitless. Love brings out the worst in us What in her do I love? Her violent temper reminds him of his father. Her emotions swinging from warm to cold in the batting of a lash, unpredictable. She is arrogant, self-absorbed in many ways—a bitch, the face of an angel and the heart of a murderer. She knows me as I never knew myself. Yet she loves me. Not with a love like a carnival played at dance parties in country estates but with a love that haunts and gurgles over rocks in an ancient forest, a love that will never perish but will exist through hunger and cold and like a gaping wound cutting into my heart.

Despite all, she is the only one he could ever love. He knew like the light fading in the October day that there was tragedy in that love, the face of an angel and the heart of a murderer. The game is over. *"We are finished, both wounded. The game no longer vague, as certain as death."*

The evening was cold and damp, but he decided to take a walk. Exiting the woods opposite the women's dormitories, he remembered Ulrich's words: "Rebecca's there. They keep them to entertain the officers."

A bell hung outside the door of cottage number three marked Women's Quarters. He pulled the string.

"Yes, Colonel, what can we do for you?" The matron, a large woman in uniform, was obviously annoyed at having been roused at that hour.

"Rebecca Meyer?" he asked absently. He pushed by her. She stared at the SS lightning bolts on his lapels.

"Yes, one of our best."

Would Rebecca even remember him? The small hallway leading to the rooms was guarded by a curtain of beaded rope. It rustled like a sudden rain shower, and Rebecca stood in front of him, thin and sallow.

"Andreas," she said softly, she, still a child in many ways. A figment of hope still within withered in front of his eyes. He'd had sex in rubble, in burned-out buildings, with whores. Never had he felt this dirty.

"I am sorry about Ulrich," he stammered, afraid she might start to undress.

"Don't be," she said. "It was a matter of time."

She suddenly burst into tears and turned away...

The matron waited expectantly. "The bed is freshly made."

Laughter, high-pitched and desperate. The room, sparse—a metal bed, a dressing table, a chair, a small clock. On the chair sat a flop-eared rag dog, Rebecca on the edge of the bed. Used, as used as the dog. Her lusterless black hair hung around her face. He put his hands on her shoulders. *How thin they are.*

"Rebecca," Andreas whispered, "I'll get you out of here."

"Where would I go, Andreas? I am a Jewess."

A Jewess. A bitter, unsparing name. There wasn't a part of the earth where the word wasn't a taunt, didn't carry despise and scorn. *But*, he thought with bitterness, *there was a time.*

A cold October day. He was at school. The days were getting shorter. He was on a lane going toward school. Afraid. *Why am I afraid? I should be happy. Soon, I'll see her.*

A bang. A voice clear and crisp. Rebecca billowing into the sunlight, her skirt swirling around her legs and her lips sparkling in the sun. "How could the Lord have created such beauty in a Jewess?" he asked as did the school's headmaster.

"Let him try," said Rebecca. "He'll be missing a few ornaments."

He remembered her defiant "It isn't your problem."

"But it is," he said. "Don't you see?"

"Why?"

"Because you smell of sunlight and sweet grass."

They took the same path from school every day, past the meadow. She put his hand across her breast and unbuttoned her blouse. Her movements were unhurried.

"I want you to be the first," she said, placing his lips to her breast.

"I don't know how," he said.

"I will show you."

The phonograph in the next room startled him. "Du, Du Liegst Mir Im Herzen."

Panicked, he realized he wanted nothing more than to leave, to escape. "Du, Du Liegst Mir Im Sinn." She took his hand, pulled it toward her.

Overcome, he kneeled.

Why? She is innocent.

But are you? the mocker asked.

I'm one man. So was he. It would have been suicide.

And is your life so precious?

Every movement, everything she did caused him pain. He knew they might be her last. He heard himself say, "We will start over. You will see. Everything will be all right."

She smiled, a fearful smile. A shadow, already dead.

This heaviness in the pit of his stomach, in his chest, behind his eyes, a smoldering ash in his throat, his heart, his soul. It dragged, heavy. It was where hell was. He would have died for her, but she was wallpaper.

"You have stayed long enough, Andreas. I'll get credit— you can go," she said, letting go of his hands.

You made the effort, he told himself walking through shadows, hurrying past empty driveways. *What good does it do to wallow in pity? If only that damned dog would stop following me!*

Staggering to his room, he threw himself on the cot. Not able to sleep, he walked to the window to draw back the curtains and pull down the blinds, to shut out the day. If only he had some place to go. The churches were empty. God had left. The dog lifted its head, staring into the black silence.

He counted the days until they were to leave for Calcutta, uncertain whether they would be able to make the climb before war was declared.

He drifted from Berlin to Wiligut listless, his stomach churning. Anxious to get under way, he decided to accept the invitation to Göring's anniversary party at his palatial manor house in Charlottenberg only a few kilometers from the concentration camp at Oranienburg.

Chapter 34
Göring's Estate, Carinhall, Charlottenberg, Germany

Music by Strauss and Lehar and the tinkling of champagne glasses filled the room. An army of waiters scurried down corridors into salons, emptying ashtrays and serving bits of cold food wrapped around toothpicks, black uniforms with gold ribbons, rich, mellow voices.

Göring's second wife, formerly Sonnemann, had been an actress, and there were a number of show people at the party—most of them Jewish. Having paid Göring for their exit visas, they were considerably poorer than they had been a few hours earlier. But at least they would escape with their lives.

"Amy Trotman did make it out, but it cost her most of her savings. Exit visas are not cheap, you know."

"What's going to happen when the visas dry up?" a short, mustached man asked. "All these Jewish actresses will have to make do, won't they?" He leered.

"This latest accord between Hitler and Stalin to divide Poland means war. France and Britain are committed by treaty to Poland's defense. War has to be the result," said a particularly officious gentleman. "Then they can be had for nothing."

"The British will find a way to back out," said another. "In the end, it won't matter, won't interfere with the season, and certainly not with our vacation in Deauville. In fact, it should be the gayest season ever. Look around you. Germans and British alike have never been happier, never more carefree."

"It certainly won't interfere with our, or his, profits," said a meticulously attired gentleman running one hand over his glistening pomaded hair and clicking his false teeth while pointing to a man in white tie and tails.

Andreas had seen him before, an art dealer who supplied Göring with treasures—extorted from the Jews. Approaching him, he asked, "Do you feel it? I mean, there's something very strange going on."

"No, not yet. The nude boys and the white horses will come later when everyone has had a little more to drink."

"There's certainly excitement in the air," said Andreas.

"Not so strange," the art dealer answered. "There is the same excitement before hangings."

Andreas felt a tug on his arm. She had wandered around the room, her eyes on Andreas for the longest time, trying to decide if she wanted to open an old wound. Finally, she'd screwed up her courage, decided, and had come up beside him.

"It's been a long time," said Mrs. Bose, pressing her body full against his. He knew Diana has been invited but hadn't seen her. *Why do I care? She obviously doesn't. And it would be good to make Diana jealous.*

The music started. Andreas bowed and extended his arm. He felt transported back in time, to India, the glorious days of the British raj. She brimmed with girlish laughter. He, the handsome colonel in a Hollywood film, would return to his regiment and be mortally wounded in a cavalry charge. She would weep over him for the rest of her life. Kongdzengchenga seemed far away.

They whirled onto the dance floor. His feet were light; his heart beat faster, and the room spun. Out of breath, he stood close to her aware of the glitter in her eye and her flushed cheeks.

She looked into his face. *Do you love him? There is so much that separates you.* Determined not to worry, she would leave it to dharma to decide.

Andreas saw the question in her eyes. "Can I get you a champagne?" he asked, leaning against a banister, a defense against the rush of idle conversation. Then just as suddenly, the moment vanished. She was behaving like a schoolgirl. Andreas would never love; he was already married—to himself and his ridiculous quest for that weapon. *Well, so be it. The fates have willed.*

"I'd like a whiskey and soda. To hell with this champagne."

They moved onto the veranda. It was a cool, starless night with the threat of rain. Andreas removed his jacket and slid it over Devi's shoulders. As she turned toward him, he bent forward and kissed her.

"Andreas," she began, reaching for him, tears forming in the corners of her eyes.

"Devi," he interrupted, "there's something I have to say—should have said a long time ago."

Hurriedly, she put him off. "No, Andreas, there isn't any need. We are very much alike. I don't want a husband, and you don't want a wife. That leaves us free. Let us leave it that way. For a moment, I let my imagination run away with me. We are too much in love with illusions to have time for love. Lancelot and Arthur are your kind of love, Kali and Shiva mine. All illusions."

Her chin raised, she arranged her sari. "I think it's stopped raining. Would you mind getting my wrap?"

"Why are you going to make the climb?" Andreas asked as they left the ballroom. "It's suicide." He followed the hollow click of her heels on the marble stairs.

"I always do what people say I shouldn't. It's the story of my life. Besides, it's only to first base camp."

"Even that's sixteen thousand feet."

"India, Tibet, they are my countries, they are not Britain's or Germany's." Her face was a mixture of antagonism and remorse. "It's as if someone is daring me, as if all of India is daring me. I'm sorry to be such a spoiler." She shrugged. "I just don't feel like partying."

You are young and beautiful, and your flesh is soft, and there is so little time, he thought.

She stopped at the bottom of the stairs. "Andreas, you are fighting a devil only you know."

"I am fighting my own demon as old as India itself."

"Please, Andreas, don't interrupt me. I may not get the courage to say this again. We refuse to see the truth. We are selfish, you and I … We must be selfish to win. Christ knew that: 'Your enemies shall be of your own household.' You must demand total allegiance. If you want to be God, don't talk to him or worship him. Be him. That is why I admire Hitler. If you are to be God, you can suffer no one else in the room. All must be sacrificed. There can be no time for love."

At that moment, Inspector Oberman was sitting in a library in Sienna, Italy, poring over manuscripts—in particular, one of a German major, Hans Heydrich. He smiled having found what he had been looking for. The major in his distant past was rumored to have had a Jewish great-grandmother and subsequently to have married a Jew. Heydrich had wiped his boots clean, but not all. He left the library. Getting into his Citroën, he drove to his farm in Vico d'Arbia just outside the city.

The sun had set, the wind had subsided, and a pleasant breeze brushed against him. He walked toward a small grape arbor. A sudden gust of wind shook the arbor, rattled the windows, and hurled leaves, dirt, pebbles. As suddenly as it had risen, it ceased.

The inspector sat back. Searching his pockets, he found his pipe. Carefully filling it, he studied the leaves collected at his feet and the sun filtering through the bare branches. "There are more things in heaven and earth than are dreamt in your philosophy," he said aloud with a satisfied smile.

Chapter 35
Cairo, Egypt

"HAD I KNOWN OF thy coming, I would have poured thee my own heart's blood or the blackness from my eyes. I am alone even in the depths of loving you," he whispered.

Tara's plane had taken her to Cairo; from there, she had taken a taxi across the Al Ahram Bridge to her lover's apartment.

"At last the queen of the desert has come home," said Hassam, closing the door to the apartment and slipping naked into bed beside her. "It has been a long time. You are changed, but not your beauty. How can such beauty exist with such wickedness?"

Her eyes flashing out of the dark caught and held his. Light filtered through the windows, bright and destructive, devouring all color and leaving the room white.

"The unfathomable thing that comes alive when lying next to a woman, is that truly love?" Hassam asked, stiff as a plank and pulling the blinds.

"I love you dearly. Not now. Make me a drink," she answered.

He slid from the divan, his erection subsiding.

"Gin and lime juice?"

Tara nodded, and he proceeded to make the drink. "Be warned," Hassam said. "This man you are going to see, Khalid Rashid, the leader of the Shammara tribe, is a viper. But he is the only one powerful enough to unite the tribes," he said, searching the icebox.

"What are you looking for?" she asked.

"This," he said, lifting a tray of ice.

She inhaled as the ice slid between her legs. "Hassam, I said no."

He followed the melting cube with his tongue.

"Where did you learn that?" she asked, her breath still labored.

He took a cigarette and rolled onto his back, listening to Cairo, a painful smile forming at the corners of his mouth. "You can seduce me with your beauty, but you will not seduce the Arabs. Never again. Lawrence, lying next to me just as you are now, made the same promises. Göring will never give us the oil. As it is written, 'Fear you not, nor grieve … but receive the glad tidings.' Paradise is under the shade of swords. Death is a welcome release. There is no deed in this life that can equal jihad."

Chapter 36
Arabian Desert, 1938

TARA LEFT FOR HER meeting with Rashid. For two days, she and her guide had been traveling in an amorphous magma of sand and heat under a sheet of ash-colored sky. Her camel began to grunt and bray.

"Quickly, wrap your kufiyah about you," her guide said. "Whatever happens, do not stop. Keep moving."

The dust storm enveloped them. Grit cut into her skin and filled her nose and mouth. It took only a moment for the sand to drift up to the camel's knees. As quickly as it started, the wailing died. Groping for her flask, she shook it, turned it to her lips, drank, and spat away sand.

She awoke under a white sky. The cool night air playing on her legs. She turned her head toward the only light, a fire burning in a large pit in the center of the tent.

He sprang out of the edge of the shadow. His voice rich and deep, his face shaped like a flint narrowed to a pointed goatee. Kneeling, he took her hand and brushed it with his lips.

"I am Khalid Rashid," he said proudly. "We have been expecting you. When you didn't arrive, I and my men started out to look for you." His black eyes burned into her. "Your beauty exceeds even what I've been told," he said. His face lit by the fire, he kneeled in front of her. "I will not waste time. I will speak plainly. You are here because you hate the Jews, and Göring hates them too, yes?" he said, stirring the fire. "Just what is it that you hate about them?" he asked, suddenly holding the red-hot tip of a stiletto beneath her throat.

"The murder and the torture of innocent people."

"And so you wish to atone for their suffering by being a martyr?" He smiled, fingering the hot point of his knife. "Or have you decided to join in?" He wiped the stiletto across his leather boot. "No matter. You see, I don't hate the Jews. Perhaps a few Zionists. The Jews have made me a rich man. Without them, I would still be a poor leader of nomads. The Jews have made me my brother's keeper. I provide the guns. And the Jews and the British ignore the trade—opium for guns. The British look the other way because they think the guns will be used to shoot Arabs. The Arabs think the guns will be used to kill the British and Jews. And so, a pretty penny is made by all," he said with a broad smile. "Soon, the Arabs will realize that no matter who wins, promises won't be kept. Then the rush for control of the oil will begin in earnest."

Rashid stood, magnificent, almost regal, in his colorful robes and silk turban, a German automatic pistol tucked in his sash. "We Arabs live under one tent and share the same pasture, but we have been strangers to one another. Though we may turn against each other for profit, we will never turn against Allah. That's the difference. If the day comes when we are united in Allah, the Crusades will look like child's play.

"The Jews want my homeland. Why? Not because it is sacred but because it has oil under it. We Arabs are like a large family. The Jews have a long history much like ours. That is why we hate with such passion and why this war, once started, will never end. It will usher a new kind of war—terror—when a single man and his interpretation of God's will become the instrument of God's justice. So tell me, what do you get out of it?"

She considered how much to tell him, how much he already knew.

"Oil," she said, "We get control of the oil."

"Don't play with me. And Hitler's head?"

She smiled. "I will deliver it personally."

Outside the tent, the men ate toasted locusts and gossiped. The camels chewed desert rabia. The women set the tent poles, washed the clothes, prepared the meals. The men drank tea.

In kaftan and sandals, Rashid heaved the heavy bag into the rear seat and drove the undulating road past squat villages and fortifications and on to the Mediterranean. He approached a watchtower surrounded by barbed wire.

"Welcome, Rashid." The figure's face and neck were covered by his kufiyah.

"Where are they?"

"In the tunnel."

A hole in the side of the mountain, the tunnel had not seen a drop of moisture, and the dust, stench, and heat were overwhelming. A shadow uncoiled from the floor of the tunnel. His eyes were sealed with a gray film. He was blind.

"What is the name of the man you want us to assassinate?" the blind man asked.

"Adolph Hitler. I don't think you are acquainted with the second one, a Mr. de Signac," Rashid answered.

"Why do you want us to kill him?"

"That's none of your business. Let us just say we want him dead. That's all you need to know," Rashid said, pointing to the gold.

"We never kill unless we know the circumstances," said the blind man. "Why don't you kill him yourself?"

"If it were up to me, I would, but Himmler wants you to do it," said Rashid. "Look, if you want the money, kill them. Leave lots of clues that you were behind it. That's the only reason we are not doing it ourselves. We don't want the British to suspect we are involved. If you don't kill him, I will. For that kind of money, I'd kill Christ."

A moment of anger flickered across the old man's face only to be quickly replaced by a smile. "So it shall be," the old man said.

"I thought so," Rashid answered. "So long as you are happy."

"Where?" the old man asked.

"De Signac will be on a boat, the *Raphael*, in the harbor in Alexandria. We want his ring finger—with the ring attached. Hitler is up to you."

"An unusual request. Heads, other more personal parts, but a finger?"

"Let's say it has an emotional attachment."

The old man shrugged. "It is your money."

"I'll meet you in the harbor before you board," the old man said, his smile growing to a grin. "I'll have someone there who will take good care of you."

"As long as we have the finger," Rashid said.

Rashid watched the valley drop away as he drove toward Askelon. He stopped at the post office and retrieved a message from Colonel Heydrich detailing the course for the *Calypso*, a Greek freighter sailing from Piraeus. Rashid read the letter from Heydrich, tore it up, and flushed it into the wind. Crusades. Assassins. De Signac would not make it off the boat.

Chapter 37
Heydrich's Apartment, Max Ebert Strasse, Berlin

"What can I do for you, Monsieur de Signac?" Heydrich asked.

De Signac had managed his disguise well. He leaned forward and fixed Heydrich with his small, blue eyes.

"You can speak in confidence," Heydrich said, trying to conceal his amusement.

"It's more what I can do for you," said de Signac, twisting a large ring on his index finger.

Pompous ass, Heydrich thought. *Ought to shoot the pygmy here and now. Save the Reich some trouble.* Heydrich hesitated. There was something about him that was familiar. He had seen him before—in the circus. He smiled. *Where do I put the first bullet?*

De Signac continued. "It was my ancestors who doled out pardons to the Knights Templar and Roman centurions and who might remember where certain articles of treasure were buried, such as the sword that pierced Christ's side and the blood that burned and set fire to the trees."

Heydrich slid the pistol back and waited. "Please go on," he said, not exhibiting the faintest interest.

De Signac was shaking with fear but managed to continue. "It was my ancestors who ordered the Jews arrested. Many were guards under Herod."

De Signac was trembling, but he managed to maintain a semblance of calm. So far, things had gone well, as planned, and the immediate danger had passed.

"If you are thinking of killing me, forget it," de Signac said. "Why go to the trouble?" His eyes moved rapidly from the gun to Heydrich.

"It's you who doesn't understand," said Heydrich. "There are no promises on Kongdzengchenga only ice, snow, and death. We will let the devil decide. I'll talk it over with Herr Himmler."

De Signac was no more out the door than the telephone rang.

"Yes sir, everything has been arranged. He won't make it off the boat."

Chapter 38
Paris, 1938

OUT OF THE BLUE, Diana called. She had to get away or go mad. The tapestries smelled of mold, the plaster was peeling. "Bellows Castle has become depressing and a bloody bore." Behind the complaints, there was desperation.

"Father may be arrested for treason. I must get away, Paris, somewhere gay and romantic."

March in Paris? He asked himself. *Wet, cold, and rainy.*

"Well, it's almost April," she said with a laugh. "You and I have never been away together. Take me to Paris."

Jesus, Paris of all places, Andreas thought. *With war about to break out any minute.* But he knew people were still traveling to France, to Deauville, to St. Tropez for the season. After Munich, things had returned to normal and the French to their main amusements.

"Do you realize what you're asking? We will be going right into the eye of the storm."

"That's why I want to go," said Diana. "It will test our love."

She was still a spoiled little girl, but he could tell it was important to her. And they could manage it, and he wanted to see her. If their love was still alive even the faintest spark, it would be reincarnated in Paris. Just a slight alteration in his passport.

Diana, desperately alone, had fallen in love like an actress, with the words, with the sense of love. She had reread the novels of George Sand and Victor Hugo and the poetry of Byron and Shelley. Love, true love, was the salt that would return flavor to her bitter world.

"I'll meet you under the Eiffel Tower! It's where all lovers meet," she declared. "Oh, and I have something important to tell you."

That certainly hadn't been his experience. She probably got it from some movie, he thought correctly.

Five days later, Andreas boarded the train for Paris. There was only one other person in his compartment. Huddled in his coat, his traveling companion furtively glanced around and fixed his stare on his shoes. Andreas introduced himself, and the man replied that his name was Allard Weinberg, traveling on business. Andreas felt that he had seen him before. *But where?*

"Do you have a match?" Andreas asked.

"I have a lighter," said Allard.

It was gold, engraved with the German imperial seal. He declined a cigarette with a wave of his hand.

"Are you going on from Paris?" Andreas asked.

"No."

Men in black uniforms started to walk through the cars "Passport control for France. All passports please." Weinberg took an enormous handkerchief and wiped the sweat that had broken out on his face. He reached into his attaché case for his passport, dropped it. Andreas reached over and picked it up. It fell open; "Saul A. Weinberg" was clearly typed under the photograph. *Of course. The Jew and the chorus girl.* Although Mr. Weinberg had taken the precaution of using Allard, his middle name, and wearing a wig for the photograph, it was clear that he was a Jew.

They arrived at the Gare du Nord and passed through customs without difficulty. Andreas, his eyes meeting Allard's, said goodbye, and he went to meet Diana under the Eiffel Tower. It had started to drizzle. Andreas bought an umbrella. It bulged like a large jellyfish with pointed ends and let the rain fall straight down so that he carried his own puddle with him. Arriving, he put it over her, and she threw her arms around him. She was pale, and when she pulled away, he saw tears in her eyes.

An older woman moved toward them. She carried a small bunch of violets, and there were several more in a basket. Stepping over dirty water filtering past the cobblestones, she stopped and pointed at a pin she wore on her sweater. Andreas had seen many pins like it, medals worn for fallen soldiers.

"My son," she said, pointing to the medal, "at Ypres in Flanders. Jacques would be only thirty today."

Jacques had been killed by machine-gun fire in the Great War; he hadn't lived to see the tables swarming with chic people, nor had he a tryst along the Seine.

Men and women drifted past and disappeared into nooks or simply made love on the steps.

Diana tired quickly. Several times, she started to speak, searching for the words that would dispel guilt. After all, it was a question of responsibility. She grew angry but was determined to see it through. It was Andreas's child, his responsibility. He had taken advantage of her. She insisted on blaming him though it might also kill any chance they had for a future. Sooner or later, their love would dissolve into boredom and blame as it had with Sloat. *I want you to prove you love me*, she thought, fingering the small medallion Andreas had purchased from the old woman on the Place Vendôme. "For myself, me, damn it, not because you owe me."

Andreas turned to her. "What did you say?"

"Nothing, Andreas," said Diana.

They walked past the Pont Neuf, and he suggested they take one of the barges down the Seine. They boarded at the quay near the Place des Invalides. Words repeated in whispers along the banks—*Je t'aime, Au revoir*—carried in the mist. All over Paris, men and women were saying, *Je t'aime, Au revoir!*

The barge drifted quietly. Huddled against the city and the past, no one was interested in the monuments. Diana rested her head on Andreas's shoulder. A war seemed far away.

Two days later, they stood on the station platform. It had been a glorious weekend. Diana lifted her face and kissed Andreas, attempting to hang onto the dream. Saying goodbye, she decided to say goodbye to her sadness as well. She would not tell him she was pregnant.

Andreas refused to deal with Diana's possible pregnancy. After all, she was the one who should have taken precautions, and she should get rid of it. All it would have taken was a coat hanger. If she chose to play the mother, that was her problem. He'd be happy to pay.

Despite himself, Andreas dreamed about his meeting with the old violet seller many times, remembering and hoping to find the reason for her quiet dignity, each time waking in a cold sweat.

It was four o'clock. He'd been up for hours. The train didn't leave until six. The lines from "April in Paris" running through his head, he walked down the Champs Élysées and again to the Pont Neuf. Leaning over the wall, he stared into the Seine flowing as it had for centuries, carrying the words of lovers, at times blending with the disappointment of discarded love.

Diana had kissed him goodbye preferring he not go to the airport. She had kissed him and said goodbye in such a strange way—as if it were forever and with a strange calmness as if she'd decided and was no longer troubled. He stared into the river, his thoughts shrouded in darkness as if expecting it to wash away his uncertainty.

An organ grinder squeezed out the last bars of "April in Paris." And the silence was lonely and sad. Diana was very much her own person, had barely mentioned her pregnancy. She welcomed it and didn't need his approval, help, or love. She would make it without him.

The organ grinder started to play "April in Paris" again, thinking Andreas was a distraught lover. The lemon-yellow melody drifted over the river, over the chestnut blossoms, over the tanks and lorries making their way to Belgium. They knew the way. They had traveled the same road only twenty years previously.

Andreas sipped his vermouth while a faint breeze played with the heat and the river. He didn't know where his love for Diana was going. Knew only that it was impossible to go on this way. His thoughts were interrupted by two lovers strolling arm in arm, secure and certain. If only he knew which options were real and which were imagined. The climb was real; there was no way he could get out of that. The Jews and the uranium—whether real or ghosts—had to be dealt with. He went down the steps to the river. Bending forward, he saw his face reflected in the stream. A gust of wind blew, and he saw his choices clearly. Bowing to the organ grinder and slipping him a handsome tip, he hailed a taxi.

Diana was the key. Everything else would fall into place. He was sure of it. He would call her and tell her he loved her, settle the whole thing. Why had it taken so long for him to realize?

When a week after her return to England Andreas had still not called, Diana decided to immerse herself in her own world, Bellows Castle. She derived a sort of perverse pleasure hoping Andreas was being eaten by his worry. How could he not know? He was a doctor.

Chapter 39
Kreuzberg, Berlin

THEY HAD DRIVEN TO a working-class neighborhood and stopped in front of a small stucco house. Heydrich felt the familiar knot in his stomach; staring into the woman's eyes, he fought to sort out his emotions.

She smelled of breakfast. Her hair was greasy, her short white sox that barely covered her ankles were yellowed from many washings, and her shoes needed mending. A woman who all her life had lived in stories of imagined heroes and castles only to find herself in torn clothes with a sink full of dirty dishes and a bellowing, unshaven man for her husband. Despite his constant yelling and threats, she still carried within her the dreams of girlhood romance. There was something admirable in his devotion and refusal to accept defeat. And she loved him.

She threw her arms around her son's neck. She and Heydrich stepped apart.

"You look thinner," he stammered, the words barely audible. His eyes were moist, the smell of waxed linoleum strong in his nostrils. "Has the abscess come back?" he asked.

Her husband, Heydrich's father, was close to seventy and nursed an old injury acquired in the first war. With one swift movement, he wheeled in front of his son. He was the man Heydrich had come to see.

"Father," he said, searching his face, trying to discover the virile young man who had dominated the house with his tirades, who seemed never at rest, who called him "boy," who would hover over his wife, his face contorted with rage. The man who would at other times hug her as if to squeeze the breath out of her, who took them on Sunday picnics, and who could swim the breadth of Lake Wannsee.

He wheezed, and his bull-like head seemed to sink into his neck. His arms hung limply by the side of the wheelchair. It was as if time had stood still. The wheelchair rattling across the floor broke his thoughts. It came to rest in front of the dining room window. His eyes burned with hate. He gripped the wheelchair as if it were a primeval beast and wheeled around to face Heydrich. "Look!" he shouted. "Look at what your sacrifice has brought! Peace, a woman's peace! A surrender engineered by the Jews. We had beaten them. All we needed was a little more time." It was the same story that Heydrich had heard many times since the end of the Great War.

"Father, that was long ago." He placed a hand on his father's shoulder as if to steady them both. He stopped shaking.

"We will beat them this time. And our victory will not be undermined by the Jews, the homosexuals, or the Gypsies. There won't be any of them left. Racial purity is the only way to guard against them. Break them—the polluters who shred our civilization with words. Equality! A poison that violates honor. Life is a battle from the moment you first reach for your mother's teat. Only the fittest survive." He gripped the chair and whirled toward the window, his Iron Cross catching the last of the evening's light. His face gray, his features silent and remote—listening to the stillness of battle, the stillness of death.

His wife smiled. She had lived with his illness, had endured his agony. Prying loose his hand, she gripped it in hers. His face relaxed at her touch, and she kissed his forehead.

"I remember you," she said, looking into his gray eyes. "I remember your poems and stories before you … before you said goodbye."

As if the effort to understand had drained him to his very soul, he slumped into the chair.

"How can you put up with it?" Heydrich asked.

"I will worry when it stops," she said with a wan smile. "The silence, the loneliness. That is what worries me."

Traveling back to Berlin, Heydrich's car was forced to slow to a crawl. On the seat next to him were his birth records. *Thank God she had saved them.* Everyone—even Göring and Goebbels—had had to prove they were Aryan. Or at least not Jewish.

The streets teemed with newspaper boys hawking a story: "Attempted Assassination of Hitler!" He bought a copy of the *Berliner Zeitung.* He'd known the coup was near but nothing more. He'd refused to join. Martial law had been declared. The army waited. Neither Himmler nor Göring was strong enough to seize power with Hitler still alive. *Just stick to your job and keep your head down. It will depend on whether Hitler lives and which way the army goes.*

Andreas decided the best place to hide would be in his own flat. He had had nothing to do with the whole business. No matter which way it went, he would remain a bystander.

Chapter 40
Schloss Bellevue, Bismarkstrasse, Berlin, December

THERE WAS A SOFT knock on the door. It had been a week since his induction. He had given the driver the night off. Reluctantly, Andreas got out of his chair and went to the door. There was no one there. He stepped into the hall—still no one. He returned to his room and resumed his reading. Another knock. This time, angry, he stormed to the door. He barely recognized the man facing him—von Kaltenbrun, his uniform disheveled and spattered with blood. fell into the room.

"I had no place else to go. The putsch has collapsed. Himmler and Göring have already seized control. Most of us are already in prison."

"At least Louisa and Ulrika are safe in England," said Andreas.

Tears forming in the corners of his eyes, Allard looked at Andreas.

"Don't tell me they are still in Berlin."

"Ulrika refused to go, to give up her parties," said

Allard. "They will find me soon. I'm going to make it easy for them. I know you didn't want any part of this, but you are part of it, all of Germany's part of it. Do what you can to help them."

"What about Manfred?" asked Andreas.

"He was a plant, a spy," said von Kaltenbrun. "He never intended to marry Louisa."

"I don't know what I can do," said Andreas.

"Please, do whatever you can," said von Kaltenbrun, gripping Andreas tightly by both arms.

Andreas watched him lurch out onto the street. As two men started to approach him from the opposite side of the street, he put his hand in his coat pocket, pulled out his revolver, put it to his head, and pulled the trigger. Andreas, shaken, returned to his chair. Von Kaltenbrun was a fool, an anachronism. His Germany had long since passed. He had warned him, told him he wanted no part in it. It wasn't his problem.

Andreas awoke in a cold sweat. He decided to at least walk by von Kaltenbrun's city address, Wittenbergplatz, not far from the Gedachtnis Kirche. When he arrived, it was too late. They stood guard on the house. Presumably, Louisa and Ulrika had already been taken away.

The phone call was from Heydrich. "I thought you'd like to know your old friends are going to be our guests at the women's dormitory—Wiligut."

Andreas dressed and once again found himself in front of the women's dormitory. Once again turning his face into his coat against the pinch of the wind and snow. Waiting, his mind wandering, lost in the waning December day. This would be the end. Her parents could not protect her.

Her father's cold, artificial hand, his medals, the Iron Cross, the photographs of dead ancestors were like pages from an advertisement.

He shrugged. It wasn't his affair. He could have told her that Von Gonten was a phony. His good sense had saved him again. It wasn't his affair.

He pulled the string and rang the bell. The same old lady answered, the same evil smile on her face.

"Rebecca is no longer with us," she said.

"Get out of my way. I'm here to see Luisa von Kaltenbrun."

"Yes, of course. A fresh flower—never picked. You will be the first. Come with me."

She led him through the same beaded curtains, up the same stairs, and into a familiar room.

Louisa was curled in a ball, shaking and sobbing. Naked, she clutched a thin pillow to her breast. Her skin against the green bedcovers appeared sallow and lifeless. *Dead*, thought Andreas. Rebecca, a Jewess, and Louisa, a German general's daughter—both dead. Louisa threw her arms around Andreas. She was warm—warm and innocent. He could see only too clearly what would follow.

"Please get me out of here!" she pleaded.

"Of course," he whispered gently. He picked up the pillow and placed it between them as though attempting to preserve her decency. The sound of the Luger was muffled by the pillow. She sank to the floor. He covered her and was about to leave when he felt a hand on his shoulder and a whisper: "Be careful! None of it is your responsibility."

As Andreas suspected, things returned to normal except for extraordinary security. Letters were opened, phones tapped, informants were everywhere.

It happened so quickly. He barely recalled getting back to Wiligut Castle. Two men in SS uniforms came for him; his head was shaved, and he was dressed in a white tunic, led outside and down a circular stairway. The stairs were lined with black uniforms, men chanting the triumphal march from Wagner's *Tannhäuser*. Their boots thudded on the stairs, keeping time. Then there was blood, so much blood, everywhere, and McDonald was standing over him.

Andreas let the phone ring, unable to face the effort it would have taken to answer. It had been a week since the initiation, a week since he'd been moved to his quarters off Bismarck Strasse for "observation."

McDonald should have let me commit suicide. Since his discharge from the hospital, a black car had parked across the street from his flat. He didn't care. He examined the rug on the floor and checked under the floorboard where he had hidden the amber. He'd had too much to drink and was drinking more.

He ignored the insistent knock at the door. *It's that fucking priest again.* Andreas had visited the church often following his initiation and attempted suicide. He had found solace in the light spreading into the vaulted ceiling, over the empty pews, and in the palpable, incense-laden air. But most of all, he wanted to hear the choir. Somewhere there was a choir, "Populous Meus, Sanctus Deus, Sanctus Fortis, Sanctus Immortalis," echoing into the spires as majestically as they did in the highest mountains. He vaguely remembered those words as if from a former life.

The church was empty, empty even of the choir. But if one listened carefully, one might have heard, could have heard, the brook bubbling under the sacristy and the blood dripping into the holy water. "Do you hear it, Father?" Andreas asked, dipping his fingers into the holy water.

"Wash yourself of yourself."

"But I can't get clean, Father," he said, "no matter how much I wash."

After his attempted suicide, Andreas had agreed to see the priest every day as part of his medical treatment. But there were days when he refused.

"Don't you believe in God?" the priest would ask.

"No."

"Without God, there is no hope of redemption."

"Redemption? You mean the way they saved him?" he asked, pointing to the crucifix. "I would have nothing but contempt for the God who would forgive me. Just as I would for the God who would ask me to forgive him."

"There's always a path to forgiveness, to another life."

"If there is an afterlife," said Andreas, "and if I have anything to say about it, it won't start with a show-stopper crucifixion or with original sin."

Andreas silently slipped away from the priest, out of the church, and onto the Strasse des 17 Juni. It was dusk, and the avenue was crowded. People shopped and held their hats against the wind. As he strolled, he was held spellbound by a small figure on the opposite side of the street. The next thing he knew, he was seated in a pew across from the priest recounting his strange encounter.

For the first, time the priest saw a glimmer of hope. Andreas was at peace—even cheerful.

"She was standing in front of the candy store, Father. She was shivering. She had on only a ragged sweater. Her stockings were threadbare. I thought she was an orphan. I stretched out my palm. She didn't move." The girl sat silently beside him, tightly clutching a small stuffed animal and looking up at Andreas with burning, coal-dark eyes.

"I said hello, but she didn't smile. Then I said, 'Come with me,' and I led her into the shop."

Andreas paused and looked down at the child sitting next to him, her eyes still focused on her rag doll and the face of the young priest.

"'You have arrived at last—almost too late,' the shopkeeper said. "I saw you out there. I thought you would never come in. There's still time before I close." He swept his hand over the trays of gold, green, red, and pink candies. "We have everything—ruby beetles, fireflies from Samarkand, emerald butterflies from Burma, gold-and-silver-striped canes, lovely amber chocolate." He swayed over them like a large jinni. The display cases sparkled, but the girl didn't answer; her gaze was riveted on a rag dog with a large black circle around one eye.

"'Let me have the dog,' I said to the shopkeeper. 'No, don't wrap it.' Then I placed it in the girl's hands and put my jacket over her shoulders. What should I do with her? When I next looked up, the store was closed and the lights were out. Father, that's the whole of it. It was like a dream."

The priest smiled kindly, recalling how just a week before Andreas had asked him to bury a body that was nothing more than an empty sack of straw.

"I am going to save this child, Father, and you are going to help me."

"Kyrie eleison," the priest murmured.

How to tell him? She, like so many other abandoned children, was probably Jewish. He wouldn't be able to hide her for long.

The priest lifted both hands toward the vaulted darkness. "Yes, she is real, Andreas," he murmured.

"Exactly, Father," Andreas said. "With God's help. His salvation is to let me save this one child."

"Would you like some hot chocolate?" the priest asked as he took the child's hand and led her down the aisle to the sacristy.

Andreas returned to his flat feeling as though he had been reborn. There, waiting, was a telegram from Diana. "Phones tapped. Am followed everywhere. Prisoner in my own house. Father is returning to Berlin next week. Doubt if he will be allowed back to England."

Diana decided to take the issue into her own hands; she would tell him how much she loved him, but not of the child growing inside her, his child.

She would not have him indebted to her. She stepped out of the shadows, trim in a close-fitting gray suit, fur wrap, and cloche. It was five o'clock on a Wednesday in May. It felt like winter. With tears in her eyes, she walked toward Andreas, the clop of horse drawn horses, muffled. Not many sight- seers on such a raw day, Andreas thought, as he approached her. He couldn't help noticing that she had put on a few pounds and that her usually trim waistline had a small bulge. He could see the worry in her face. Morally, I should go to her, take responsibility. But.! There's always a but when you're concerned, he thought. But how can I? I'm not going to make it off the mountain. How can I tell her? "It is your child. Take responsibility!" came the answer, swift and sure

"Any spies around?" he asked with a warm smile.

"It's no joking matter, Andreas. That man, the one reading the newspaper, has been following me all day. Father has gone over to the Germans. He's scheduled a radio address for Saturday. MI5 is planning to arrest him if he puts one foot in England."

"That makes you a pawn for both sides," he said.

"They wouldn't dare arrest me, though I'm just as much a prisoner. I'm traveling courtesy of Göring. We are dead broke." Andreas looked at the gold and diamonds dripping from her wrist. What Diana considered dead broke would take care of him for some time. She wore a small medallion on her jacket.

"A girl's best friend," she quipped. "I cleaned out the safe-deposit box. Everything I own is on my wrist. These go last. Göring pretty much owns Bellows Manor. I would let him have it, but," she hesitated, "my son is buried there."

Andreas took her hands in his, and leaning forward, told her about his visit to the church and the girl he had found wandering the streets.

Diana too had constructed a splendid vision: Andreas and a new life. "And this miracle, Andreas, does it come with a father and a mother? Who will be responsible? Who will care for her, love her, while you are away chasing a dream? Take me with you. Start over. We can find someplace where they haven't heard of this ridiculous sword."

His face grew pale. The reasons for avoiding her love were suddenly clear. There would be no exceptions, no safe houses. The blood-laden snow would fall and the boots would march. The rhythm and stomp." Tomorrow belongs to"—the Sturmabteilung, the sound of the past, present, and future marching into every cranny of life.

"Diana, I would never leave you. I will always come back for you," he said. He took her hands in his and led her to a nearby bench.

At Andreas's urging, Diana agreed to visit the church, half expecting it to be empty. At her knees was a dark-eyed eight-year-old girl, her stuffed pet tucked warmly under one arm. Diana listened to the priest's story.

"Andreas may have been mad when he came to the sacristy but yet saner than I have ever seen him," the priest said.

"What's her name?" Diana asked.

"Saskia," the priest said. "We won't be able to keep her much longer."

Diana looked away, and then rising, approached the girl, who had moved to another pew to play with her rag doll. Taking her hand, she said, "Say goodbye to Father Rizzoli. We are going home."

Chapter 41
Piraeus, Greece

DE SIGNAC LOOKED OUT the window at the stanchions, the advertisements plastered on the tenements highlighted by intermittent sparks and framed by alleys and walls. His reflection in the compartment window was lit by the overhead light as it flashed on and off with the rocking of the train. Intent with his ring, he twisted and pulled at it, wincing as each twist drew blood. The ring, Andreas thought, would leave only with the finger.

De Signac had traced the ring almost as far as the Crucifixion. At the time of Christ's Crucifixion, Eusebius de Signac was legal counsel to the Roman court—in particular, to Pontius Pilate. The disposition of Christ's remains was his responsibility, and he carried it out scrupulously—always keeping a little for himself, he'd found the cup lying among the debris on Golgotha. After the mob had scattered, after the storm, and after Jesus' blood had ceased dripping from the wound in his side, the blood—rose red—had solidified.

Eusebius wondered and wrote in his diary, "Had his blood been shed for Magdalen or Mary?"

Quietly, he'd had the stone made into a ring. When Eusebius tried the ring, however, he found that once on, it would not come off. And so it and the fingers that wore it had been bequeathed from generation to generation. De Signacs through the centuries had decided that the safest way to carry such a precious relic was to wear it.

After all, a finger was a small price to pay. Guy de Signac knew he was playing for more than his finger—his life. No longer sheltered by crosses and prayers, it was time to get rid of the ring even at the cost of his finger There was no alternative. He had grown tired of looking around corners into doorways. It was time to get rid of the ring.

He was confident he would get a good price, a fabulous price! After all, Herr Heydrich had insisted, "Money is no problem." But for safekeeping, he'd rather de Signac wear the ring. He was getting a trip to Cairo, all expenses paid. Why should he care? Contemplating the dining car menu and his taut waistcoat, he leaned back in his seat, unbuttoned the waistcoat, and drifted to sleep.

The two chess players in the compartment across from theirs had reached an impasse. The rest of the climbers were in the dining car playing cards.

"Piraeus. Next stop Piraeus." The conductor passed by the compartment followed by porters with the luggage. The train ground and jarred to a halt; squeaking and groaning, it lurched backward. Andreas rose. Checking under his seat, he found his bag and started forward. Climbers were assembled at one end of the car in various degrees of boredom.

Amid yawns and mumblings, they shuffled toward the exit. Andreas stepped onto the platform into a cold drizzle and was almost immediately greeted by a large, dark man in a wool sweater with enormous hands, a bull chest, and a smile that stretched across a face beaten and weathered by wind and salt. Andreas liked him from the start. He was the sort who would lie and cheat but always with a smile and a sense that if he sinned, he could be made pure at the cost of a coin in the confession box.

Captain Stavros Stephanidis herded the climbers aboard an old military transit, and with Andreas seated beside him in the cabin, they drove the short distance to the Piraeus dock. There, the truck jolted to a stop, and they disembarked at an aged freighter, its hard life evident from its rusting hull. The captain's sweater was pungent with lanolin and salt. He led them below into a hold that stank of seaweed and diesel.

"Hope you don't mind my asking," said Andreas, "*Calypso*?"

They were in the captain's cabin drinking strong black coffee. Above, the crew was getting ready to get underway. The captain smiled. "She used to sail the southern circuit—rum running, mostly. Was beached in a hurricane off Tortola. I picked her up for salvage costs and sort of gave her a new life you might say. Retrofitted her with a single-screw Cummins. She can do near thirteen knots at top speed. Almost renamed her the *Ulysses*, but she liked *Calypso* better."

"How could you tell?"

The captain looked away. Filling his pipe, he said, "She's a woman. You can tell."

The gear stowed, the *Calypso* left Piraeus for its first destination, Alexandria, and then via Suez to Calcutta.

The ship dipped and rolled in a southwest swell. Andreas, feeling queasy, left his small cabin and went up on deck. He settled into a deckchair and reread the last letter from Diana.

"My dear Andreas, it seems ages since Berlin. The flight home was uneventful. I am so grateful that you convinced me to take Saskia. I have fallen in love with her … I wish you could see her, so happy. I think of her as our child. I hope you don't mind. She is bright, lively, and constantly on the move.

"Father gave his radio address. I think he truly believes (as do many British people) that union with Germany is best.

"Bellows is going to rack and ruin. I can barely keep up with the main house. Göring has been very kind and offered to pay to have it restored. I think you know why. Over my dead body, but he knows that too. It is so cold, musty, and haunted.

"I am going to adopt Saskia. I look at her and think of you and our walk along the Seine. I have the medallion the old woman gave me. I wear it on my sweater next to my heart. I will cherish it forever. It is one of the few bright spots in this ever-darkening world.

"I know it is difficult, but if you can, please write. Je t'aime, Diana.

"P.S.: I have something I must tell … I think you already know—you must know. I'm pregnant. It is your child, Andreas. Our child. I never thought God would see fit to give me a second chance."

It was an odd sensation, as though a story were coming to a close. He stopped frequently to examine himself, looking for changes. His appearance hadn't changed. He was in the middle of a dream, one he hadn't chosen and over which he had no control.

People were getting ready to go to their jobs; none of this concerned them. The peeling paint, the children's bad teeth, the sore foot concerned them. A pile of Jews sitting on a mountain in Tibet burning uranium to keep warm was not something they would think about. Diana's abortion was not something they would think about, nor was her pregnancy.

I'll make the most of the hand I've been dealt. Climb the damned mountain, grab the uranium, and make off into India.

A shadow fell across the deck covering his chair and the letter. When Andreas looked up, it was into the face of a gaunt giant with long arms and hands that were tanned and scarred. His body was angular. His eyes were brown, and the light shining from them transfixed. His clothes were too large; they flapped in the wind.

"Pardon me, but your jacket is on fire," the giant said, pointing to the cinders falling from the smokestack.

Andreas struggled to get out of his chair; he batted away sparks on his clothing.

"I haven't introduced myself," the giant said. "I'm Yuri Telek Tsongay."

With difficulty, he lowered himself into the deck chair, and together, they listened to the sea gurgling beneath them. Tsongay tapped his pipe on the railing.

A Mongolian or Tibetan, thought Andreas. High cheekbones, skin drawn tightly over two cavernous eye sockets, flat nose, and a firm, square jaw. There was a scar along the side of his neck extending from his upper lip to one ear and across his forehead.

They sat together in silence. The giant rose and without a word went below. Andreas followed, but unable to sleep, he started to pace. He lit a cigarette, then another. Lying on his back, he studied the clock on the cabin door. It was three in the morning.

"Are you all right?" a deep voice asked from outside his cabin door. "I'm sorry if I woke you," said Yuri. "May I come in?"

"Yes, of course." Andreas wiped the perspiration from his chest and neck, made sure everything was safely stored, and then taking several deep breaths, opened the door. "Please, come in. Sit down." Andreas said.

Tsongay, bent nearly double to avoid the overhead, sat with his legs sprawled across the bed.

"I couldn't sleep," Andreas said. "I'm sorry my pacing woke you."

"Please, call me Tsongay."

Perhaps it was his attitude or maybe his eyes. Andreas hadn't met many people from the East, but those he had seemed to look past you into the back of your head.

"Herr Heydrich has told me you are going to climb Mt. Kongdzengchenga. I have signed on as lead Sherpa. Next to Chomo-Lung-Ma, this mountain is the most dangerous."

"Why did you decide to take the job?" Andreas asked.

"It pays well… It is my home. My people need me." He spoke as if he were some sort of king. "May I borrow the Bible in your bed stand? Mine is missing, and I find it makes good bedtime reading. It's a fairy tale, better than the *Arabian Nights*. Have you read it?"

"Parts of it," Andreas answered.

"And?"

"As you said, a fairy tale."

"Perhaps," said Tsongay. "This is the part I was looking for. Revelation 19:1–21: 'Fire will come down on them from heaven and they will be thrown into the lake of fire.' I was reminded of this when I saw the plankton on deck, like fire in the water."

A sudden surge forced the vessel to heel.

"My people are dying," he said suddenly. "Soon, there will be none left. They have been here since the beginning, but now they are dying," he said as if there were nothing shocking about it, nothing he could do—that was all.

"I don't understand. What do you mean from the beginning?"

"From as long as anyone can remember, my family has lived on Kongdzengchenga, but of course, they, like all of us, were squatters. It's really their home."

"Whose?"

"The gods."

"Awfully damned cold. How do they keep warm? You're kidding me. I mean, you can't be serious," said Andreas.

"I can see you don't believe me. I won't bore you with the rest. They keep warm by picking the coal left by the gods. Do you mind my calling them gods?"

"It's as good a name as any. As long as you don't expect me to believe it, said Andreas"

"Are any of the other mountains inhabited?"

"No. I don't believe so.. Kongdzengchenga, in particular, is reserved for the Gods."

"How are they going to take our trying to climb it? The Gods I mean." asked Andreas

"Climbing it is one thing. Conquering it another. I

mean summiting it. I don't think they'll take kindly to that" said Tsongay.

'The coal has lasted a long time. Now, it's running out, and they must dig for it. They have been getting sick— sores and awful rashes. They become living skeletons, spit blood, and die. The end is gruesome. They become images of themselves, skin and bone. The rabbi claims it is God's will."

"Sounds like good old-fashioned TB to me, or perhaps, radiation poisoning," he said to himself.

"Did you say rabbi? Andreas asked"

Yes. I don't know why they refer to him as rabbi. They aren't Jewish. They have no connection to the Jews historically. They came from Iceland. Seafarers" said Tsongay.

Like the Geats Andreas said.

Have you read Beowulf?

A long time ago I didn't understand it very well.

"No I don't think they'll take kindly to that" Tsongay repeated.

"Many have tried. None has succeeded," said Tsongay with a shrug No human has come close to climbing Kongdzengchenga.

leprosy or something like it, is eating away at them," continued Tsongay.

"And you've talked to them?"

"In the Tibetan way," he answered. "I don't think you'd understand."

"I thought not," said Andreas. "Give me a clue."

"We put the message on the wind, and it is transported."

"You mean like a drumbeat."

"It could be a drum, a horn, or simply a voice—a prayer."

Andreas could see he was getting nowhere and opted to change the subject.

"There are no leper colonies this far north," said Andreas. "I am a doctor, and I know."

"There are many kinds of leprosy," said Tsongay, "and we are all lepers. That which is nonexistent can never be and that which is can never cease to be. We do not mourn death. Worn-out garments are shed."

"There is only one kind of death," insisted Andreas. Lighting another cigarette, he offered one to Tsongay, who declined. "Are you a priest?" Andreas asked. "You talk like one—your people, your flock."

"I guide people. I'm a lama," Tsongay responded.

"Ah, I knew you were some sort of priest. If we are going to be friends, please don't try to convert me. Let's be clear on that from the beginning. I believe that once we die, we don't exist. It's as if we had never lived," said Andreas.

"Exactly," said Tsongay. "I have no problem with that. We are nothing more than what we are." After a pause, Tsongay started to speak again. "I will go you one better: you are nonexistent now, and you have never been."

"If you say so," said Andreas, amused.

"We have been traveling for almost eight hours, cutting deep grooves in the ocean. Look astern. Do you see a path? Bits of sea have been jostled, colliding, vibrating. The bow wave will perhaps wash up on the coast of Africa. But to the naked eye, we were never here. Only the energy imparted to the sea and passing from one molecule to the next until a wave crashes onto the beach. It is wonderful to think about even if it turns out to be only a dream. You are nowhere and yet everywhere."

"Yes, you are certainly a priest. There's going to be no way to shut you up," said Andreas good naturedly.

The giant lama laughed at the reproach. "Why are you willing to risk making the climb?" asked Tsongay.

"Damned if I know," said Andreas, avoiding his gaze.

"You were called?" asked Tsongay.

"You might say that, but then, you are a priest. In the real world, particularly in the army, you are ordered."

"Sometimes in the other world as well," Tsongay mused. "We always have a choice."

"You don't know Himmler. My choices would have been go or face the firing squad," Andreas said. His words were barely audible. "It's my responsibility."

The word barely out, he caught at it trying to bring it back, but it hung on the air mocking. Responsibility. A word he had sworn never to use. It had lain in wait and tumbled from his mouth without warning, a word that always meant death.

Tsongay studied him. Throwing his legs off the bed and sitting up, he said, "It's time for my meditation. I must be going." He stood a moment, bending to accommodate the low ceiling. "Climbers live in a small world," he added matter-of-factly. "To clear the air, I know about the Eiger."

"I thought you might," said Andreas. "That's not why I'm going. I don't know why I'm going, not really. I do know that once this is over and I've climbed this mountain, I'll be free of the whole damned mess."

"Yes, you will," said Tsongay. He left.

Andreas rolled off his cot and watched the sea wash

over the porthole, listened to the hull groan as the ship heaved in the swells. Compound three—Wiligut. The ones in compound three were lepers, radiation lepers. A shrug. *Things happen.* Tsongay hadn't just wandered into his cabin and picked up the Bible for a little night reading. The visit was intentional.

Andreas lay back on his bunk and tried to meditate; breathe in, pause, out, pause. He began to feel dizzy. The wind coming out of the northeast suddenly turned into a gale. The ship dipped onto its side. Andreas was thrown from his bunk onto the floor on all fours.

Someone yelled, "Oh Lord!"

He didn't see Tsongay that day or the next. His dinner tray was left untouched outside his cabin. Heydrich, too, remained in his cabin. The ship made good progress and would arrive in Alexandria the next day.

Andreas finally saw Tsongay. He seemed miles away. Andreas knew the lama did not drink, but he behaved as if he were hungover.

"There's something I have to do before I leave the ship," said Tsongay.

Andreas was puzzled, but Tsongay said nothing further and walked away.

Tibetans and Jews, they both spoke in riddles, he thought as he watched the large priest navigate the narrow passageway.

Chapter 42
Alexandria, Egypt

ONCE IN ALEXANDRIA, THE climbers, freed from the boredom and claustrophobia, eagerly went ashore. Heydrich elected to join the ship's crew and vanished into the fog.

He's up to something, thought Andreas, who had elected to remain alone on deck. Every sound was magnified by the fog, and he heard the muffled voices of crewmen on other ships. Nothing moved—not a bird, not a cloud—a tide of darkness, a city of stars, and the night. A watchman playing a mournful tune on his hornpipe.

Immersed in the music and the *Calypso*'s rhythmic bumping against the dock, Andreas barely heard the oar strike the side of the ship. A skiff gliding past left ripples in the water.

A tall man standing in the stern wore a long, black cape thrown over one shoulder and a hood that covered most of his face. Only when he turned were his features distinguishable. Khalid Rashid handed the oar to his companion, the blind leader of the assassins. The leader had kept his promise to Rashid and had met him in Alexandria. Rashid leaped ashore and secured the skiff.

Searching the fog and seeing only a beggar, Rashid set off toward the *Calypso*. Andreas lost sight of him. At first, he thought nothing of it, but then, worried about the equipment, he hurried down the passageway and crept into the hold.

A shot exploded. Andreas felt a sharp, hot pain slash into his chest; he spun to the floor.

Someone, as if possessed, bent over de Signac's body and slashed at his hand.

Andreas lay on the floor, dazed. He'd heard de Signac's scream when he first entered the cabin, but it was so far away. He shook off the dizziness, sidled onto his side. The shot had glanced off the stanchion and creased his chest. He lifted his hands from the mat of blood forming on the deck. It belonged to de Signac.

De Signac, his mouth ajar, his head nearly separated from his body, bumped against the stanchion. Cut away, too, was his ring finger.

Something moved. Andreas spun and fired in the direction of the sound. He raised his pistol to fire again. Someone outlined against the light tore past him and melted into the fog.

Tsongay watched and waited for Rashid to leave the steamer. Shedding the beggar's clothes, he buried his knife in Rashid's throat.

The blind man loosed the painter, and the small skiff drifted into the bay. Tsongay melted into the fog.

Andreas had followed after the stranger as far as the gangplank and then returned to the hold. He searched in the blood for de Signac's finger and the ring but found nothing. He scoured Heydrich's cabin. Neatly piled on the bedside table were a Bible and several books including *The Will to Evil and the Power of Terror*. Andreas knew that Heydrich's absence meant that he had known the murder would take place. Otherwise, he would never have voluntarily joined the crew. He knew too that he had to dispose of the body quickly and silently without alerting the police. Police involvement would result in a disastrous interruption of their schedule.

The crew sang and joked as they returned to the ship. Heydrich made a show of yelling to him from the deck of the *Calypso*.

"How did you get back without my seeing you?" Andreas asked.

"You must have missed me in the fog."

"Quickly. Come with me," Andreas said.

They went down into the hold.

"Looks as if de Signac was in the wrong place at the wrong time," said Heydrich. "Where's his finger and the ring, the one he was always twisting?"

Andreas shrugged in response.

"We will have to get rid of this body. Pay the captain off," Heydrich said. "See if you can find him. Most of the bars are on Cat Street. The Cat-o'-Nine-Tails, it's a whorehouse at the end of the street. That's where he's most likely to be."

When Andreas entered the room, the captain stood at the end of the bed, his trousers around his ankles, a naked woman lying on the bed.

"I have to see you, Captain. It's urgent." Andreas said from the doorway.

"It had better be," Stavros muttered. "This is not a particularly good time, Doctor!"

His trousers secured, Stavros joined Andreas in the halfway. "Damned Germans, always a crisis. What the hell is so important?" he slurred.

"There's been a murder."

"So what? Blute? I wondered how long it would be before they killed him. Well, good riddance. I won't have to listen to his whining." He shook his head as if trying to find the proper channel. "Onboard my ship?"

"Yes, Captain—but not Blute."

Andreas briefly described what had occurred.

"Shit. So let me get this straight. You found one of your guys with his throat slit and his fucking head cut off and you don't want me to notify the police. Is that right? This is Alexandria, and the limeys run this town. They are going to have a ball with you krauts. How much is it worth to you?"

Andreas knew it wouldn't be cheap.

"Let's get out of here, and then we can talk," said Stavros.

They made their way to the old Greek section and stopped at a café. Stavros banged on the table and ordered two beers.

"So who was killed?" he asked.

"Guy de Signac. The pudgy guy, seasick most of the way. You know, the one always fiddling with his ring."

There was silence at the table as Stavros struggled to recall the nondescript de Signac.

"I'm not putting my head in a noose. I don't want those bastards coming after me."

"Who?" asked Andreas.

"You know who," said Stavros. "The bloody assassins. This is their work. It has their name stamped all over it. Of course," Stavros said smiling, "if it pays enough."

"Five hundred marks—in gold," said Andreas.

"Gold. Now you're talking. In a few days, pounds, marks—they won't be worth toilet paper."

"Himmler would gladly wire a draft on the Deutsche Bank. You could cash it here in Alexandria before we leave."

There was silence, the only noise coming from an argument raging in the kitchen. Stavros pushed back from the table.

"And five hundred more if you can get me a lead on this," Andreas added, removing the amber from around his neck.

"I warn you, if you are fucking with me—" said Stavros. Passing the amber over his fingers and closing his eyes, he said, "Good quality, but not worth anything like five hundred marks. What's so valuable?"

"That's my business, captain."

"And so it is." He smiled. "I got this guy here in Alexandria, knows more about antiques than anyone. He's bought some stuff from me. Honest too, believe it or not. If he weren't, I'd have killed him by now. He might be able to tell you about the amber. What about your man's ring? That looked like it had real value."

"Still searching for it."

"Sure. Probably took it with them, whoever it was."

The next morning, Guy de Signac was weighted down with ballast, rowed out from the *Calypso*, and quietly pushed overboard. Andreas had second thoughts about the antiques dealer, but though he knew Stavros was devious, Andreas trusted him to hold to his word.

"This is the address," he said, "but I haven't been there in a long time, and he may have moved. When you get to the El Salamik Hotel, it might be best to ask. Tell him Stavros sent you."

"If I go ashore, can I catch up with the ship in Calcutta?" asked Andreas.

"Plenty of time," Stavros answered.

He had just enough time to write a short note to Tsongay. *Why?* he asked himself. *Is it important to let him know?* He wasn't his guardian, nor had he promised anything, but somehow, he felt it important.

Andreas checked at the El Salamik Hotel. "War is Imminent!" was plastered across newspapers and whispered over martinis. Love affairs kept secret burst into flame. The excitement was palpable, an anxiety heightened by the hectic movement of planes and trucks as well as young men with rifles firing into the night sky.

With directions from the hotel, Andreas walked down the Shar-al-Horroya, turning several times to make sure he wasn't being followed. At last, he found the antiques shop. A small bell tinkled as he opened the door. Mold and dust hung in the air as if nothing had stirred in the shop for decades. A hoary head appeared, and an old man approached the counter. With a sigh, he asked, "What can I do for you?"

"I'm searching for some old records."

The librarian looked at him with a questioning smile.

"And I know this is going to sound ridiculous, but I'm trying to chase down some Jews who left Palestine—a very long time ago."

"Many Jews have left Palestine."

"I mean in the third century BC."

Andreas told him of Ephraim and the exodus that might have taken place. The old man smiled. He felt idiotic. He was asking to trace a group of Jews who might have left on their own or who had been forced to leave for a part of Europe, to no specific place—simply somewhere in the north.

"Have you tried the Jewish library?"

"Captain Stavros has recommended you," Andreas said in desperation.

The old man's black eyes stared from beneath his white eyebrows. He hunched, and still not ready to commit, asked if Andreas had something he wished to sell.

Reaching into his shirt, Andreas showed him the amber and the note from Stavros. The old man passed his hands over the smooth stone. There was a flicker in his eyes, and moving with surprising agility, he led Andreas down several flights of stairs into an airless cellar.

The odor of mold and decaying paper sweated from the vault. The old man lit a torch made of pitch. It too hadn't been used in some time. The torch illuminated a cubicle. There was a cot, a washbasin, and a large stone tablet. Books and manuscripts lined the walls from floor to ceiling.

There was barely enough air to nourish the torch, and it grew dim. The old man inserted a key into the lock of one of the small crypts. The lock tumbled, and the door swung open. He withdrew a yellowed parchment and laid it on the altar. The hieroglyphics were in curling black script. Each corner had been hand-painted with vivid color, and in the center, a mountain was circled in deep red, its twin peaks and shape an exact replica of the amber—except that between the peaks was a blue lake.

The old man traced the script with the tips of his fingers line by line encircling and embracing each word. "This writing was done by my friend, Eudoxus, in the third century BC. I knew him while he worked on it. Do you have the ring?"

"What ring?" asked Andreas, his thoughts racing to de Signac's missing finger.

"The piece of the puzzle, the ring," the old man replied harshly, "But is it the final piece? The ring," the old man said, aware that if it were, his vigil would soon be over. "Many lives you and I have lived. I remember them all, but thou dost not." The old man kneeled by the stone tablet, running his fingers over the papyrus.

"We must have the exact time. Then the last trumpet will sound, announcing his return and his judgment. Then the sun will be directly over the place where Sambhava jumped, where the sword is hidden."

"All of them jumped. Was it a mass suicide?"

"Yes and no. You are assuming they were forced to jump. This was ecstasy. There was no fear, no death. It wasn't suicide, not if you believed. There was joy. It was a jump into belief, into nirvana." The old man's face seemed to glow as he spoke. "For one instant, the position of the sword will be marked by the sun. The sword cannot be removed until the exact time, to the minute and second. At that time will it be so—God's final judgment. The minutes and seconds are still hidden in the ring. The Jews you are seeking are the keepers of the secret."

Andreas remembered what was left of de Signac floating in the bay. He put his fingers on the numbers 666. "What about these?" he asked.

"These are the devil's numbers."

"Why the devil's?"

"Because he too has a right to it. Satan owned the sword and the ring but surrendered them when he lost the battle and was thrown out of heaven into the lake. You will have to find it. You must find the ring before Satan does. We must know the exact time."

The caretaker became a blur and faded away. Andreas stared at the vaulted columns and the stairs stretching up as far as he could see. *Go*, a voice said from somewhere within. He grabbed for the papyrus and hurried up the stairs, two and three steps at a time; he tripped, striking his knee. As he passed each flight, a metal door slammed shut behind him. When he arrived in the shop, it was empty. He opened the door, expecting the sound of the bell, but there was no sound. There was no bell.

His legs tired and his mind numb, he turned his eyes toward the setting sun. Out on the pavement, passersby stared at him. Perhaps he had dreamed it. His knee hurt, and the bruise was no dream. He carefully folded the papyrus and put it in his pocket. *Sambhava? A leap of faith?* He needed to touch something human, alive. He walked to the corner and turned back onto the intersection with

Shar Nabi Daiel, the site of the old library. Uncertain, he ran his hands into his pocket, felt the bulk of the papyrus.

Night was closing swiftly around him. Every time he looked up, it seemed to have grown darker. Numb, he looked for a place to rest. He needed time to think. He looked back. The row of low, whitewashed studios was still there, and so were the two people who had been following him.

Pastroudis, a favorite place for Europeans, was too crowded. Instead, he chose a small Greek café across the street intended for local working people interested in a quick lunch, not for the Mayfair crowd. He opened a newspaper but had to struggle to concentrate. The political situation had deteriorated, particularly in the Middle East. There was no organized army, only sporadic bands of militia. There were reports of German submarine sightings. Airplane hangars seemed to have sprouted from sand dunes.

India was in turmoil; gangs roamed the streets looting and shooting. Women had been raped in broad daylight. Things were very bad in the Hindu Kush and in Afghanistan. Telegraph lines had been cut south of Dharamsala. There had been isolated bombings; someone had blown himself up at the Vatican, and in a railroad station in Switzerland, sepoys had mutinied and turned on their officers.

Putting down the paper, he felt safe seated in the comfortable café among the bustle of the diners and the wait staff in their brightly starched whites. He stared at his watch. The second hand jumped, reassuring him. He was living in the present, that particular day. His watch worked; it was keeping the correct time—Wednesday, 4:00

p.m.—not yesterday, not hundreds of year ago. Far away was the emptiness, the darkness, the mountain, and the passing shadows. *He's not coming. You never thought he would. He said he'd be here.*

Chapter 43
Pastroudis, Alexandria, Egypt

IAN MCDONALD HAD LOST track of Andreas. He had arranged his flight to Beirut with a layover in Alexandria hoping to catch up with him. The dust and heat made the drive from the airport interminable. McDonald reached into his pocket for his flask. "Damn," he said, spilling it on his trousers.

His best chance of running into Andreas, he knew, would be at Pastroudis. His editor had fumed, "When all hell is breaking loose in Berlin and Göring and Himmler are ready to face off against each other, you're going off on a wild-goose chase to Lebanon!"

McDonald was certain that the British and his old MI5 bureau chief, Somersby, were behind the unrest. He and Somersby had unfinished business and old scores to settle. T. E. Lawrence, a bastard shunned by the aristocracy, had adopted the Arabs and had promised Mesopotamia to Sharif Hussein. The British Foreign Office had stabbed Hussein and Feisal in the back by making secret treaties and deciding together whether to keep them and who would rule.

Perfidious Albion together with even more perfidious France had concocted the Sykes-Picot treaty dividing Syria, Mesopotamia, and Iran between the French and British while both countries were still guaranteeing the Arabs independence. Hitler had sealed a deal with Russia and was planning the invasion of France while still talking peace with Chamberlain. And so round and round it went.

McDonald checked Pastroudis but with no luck. He then hurried to the café across the street and found Andreas sitting at one of the tables. He clapped him on the shoulder, causing Andreas to leap up and reach for his revolver..

"What the hell are you doing here?" Andreas asked, regaining his composure.

"I was on my way to Beirut. I have a four-hour layover in Alexandria."

"As usual, you are just in the nick of time," Andreas said, lowering his voice to a whisper and studying the man in the white slacks sitting at the next table.

"I noticed him when I came in," McDonald said. "He doesn't know how to carry a gun. It sticks out like a sore thumb. Of course, plenty of people are carrying guns these days."

McDonald patted his jacket to be sure his was still there.

A car careened around the corner. Young men shouted and fired their guns into the air, then disappeared.

"Thayne's dead," said McDonald.

"Who?"

"Just in case you forgot, he was an old MI5 who thought there was a war brewing in the Middle East and Göring was behind it. Even offered proof—for a price. Proves you can't be too right too early. You had a meeting with him before I left—some pub in Kreuzberg. Remember?"

Andreas nodded. "Ah, yes, I remember. I thought he was crazy."

"They found him at the bottom of an elevator shaft."

"What made you think of him?" asked Andreas.

"He predicted it."

"What?"

"Chaos. People blowing themselves up. The explosions in Switzerland and the Vatican. I never liked the man, but you know, I almost wept. He was right," said McDonald. "He tried to be something he wasn't, a hero. In fact, he was simply a survivor. Who am I to criticize? You have to be willing to throw yourself in front of the train."

"You first," said Andreas. "I'm just trying to survive."

"Well?" asked McDonald. "I suppose this witch-hunt for uranium is just part of your job."

"As a matter of fact, yes. Himmler has a way of putting things so that you can't refuse."

"Thayne thought he was a martyr. He was broke, disillusioned, scared, and," added McDonald, "homosexual."

"Is that all?" asked Andreas "Was he pushed, or did he jump?"

"Down an elevator shaft? I mean it's not exactly from the top of a building or a bridge," said McDonald.

"So? Is there something magical about those places? If you jump from a bridge, it's all right?"

"Don't be an ass," said McDonald.

"Anyway, he was a fool, and I never liked him," said Andreas. "He'd seen the future, and it wasn't pretty.

There wasn't a damned thing he could do about it, so he committed suicide."

"I think it was the past he saw. He wasn't that brave," added McDonald.

Something in McDonald's voice or perhaps his gestures worried Andreas. "What do you mean?"

"At times, life gives you the opportunity to become a hero. It's up to you to accept it or not. Thayne found out about Farouk, the Arabs, and the grab for oil, and he elected to blackmail Farouke—Somersby to you. Never a good idea unless you have the balls to see it through. To make things worse, his wife was a nymphomaniac. She had practically taken on everybody in MI5. She was divorcing him."

"You think that's why he did it?" asked Andreas. "Hard to reach for the stars when your legs are mired in muck."

"No," said McDonald, rearranging his knife and fork. "Never can remember which goes where," he mumbled. "It gets complicated. You get drained, the sense of failure. I think he was just tired." He pretended to study the menu, not taking his eyes from Andreas.

"So are you still hunting the Jews and that doomsday weapon? Have you run into Chaim Lowenstein?"

"No, nor am I looking for him. Why do you ask?"

"Bad news. That pretty wife of his, the one you were chatting with at Bellows Manor that weekend we were both there. Well, she's dead, another victim of Hitler's henchmen. Seems she agreed to work for the government. You know, secret agent and all that. Must have sounded like fun to a young woman looking for a little excitement. Until you discover that it isn't a game at all but real life and death."

Andreas shook his head in disbelief. *Kirstin dead!*

"Her husband is trying to trace down the Jew killer, Heydrich," continued McDonald. "The Nazis have decided to jettison him and the Allies to forgive him. He has too many secrets and dirty linen. People on both sides don't want him to see the light of day."

"Why don't they just kill him?" said Andreas, turning away.

"They want to. First, they have to know where the evidence is buried."

"Why should it matter to Lowenstein?"

"Heydrich's his father."

Andreas looked as if he had been struck. "His *what?*"

"You can never be sure where the cat's going to roam," said McDonald. "We are not sure about being his father, but definitely his mother's lover. I wrote the article, but my editor killed it, the dumb bastard. Said it couldn't be substantiated, but I know better. I have my sources."

"But he can't be. Chaim would have to be at least forty."

McDonald nodded. "More like fifty. Heydrich was thirty when he met her. He was a student in Leipzig. She was born in Lithuania. Remember, the Nazis have been parading through Europe under different guises for a long time—Holland, Lithuania, Denmark. He's an accomplished violinist, by the way. Reinhardt Dieter Tristan Heydrich. Not something you'd associate with murder, is it?"

McDonald paused long enough to dig into a plate of hummus that had just been put in front of him. "We pigeonhole people—a murderer is sadistic but never intelligent or gifted and certainly never a musician. Interesting history. He started in the navy working for

Admiral Canaris. It's a long story. I'm not sure you want to hear it."

"Go on," said Andreas. "I have time. You're the one who has to catch a plane."

"Well, Heydrich was smart, an excellent skier and fencer. He had only one problem—a high-pitched voice. Two problems, actually. He also had a knack for making enemies. And a taint to his blood."

"Jewish?" asked Andreas.

McDonald shrugged.

"Is that it?"

"Not quite. As you know, this is no time to be labeled a Jew."

"What are you saying? Well, was he?"

Andreas was enthralled by the story and envious that a newspaper man could get information that he, an SS officer, could not.

"He was cleared by the SS. That's when he joined the navy and was commissioned under Admiral Canaris. But here's where it gets interesting. Seems the Lowenstein family owned a Stradivarius worth, some say, three to four hundred thousand American.

"Elisha, not a household Jewish name, but she was Jewish I guarantee you, sneaks back into Germany to retrieve it, is nailed, and marched away to Sobibor. Guess who the camp commandant is? None other than Heydrich. They fall in love. By that time, he was in his forties. Heydrich saves her, and she winds up his mistress and as fate would have it, Heydriich his father."

McDonald tapped a cigarette out of a pack of Camels and lit it. "Life is strange. At any rate, Heydrich is still in love with her. But then he disappears, becomes a ghost. Heydrich's son, Chaim, is intent on killing his father and making him a dead ghost."

Christ a Greek tragedy Andreas said. He started to add something but thought better of it. "Anticipating Andreas's thoughts, he said, "That's how it started.. As I said, Heydrich knows too much, too many dirty secrets. Both the Jews and the Nazis are after him. Are you?" asked McDonald, looking him straight in the eyes.

Wait a minute. Are we talking about the same Chaim? The head of the Irgun? said Andreas

"But…" He let the sentence hang unfinished.

"Come on Mac. It can't be.

McDonald smirked "Can't it? The British have hired Chaim to find Heydrich, his father. But not kill him … They, of course would rather have him in one piece. Chaim wants his pound of flesh. Wants him dead.

Wouldn't you? said Andreas.

Mac shrugged. "If he can bring in other high-ranking scientists, Nazis like von Braune, Heisenberg? What's going to do more good? I mean shorten the war."

"If I were Cahim wouldn't care much about shortening the war. I'd want to see Heydrich dead."

"So would I" said Mac.

"The allies want to throw a wreath around his shoulders, make him a hero. The sky's the limit - -if Chaim will bring his father, back alive" said McDonald.

He won't hear of it. Wants him dead

"I knew there was something I liked about him, said Andreas

"Besides his wife' quipped MacDonald"

. Leaning forward, his elbows on the table, McDonald fixed his eyes on Andreas. "You have to ask yourself why.? Why are we rushing toward another war? Why is the Luftwaffe involved in Spain? And why are Jews living in fear of their lives?"

Andreas was silent, listening to the wind rustling the magpies just outside the cafe. They flittered back and forth looking for a stable perch.

"They, Chaim and Kirstin, a goy and a Jew, were so close to making it. Everything by the book. Kids. Yeshiva, Charities. What else could you ask?"

What else? Andreas sat quietly, thinking of Kirsten. "You know, those things: sex, love, desire," he said, turning toward McDonald.

McDonald stared at Andreas. "I never knew you, Horatio."

"Well, anyway, you'd be doing MI5 a great service if you run across him."

"And do what? Kill him?" asked Andreas.

"No! Tell him to go home, his mother's looking for him. Of course-- kill him."

Without being asked, the waiter set down a pot of coffee, strong and sweet, and a dish of pistachio pastries. McDonald poured for them both.

"I treated Chaim's father," Andreas began. "He was brought to my hospital after being hit by a car. Died."

Andreas looked into McDonald's eyes. McDonald seemed far away. There was something dangerous behind those eyes.

"Pardon me, Mac. I have to go to the john."

Andreas stood outside the lavatory and leaned against

the wall staring into a remorseless sky. The branches of a fig tree waved in a gentle breeze. He raised his head and asked, "Why?"

A toilet flushed, and a tall man came out zipping his fly. He cast a satisfied look at Andreas and walked on.

Andreas laughed. *That's it. That's the answer. There's no more meaning than that.* He moved his back flat against the wall knowing that a thousand years from now, it would be no different—the same question, the same answer.

"I thought Lowenstein was looking for uranium," said Andreas.

"Mention a weapon no matter how fantastic and we'll start looking for it," said McDonald, eyeing Andreas. "That's the reason you're here, isn't it? To find the uranium?"

"It wouldn't do much good to say I wanted to try the cuisine, would it? And by the way, what the hell are you doing in this rat hole?"

"I just lucked out," said McDonald. "When you weren't at Pastroudis, I just happened to try this one. Christ, talk about committing suicide."

Andreas rearranged his knife and fork, leaned forward, and whispered, "Himmler sent me to see a Mrs. Bose, something about declaring that the Aryans were Brahmins. Why is that so important?"

"For Christ's sake, it makes the Brahmins Germans and gives Hitler the moral high ground. The British would be seen as attacking Brahmin priests, destroying age-old temples. You know the drill. Tibet is going to be very important in this war."

"You think there's going to be one?"

"No, I'm certain," said McDonald, refilling his coffee

and choosing a pastry from the plate. "Tell me, what are you really doing in Alexandria?"

"Picking up some papers," said Andreas. "I'm flying to Calcutta from here. Would you like to see my tickets?"

"You bet," McDonald said, raising his glass and pretending not to notice the silence between them.

Andreas knew his old friend, knew he was troubled. Not able to contain himself, he leaned forward till their faces were no more than inches apart. "Come on, Mac, unload it. There's something else bothering you."

"Diana is in Alexandria," he blurted.

Andreas could do nothing to conceal his shock.

"I just left her minutes ago at the El Salamik," continued McDonald, not giving Andreas time to ask. "At first, I wasn't sure it was Diana—she looked so harried. I tapped her on the shoulder, and she almost jumped out of her skin."

"Jesus, Mac, tell me everything. What's she doing here? What did she tell you? How did she look?"

"She seemed so changed. Difficult to put a finger on it. Her appearance—those blue eyes were cold, and she'd put on some weight. She took one hell of a chance coming here."

Andreas had withdrawn into his own world and was listening to a different voice. Paris, strolling the Seine, so many kisses never given, waiting. So much of life waiting. The world would soon be on fire. The moment would not come again.

His coffee untouched, Andreas stared into the cup as into a mirror.

"You'd better phone her," said McDonald. "You can't just ignore her, pretend she's not here."

"You don't know her. She won't be put off," said Andreas.

"The British will never let her leave now that her father has defected. They'll take her prisoner and use her as a bargaining chip," said McDonald, glancing at his watch. It was time. As he rose to leave, he turned toward Andreas and fumbled for the words. "You can tell me to go to hell, that it's not any of my business, but she will not come again, Andreas. This is your last chance."

McDonald tossed some bills on the table. "Well," he said, clearing his voice and looking at his watch. "I'm sure we will meet again. In hell," he added with a smile.

Andreas watched McDonald leave, his large athletic frame swinging between the rows of tables. Mac had to pass the man at the next table. He stepped toward him, hooked his foot in the rung of his chair, and sent him sprawling to the ground. The revolver slid out of its holster and spun under the table. McDonald bent, picked it up, quickly spun the chamber, pocketed the six shells, and handed it back to him.

"Excuse me, old man," he said. And turning toward Andreas, he waved.

Andreas felt Diana before he saw her, and his pulse quickened. She walked to the table and sat gingerly, her small, delicate hands pressed together, a question forming at the edges of her mouth.

"You've found me," he said. She looked at him quizzically. She had never looked lovelier.

"Magic, fate, karma," she said.

"You have no idea how good it is to hear your voice," said Andreas. "Why have you taken the risk to come?"

"It's simple. I'm a woman in love. I'd rather die with you than live alone without you. I have left the girl you knew behind."

But not the sadness, not completely. It was still evident in her voice. Andreas heard her simple explanation and knew that though he practiced "love," he didn't have the faintest idea what it was.

With his eyes on the menu, he said, "Go. Ask for the loo and make a run for the entrance. I'll meet you outside."

She rested her chin on her hand and studied his face. "I'll do no such thing," she said. "Don't play games to avoid answering me. No more games, Andreas. If you don't love me, I'll go back to London. You'll never see me again."

"Please, Diana. I'm not playing a game. There is very real danger here, for both of us. I don't want you to be involved."

"All right, but not much longer," whispered Diana. Then, more loudly, "Would you excuse me? I'd like to freshen up."

Andreas caught up with Diana, and they stumbled toward a taxi. He looked back over his shoulder and saw two men get quickly into a car and follow them.

"Lose that car," Andreas ordered. "It's worth five hundred piastres."

They drove off, leaving a patch of tire on the hot asphalt. The taxi lurched around the corner, the second vehicle close behind.

"I will lose it," Assad, the driver, said, "not to worry."

They careened down the alleyways of the old district leaving a trail of havoc. Fruit carts tumbled, lemons and tomatoes bobbled and bounced on the pavement down the alley. They exited along the waterfront. A burned-out shell, a car, had been left on the causeway. A crazy-quilt pattern of machine-gun bullets pockmarked the cornice. *It has started*, he thought.

The sharp bark of gunfire shattered the windshield, and the driver, with a quick glance over his shoulder, turned the steering wheel first in one direction and then the other. The car careened onto two wheels and then back, swerved sharply toward the seawall, and threatened to fly into the Mediterranean.

"One thousand piastres," shouted Andreas. The driver swerved the car onto the divider, crossed it, and dove into the oncoming traffic. Startled drivers slammed into each other amid a cacophony of horns. The driver seemed to take pride in the junkyard he'd left behind. The other vehicle was nowhere in sight. Quietly, they coasted into an alley. "My cousin is the owner," he said proudly. They waited, listening to the click and ping of metal as the car settled.

"My cousin has rooms for hire," the driver said, surveying a bullet hole in the trunk of the taxi and the shattered windshield. They waited, listening to the sound of surf breaking on the sea wall. The driver left the taxi and returned minutes later. "No piastres. Fifty pounds." He pointed to the windshield. "There is danger?" He turned his palms upward toward Allah.

"All right," Andreas said.

They entered a tiny living room overflowing with children, some clothed, some naked, some crying, others playing on the dirt floor. An older couple stared straight ahead pretending not to see them.

"What they don't see, they can't identify," said the driver.

They were led to a small room with a cot and a single window covered with sheets of plastic. Andreas put his arms around Diana and kissed her softly on the neck.

"I love you," she whispered, holding him tightly. She knew he could feel the life growing in her womb.

"Love." A word he'd been careful never to use, unsure of its meaning. Devotion, adoration, worship. Certainly, he didn't feel any of those. Passion, yes. *Is that enough?*

It had grown cooler. The soft Alexandrian light had dimmed. In the distance, they could hear the surf beating on the shore. Andreas kissed her again, tasting the salt on her lips and trying to weigh the meaning of his feelings whatever they were.

"Can't you tell?" she asked, looking down at her waist. "I'm pregnant—I'm carrying your child."

"I thought you looked pale. How many months?" he asked absently.

"Since Berlin. You remember?" She gently pulled his head to her abdomen. *Is this too much to expect?* "Why was that car chasing us?" she asked.

"Someone thinks I'm carrying a secret," Andreas said, "but I am not."

"This will be our secret, our future," she said. She was a woman in love. Her thoughts were in love, her music was in love, her imagination was in love. "I meant to get rid of it," she said, pleading, "but I couldn't. It was your child, yours, and I wanted it."

So you made the decision for us both, he thought grimly.

The night was cool. He put a cover over her and walked to the window.

"Why didn't you take precautions?" he asked. *Why am I angry?* An instinct he didn't understand was leading him to purposely destroy their love.

When he returned to the cot, Diana was propped up on one elbow. She turned away from him, her eyes withering, a burning sadness and aloneness scarring her face. Then she was standing. A dull slap. It was the moment she left him, the moment she severed her love. Years later, no matter where, the sound of the slap would awaken him.

"It's all about you. It's always has been," she said, sobbing. A torrent of words flowing from her through lips that only moments before had kissed him. A mouth that held the promise of love was ejecting words of hate powered by the hatred in her eyes, each word surrounded by spittle from a mouth screwed into hate, arms that were rigid by her side. The words stung and seared when they hit. He rubbed his face to get rid of the pain, but the hurt stayed.

Her hands moved aimlessly over the bed, and he knew if a knife or gun had been within reach, she would have used it. She quieted, and he thought the storm had passed, but the pain suddenly returned, and she howled and scratched at him.

They fell asleep, she from sheer exhaustion, he from the weight of his emotions. In the darkness, he reached for her hand. She pulled away.

The night was still and cool, and sleep was deep and reviving. Perhaps the morning would make things right. Perhaps it would somehow all sort itself out.

Suddenly, Diana sat up. Bending over and holding her abdomen, she let out a high-pitched scream. Her face contorted. She fell from the bed onto her knees and grabbed for the nightstand.

"No, it can't be! It's too early."

The sheets red, then black.

The nurse had left. Diana's eyes were cold. She felt nothing. The bloodied sheets were rolled into a pile on the floor. "The baby was yours, Andreas," she said softly, so softly he barely heard. Each word separate, distinct as if plucked with guitar strings. "Not that it matters any longer. An abortion is no one's child." She no longer had any reason to hurt him. Hurt and pain were for lovers. "Funny, I swore I would never have another abortion."

Another contraction, and she lay doubled up on the floor.

He checked her pulse—rapid. But the bleeding seemed to have stopped. He kneeled beside the bed and stroked her. It was too late, but he realized how much he loved her, knew what the words meant. None of the explanations did justice. They'd left out pain, suffering.

Andreas shook his head. "It's too early to tell. Placental separations aren't unusual, but at this early stage, the prognosis isn't good. The safest treatment is to complete the abortion. But if you choose not to, we need to keep you in bed. And quiet. Diana, I must tell you that if the separation continues, the baby will be lost—and you could die as well."

Diana heard the words but was too tired to respond. "I don't care," she said. "I will not have another abortion."

"But this time, it isn't your fault. This was a miscarriage," said Andreas. "Don't be a fool!"

A week passed. They waited for Assad to return. They waited, two lovers trapped in a love that had turned to hate. Alone. Strangers to each other. He remembered her, flowers, a young woman in springtime.

At first, Diana was too weak to care. The anger gradually subsided from her voice only to remain in her eyes. Weariness and gloom surrounded them. Simple sounds, words, frightened him and became harbingers of death—the hum of the refrigerator, the tick of the clock, the agony of time slipping away. He had wanted to say, "If you leave me, I will be alone again." But instead, the words he spoke had been intended to hurt. They did—and they could never be called back.

"Andreas, you are the director in a play you have written," she said coldly. She turned her face to the wall. "No, not the director, an actor." The words hit and sting. "You have wrapped yourself in death as protection. Not a word can be shouted at you. You have kept yourself private, independent. You are not accountable for a single death nor in fact for a single life."

Chapter 44
Egypt, 1939

THE HORN ANNOUNCING ASSAD'S return was loud and riveting. Andreas and Diana had fallen into an acceptable routine. She had passed the remainder of the placenta, and like a signal, it seemed to portend the end to many things: anger, love, and feeling. Two strangers thrown together, sharing a room, mistrustful but without fury or consideration.

Assad and the two younger children jumped out of the car laughing and skipping into the house. Andreas met Assad in the street. "Is there a private place where we can talk?"

"The English always want privacy," the driver said with a shrug. "What could be more private? In Egypt, we have many secrets but no privacy, in England, privacy but no secrets."

He motioned Andreas into a room with a hole in the ground and the odor of urine and soap.

"You said you could get us to Cairo. Can you arrange for two tickets to Calcutta?" Andreas asked.

"I can try. The flight to Cairo continues to Calcutta. Perhaps just a little more money." Reading the fear in Andreas's eyes, Assad asked, "Who is after you, my friend?"

"I don't know, Assad. I honestly don't know."

"You British. Someone's trying to kill you, and you have no idea?" he asked, incredulous. "In Alexandria, we know. It's usually family."

"It could be several people," Andreas said.

The driver laughed. "Well, that makes it simpler."

"Probably British agents," said Andreas.

"I have a large family to feed, my friend, but I will be fair. A hundred pounds. I will get you the tickets, and what is left is for me. This is good?"

Andreas had run through most of his money. This would leave him with next to nothing. *Do I have a choice?*

"Tomorrow might be a different story," Assad said, not untruthfully. "And the memsahib?" he asked. "She will go with you?" Assad saw the pain in Andreas's eyes, shrugged, and waved his hands toward Allah.

"I can get you to Calcutta, but from there, the British are not letting anyone leave. It will take at least two weeks."

"We don't have two weeks," Andreas warned. "Is there a telephone I can use?"

"My uncle has one. He can let you borrow it."

"Borrow?"

"Where he works," he explained.

"I want to place a call to Calcutta. I will pay you half now and half when it is done."

He shook his head. "Your visas must be paid for in advance. I warn you, it will take time," he said as he turned to leave.

Assad was as good as his word. Three weeks later, Andreas had the visas.

"Getting into Calcutta will not be a problem," Assad had said, "but getting out—practically impossible."

Andreas had no clear idea what he was going to do once they reached Calcutta.

It was a chilly evening when Assad led them, their teeth chattering, along a narrow alley, the rooftops covered with barbed wire. Young boys, guns their constant companions, moved stealthily over the roofs. Walking in sand, their backs to the sea, they reached the car Assad had left parked along the side of the road.

"This is where we part," he said, "Salaam, my friend. We will meet again." He turned and quickly disappeared into the dark.

The spray blew off the sea wall. There was machine-gun fire, high-pitched; closer was the dull thud of mortar fire. The firing was too heavy and sustained to be an isolated guerilla attack. Not one shutter opened; not one person looked out.

Andreas wired the address in Calcutta that Captain Stavros had given him. He told Tsongay to keep in touch via that address.

Driving without headlamps, Andreas and Diana crawled through the narrow streets to the airport.

There were only three other people on their flight to Calcutta: an older gentleman and two younger men. The plane climbed, banked, and headed east, the ribbon of the Nile below.

The cabin lights dimmed. The sky was pitch; the moon was hidden behind overhanging clouds. Andreas reached for Diana's hand, and her fingers closed gently around his. The piston fire of the twin engines lit their way in the dark emptiness through a hundred dreams and a thousand tears. As if all the stars and moonlight had been sucked into the plane. Even the sound of the engines disappeared. He carried nothing, nothing. Only the fingers wrapped around his were real, and soon, they too would be gone.

Chapter 45
Calcutta, India

A LIMOUSINE SQUEEZED ITS way up the hill, chasing large blackbirds from their kill. Grizzled and unshaven, Chaim, alone in a blistered wilderness, in the middle of a crowd of pariah dogs, ran his hand over his face.

Quick and painless. The quicker the better. Easier said than done. The assassin slipped a shell into the chamber, and it snapped shut, sudden, sharp, and final. Sliding onto one knee and balancing the rifle, he presses the stock to his chin. Bringing the sight up, he stopped and focused past a praying mantis eyeing a large caterpillar. Chaim was clearly outlined in the crosshairs. He waited. *Steady now.* He reached into his coat and moved the envelope to a spot where it wouldn't interfere with the shot. A half million, too much to turn down. *Even you, Chaim, would agree.* Perhaps at an earlier time, when things were clearer, when the sides were more defined.

A loneliness settled into his eyes, and he remembered he and Chaim and Kirstin together. Kirstin—young, blond, and angular in her beauty. Chaim—strong and steadfast in his belief of a homeland, an idea that had tarnished with the passage of time but like a dream would never disappear.

His leg began to cramp. He changed his position, and pebbles cascaded down the hill. The wait required patience and a calm hand on the trigger. A sterile sun drilled into the afternoon quiet. He had learned to be patient.

Chaim knew he was being stalked. By temperament nervous, he was strangely calm. *The dawn of my last day, no different from the others, no trumpets, just another day, another instant in the march to eternity,* he thought almost with a sense of joy. The years had sucked the sap away and stolen the strength.' but. *you can't kill a corpse.*

His killer had promised to have Kaddish said over his body. Soon, it would be Passover, the first week in October. He would leave no blood on the corners of his door, nothing to recognize his sacrifice, no one to attest his loyalty to God. *There must be ten Jews present.* He didn't even know ten. Perhaps someone would attend and recite yizkor, someone would say, "Alav ha-shalom," "Peace be upon you."

"How will they learn of our fight to be free without the Haggada, of the Messiah without Elijah's cup? Of the missing Jews?"

"They will need us to teach them."

"Do it," his mother said. "Kill him. It will not change anything. You are still his child. He is not a monster. You have no idea what kind of man he is."

"He's the kind of man who stands at the gate playing a violin while prisoners are brought to be killed—women and children," he'd answered.

"They would have been killed anyway. He tried to make it more pleasant."

"Pleasant?" he'd shouted.

"What would you have him do? If you knew what they, Himmler and Roehm, had planned—the experiments, the tortures."

"And he saved them?"

"Courage is not always what you think."

"He is not a coward, a murderer. He's an artist, a musician."

"He's your father, Chaim. He dances, laughs cries—prays."

Her voice receded into the clamor coming from below and was replaced by a softer, stealthier one to his rear.

The spoils of war. *Women used and frightened. Children, shovels to be used and discarded. Money, riches, are the only things that last. The dead are the only ones fit to judge the dead. Who will bury you? Who will tell them?*

He'd allowed for everything but his own burial.

He's a Nazi. I'm a Jew. We are the same when we are dead. Throw us into the same pit. But I had the purer motive. How have I come to this—suicide? I was caught in the current. Hitler Göring Heydrich. Killing becomes habit, a thing in itself and sweeps everything before it.

He looked at the mute, silent sky.

You are God, and these are your rules. What of the rules of men? I never knew you. I have an acquaintance who claims to have met you, Andreas Eckhart. I have never done harm except in battle. Am I to be condemned for fighting for what I thought to be right? For wanting revenge for my mother?

But she does not wish to be avenged. She doesn't consider herself wronged.

How can she not be wronged? Heydrich killed women and children and rejoiced while doing it.

What of the Arabs you have killed? Are your hands so clean? Can you deny it is their land as much as yours?

The sky is red—blood red.

There was no answer. Just the wind in the trees.

They need me to teach them. They won't know.

You are creating reasons. There are others who will teach them how to kill. There are always others. You have killed many. Why are you grieving?

I want to be free of it, rising in the morning to death, waking at night to death.

The wind ruffles the grass. *All those corpses. This must end. I have nothing left. It has to be done.*

His head explodes.

Moshe disassembled the rifle, carefully wrapped the parts, and slid them into the specially upholstered traveling case. He was weary. Turning carefully so as not to step on the wild violets, he left, stepping over discarded tires and the occasional condom.

Moshe dialed the number of the Irgun in Palestine and left a message. It was half past noon. Shades of gray colored the sky.

Chapter 46
McDonald, Beirut

MCDONALD LOOKED AT HIS watch and wondered if Andreas had been able to make it out of the restaurant. After leaving, he'd gone straight to the Alexandria airport. Landing in Beirut, he'd taken a taxi to the Royal Beirut Hotel, the cheapest in town. He checked in under the name Grimalkin. His instincts told him that something about this uprising smelled; there was something phony about it, a decoy for something bigger. Nothing went on in this part of the world that his old friend and enemy Farouke wasn't part of. The name fit him better than Somersby.

He'd brought a bottle of Scotch. Pouring himself a drink, he fell back on the bed. He had already spent a sleepless night scratching bedbug bites. Walking to the window and pulling the curtain aside, he settled back and waited for the phone to ring.

The phone rang just as he fell asleep. There was only silence on the other end. "Who the fuck is this? It had better be important," he snarled. "Farouk, you bastard, say something or hang up," he yelled into the phone, scratching his leg savagely with the other hand.

"Hello, McDonald," an accented voice answered. "Welcome to the Middle East. I'm glad to see your temper hasn't changed."

"When are you going to drop that phony French accent? And where the hell are you?" McDonald asked.

"Never mind. Just write down what I'm going to tell you. Bus number nineteen from Isaad Street leaves at six-thirty in the morning. Take it to Passim Road and then switch to bus two. Go to Qatar Road, and then take bus thirty-three to the end of the line."

"Christ, okay. And then what?"

The caller hung up.

McDonald set his alarm and moved to the chair, cursing and scratching.

All too soon, the alarm clock went off. From his window, McDonald could make out Tripoli and the sea, blue-green and sparkling, in the distance. He got dressed and went down to the square alive with small shops selling apricots and the ever-present soccer ball. Business conducted over baked dust and buzzing flies. He sat at a metal table and ordered a cup of mint tea and a bowl of pistachios. He had gotten off in a ghost town—hot, breathless, quiet.

With a little help, he found bus nineteen and followed his instructions. Nearly two hours later, he disembarked bus thirty-three at the end of the line. Two men in Arab dress approached; one motioned for him to follow. They walked across the square, and McDonald was ordered into a car. A blindfold was wrapped around his head. The car stopped in a gravel driveway. He was pushed out, up three steps and into a cool room, and was left alone.

The door creaked open, and his blindfold was removed. He could make out a figure in traditional garb—the ogal around his head was made of gold with an inlaid crescent.

"Now, Ian, why have you come all this distance?" asked the man known as Farouke to some and Somersby to others. Satan whispered by many. "Certainly not because you miss me. Good God, you must realize that your coming here was foolish. It compromises me and makes you an obvious target."

"Target? What are you getting at?"

"I'm not getting at anything."

Somersby motioned a young woman toward McDonald's legs swollen with bedbug bites. She reappeared with an ointment. Almost immediately the itching subsided.

"I will love you until my dying days," said McDonald.

Over a cup of mint tea, the two men rehearsed old times. Suddenly and without warning, Somersby stood; looking into McDonald's eyes, he asked, "How long has it been since the last Crusade?"

"I don't know. I guess about eight hundred years," said McDonald.

"Time for another?" asked Farouke. He refilled their teacups. "What started the last one? And don't tell me it was to recover the Holy Grail."

"How about gold and the Holy Grail?"

"Sounds better. Can't have Christianity without gold cups and crosses. The real reason was to use religion and the church to enrich Rome's coffers and steal some land. The knights clunked around, screwed the inhabitants, and grabbed the land, the jewels, and the gold—not to mention women. In short, a good time was had by all."

A polite knock. The door crept open. A German soldier was outlined in a shaft of light. Clearly used to command, a swagger stick in his left hand, he dominated the room by his presence alone. Many men had bid farewell under his gaze. Only priests and hangmen had such a gaze—those who had the power to fulfill a wasted, empty life with death.

"Mr. Ian McDonald, may I introduce Hans Tristan Dietrich Heydrich of the Sturmabteilung. Unfortunately, he is not able to join us. He has a plane to catch for Calcutta. But I wanted you to meet him."

The major stepped forward, clicked his heels, and flashing a Nazi salute, smiled. McDonald was taken aback, surprised to be in the presence of the famous Colonel Heydrich. "Quite a mouthful," he quipped, breaking into a broad smile. McDonald would have sworn the tall figure standing in front of him was indeed the devil—tall, bent, with dark jowls and a spear-tipped face with pointed goatee. And the eyes—like two red-hot coals.

"I can't stay long," he said in a surprisingly high-pitched voice. "I merely wished to take my leave of Sir Somersby and to meet the famous journalist, Ian McDonald." Heydrich bowed with what appeared to McDonald as cynical mockery, but the journalist knew better than to provoke the issue, and fascinated and even amused, he thought, *Chaim has his father's eyes.*

"You're a journalist, Mr. McDonald," he said. "I feel as if I should know you. You've written several articles about me. One thing is obvious: You don't know me. You don't come close to knowing me. You've called me a murderer. Perhaps I am. I've tried to be honest and manly all my life. This Nazi business. I believe you've referred to it as a homicidal derangement. Homicidal? Yes, without doubt. Deranged? Not as certain. I believe logical would be better. There can be no doubt that what started as one madman's dream fell on fertile soil and has turned into a murderous scream, a tidal wave."

Leaning forward, looking into McDonald's eyes and with a slight quiver in his lips, he said, "Tell me if the cause of destruction lies in its birth. Who gave birth to this creation? This dream? This nightmare? This life? Why? Not for justice. Not even for food or water. What for, then?

"You have portrayed me, the Nazis, as madmen. I thought as long as I was here, I'd introduce myself. There are no hard feelings. Much of what you say is true, but there is a fault line that many, including you, don't want to cross. It shines a light into their weakness. You must ask yourself, as have I many times, who put the poison there? Was it in the same cup? That we are doing God's work is unmistakable.

"Is he coming, Mr. McDonald? Do we want him to come? Perhaps we in Germany no longer care. We have found someone else?" With a click of his heels and a slight bow, he smiled. Leaving behind the demons and corpses, he turned and left.

"Well, that was certainly interesting," said McDonald after Heydrich had left. "I don't get it."

"Just a way of introducing him," said Somersby, trading his French accent for a clipped British one. "You must admit that's why you are here, isn't it? To meet the players, and the game. You must have known there was a reason for all the guns and guards. Heydrich and I are friends. Well, if not friends, acquaintances. We have known, disliked, and admired each other for a long time. Have you noticed anything strange?" Somersby asked. "The odor. Like a lit match."

"Doesn't make sense. I don't have the whole picture. Something's missing."

"You do, but don't want to believe it," said Somersby. He chewed a betel nut and spit the husk into a bowl. "You said it in one of your editorials, Mac. All the stories will turn out to be true—Christ, the apostles, Satan, the Apocalypse, redemption. All true. Hellfire, damnation, is true. So is a dirty uranium bomb small enough to be carried in a suitcase. And you, I, anyone can buy it for maybe three—five million. The fuse comes free. 'I am my own vengeance,' sayeth the Lord. We should pay more attention to scripture. If what Christ said is true, man will destroy himself, the poppy seed in the pipe. When revenge becomes individual, the man next door, depending on what side of the bed he got up on that day, is able to take out not only his neighbor but also a whole community, a state. Revenge becomes the means for murder. Anarchy is ready-made for the Nazis," said Somersby.

He stopped, waited for a response, but McDonald only stared with a look of exhaustion and pain. "The murder and mayhem that Hitler has unleashed is miniscule in comparison," he continued. "No society could survive for long. We will all be living in caves behind concrete walls. Are you going out to dinner tonight? Be sure to take your radioactive protection with you. Is there someone who thinks you are Jew, a wop, a Pole? How do you protect yourself?"

"You don't," Ian said.

"Unless … of course! A worldwide protection agency. That's it, isn't it? That's what's behind it. Bingo! Give the man a cigar! They will beg for it," said Somersby. "We will own the world's oil and uranium, its justice and penal system—and the caves. Thanks to the Germans, the organization is already in place. A united world order. All we have to do is change the name on the doors to International Control."

"And you of course will be the head of the organization replete with all kinds of committees and safeguards. All phony and on the take," said McDonald.

"There will be no stopping us. We can claim the power and the money. Hitler's assassination will provide the excuse."

"Christ's already been assassinated," said McDonald.

"Yes, but he's not dead. Of course, he will die. He's hanging on by a thread. Soon, the Nazis will finish them both off. Watch the turmoil that will follow when he finally dies. Armageddon! Hitler will leave the list of survivors, not Christ. Nothing will change, really. The donation will have to be larger and made out to the committee instead of the church. Himmler and Göring will be at each other to divide the spoils."

He stopped, perhaps waiting for McDonald to respond. But the Scotsman's only reaction was to take a Camel out of a pack, tap both ends on the table, and light it.

"Göring thinks he's sewn up the Middle East and the oil," Somersby continued, talking to himself as much as to McDonald. "He's a lot to learn. We are about to start a holy war. A jihad."

Somersby's eyes told the story; McDonald knew too much. There was no way he could leave. "Will you reconsider?" he asked, a tone of genuine entreaty. "You knew when you came, Ian—unless you'd like to join us."

There would be no ceremony. His leg began to pound and itch again.

"Would you like a drink of water?"

He handed a glass to McDonald, who received it with resignation. He drank. The water tasted slightly odd, but it was clear and cool, and he finished the entire glass.

"I'm ready," he said, looking directly at Somersby. He nodded and extended his hand.

"Well then, goodbye."

The throbbing in his leg was getting stronger, and he had trouble keeping his eyes open. The will to live, the difference between life and death was the same as that between lives and lies. One can go on only as long as the other survives. *I've run out of lies*, he thought. *I'm ready.*

He was driven to his hotel. Across the square, a light burned and a lathe was turning. The wheel turning and grinding, sharpening, throwing off a shower of sparks. A face hidden in darkness illuminated by an occasional spark.

Soon, it would be over. He would meet her again. It was time. It was the reason for his journey.

A dim, naked lightbulb burned in the telephone booth in front of the shop. He stepped into the booth and dialed Somersby's number.

A deep voice answered. "There is no Farouke here."

He heard the soft footsteps behind him, a hand reaching for him. And he heard the voice—his wife, Kashmir—calling him to come home.

Chapter 47
Airport, Calcutta

ANDREAS AND DIANA WALKED toward the terminal. The air was hot, sticky; it carried the odor of dead carrion. Neither Andreas nor Diana saw the black Mercedes waiting in the dark at the end of the runway. Two men got out of the car and followed them.

A sharp twang, a wire pulled taught, a head wavering, tumbling, and bouncing onto the tarmac. Seconds later, a second head followed. Not realizing they were dead, the two men took a few more steps before falling to the ground, kicking and squirming until their blood ran out. It was several seconds before a second car drove onto the tarmac.

"Where the hell did you come from?" Andreas asked as Tsongay turned the car onto the highway and followed the Hoogli River.

"I've been here arranging for the Sherpas for the climb, or did you think we were going to sprout wings? The two behind you were hired to kill you. The amber you are carrying around your neck would have come off easily without your head. They are professional assassins. In India, they are known as Thuggee. I think you know their employers." He smiled. "At least one of them—Devi Bose. The other you never had the pleasure of meeting. Rashid-al-Din. He's dead."

They drove in silence. The car lurched to a stop in front of a dimly lit marquee, the Raj Palace Hotel.

"How long have you known about the amber?"

"For some time. You talk in your sleep."

"Would it be possible to skip Calcutta and leave directly for the mountain?"

"We will need visas, one for you and one for the memsahib. Your way back would be blocked. There's only one way, and that is by train to Dharamsala, in the Hindu Kush. From Dharamsala, I can get her out. I have friends in Shigatsa."

Other than the brief moment of warmth on the plane, Diana had shown no sign of emotion. She might as well have been sleepwalking. If only she would say something— yell, accuse him, stop playing the martyr and listen to reason. She would come around; he knew she would. Those centuries of Bellows toughness weren't going to fray over such a small thing.

"Remember, we are to meet with Miss Bose in the morning," said Andreas.

They were in the hotel lobby, a noisy fan vainly attempting to drive away the heat.

"Don't worry, I won't embarrass you," said Diana. "My belly is almost back to normal."

She fought to hold back the tears, and for a moment, he felt she had forgiven him and was coming to sit by him.

Without warning, she rose, slapped his face. She reeked of violence, her hatred spewing from her eyes her mouth. Andreas hadn't seen that coming.

Love—a phrase, a melody. Imagined? Her anger is, must be, a momentary aberration, a testament against the wind. A long silence. "They could start again."

Numb, the heat and the haze, the dead dogs along the road, the dirty handprints on the wallpaper, the torn rugs, his jacket hanging on the nail in the door were not real, didn't belong in a place where love existed. Love is pure, without violence or hurt.

No! You are a dreamer. These are dreams. There is no other world, no far-off heaven. This is the real and only world, and love is where the blood and the hitting and the fucking take place, the real world. You can't hide forever. If I only knew what it is I'm running from. Can it be that love is ten seconds of epileptic insanity? And the emptiness and bitterness are the true, lasting reality?

"What about Devi? Maybe she's heard from Heydrich?" asked Andreas, tired and uncertain, his eyes unfocused, his voice far away.

"Perhaps. Heydrich is too smart to trust her. Devi would rather none of us made it. She's made her own deal," said Tsongay.

"With whom?"

"The assassins, Heydrich, Himmler. Remember, she is to think you are going by boat as far as the Testa River. She won't have her assassins try again if she believes you are going to run the rapids. They have never been run. She will think the river will do the job for her. An accident is cleaner and removes your death from her shoulders."

And from yours as well, Andreas thought. "If you killed me, the amber would provide the path. What is it you'd need? What is the final piece of the puzzle you are missing? Whom are you working for, Tsongay?"

"I'm searching for the same man you are," he said.

"I don't know whom I'm looking for," said Andreas.

"I think you do. At night when you suddenly awake to silence."

Andreas knew better than to continue the conversation; he settled himself on the sofa.

The following morning, weary, they drove in silence to the Bose mansion surrounded by a network of barbed wire and corrugated iron and separated from the Hoogli River by barking dogs, huge frogs, car tires, and the moaning of the dying. The Chandelas, their feet covered with dry mud, their dhotis torn to shreds, scoured the hill and crawling along the riverbank searched for worms. They had no reason to hope and nothing to lose, so they pecked at and inspected every shiny scrap, anything that moved or wiggled; whatever they found would be saved or eaten or perhaps used next time when they'd be born into a better life.

A police car stationed at the top of the hill blocked the roadway.

"What are they looking for?" asked Andreas. "They're giggling like a bunch of teenagers."

"Whatever they can find—a scrap of paper, a button, makes them richer than they were a few minutes ago," said Tsongay. "Seems someone was shot here yesterday."

The sporadic crack of rifle fire could be heard in the streets.

The British suspected everyone. Diana, if caught, would be treated as a spy and detained in an Indian jail. Escape through Dharamsala in northern India or Lhasa in Tibet were the only alternatives.

What the hell had happened to Heydrich? Devi guaranteed that the climbing gear had been off-loaded from the *Calypso* and had been stored in a warehouse in Calcutta, but it had since gone missing. Heydrich must have collected it. Both he and the two climbers with him had disappeared.

"If I were Heydrich, I wouldn't want Devi to know I was still alive," said Tsongay.

"What do we do without the gear?"

"I have all you will need. It's stowed in one of the monasteries."

"Heydrich is much too smart to be taken in. He realized from the start that Devi had been bought out by Göring."

"If we do find Heydrich, I doubt he will be alive," Tsongay said, bending to pick up something in the dirt.

"What's that?" asked Andreas.

"Nothing. Just a piece of metal," he said, putting a shell casing into his pocket. "Göring has made sure that no one, including Heydrich, will make it off of Kongdzengchenga. I doubt if even Himmler will be alive. That was the plan from the beginning. Neither Göring nor Devi is anxious for us to find this weapon. If we do find it, so much the better, but if we don't and there is no one left to tell, the threat that it exists will be as good as the fact."

"Well then, what are we doing here?" asked Andreas.

"Trying to stay alive," answered Tsongay. "We need

exit visas, and Devi is the only one who can get them for us."

"Why would she do that if she was going to kill us anyway?"

"First for cover, and second, it frees her of responsibility for your death."

"Why my death?" asked Andreas.

"She couldn't care less about the rest of us. She's in love with you. She'd rather we burned in hell, in particular, your Diana," Tsongay said.

The next morning, they followed Devi's directions across the Hoogli River and to the edges of a shantytown. Their driver turned off the highway onto a dirt lane and drove to a wooden hut crouched in the middle of overgrown bushes and black snakes.

"Please, sahib, how good of you to grace my humble dwelling," said the occupant, Pranfari, a short, balding man of the untouchable caste. "How can I be of help?"

"I am the fellow who sent you a message earlier today," Andreas said.

"Yes, yes," said the man as if he had just remembered. "Can you do it?"

"First, as in all things, one must assess. A person of my caste must be careful." His hands were pressed together, and he made short bows from the waist. "Yes, one must first assess the risks. I understand that you are a German officer, a colonel. And you, dear, beautiful lady, are his wife and the daughter of the British air attaché. It is out of courtesy for Mrs. Devi that I have considered your proposal. My advice is that you will never be able to fool the emigration people.

Remember, both the British and the Indian officials as well as the Germans may be looking for you. My advice is not to try."

"We have to try," said Andreas. "We have no choice."

"Yes, we have to try," Pranfari said with the readiness that comes from a life of obedience. "It is off my hands. I do have a plan. If you, Colonel, were to travel third class and your wife first, the British might not be looking for a single memsahib. Of course, you will not be Hindu. Because of the lightness of your skin, you will be Kashmiri, Afghani."

Pranfari beckoned with a single bent finger. "We are wasting precious seconds. Come with me." He slid back a rug and lifted a trap door. They climbed down a rickety ladder. "Germans make the best cameras," he said. "Remove your watchband, please." He covered Andreas's hands, face, neck, and ankles with a bronze paste, dressed him in a large sun hat, baggy cotton pants, and a loose shirt. "Not exactly Gandhi," he said, "but it should do. So now you are Afghani traveling to Dharamsala and on to Kashmir. Your wife has become the memsahib of one of the Bengali horse guards stationed in Kashmir, the Bengali Grays. Come back tomorrow night. I will have everything ready."

They prepared to depart but stopped when the little man loudly cleared his voice. "Forgive me, sahib, but I wish to be paid in gold, please. Five hundred dollars' worth."

Diana had paid out the last of her pounds. She removed her diamond ring. "Can you pawn this?"

The Hindu's enormous smile revealed a chaotic mouth of crooked and missing teeth. "An excellent diamond worth twice what I asked! I will do the best job."

"Remember," said Andreas, studying the Hindu with menace, "as far as you know, we are going by ferry. You know nothing about the train."

It had all been too easy, rehearsed. *I don't trust him,* Andreas thought. *He's a Shudra, an untouchable. Why would he let us go? We are everything he detests.*

Chapter 48
Train Station, Calcutta

ANDREAS MOVED DOWN THE platform to the section marked Third Class to Dharamsala and into a mass of surging, sweating humanity. Carried along, Andreas gripped the fake passport. His hands were sweaty, and he left dirty thumb prints on the edges.

Where have they come from, this teeming aboriginal invasion? Hoisting his cotton duffel, he realized they'd been there all along, invisible.

Someone behind him said, "I see you are not an experienced traveler. It is best to wait until the train arrives. Choose your car, and run for it. You will have to climb over children and old women, but it won't matter. This is Calcutta."

Diana, pale, feeling sick, waited in the first-class section. She tired quickly. She had lost a lot of blood and continued to spot. She had taken the precaution and worn a loose-fitting skirt.

Next to her sat a cheerful-looking man in his sixties, well dressed in a spotted bow tie and white linen suit.

"I am Doctor Leonard Savoy," he said, removing his fedora. "Don't worry, miss, there will be plenty of room in first class. The compartment is never crowded. Most of them have already left for the north to escape the heat." Returning the hat to its rightful place, he added solicitously, "Is there something wrong?"

"No, no, just the heat," protested Diana, dabbing at her forehead with a hankie that was by then far from fresh.

Dr. Savoy returned to his paper. The headline read, "War Imminent. Göring Claims Doomsday Weapon."

Diana lifted her portmanteau, struggled to move it closer to the edge of the platform, and felt the immediate pain and cramping in her abdomen.

"Don't," protested Savoy. "Please, allow me." He placed his hand above hers on the trunk, and she noticed that the initials on the cufflinks were W. L. "I will see it onboard."

"Are you traveling together?" asked the porter.

"Yes," said Savoy. He motioned to the porter to take her luggage with his. He handed the porter a few rupees. "Ice," he said and motioned to the compartment floor. Diana fumbled in her bag for her purse.

"Dear lady, I wouldn't think of it," he said. "Forgive me, I didn't get your name." His broad smile revealed two rows of perfect teeth.

"Miss Fellows," she said. "Miss Diana Fellows."

Once on the train, Diana found herself alone with the doctor, who clearly was not going to leave her unattended. *Merely the kindness of a countryman.* She shrugged. *Has Andreas succeeded in boarding the train in third class?*

The tropical landscape slid past. "Looks as if we are in for it," Savoy mused without looking up from his paper. "I mean, for war. What do you make of this headline about this new weapon?" he asked, his face impassive.

"I'm sure I don't know. It's the first I've heard of it. May I borrow the paper when you are finished?"

"Of course." He withdrew the page and handed it to her. "Germany Divided. Fuehrer Still in Doubt," she read.

"Reich Minister Hermann Göring today claimed to have possession of a doomsday weapon that will make conventional war obsolete. Capable of destroying entire cities, it will render the Reich invincible. Attempts to contact the heads of foreign governments were met with silence. Himmler was not available for comment."

It was the *Manchester Guardian*. Diana searched for the byline expecting to see McDonald's name, but curiously, it had been written by an Anthony Ewart.

"Looks as if they will be goose-stepping through Hyde Park," said Savoy. "Here," he said, and offered her a pillow from the rack above.

Andreas, in third-class, settled on the floor of the compartment, on top of his bag, amid a tangle of feet crusted with dirt.

"So, English, where are you going?" said the gray-faced man with a twisted mouth who'd spoken to him earlier. Andreas winced, his revolver pushing against his ribs with each roll of the train.

"No need," said the stranger, motioning toward the gun.

"I am Afghani. I have friends in Dharamsala," Andreas said.

"No matter to me," said the stranger, the touch of malice in his voice barely audible.

"Who are you?" Andreas asked after a long pause.

"I am one of them," he said, pointing toward the crowd of brown faces and black, unseeing eyes.

Slowly and solemnly, a woman groped her way along the car, a bundle under one arm, holding onto each seat to prevent her from falling. With great deliberation, she unbuttoned her blouse, unwrapped the bundle of rags, and placing her child's lips to her breast, she started to chant a lullaby, her frail voice barely audible. At the far end of the car, a lantern swayed from the ceiling. A priest rose in mythic blackness to sprinkle the congregation with incense.

Andreas tried to discern some flicker of humanity in the faces but saw only empty stares. The train rounded a curve, and he was thrown up against one of the women seated on the floor. She didn't notice. He realized he was separate from this horde of humanity. His failings and his virtues, his desires and frustrations mattered little to them. Christ, Jews, Himmler, Hitler … all mattered little—if at all. And yet their ignorance would not shield them. Death would visit them unseen, quiet. They would pay it no notice.

The train began to slow as it climbed ever higher, the air thinner and colder. The stranger was practically naked in his moth-eaten dhoti. The bandage on his leg had reddened with fresh blood. The crush of passengers had disembarked with each stop until the car, once bursting with the refuse of humanity, was nearly empty.

"What's happened to the baby?" Andreas asked.

"Under the seat," the stranger said.

Dimly, Andreas could make out the outline of a small heap at the end of the car. The mother had carefully placed the baby, dead, wrapped in dirty rags so it would be warm in the next life.

Chapter 49
Sikkim, Tibet

"TELL US WHAT WE want to know."

"I have!" They plunged her legs into ice. Diana screamed. "Please," she pleaded. "I've told you everything."

"How do we know?" said the man with the hint of an English accent. "She could tell us anything and we wouldn't know the difference. I think she's lying."

A livid sky rushed by, and garbled voices and shouts grew louder. The train climbed higher.

"No, not again, please!" Diana's eyes meet Tara's for an instant, but in that instant, Diana saw a flicker of pity, hesitation, and sadness.

"I tell you, she's cheating us," said the man, his mustache sagging against his red cheeks.

"Where is the sword?"

"In the trash," Diana answered, delirious. "Andreas buried it. Everything I touch dies."

The pain, the smell of unwashed skin, of iodine, mingled with the heat of the cabin and the cold mountain air. They climbed higher amid a chorus of frogs and the grunts and snorting of buffalo.

"You will never see your child. He is dead. The seed sowed in you is dead, and it has soaked up everything you had to give—all life," said Tara with an antipathy born of tears and fear and anger against men.

It was a warm day. Tara opened the window, and the flow of fresh air revived Diana. The branches of a chestnut tree scratched and grated against the side of the train. She saw many shapes, always imprecise and undefinable. Mouths, always feeding, a child staring from under the slats of a seat, his small mouth working on his dirty thumb. She woke in a frenzy of fear, realizing the child was dead and no one cared. *No one to cry out in the night. Thank God for Saskia! She will miss me, cry out for me in the night. That's the important thing. Someone to remember that I existed. Someone to cry out for me in the night!*

The train whistle screamed; the noise covered her sobs.

The train slowed, jolting Andreas awake.

"There will be a passport and papers check. This is the end of the line," his companion said.

Panicked, Andreas looked for a way to run.

"Don't even think about it. They will shoot you on the spot. Give me your bag and some rupees." As the train lurched to a stop, he returned holding some pieces of colored chalk. "A gift from the dervishes. They paint themselves before they dance." Carefully, he painted Andreas's face with splotches of black, red, orange, and green.

"Give me your arm," he said. "Be quick about it." Making a small cut in Andreas's arm, he squeezed out some blood and applied it to the painted skin.

"Now you will pass for a leper. Limp. Remember, you are close to death. Your nerves are infected. Stumble. They won't want to touch anything of yours."

With a smile that was as much a grimace, the ragged companion jumped from the train and was gone. The policeman herded the passengers into line. Andreas, dragging his leg and holding his hand like a claw, stumbled and grasped for support. At the sight of him, the policeman staggered back and covered his face against the mass of open sores.

"You filthy leper," he spat, raising his baton and striking Andreas across the face. Andreas was reeling. "Get out!" The policeman threw the baton on the floor in disgust. Andreas crept off into the bushes.

Unseen by him, the stranger who had helped him changed out of his dhoti and stepped into a waiting car.

A hand closed over Andreas's mouth, and he was quickly and noiselessly wrestled to the ground.

"Quiet!"

"Tsongay!" Andreas whispered.

"Stay down!" Both lay flat in the underbrush. "They have followed us," Tsongay whispered. "They know we are here."

"Who?"

"The Thuggee. They are still in the car. I followed you on the train. You remember. The blind man when you got on. I bumped into you."

"It seems Miss Bose and Mr. Pranfari are not as forgiving as we thought."

"You had help on the train?"

"Yes, a Hindu."

"An untouchable, a Chandela who spoke excellent English," Tsongay said with sarcasm.

Andreas was angry and suspicious. "What devil are you working for?" Andreas asked. "Who's in it with you? Rub the magic lamp and you appear. Who the hell are you?"

"I'm your guide, your Sherpa," said Tsongay.

"What will you do with the uranium once you find it?" Andreas asked. "Put it in a sack and carry it home? The uranium would have eaten through a foot of lead or whatever you planned to carry it in. You'd have been a mass of sores before you got halfway."

"Exactly" said Tsongay, "a mass of sores."

"Of course! The leprosy is coming from uranium decay." It was all suddenly so clear.

"If I fail, they die." said Tsongay. "I am their fate."

"Some more Veda bullshit," said Andreas.

"Not the Vedas, the Bible."

"And they lived happily ever after. The Vedas, the Bible—pure drivel. You can't believe that nonsense, Tsongay."

"If the sword exists, it has the power to heal. And all the fairy tales are true: The Apocalypse, Christ's birth, his death, Christmas and Easter, they are all true."

"If the sword exists, it has the power to destroy. Fire, hell, and damnation exist, and Armageddon will come," said Andreas.

"Then it doesn't matter. None of it matters," said Tsongay. "This Chandela you met on the train, the one who helped you, also set you up to be killed, and he is probably one of the men in that car. Mr. Pranfari is probably dead.

If not, he would rather be dead than to have helped an Englishwoman."

"Someone has arranged for us all to die. No one on this journey will return," said Andreas.

He was certain of his own death.. It made Diana's separation seem eternal. He thought of her blue eyes. Her voice, a cry in the darkness, emitting light, warmth, and love.

"I'll deal with what I can see and touch," said Andreas, pronouncing his final judgment.

Tsongay shrugged, rolled over onto his side, and studied the car outlined in the moonlight. "You will soon have your chance," he said. "They are not after your Diana. They want me. They think I know where the uranium is hidden. I don't. I was led into the mountain blindfolded. I don't know the way back."

The car began to move, slowly at first, the tires crackling on the gravel road. Gaining speed, it slid over the outcropping and catapulted into the ravine. Bouncing like a rubber ball, it settled at the bottom. Three bodies lay in the rubble. One was still alive. A monk stood over him, a knife in his hand. He raised it as if to acknowledge Tsongay, then nodding, he cut the man's throat, bowed, and limped away.

Chapter 50
Chomba Monastery, Shigatze, Tibet

Andreas and Tsongay climbed through the night and into the next day. Tsongay, like a mountain goat, chose the trail marked by piles of rocks and surrounded by poles with colored rags attached to them. The tatters, colors, and rocks were often not what they appeared. A pile of rocks could be a stupa, holy, and a representation of "the path," often one chosen by a saintly lama.

"Like the Stations of the Cross," Andreas said, stopping to rest by one of the mounds. As he laid his walking stick against the mound, he noticed that the mound vibrated ever so slightly. *An avalanche perhaps.* But the mountain was quiet. Tsongay had gone on ahead and didn't seem to notice. Andreas trudged on. Six steps to either side and he'd either be buried in an avalanche of snow or hurtle down the side of a cliff.

"Small differences become large ones in Tibet," Tsongay explained. "Things that seem to be decorations have hidden meanings. But consider that there is one thought that will see you through—life is the one thing we share even with the smallest thing that crawls. Each color has meaning and stands for a different element—yellow for earth, green for water, red for fire, white for air, and blue for space. Sounds may have no written meaning and are called mantras."

"Like runes," Andreas said.

"The sound from the mantra contacts invisible energies," Tsongay said. He stopped and faced Andreas. "Listen, Andreas. Stop and listen. Turn off your arrogance. You won't be a lesser man. I'm telling you. It will free you. Revenge, death—they have no reality except in your own mind."

"It was real enough to the poor bastards back in the ravine," quipped Andreas, though even as he spoke, he realized he was doing so in defense of his own weakness.

"You must separate the act from the reason for the act," said Tsongay. "If the reason for the act was good, then the act was justified."

"Who determines if it was good?" Andreas asked.

"Om Mani Padme Hum," Tsongay answered. "Remember it. You will hear it often in Tibet."

"Like Kyrie eleison," said Andreas. "I remember. The little bell would ring, and I would clap my chest and say, 'Lord, have mercy; Christ, have mercy.'"

"The bells you are hearing now," said Tsongay, "are echoing from cattle hundreds and hundreds of meters below. It took time for the sounds to reach us. Like the mantra carried on the wind, a wave of energy that awakens that deity to the caller. The wind picks up the mantra and carries it through the universe."

A clap of thunder. A flash of light struck the mountain. That time, Andreas was certain the mountain shook. He cast Tsongay a worried look. Again, the tremble passed.

The air became tissue-paper thin, their breath coming in short gasps. Ahead, set on a high ridge, was a series of lanterns. Behind them stood a dark, squat structure, the Chomba Monastery.

"That's where I left my climbing gear when I attempted Kongdzengchenga. What happened?" asked Andreas.

"I ran out of strength—and courage," said Tsongay. "The lama is a friend."

Andreas was almost out of breath and didn't think he could go farther. The monastery was in the midst of a village. They entered beneath a *chorten*, a large, stone rectangle topped by an inverted crescent. Offerings had been placed beside a small wall inscribed with the mantra Om Mani Padme Hum.

Andreas followed the path alongside the wall, stumbling as he went. Tsongay grabbed him by the arm.

"No. You must always take the left fork and hold your right side toward Buddha, pass clockwise with your right side. Remember, Buddha circled the bodhi tree, the tree of wisdom, clockwise ten times. In Tibet, all religious things are circled clockwise with the right side toward the holy object."

The path led to a courtyard, the temple in the center. A tall figure in a loose-fitting robe stepped out of the shadows, and placing his hands together as if in prayer, he held them to his forehead. His large, hanging sleeves made it seem as if the robe were inhabited by a phantom. He was the high lama.

Tsongay bowed and extended his hands. He and Andreas were ushered by two young men, barefoot despite the cold, into the temple. Brass lanterns threw a dim orange light, sweet incense drifted from a large kettle, and the chanting of "Om" came from every direction.

"They are called thanka," Tsongay said.

Andreas's gaze fixed on the painted figures hanging from the walls. Buddhas, ogres, and demons painted in bright blues and reds like none he had ever seen.

Tsongay had fallen to his knees before the altar, his head touching the ground, and had pulled Andreas after him. Arranged around the altar were a large mirror, two pairs of cymbals, a conch shell, long copper horns, a pair of human thigh-bone trumpets, a kettle drum, and a pitcher of holy water. The room was lined with teak that had been lacquered red.

"We are in the middle of the ceremony for the dead," Tsongay whispered.

A corpse lying on a white sheet spread over a wicker framework was carried into the temple by two men. Tsongay explained that the third man was an astrologer whose job was to declare what kind of evil spirit had caused his death.

Drifting in the incense-laden air, Andreas was suddenly seized by a surge of panic. Cardboard figures, replicas from his past, came back, passed before him. Claire, her throat open and still bleeding, the man in the morgue, the knife still in his chest. A woman placing a dead child under a wooden bench.

No one had threatened him or even acknowledged him, and yet Andreas was frightened. The water in the small ewer dimpled, and the butter lamp sputtered and almost went out. Andreas leaned forward to speak to Tsongay, but the Tibetan was intent on the dead.

Wake up! Andreas said to himself. The wrinkles in the water faded as if they had never been there. Cautiously, he approached the mourners, but as soon as he was close enough to read their faces, they vanished. Bellows, the prophecy: "You will lie down and die." Was he the one on the bier? He had the uncontrollable urge to get up and look.

"There's no mystery," said a figure stepping out of the darkness. "Surprised?" Heydrich asked. "Bet you hoped I'd fallen into a crevasse. I ran out of supplies and came back for some. These monks were only too happy to oblige," he said, pointing to the two dead men. His jaw was unshaven, his hair straggled down the back of his neck, his smile a rosebud red.

"Heydrich!" Andreas hissed.

"Glad to see me, are you? Tough to kill evil spirits," Heydrich said, pointing to the bier.

"Why did you kill them?" Andreas asked.

Heydrich smiled. His image, reflected on the wall, seemed to come to life, speak, and move while Heydrich remained still.

"The bastards wouldn't leave well enough alone, kept asking me questions. Where did we come from? Where were we going? I'm a soldier, and that's classified information. And that goddamned moaning! I shot two of them. One got away, but I didn't think he'd get far. This must be him."

An old woman, her hand trembling, deposited a large blue stone in the offering box.

"What was that?" asked Heydrich.

"An amethyst," said Andreas.

Heydrich rose and started for the box. "Son of a bitch.

I could make a fortune just sitting here." No one made a move to stop him.

Andreas shook his head in disbelief. Heydrich had killed the lamas, and they were sipping tea with him.

A monk struck a gong. The sound was followed by a growl, like the timbers of a ship going aground. It gained pitch as it rose: *hum, hum, hum.* The high lama, dressed in his flowing robe, stood in front of the altar. He dipped his fingers into the holy water and touched a bell to his forehead. "Om."

The mourners lifted the bier.

"What are they doing with him? Where are they taking him?" Andreas asked. "They are not going to just take him away and let the bastard get away with it. Aren't they going to do anything to his killer? If not, I will." He started at Heydrich, who had raised his gun and flicked off the safety.

"No, not here, not in this house," said Tsongay.

"Then where, when?" said Andreas.

"Do you think we have survived solely by turning the other cheek? We have learned to wait. Now is the family's turn to grieve. Justice, revenge will come later. We must not interrupt his trip. In two or three days, he will recognize he is dead. Then will begin the second stage, rebirth. His consciousness will seek rebirth in this world or another. The second stage is the most dangerous. It is when the hallucinations occur and he sees the symbols of his actions on earth."

Turning to Heydrich, Tsongay said, "You will be punished. You will pay the price. And when you do, it will be horrible. One by one, you will relive the murders and spilled blood. They will blossom and pass before you, as you have never seen them before."

"Don't tell me, hell," scoffed Heydrich. "I know all about it. I'll look forward to it." His laughter echoed off the temple walls and mingled with the intonation of the sacred Om Mani Padme Hum.

"What do the words mean?" Andreas whispered.

"Om is from the Sanskrit and stands for Brahma. It's the sound of all sounds. Mani means a jewel, a precious thing. Padme means the lotus, a flower that sits on water but never touches it. It is the world that surrounds the Buddhist teachings. Hum is an utterance in defiance of ogres and demons."

"It's like the swastika. They scribble it everywhere," said Heydrich.

"The temple is open to all who wish to come," said Tsongay. "It doesn't belong to us—nothing does."

"I think I'll get a night's sleep. I've got an early start in the morning," said Heydrich. "Don't try anything. I won't hesitate to use the gun—on the lama."

He walked away, and with him walked a shadow, not his.

Unable to sleep, Andreas stood once again in the courtyard. Heydrich had left to finish packing and taken a lama as hostage. Tsongay removed his shoes. Andreas shrank back.

"Christ, how do you walk on those feet? What happened? Did a truck run over you?"

Tsongay winced as he stepped onto the icy stones. "No," he said. "They shattered the bones. They weren't good at driving nails."

"They?" said Andreas.

Without replying, Tsongay motioned for Andreas to follow. They entered a simple but handsome stone structure.

"Welcome, my son," said the high lama as they approached. "I have been expecting you." The lama was seated on a rug, cross-legged, his hands folded in his lap, a knot of hair tied at the top of his head. One shoulder was bare, but he seemed unbothered by the cold. His shadow on the lacquered wall was enormous. For what seemed an eternity, he did not speak or move, and then, with the slightest movement of his hand, he gestured for Andreas to join him at his side.

"Pardon me, Father. I mean—I'm not sure what to call you," he stammered. As he sat next to him, Andreas felt as if the seat had been reserved for him for a long time.

"I apologize for Heydrich, and for your dead friends. Heydrich would not be here if we hadn't come."

"Heydrich would have come whether you did or not. It was destined," said the lama. "He has wanted one thing all his life, and now it's almost his. But the path does not go on without end. It does not endure. When the stars we see above fade away, they shine elsewhere. Heydrich is destined to live in darkness and deadly fumes."

Andreas waited a long time before asking. "And the Jews? Are there Jews on the mountain?" he blurted, carefully watching the holy man for some indication.

"My son, you do not grasp the truth: I do not know if there are Jews. I do not know because it does not matter. How do you tell if they are Jews? We are all the same."

Andreas laughed. "Yes, the same, except some of us have sloping skulls and big noses and hairy jowls."

The lama looked at him as if he'd arrived from a different planet.

"Is that what a Jew is?"

"No. But that's how you identify him," said Andreas. "Then you find out he believes in all sorts of things—blessings and things you can and can't eat. A Jew could never be a Buddhist, all sorts of blessings and rights to perform."

"Like not eating the meat of cows and marrying outside the caste," the lama said, smiling. "We call it karma and the right way, dharma. The Jews call it Mishnah and the way of the Talmud."

"Like not having sex with my sister," said Andreas. "But it wasn't that I didn't care. I didn't know!" The words poured out like lava from an erupting volcano.

"I know," said the lama. "First, there is nothing that is beyond forgiveness. And second, she was not your sister."

"That's your answer? How would you know? You know nothing!" said Andreas. "You are stumbling in the dark as much as me. I should be punished. I want to be punished."

"For what?"

"What I am! For not accepting what I am," said Andreas in a burst of grief and anger.

"You are Andreas," the lama continued, "like the name on a front door. There have been many Andreases. Yours is a unique combination of sins that open into a different house. The difference is that you dwell on them, wallow in them, and use them. An excuse not to do anything about the evil you see around you. You cannot act. Your feet are nailed to the floor. Your father drove the nails one by one."

Andreas heard the rumble of chant echoing from somewhere in the background, the words from the lama echoing within him.

"And my child who struggled for life," said Andreas. He paused, "dead before it lived. I'm sure you will tell me there is some sort of divine justice. That I deserved it, and there was nothing that could be done. I swept him into the garbage."

"What you swept into the garbage was a clot, but it wasn't your son," replied the lama.

"That's the trouble with you priests, lamas, and rabbis. Your job is to find excuses, solace, not justice."

"You've already judged and punished yourself, Andreas. You have kept yourself safe from the one thing that you feared most—failure. That, Andreas, has been your greatest fear. You ran through life with your hands over your ears fearing your father's voice, denying life and love. You have punished many others who wanted your help."

"What do you mean? Diana's alive," said Andreas, grabbing the lama by his robe.

"Yes, she is alive, but she is dead. Dead love is like a bite into an apple of wax," replied the lama unflinching, his voice as soft and tranquil as before. "Andreas, did you believe in your soul that you loved her? Have you ever loved anyone?" The lama pulled a jeweled comb from his hair and let the knotted braid fall. It rested in his lap, touching his cupped hands.

"Eight weeks. He would have been no bigger than a speck of sand," said Andreas.

The lama smiled. "Exactly. A few cells, a purple dot under the microscope. But with a difference. Nothing, not even death, can interfere with his destiny."

How easy, thought Andreas. *He was destined. Who destined that he should die before he ever lived?*

Heydrich stepped out of the darkness, his tall figure bent forward at the waist, his unshaven face and goatee incongruous, his clothes tattered as if by a hurricane. The lama didn't turn or acknowledge his voice but continued to look at Andreas.

"That pistol won't be necessary," said the holy man.

"I'll take one of your lamas with me just in case."

"I give you my word they will lead you to your destination," said the lama.

"Your word?" said Heydrich. "You bet they will. I'll take him as insurance. Andreas, I'll look for you in hell."

The lama watched Heydrich and the Sherpa until they passed out of sight. On his face was a quiet smile. "When we enter the stream, the crossing over from one life to another, we are judged by our past over all the lifetimes of our existence. Heydrich will be judged."

Andreas sat gazing at the bowl on the altar. It reflected the image of the Buddha broken into many colors and lines. "If the world is a bag of mirrors, why am I risking my life chasing this uranium? Does it matter? I was right from the first."

"Yes," said the lama, "But is it really the uranium you are chasing?"

Andreas realized that the conversation had come to its end. Exhaustion threatened to overwhelm him. Taking his leave, he climbed the rickety ladder to the attic that served as sleeping quarters.

No sooner had he put his head down than he was awakened by Tsongay. It was morning. There had been no news, no ransom demand. A monk from a neighboring monastery had seen smoke coming from an abandoned shed, and the lama had sent out a search party.

"We are running out of time. Soon, the monsoons will decide," said Andreas.

Quickly descending from the loft, Tsongay presented himself to the high lama.

"Holy one, a lama gave me this book. I've been waiting to give it to you. A page is missing. He told me that the holy one, Sambhava, owned it."

The lama lifted his head, his eyes alert.

"Sambhava tore the map in half as soon as it had been written and took one half with him. The other half was left in a vault in Alexandria. We have found the two halves. I believe Andreas has the other half," Tsongay said, smiling.

Andreas appeared with his half of the papyrus and placed it next to the remnant that Tsongay had given the lama. There was a glint of pain in the lama's eyes.

"Six, Six, thirty-nine, twelve. The page foretells the coming of the end, the Day of Judgment. On that day, the last trumpet will sound," the lama said. His eyes were fixed on Tsongay, but Andreas couldn't tell whether he saw him. "The amber will show the way on the sixth day of the sixth month in the year 1939, at twelve o'clock. The sun will shine directly over the place from which Sambhava leaped.

At that time and place, the trumpet will sound, the sun will come to rest, and time will cease."

"What is the sword? Is it real? I mean, can you touch it?" asked Andreas.

"The sword is the instrument of God's judgment."

"A trumpet will sound? The sun will come to rest? Time will cease?"

"You will know," the lama continued. "There will be a white flame. There will be fire in the lake. The seventh and last trumpet will sound. The sword will rise out of the lake, and there will be blood on the lake and in the mountains. The way of return is illusion, wondrous, full of hardship and terror. Do not ask the way, but follow those who have passed before. A woman's love will light the way. Those who survive will guard the secret. Hidden in the answer is the answer."

Tsongay held the amber against the light coming from the candles. "Today is the ninth day of the fifth month," he said. "The path isn't clear, and there is only emptiness beyond."

"Now the ring," said the lama.

Tsongay reached into his robe and handed Guy de Signac's signet ring to the lama. He held it cupped in his hands. Taking the ring, the lama stamped it on a corner of the papyrus and stood back as if expecting the parchment to burst into flames. The papyrus started to turn red, and then the seventh seal appeared and the lion lying down with the lamb. Slowly, numbers appeared.

The lama stared across the table straight through them. His voice was clear, but Andreas could detect a faint trembling. "It is the last warning. Fifteen minutes and forty seconds after the sun reaches high noon will be the time. The amber will tell you the place."

"But what does he mean by the answer is in the answer?" asked Andreas.

"Faith is the answer. It will take a leap of faith."

"What about the numbers six-six-six over the blue circle?"

"The lake of fire—the devil's sanctuary," he said. "The path leads to him as well. It depends on which fork you choose."

Heydrich has already chosen, thought Andreas, recalling his parting words, "See you in hell."

The next morning, Andreas and Tsongay prepared to leave the monastery. The lamas had found where Diana's captors had hidden her.

The high lama's robe swirled about his bony legs whipped by a gust of wind. The prayer flags snapped, and bells echoed up the mountain. Andreas asked Tsongay how the ring had miraculously come into his possession.

"It's simple," Tsongay said, smiling. "You are too ready to believe in miracles. I knew Heydrich wouldn't let the ring get away. I knew, though not why, that the ring was a key to the sword. Rashid made quick work of de Signac—amputated his hand and finger and stuffed them into his pocket. That's when you interrupted him. I was hidden right in front of you behind the stanchion. After Rashid took a shot at you, I ran after him and killed him. Then I took the finger with the ring."

The sun had barely risen; the peaks were violet, the sky a surreal blue. Tsongay and Andreas, accompanied by five monks, set out from the monastery. They head toward the small village of Shigatse, Tsongay in the lead.

It started to rain heavily. Worried that it might be a precursor to the monsoons, they trudged on.

Any minute, we will meet the Mad Hatter or at least the Red Queen, Andreas thought. *This scene is out of a bad play. What do we really have? A piece of old paper, a piece of amber with a line scratched in it, and a story about a man who committed suicide by jumping off a mountain. It's a dream, a nightmare. If I pinch myself, it will go away.*

Every minute counted. Tsongay hurried across the spree, the loose stones tumbling into the valley. They climbed a steep embankment, keeping their eyes on the hut beneath them.

"She is in the hut. There are three others, two men and a woman. Diana is in the back, where they stable the horses. The woman is Tara," Tsongay added softly.

"I don't know her," Andreas said, again denying her while at the same time remembering her as if in a forgotten dream—her face aglow, her eyes bright. *Whoever brings the ring must be given the wish that comes with it.*

The lamas lit incense and floated pieces of paper into the wind, sending prayers to the Buddha to guide them. They prayed for those they were about to kill. A door thrown open shone a flash of light on the wall. It was over in seconds. Racing into the valley, the lamas burst through the door. Small swords whirred, and two men fall headless. Tara was wounded, and the lamas moved in to finish her. Tsongay waved them off and motioned them to leave Andreas backed away against the wall.

"So, Andreas, the moment is at hand."

She was if possible even more beautiful than he'd remembered.

"Have you brought the ring? Remember the ring. Will you, as you promised, save me?" She let her dress fall from her shoulders. The blood from her wound was black against her white skin. "Will you slay passion for sweet love? You would leave your precious Diana in an instant if I offered you myself here, now, aroused and burning with passion. You forget, Andreas, that I am part of you, that the ring binds us. You have turned your face toward love. Are you sure?"

"Tara!" he cried, shrinking back. Pale and bewildered, Andreas started for her.

Tsongay, appearing in the doorway, uttered a single word, "Diana." Light ripped through the darkness.

"Go to her, your sweet Diana. We are at a draw."

Growing weak, she grasped her side. Andreas placed the ring in her hand, and the bleeding stopped, the wound began to close. Like the hawk perched on the tree limb just outside the window, she soared into the air, a black speck in the sky. Her hallucination was all that remained.

"It is nothing to fear," said Tsongay. "She is—but is not."

Andreas opened the bedroom door, and a sliver of sunlight passed into the dark room. He lifted Diana from the cot and with his finger traced a lone tear that had traveled down her cheek and dropped softly onto her neck. He wiped it with his finger. His tears came in a rush. Her voice soft, returning from another world. Her world was green—hills climbing and rolling, forests of oak and chestnut, horses and raiment, bunting and the bustle of leaves in the wind. How strange it must have seemed, this world of white, endless snow, men in flowing tunics, shadowed halls lit by incense and candles, and incessant chanting.

"Why?" he asked.

"What's the difference? You once said it didn't matter."

"It does matter, Diana. It does." *How to tell her, "I love you"?*

The words were strange and new to him.

He could already detect the sense of the other world, the divide, the river between the living and the dead. She had already crossed and gone on ahead. He remembered her patrician face, her smile, but it was hazy, smudged, and indefinite. She was flowing out of his life. Though he loved her, he had never really known—until that awful night, a night he would never forget. *It's a delusion to think we know. Each of us sleeps in his own bed until we are awakened and share the others pain. Then we know.*

Andreas was standing on the side of the mountain on a great precipice, listening. Vultures screamed in the distance. Wind threatened to carry the burial bier off. Vultures swirled as they carried off the carrion. He was at peace. What they were carrying off was not Diana, not her grace, her voice, her smile. Her smile, here only once, would never be again. He waited before turning. Alone on the mountain, he heard her voice in the wind. *Search for my smile, Andreas.* Beneath the snow could be seen the glistening harbinger of green and blossoms of spring. "Perhaps he is coming after all," declared Andreas. Tsongay, hoisting his rucksack, smiled.

Saying goodbye, Andreas thought, *I shall have to learn how to miss you. So many things to learn.*

Ahead loomed the white face of Kongzhengchenga.

Andreas had never heard such perfect silence; it was as if a shawl had been thrown over the mountain. As he climbed, he kept his eyes open for signs of Heydrich.

The farther they climbed, the farther the mountain seemed to recede. The sun burned through their clothing, and the cold made them weep. Tsongay seemed indifferent to both.

They reached the top of a ravine, and the mountain came into full view, majestic and terrible. They pitched a tent, started a fire, and brewed tea. The tent flap, beating in the wind, kept Andreas awake. Taking the binoculars, he kneeled outside the tent and scanned the snowfield. As he lowered the glasses, a light caught his eye. Leaning into the tent, he shook Tsongay awake. The wind beat the flaps so fiercely that at first, Tsongay didn't hear him. Andreas shook him again. He pointed toward the mountain and handed him the glasses. Tsongay lowered the glasses. "It's Heydrich."

"We could bypass them," Andreas said, "but we need their supplies."

"We will solve that problem tomorrow," said Tsongay, crawling back into the tent and falling into a deep sleep.

The wind subsided. It was dawn when they crept up the moraine. The sky reminded Andreas of the desert, light blue fading to hazy white. Heydrich had made camp on the edge of the snowfield. There was no movement in his tent. They decided to approach separately, from both ends of the tent. Andreas crouched behind a boulder some meters away, wrapped his scarf around his neck, and stomped his feet. *Maybe Heydrich had gone on to a higher camp.* He couldn't stay there much longer; his legs were beginning to cramp.

He gestured to Tsongay, and they sprang for the tent. At that moment, a soldier staggered out. "Verdammte," he grumbled, searching for his fly. He stepped aside so as not to piss on the tent and leaned back with a satisfied expression. Andreas, halfway there, saw himself outlined in the snow. The soldier also saw him. "Otto!" he yelled.

A second soldier emerged from the tent, gun in hand, and managed to fire off a round. The shot whizzed past Andreas's shoulder and ricocheted off a boulder. Andreas lunged and buried his knife in the man's stomach. Tsongay pulled the rope tightly around the first soldier's neck.

"You are bleeding," said Tsongay, examining the wound. The shot had grazed his shoulder. "Will you be able to climb?"

"Yes," Andreas answered, though in truth he wasn't sure.

Heydrich, certain he would be successful, had stripped himself of everything, leaving behind two complete climbing packs, rope, crampons, carabineers, and ice picks. He'd also left behind a weapon, one he himself had designed—a strong bow, like the ones used in the middle Ages. Andreas was about to leave it when he considered that guns might have been of little use up there as the mechanisms could freeze in the severe cold.

At first light, two small figures silhouetted against the mountain trudged up the ice field. They cut into its steep and treacherous flanks, immense and white. A wall of mist rose between two spires of rock. Andreas's attention was drawn to an outcrop halfway up one of the spires. His fingers stiff from the cold, he steadied the amber and measured the sun's angle. It was 10:00 a.m., June 5. He and Tsongay huddled on the precipice. *What if the sun passes us by and nothing happens? What if this is a hoax after all?*

The sun crept higher. Andreas took the amber from around his neck and handed it to Tsongay. The amber sparkled, the sunlight refracting into all the spectral wavelengths. The gem selected only one. The path scratched into the amber glowed blood red. Clearly outlined, it led over a ledge to the twin spires directly in front of them.

"What do you think?" Andreas asked.

"Impossible," Tsongay answered. "The spires are at least two hundred meters straight up. We have no idea what's on the other side."

"Which spire?" Andreas said.

"The left one," Tsongay answered without hesitation. "It's the left one. Sambhava turned to the left and saw," he repeated.

It has become unaccountably warm. They shed their parkas as they made their way up the steep face, fixing pitons as they climbed. Andreas anxiously searched for footholds. The rock sparkled in the sun like a huge diamond.

The mountain shuddered, and a wall of snow hurtled over them; rocks carried along in the avalanche bounced crazily off the mountain and into the glacier below. The wind rose. *You remember,* said the dark-gray, scudding clouds. *You remember my face.*

"I had to cut the rope," Andreas whispered. He struggled to unhook himself from the rope and follow the voice.

Tsongay grasped his arm.

"You don't understand," Andreas said. "I have to go to him."

"No, Andreas. It's your reality, but none of it is real except that Ernst fell. The rest is deception. It is maya, a false temptation. It is only the first. You will see many before you cross the stream."

If the temperature fell any further, ice would make it impossible to drive pitons and to obtain footholds. The sky grew dark. As quickly as it had risen, the wind died. The mountain made its own weather. A blanket of fog descended.

"I hope this fog is maya," Andreas said to Tsongay. He could hardly see a meter in front of him. The avalanche had left a hushed silence in its wake. The mountain appeared dead, but Andreas could feel it pulse beneath him. They were alone on the back of a primordial beast in the middle of vast desolation. Their world extended less than a meter to each side.

Andreas climbed up to Tsongay. Their odds were better; the weather was warming and softening the ice.

"We will bivouac here," Tsongay said, oblivious of the height and danger.

Driving in two ice screws, they fixed a rope, secured a foothold, and leaned back into a sort of hammock. They ate chocolate and biscuits and spent the night suspended twenty thousand feet over the earth. Andreas drifted into and out of a fitful sleep. Awakened by the vibration in the rope, he turned anxiously toward the ice screws. The vibration stopped, and Andreas fell asleep.

June 5, the next day, they continued to climb until an overhanging ledge blocked them. It was too high to reach to place screws or pitons.

"We have to make it over that ledge before it gets dark,"

Andreas said, gathering the rope beneath the overhang. "The only way to get over it is to somehow pull ourselves over it. If I stand on your shoulders, I just might be able to drive a screw into the base of the overhang and slip a rope through it."

They drove pitons on either side of Tsongay for him to steady himself against the face.

"If I fail," said Andreas, "we will both be fish in the stream." But he was sure he wouldn't. He was convinced more than ever that he was destined to meet the face behind the smile.

As Tsongay held onto the pitons on either side of him, Andreas climbed onto his shoulders. Tsongay lost his grip, teetered on the edge, but managed to steady himself. Andreas screwed the bolt into the rock, tested it, and lowered himself. He tied the other end of the rope to the carabiner around his waist. Tsongay began to swing Andreas side to side like a pendulum, flattening himself against the mountain each time Andreas swung past. When Andreas had enough momentum, he lifted his legs and hurled himself up and over the ledge.

He didn't move for several minutes. Tsongay, realizing that the rope had not played out, thought Andreas was hanging on the other side of the needle. Instead, he has landed on a large, flat rock.

"Are you all right?" Tsongay shouted.

"Yes. Hold on, I'll pull you up," said Andreas.

Tsongay scrambled over the edge.

"Where the hell are we?" Andreas asked.

"On the beetle's back," said Tsongay, pointing to the insect trapped and imprisoned in the amber. Exhausted and exposed to the wind, they built a small fire with the rest of their yak fat, brewed tea, and waited for the sun. Andreas had taken his gloves off to warm his hands. He felt his cup wobble and saw the tea water shimmer. The mountain vibrated.

June 6 and a strange sunrise. The snow on the mountain scarlet against the rising sun. At times, flashes of yellow and white lightning boiled into the western sky hiding the light from the sun, and a deep rumble rolled out of the west.

Andreas, awakening to the warm sun on his face, pulled the amber from around his neck and checked his watch. He would have to be accurate; one second off would result in being off by sixty kilometers. Light coming over the ridge glanced off the ice and covered the boulders. The sun rose to the center of the sky—a tired, pale, lemon-colored ball lacking heat but commanding everything beneath it. Ahead, the sky was in turmoil; flashing bolts of light in the west, contending with the sun in the east.

"I've seen a sky like that once before," said Andreas, "during the war. I remember thinking how beautiful it was."

The wind had risen; Andreas could hardly stand, and he could not communicate with Tsongay other than by sign.

They had only minutes left.

Again, Andreas turned the amber toward the sun. The path was lit, but not the entire way. At the rate the sun was climbing, it would pass them and go on to the other spire before it stood at ninety degrees. He moved closer to the edge of the precipice. Forty seconds. He steadied himself and held the amber out over the edge, more than a 1,600-meter drop into a white veil of mist and snow. The amber was still dark for most of the path. Tsongay squatted placidly, his eyes fixed on the sun.

A spark lit the jewel, and like liquid fire, it spread, suffusing the entire amber until it glowed red. The path, clearly outlined, led into the void some thirty meters away and then down the side of the second spire. The amber started to crack and like molten glass to dissolve. In seconds, the light was extinguished and was gone.

"You would have to believe you could walk on air to try to jump across to the other side. You can't, can you? I mean walk on air?" Andreas asked. He had to yell to be heard. The mountain was disintegrating.

"It would take a leap of faith," said Tsongay.

Sunset. Flashes of light everywhere, rumble like thunder, darkness, sudden and complete. They mapped out a perimeter and huddled against the cold.

First light brought a sight that dumbfounded them. Thousands of feet below the peaks was an oasis, a tropical paradise. A cauldron spewed steam. Tsongay pointed to a path leading some meters straight ahead between the spires and then splitting in two—one fork leading left to a precipice overhanging the lake. Following the fork on his knees, he reached below the ledge and snared a shank of rope swaying in the wind. He let it slip through his hand until it ended still hundreds and hundreds of meters above the surface of the cauldron.

"Heydrich threw the dice and dived into the cauldron. The fire in the lake."

Andreas could not help admiring his courage. "He believed in the devil and had the faith to die for it," said Andreas.

Andreas, on his knees, continued searching. Lightning played over the surface of the lake. "We can't go back, and if we stay here, we will freeze," Andreas said.

"You are right. Maybe the amber was off, or your watch was," said Tsongay. "It's started," he added, looking at the western sky. The mountain shook, and flashes of red and purple lit the sky.

"Do you remember? Do you remember, Andreas?"

"You refused. It was not your affair."

"Gunfire," said Andreas. "Yes, I remember. I didn't have the strength. Another war. I wanted to live, to stay alive. I feared the darkness, the loneliness."

"Where the hell is that bugle call coming from?"

"It is the last trumpet. After, the doors will be sealed."

Andreas started to laugh. A malicious laugh, half fatigue. "You know," he said, "I'm going to die on this mountain. I don't care. It is summer, and I am free. It's just a matter of hanging on until he's ready."

Tsongay settled against the rock, at peace.

"It's a long shot," said Andreas, "but if we attach a piton to the end of one of these arrows, we might just be able to get it to lodge in the rocks on the other side near that cave."

It took two of them to stretch the bow.

"Where do you want me to aim?" asked Tsongay.

"At the crevice, between those rocks. It might wedge itself in the base. It just might hold."

A loud thwack. The arrow shot across the ravine and landed with a hollow thud in the crevasse. It started to tumble, but then it held, wedged at the bottom. Andreas stared at Tsongay in disbelief.

"If we try to cross when the wind is up, we will never make it," yelled Andreas.

"Have faith," Tsongay said, pointing to the sky. "You must have faith. We have to leap. Now or never, before it gets dark. You are lighter. It might not hold my weight."

The wind rising, the rope danced and the piton started to wobble. Andreas was unable to see the other side of the spire. If he cut the rope, he would be safe. He was close enough to reach out for the rock. It would leave Tsongay marooned. The rope began to dance and threatened to throw him into the valley below.

Falling, falling.

"Cut the rope! You have to cut the rope!"

"No!" Andreas yelled into the face of the mountain. "I will save him. I must save him!" He leaped for the ledge.

A vast scope of rock, ice, and snow—coming nearer. The mountain loomed. The sun, a fireball, climbed higher.

His hands were heavy with blood. His face bruised. The mountain shook. There was no lake. There was no mountain. Only the sky.

A woman's voice:

> *"Uprise and see and hope.*
> *Seek and ye shall find me*
> *As a man's courage is, so is his destiny.*
> *This is my promise."*

Silence. No air moved—not a breath. The mountain, like wax, melted—swept bare, the last echoes dead on the white slopes. The fresh earth glittered and lay still. A door closed. The seventh seal had been broken. The last trumpet had sounded. There was silence in heaven and on earth.

> "Many lives you and I have lived.
> I remember them all, but thou dost not."
> —Bhagavad Gita iv.5.

Synopsis

The novel follows the tortured and brilliant main character, Andreas Eckhart, from the birth of Weimar Germany to the nation's descent into Nazi barbarism and the coming of World War II—a descent aided and abetted by an exhausted Europe.

Andreas is a physician practicing in London. He is a physicist who has worked in the developing field of atomic energy, a famed mountain climber, and a womanizer.

The nightmare and mordant humor of Europe in the 1930s is mirrored in Andreas's story, which parallels some of the most significant events of the twentieth century. The characters include historical figures and others unknown to the readers until they encounter their vivid personalities in this highly cinematic book.

The heart of the story is the attempts of the Nazis to enlist Andreas—the profligate son of a German general—to find the lost tribes, Jews who had been lost to the world centuries ago—and a weapon hinted at in the Bible as the sword of destiny, the significance of which becomes clear in twentieth-century science.

The reader is taken from Berlin, where the novel starts, to the gritty streets of London, to conspiracies in the teeming cities, to scorching deserts of the Middle East, and finally to the Himalayas.

A Western culture unable to come to grips with its own history is revealed in this odyssey, which leads Andreas to Tibet. The reader will not forget the characters and the incidents in this exciting and provocative historical novel.